A CANDLE I

A CANDLE IN THE WIND

Audrey Willsher

ARROW BOOKS

Arrow Books Limited
20 Vauxhall Bridge Road, London SW1V 2SA

An imprint of the Random Century Group

London Melbourne Sydney Auckland Johannesburg
and agencies throughout the world

First published in Great Britain by Century 1989
Arrow edition 1991

© 1989 by Audrey Willsher

The right of Audrey Willsher to be identified as the
author of this work has been asserted by her in
accordance with the Copyright, Designs and Patents
Act, 1988

This book is sold subject to the condition that it shall
not, by way of trade or otherwise, be lent, resold, hired
out, or otherwise circulated without the publisher's
prior consent in any form of binding or cover other than
that in which it is published and without a similar
condition including this condition being imposed on
the subsequent purchaser

Printed and bound in Great Britain by
Cox & Wyman Ltd, Reading

ISBN 0 09 972840 0

To John, Derek, Elizabeth, Kim
and, of course, my Mum

1

Tess had known she would always loathe it there the moment she stepped through the gates. It was so huge and forbidding, the factory, and cast a long, dark shadow over the whole area. Then there was the noise, as hundreds of women laboured at machines, and heat and dust. But what she hated worst of all was the sulphurous smell that infiltrated every corner of the lucifer factory and made her feel sick in her stomach.

At one point as she trudged between drying room and work benches with trays of matches balanced on her head, she felt so dizzy and ill she had to close her eyes and clutch at a bench for support or she would have fallen over. After a second or two she cautiously opened her eyes and found one of the girls who was cutting and boxing matches staring at her curiously.

Tess gave her an apologetic half smile but the girl looked away and, bending her head to her work, continued to fill the boxes with a speed that left Tess gaping in silent admiration. Occasionally a match flared into life but her nimble fingers would quickly extinguish it. The women here were on piece work and with three gross of boxes to be filled for two pence three farthings there was not a moment to be lost.

The nausea came again in great waves and Tess could feel the blood drain from her face and sweat bead her forehead and upper lip. She was going to be sick, she knew it, and on her first day at work, too.

'You gonna stand around all day like a spare dinner?' the sallow-faced girl hissed in exasperation, her tone of voice making it perfectly clear Tess could expect little sympathy there.

'I feel ill.'

'There ain't no time to be ill. He's watchin' yer.'

Tess glanced nervously around. 'Who is?'

'Him over there. Ol' potater face.' She motioned with her head in the direction of one of the charge hands. 'Makes 'is day if 'e can fine someone and I don't want no trouble, see.' She glared at Tess to emphasize her point.

Tess could see that the girl wasn't much older than she was, perhaps fourteen, but she spoke with the authority of someone who had several months' experience behind her. So, ill as she felt, she pulled herself together and went scurrying back to the drying room. If she earned half a crown that week she'd be lucky, a fine as well and her ma would skin her alive.

Although, with its oppressive heat, it felt like it, Tess knew that the drying room, where she had to go for the trays, wasn't the worst place in the factory. The dipping room enjoyed that privilege. There men and boys worked in a haze of noxious fumes, dipping coiled wooden splints into the yellow phosphorus that would turn them into lucifers. But the knowledge in no way consoled her. I hate this place, Tess thought, staggering under the weight of trays as she hurried to keep the women supplied with work. Any slackening of pace soon produced loud-mouthed abuse and one woman, a hunchback called Elsie Leggatt with a chin like a shovel, picked on her continuously.

A few spilt matches, nothing more, and the woman had really gone for her. 'What you wanna do that for, you silly little moo?'

Unable to think of any good reason, Tess remained silent.

'Cat got your tongue?' Elsie demanded aggressively.

Tess had had enough. 'No it ain't, an' leave me alone, can't yer?' she shot back defiantly, and for her pains got such a cuff round the ear that the world went into a spin and the tears started in her eyes. But she squeezed them tightly shut and bit on her lip. No one here would see her cry, not never, she thought with a deep mutinous anger.

What with one thing and another, by dinner time she'd had enough. Collecting her shawl and dinner bag, she hurried outside.

A clean, fresh breeze was blowing in from the Lea Valley and she took deep, grateful gulps of it, letting it fill her lungs. Then spreading out her shawl, she sat down on the grass and drank thirstily from a bottle of cold tea. The fresh air and tea helped to clear her throat of the fumes but they did nothing to remove the tight, restricting knot of misery; and although she was starving, when she started on her dinner of bread and cold bacon, it almost gagged in her throat.

Surely her mum could have let her do something better than this, she thought with an unhappy sigh – apprenticed her to a milliner, got her a job in a shop ... after all, she wasn't stupid, she'd been good at her letters and numbers, got her fourth-grade leaving certificate. So why had Mum sent her to this awful place? She knew why, of course, it was because of her dad. But it was a bad enough day without thinking of him, too.

She was moodily chewing on her last piece of bread when she became aware of someone standing over her. It was the thin-faced girl who'd spoken to her earlier.

'Hello,' said Tess a little warily.

'What's yer name?' inquired the unsmiling girl.

'Teresa Kelly, what's yours?'

'If you want to know, it's Sarah Atkins.' She studied Tess in silence for some moments then with her small bitter mouth pursed into a thin line of disapproval, she said, 'You must be one of them, then.'

'One o' what?' asked Tess innocently.

'One of them bloody Irish folk who ought to go back to where they came from. Troublemakers and scum, that's what you are.'

That was it! Tess had had enough for one day. The unfortunate Sarah never knew what hit her. For there she was, at one moment confidently in charge of the situation and in the next she'd been grabbed by the ankles and sent flying, to land with a surprised bump on her backside, legs in the air and displaying a rather improper amount of grimy petticoat.

She tried to struggle to her feet, but Tess was up first and grabbing hold of the girl's wispy bun, she screwed it so

9

tightly against Sarah's scalp that the pins went flying in every direction.

Sarah let out a shriek of pain. 'Lemme go, lemme go!'

'Not until you've said you're sorry,' Tess snarled into the girl's ear. 'If you don't, I'll pull every single hair out of your rotten 'ead by its roots, make no mistake.' Her anger was white hot now and there would be no stopping her.

Soon a small crowd of girls had gathered round but no one sought to intervene, a fight was always an enjoyable diversion.

'Serves yer right, Sarah Atkins,' a voice from the crowd shouted. 'Yer mouth's bin gettin' the better of you again, I shouldn't wonder.'

'I didn't mean nuffink, honest,' sobbed the unhappy girl, who was now kneeling by Tess in an attitude of total submission.

Tess's temper burnt itself out just as quickly as it flared, and she began to feel slightly ashamed of herself. She let go of Sarah's hair and almost immediately the knot of girls began to drift away. Tess and Sarah were left on their own.

Sarah looked terrible. Her face was blotchy and red from crying and her hair, now loosened from its bun, stuck out crazily from her head. She was such a wretched, miserable sight that Tessa's heart went out to her.

'You shouldn't have said what you did, you know,' she explained to the girl who, sobbing noisily, was searching the ground on her hands and knees for lost hairpins. ''Cos when I gets riled I hardly knows what I'm doing.'

The girl said nothing but only continued to snivel. The sound began to get on Tess's nerves. To shut her up she thrust the bottle of cold tea at her. 'Here, have some of this, there's a drop left.'

Interrupting her search, Sarah took the bottle and drank it dry. Then without even a murmur of thanks, she handed it back.

'Here, let me help you with your hair,' Tess volunteered. Now that her anger had abated she wanted to do something for the girl.

10

'Don't bother, I can do it meself,' Sarah replied huffily.

Tess gave up trying then. 'Please yourself,' she said with a shrug, and picking up her shawl she started to walk back to the factory, aware that Sarah was trailing after her, silent and reproachful.

Deciding to give her one last chance, Tess slowed down long enough for Sarah to catch up with her. 'Been 'ere long?' she asked.

'Two months,' mumbled Sarah, wiping her nose on the corner of her shawl.

'First job, is it?'

Sarah gave a derisive laugh. 'No, course not. I was in another lucifer factory afore this one, wasn't I? It's better 'ere, though, they look after yer better and yer not so likely to get the jaw disease.'

Tess stopped and looked at Sarah with a puzzled expression. 'Jaw disease, what's that?'

'You know, phossy jaw. You gets it from the compo.'

'Is it bad?'

'Silly cow, course it's bad,' replied Sarah, beginning to sound more cheerful. 'It gets in yer teeth, see, they turn black, then yer jaw bone starts to rot. Rots clean away, it does,' she finished with some relish.

To Sarah's considerable satisfaction a spasm of fear crossed Tess's face. 'And another thing,' she continued, 'carrying them trays around on yer 'ead don't do no good, neither, makes yer 'air fall out.' She studied Tess objectively. 'I shouldn't think yours would last long.'

Tess lifted a hand protectively to the dark curls she was so proud of. That was it, no matter what her mum said, she wasn't coming back to this awful place tomorrow. And she wasn't going to stand and listen to any more of Sarah's horror stories either. 'I'm off,' she said and took to her heels.

In most respects the afternoon was very much like the morning, except for one thing. The bullying stopped. Although she was glad of this, Tess couldn't at first understand why. It was Elsie Leggatt, the hunchback, who finally put

11

her right. Tess was emptying matches on to her bench when Elsie gave her a sharp nudge in the ribs.

'Sorted that Sarah Atkins out good an' proper, didn't you? Serves 'er right, she's a real miserable bitch.' She gave a loud mirthless laugh.

Listen to who's talking, Tess felt like saying but wisely held her tongue. Still, it obviously paid to stand up for yourself here. Not that she was staying anyway, she reminded herself.

When the hooter finally sounded Tess gave a great sigh of relief. The day had seemed endless and a pain was now pulling at her stomach. What if the compo had already got into her body and was at that moment gnawing away inside her? She shuddered at the horror of it. She had to get away from here, get home and tell her mother she wasn't going back. Quickly she gathered up her few belongings and headed for the factory gates.

A woman came out of a house and carelessly emptied a pail of slops into the gutter, missing Tess by an inch. But then, as she knew, it was always as well to walk carefully once you left the main thoroughfare behind. Crossing sweepers didn't waste their time in the back streets of Bethnal Green.

There was less sky here and buildings seemed to rise rotting from the ground and lean darkly, blotting out light. But even so people spilled out of their houses and on to the streets. Women, some of them nursing babies, gossiped and argued on steps while their children happily shared the gutter with decomposing vegetables and steaming horse dung.

At one of the doors a woman sprawled with her arms hanging loosely between her legs, her head almost in her lap. As Tess passed she looked up with bleary, unfocused eyes, hiccuped once and then her head rolled forward again on to her chest. Inside the house a baby cried hungrily.

On the opposite side of the road was the Kentish Drovers. Crossing, Tess pressed her nose against the frosted glass and tried to peer in.

This was her father's favourite tavern and he was probably somewhere inside. With a bit of luck and if he was only half drunk, she might be able to cajole a fistful of coppers out of him. It was the only time he was inclined to display any sign of generosity towards her and she exploited it to the full. There was the normal racket going on inside, the raised voices, the false bonhomie of the inebriated which as the night wore on, Tess knew, would turn to violent argument and end, inevitably, as a brawl in the street.

Unable to see much of the smoke-filled interior, Tess walked on, wondering, not for the first time, how her mum and dad had ever come to marry. She'd even, rather boldly, asked her mother once.

'Yes, why indeed did I marry him? It's a question I've asked myself often enough,' was her mother's bitter reply. 'But I was young and foolish, I suppose, and your dad was handsome with a glib tongue. Girls have fallen for less. But I could have done a lot better, Tess, a lot better.'

'Better' had been the young nonconformist minister who'd come calling on Florence's parents. But instead, she'd chosen to marry the black-haired, black-souled Patrick Kelly, who was both Irish and papist, albeit a non-practising one. Her parents never spoke to her again and had gone to their graves unforgiving to the last.

But that had been Florence's only lapse and respectability was the code she now lived by. She saw no virtue in dirt, abhorred drink and as for sex . . . well . . . and the lust she'd felt for Patrick Kelly at twenty had long since been deadened by numerous stillbirths and miscarriages.

The sky was darkening when Tess finally turned into Golden Court where cramped, jerry-built dwellings faced each other across a narrow alleyway and open gutter. The one gas light suspended from a wall bracket barely penetrated the gloom and threw into relief only the grimy washing hanging from an upstairs window.

Tom, her eleven-year-old brother, was sitting on the step waiting for her, his small face pinched and tired in the dim light.

13

'Mum says we're to take the washing to Mrs Chadwick,' he said, standing up and opening the door. Tess, wanting only to sit down, sighed audibly and followed him into the house.

There was a bit of a fire in the grate and taking a taper from the mantelpiece, she lit the lamp. The room, with its deal table and chairs and bed pushed against the wall, was probably no more impoverished than any other in the neighbourhood, and some effort had gone into making the room homely. Pegged rugs covered the holes in the lino and framed prints did the same for the cracks in the wall. Various ornaments lined the mantelpiece, along with a nickel clock that had to be shaken violently to make it work. It was also obvious that a great deal of energy was expended in trying to keep the place clean, against impossible odds.

On the table stood a large wicker basket full of freshly ironed linen and yet more was steamily drying on a line across the room. Tess sighed again. Washing, always there was washing, it seemed to dominate their lives.

And her stomach ached and she was tired and she was hungry. She also needed to talk to her mother about the factory while the horror of it was still fresh in her mind. But, the washing had to be delivered. There wouldn't be anything to eat until Mum got back from her charring job anyway. 'Come on, let's get going then. At least it's Mrs Chadwick's.'

Between them, Tess and Tom swung the heavy basket off the table but even the thought of the treat that lay in store for them couldn't lighten the load or shorten the journey for Tess that night.

Tess just knew that Mrs Chadwick was very rich. She'd have to be to live in a house that had such black shiny railings, lace-curtained bay windows and green blinds that could be pulled down in summer to keep out the sun.

As always, she stopped to admire the trim exterior and as always Tom raced on ahead to pull the bell.

'Come on, Tess, don't 'ang around,' he called impatiently. 'If Mrs Chadwick's going out we won't get nuffink.'

Mrs Chadwick opened the door just as Tess, urged on by hunger, reached the top step.

14

'How nice to see you, my dears,' she said with a smile. 'Now bring the washing through to the kitchen and I'll see what I've got for you.'

Their saliva glands already working in eager anticipation, the children followed her down the hall. Mrs Chadwick was wearing her shiny blue dressing gown with a red and orange dragon embroidered down the back. She was usually dressed like this when they called. But Tess knew why, of course, her mother had told her. Mrs Chadwick was in the theatre and only worked nights. And Tess could see she would look well on the stage for she had well-rounded bosoms, blonde curly hair and rosy lips and cheeks. And she smiled a lot, spoke in a very refined voice and hardly ever dropped her aitches. Tess tried hard to speak like her. She really admired Mrs Chadwick.

Taking the washing, she sat them down at the kitchen table. 'Fancy some ginger beer and Madeira cake?'

Their faces lit up. This was a favourite treat. 'Yes please,' they replied in unison and their eyes watched hungrily as she poured the foaming drink into glasses and cut through the soft yellow cake. Tess's mouth was really watering now and her tummy rumbled audibly.

'Here you are, my lovelies,' she said at last, 'tuck in.'

Tom immediately stuffed his cake greedily in his mouth, but Tess ate hers slowly, savouring each buttery mouthful and trying not to let hunger get the better of her. Unlike Tom she didn't gulp down her ginger beer either and when he finished his with a loud burp, she frowned at him reprovingly over her glass. When she'd finally finished, she leaned back with a contented sigh. For the first time that day she felt almost cheerful.

While they'd been eating, Mrs Chadwick had collected together some dirty washing for them to take home. Tess was greatly impressed by Mrs Chadwick's cleanliness and she'd worked out that she changed her bed linen at least three times a week.

The soiled linen was bundled into the basket, Mrs Chadwick poured herself 'a small glass of something' as she liked to call it, and then sat down with the children.

'Well, how was your first day at work, Tess my love?'

Tess shuddered. 'Horrible. I'm gonna tell Mum I'm not going back.'

'Is that so?' replied Mrs Chadwick but she only just managed to keep a straight face. 'Well you can tell your mum there's always a job for you here. I've been thinking of getting someone to answer the door for a long time.'

Tess's face brightened. 'Do you really mean that?' she asked eagerly.

Mrs Chadwick took a dainty sip of her drink then replied casually, 'Of course I do, duckie.'

That was it! There was nothing to stop her leaving the factory now. Even her mother couldn't object if she had another job to go to. The day seemed to be getting brighter by the minute.

Amid all this excitement Tess had to remind Mrs Chadwick about the laundry money and while she went to collect it, Tess had a tantalizing glimpse into the front parlour with its deep, comfortable armchairs, red Turkish carpet and small round table set with glasses and a decanter.

'I'm gonna have a home like that one day,' Tess announced as they trudged home with the heavy basket. 'And when I have I'll eat Madeira cake every day.' She sighed dreamily. 'I don't think I could ever get tired of Madeira cake. In fact I'll probably eat it at every meal.'

'You can't eat it for breakfast,' said Tom practically.

'Oh yes I can,' Tess replied firmly, and this struck them both as so funny that they began to laugh and in a sudden spurt of high spirits they started to run down the street, swinging the basket recklessly, daring the washing to fall out.

But with a sudden jerky movement, Tess stopped and dropping the basket she leaned over, clutching at her stomach.

'What'sa matter, Tess?' Tom asked, his face puckering with anxiety.

'I dunno. I keeps gettin' this pain in me belly, it's like cramp.' The pain frightened her and she began to wonder if she had one of those diseases that killed people . . . perhaps the cholera.

'Let's hurry and get home, then,' Tom urged. 'I'll carry the washing.' But Tess knew he'd never be able to manage on his own, the basket was too large and Tom was too small.

At first glance there didn't seem to be any great resemblance between brother and sister. Tess was sturdy and tall, Tom small and slight. And his eyes were brown while Tess's were as grey as an Irish lough and often as sombre. Tom's hair had a copper tint to it but Tess's was black as liquorice and very curly. 'Like an Irish tinker's,' her mother would mutter with disgust as with harsh brushing and tight ribbons she sought to groom the rampaging curls into submission.

It was only on closer inspection that the resemblance between brother and sister became apparent: in the pale Celtic skin and the short, full upper lip, but most of all in the very determined set of the chin. Tess had fine dark brows which were accentuated by the paleness of her skin. And perhaps not a pretty face, although one day it would be an arresting one.

They knew what there was for supper halfway down the street and the smell of herrings frying propelled them eagerly forward. Tess forgot the factory then, the pain in her stomach, and remembered only her gnawing hunger.

Their mother, bent over the fire, turned as they opened the door. There was no word of greeting, instead wiping her hands on her apron she said, 'Got any money for me then?'

Tess handed her two shillings. She took it, then handed tuppence back to Tom. 'Go and get a pinch of sugar and a twist of tea,' she ordered brusquely.

'But Mum, I'm hungry,' whined Tom. 'Can't I get it afterwards?'

'Do as I say, that's if you want any supper,' his mother snapped. By her tone it was obvious that Florence was in no mood for arguments, and Tom quickly did as he was told.

'Here, you sit down and eat this.' A plate with two herrings on it was banged in front of Tess who, forgetting her manners, fell upon the food ravenously. When she'd finished she carefully wiped the enamel plate with some bread, then pushing it away from her she cushioned her head on her arms and fell into a deep exhausted sleep.

The next thing she knew was her mother shaking her vigorously. 'Come on, Tess, drink this,' she urged, handing her daughter a mug of hot, sweet tea. 'Then off to bed with you. Tom's been gone ages.'

Rubbing her eyes Tess peered sleepily at the bed in the corner. As usual Tom had all the blankets.

'I'm off upstairs myself now,' said Florence, lighting herself a candle. 'Heaven knows when the old man will be in.'

When her mother had gone Tess finished her tea and began to undress, laying her clothes neatly across the chair. From an early age modesty and a sense of propriety had been dinned into her by Florence and even though Tom was asleep she was careful to put her rough calico night shift on before removing the last of her undergarments and black stockings. She was just about to blow out the lamp and jump into bed bedside Tom when she felt something warm and sticky oozing down the inside of her thighs.

With a feeling of panic she began to pull at her nightgown, touching the stickiness warily. She lifted her hands to the dim light and saw that her fingers were covered with blood. Dear God, she was dying, bleeding to death. Dropping the shift she held her hands to her face and started to scream, a long, loud scream of pure terror.

The noise woke Tom who shot up in bed and started to howl. Florence Kelly came rushing downstairs, took one look at her hysterical daughter and went over and brought her hand sharply across her face.

'Stop it, Tess, do you hear me, stop it!'

Tess's scream gradually subsided. Great shuddering sobs shook her young body instead and the tears came, searing the red weals on her burning cheeks with their salt.

'Oh Mum,' she cried at last with a passion born of despair, 'do something, please, get me a doctor for Gawd's sake, me liver's dropping out!'

2

Shock, bewilderment, dismay were Tess's own particular emotions as she took that irrevocable step into womanhood. She wasn't unfamiliar with the ways of the world, that would be impossible in Bethnal Green, but her mother had kept her in ignorance about the workings of her own body. And listening to Florence's angry strictures, she decided that these monthlies would never be anything more than a tremendous burden.

'Now, you are to stay away from men, do you hear me?' Florence ordered fiercely, waving an admonishing finger at her. 'They're beasts most of them and not to be trusted an inch. And I don't want no kids on my step, understand?'

Confused and unhappy and not understanding at all, Tess could only sniff and nod her head dumbly, her mother's obvious irritation making her feel that this visitation was somehow her own fault.

'And you'll have to sleep with me now,' her mother continued. 'The old man can go in with Tom.'

Although exhausted, Tess was too overwrought to sleep and she lay tossing and turning beside her mother, her bones aware of every lump in the flock mattress. Exasperated by her restlessness, Florence finally snapped at her to lie still. Tess had dozed off then, only to be woken by her father stumbling drunkenly around the room, crashing into furniture and cursing loudly. When he tried to get in beside her, Florence gave him an almighty shove, which sent him tumbling heavily to the floor. Clambering out of bed, she then ordered him back downstairs. Surprisingly, he went meekly as a lamb.

Not unnaturally, by the next morning Tess found it needed superhuman effort to drag herself from bed, into her clothes and downstairs where her mother had already raked out the fire, lit it and put a kettle to boil.

20

Tom was still asleep and her father lay snoring next to him. Going over to the bed Florence shook her husband roughly. 'Aren't you going to try and get some work today, then?'

He pushed her hand away and rolled over. 'Lemme 'lone,' he mumbled.

'Come on, you lazy beggar, get up.' Florence shook him more vigorously this time.

Suddenly and with a roar, he jumped out of bed and grabbed his wife's arm. 'Leave me alone, woman, do you hear me!'

Florence stood glaring up at her husband with unflinching contempt. Tess held her breath, terrified of what would happen next. One blow from those great fists and her mother would go flying across the room, as they all knew to their cost. Hurriedly she poured her father a mug of tea. 'Here Dad, drink this,' she said, thrusting the mug into his free hand and almost expecting it to be smashed into the fireplace. But this time it wasn't. Instead her father let go of his wife's arm and slumped down heavily into a chair and, looking gross and unkempt in his combinations and shirt, gulped noisily on his tea.

The atmosphere in the small room was thick with animosity and tension and Tess longed to be away from it. But she didn't want to leave her mother – or Tom – who was now awake and crouched fearfully on the bed.

There was no doubt that her father had once been a handsome man, but drink had taken care of that and now the eyes were pouched and bloodshot, the skin coarse, the nose red-veined. And the hair which had once been as black as her own was now prematurely white although it still curled thick and strong as ever. His large burly frame had once earned him good money at the docks as a stevedore. Now he got work there when he felt inclined or when they would have him. Sometimes he even brought money home. Sometimes. And when he didn't Florence would wait until he was in a drunken stupor then rifle his pockets for any loose silver or copper.

Tess watched him with a veiled hatred as he lumbered round the room searching for discarded clothing from the night before. 'Where's me bloody boots?' he thundered, kicking at a chair.

'Where you put them, you great oaf,' was her mother's reply and there was such scorn in her voice Tess really feared for her safety.

Tess looked at the nickel clock on the mantelpiece and knew she'd have to go. Although she didn't like leaving her mother and Tom to cope on their own she slipped out of the house with a guilty feeling of relief. Work was almost welcome that morning if only to get away from the brooding malevolence of her father.

Not that their circumstances differed very much from many other families in the neighbourhood. Almost without exception the men drank, and often the women too. Sober, industrious families soon moved out to the more respectable areas of Hackney or Stratford.

Only Florence's unflagging determination had prevented the Kellys from being reduced to the squalor of living in one of the rookeries and lodging houses that dotted the district like a plague. She would do anything to earn a few coppers, as long as it was honest, and she'd never encouraged idleness in her children either. From an early age Tess had been put out to work after school, washing steps or baby minding.

Her mother was a hard woman, her life ruled by the need to survive and with little time for tenderness or affection. In spite of this, Tess recognized in Florence a courage and inner strength which inspired in her a fierce, protective love. She would have done anything for her mum.

And she was proud of her too. Proud of the fact that she could read and write, never drank, never used bad language and despised those who did. In fact she fancied herself a cut above her neighbours and was inclined to adopt a rather haughty manner. This did little to endear her to them and, hoping to bring her down a peg or two, they'd nicknamed her Ma Gladstone. In fact it had precisely the opposite effect, confirming for Florence her own superiority.

22

Her only transgression, it seemed, had been marrying Patrick Kelly. But Tess knew enough about his past to see that fate had dealt him a fair share of blows. There'd been the loss of his parents from cholera after they'd managed to escape from the famine in Ireland. Then the Infant Pauper Asylum where he'd been subjected to systematic beatings and near starvation. At twelve it must have come as a relief to be let loose on the world to fend for himself. Sometimes Tess almost felt pity for her father. Sometimes, but not often. But she saw how adversity had shaped and moulded her parents differently; her mother fought against it with the valour of Joan of Arc while her father had capitulated and was brutalized by it, to his eternal damnation.

She saw suddenly that if she didn't hurry she would be late for work, which could mean a fine. Lifting her heels, she started to run and by the time she joined the crowd of men and girls surging in through the factory gates, she was panting and out of breath.

But she felt she had too much on her mind to care about the dreary, monotonous work. Her mother's dire warnings still rang in her ears and the thick rough material between her legs made her awkwardly aware of her own body.

She nearly jumped out of her skin though when she heard the chargehand's voice and felt his warm breath against her ear.

'I've bin watchin' you, Kelly,' Bert Higgins snarled, 'and you'd better buck your ideas up or you'll be out of a job.'

Struck dumb with fear and forced into close proximity, all she could see was his greasy skin cratered with blackheads and spots. No wonder they called him potato face, she thought.

'Something wrong?' He pushed his face even closer and she could smell last night's beer on his breath.

Instinctively she drew back from him, trying to hide her disgust. 'N . . . no . . .' she stuttered unconvincingly.

He glared at her threateningly. 'Well get a move on, then. You're paid to work, not sit on your arse all day.'

Tess was about to point out that she hadn't been sitting down but changed her mind and, thankful to have got off so lightly, she hurried away.

'You haven't got much to say for yourself,' Sarah commented later as they sat on the grass eating their dinner. Tess could have done without Sarah's company that day but, quite insensitive to Tess's monosyllabic replies, she'd plonked herself down without as much as a by your leave, and Tess couldn't summon the energy to send her packing.

Tess plucked moodily at the grass. 'I don't feel like talkin'.'

'Why not?'

'Lots of reasons.'

'Well tell me one of them.'

Suddenly Tess felt a desperate need to unburden herself. 'Oh Sarah,' she cried unhappily, 'I'm, you know . . . not well. I've got me monthlies.'

'Is that all?' Sarah looked disappointed.

'But I can have a baby now . . . can't I?' Tess ventured, still hazy about anatomical details but not wanting to appear ignorant.

Sarah looked at her with more interest. 'Do you do it with men, then?'

'Do what?'

'Let 'em put their thing in your crack.'

'Course I don't,' replied Tess, bridling with indignation and going very red.

Losing interest, Sarah shrugged. 'Well you're arright then, cos if you know of any other way to have kids, you'd better tell me.'

Tess's grey eyes widened and cleared with relief. This was a great weight off her mind and she felt immensely grateful to Sarah. She stood up, brushing the crumbs from her skirt. She was quite safe, she would never let a man do that to her. Never.

'You are not going to work for Mrs Chadwick and that's final,' Florence snapped. They were in the small steamy wash house, Florence up to her elbows in soap and her hair

24

hanging limply around her tired face. Tess was so surprised at the force of her mother's rejection of the idea that she couldn't speak for a moment and just stood staring at her open-mouthed. After all, what could be wrong in working for Mrs Chadwick? She'd have thought her mother would be pleased.

'But Mum,' she wailed, 'I hate it at that lucifer factory, you know that . . .'

Florence Kelly paused for a moment and brushed her hand wearily across her forehead. 'Who ever said anything about enjoying work? Do you think I enjoy slaving away here? You've got regular employment, so get on with it and don't start getting any fancy ideas.'

Florence wasn't a patient woman and Tess could see by her set features and the way she banged the washing angrily against the scrubbing board that dangerous territory lay ahead. But she was moved by a sense of injustice and detestation of her job that made her reckless. Besides, she reasoned, just because her mother's life was awful did that mean her own had to be too? Not seeing the sense of this, she formed her thoughts into words of protest.

'I don't see why . . .' But a wet, swinging pillowcase stopped her in mid-sentence and she had to duck hurriedly to avoid it.

'Go!' her mother shrieked.

Wisely, Tess took her advice, just in time to hear the thump of wet linen against the closed wooden door.

Bewildered and resentful at her mother's attitude, Tess nevertheless knew that, for the time being anyway, she would have to accept boredom, drudgery and danger. But no power on earth would keep her at the factory. She was just biding her time, she told herself, and one day when she had more control over her life, she would do something to change it. She could not, would not, allow it to be a repetition of her mother's miserable existence.

If she complained about conditions to some of the other girls at the factory, they would laugh and call her Miss High and Mighty and ask her what she intended doing about it. But she did find one ally and friend, a rough and ready young woman called Lizzie Cakebread. Even more surprisingly Sarah, despite their initial set-to, seemed to have taken a strong liking to Tess. Often after a day's work the two girls would link arms and walk home together.

One warm May evening they were dawdling along the Bow Road together when a brake passed, full of young men and girls. From the look of them Tess guessed they'd been on a picnic for there was a great deal of slightly drunken, good-humoured horseplay and the brake overflowed with bluebells.

As the tired horses with their festively plaited and beribboned manes and tails trundled past, the two girls stood watching the boisterous group enviously.

'I expect they've been to Epping Forest,' said Tess knowledgeably.

'Lucky bleeders,' replied Sarah with feeling, her gaze following the cart as it disappeared down the street. 'Me and Milly never goes anywhere.'

'We could go, what's to stop us?' answered Tess, but she spoke with a certain bravado for she had only the vaguest idea where Epping Forest might be.

Sarah's face brightened. 'Could we? When?'

'Next Sunday if you like.'

Sarah hesitated. 'I'd 'ave to take me sister.'

'That's arright. Mum likes a bit of peace on Sunday, so I wouldn't get far without Tommy.'

And so it was decided. On the Sunday the four of them would go to Epping Forest and pick bluebells.

It was going to be hot. Tess could tell that. Somehow the sun, that Sunday morning, had even managed to pierce the gloom of Golden Court. Trying not to disturb her, she climbed over her sleeping mother, noticing that even in sleep a small frown of irritation creased her brow, and wondered briefly if there'd been a time when her mother was happy.

26

She dressed quickly and crept downstairs to rouse Tom. The place beside him was empty, their father hadn't come home last night.

Tess heated water on a small paraffin stove and made tea which they then drank, heavily laced with condensed milk. What was left she poured into a bottle to take with them. Bread and cheese were wrapped in a cloth, Tom was persuaded to wash his face and comb his hair and then they quietly let themselves out of the house.

Already costers were putting up stalls and arranging their goods for sale. Soon the street entertainers would arrive, the pubs would open and it would be as noisy as any other day. But at that moment there was a pleasing quiet to the morning which Tess relished. And they had a whole day of freedom in front of them too.

'Come on,' she said excitedly, grabbing Tom's hand, 'let's run,' and then laughed as their tapping feet echoed loudly in the peaceful streets.

They were to meet Sarah outside the Wesleyan Chapel and soon after they got there she came hurrying down the street pushing a very old and dilapidated baby carriage in front of her. This surprised Tess. She'd imagined Sarah's sister to be about Tom's age. But as the perambulator drew nearer she saw, propped up in it, a girl of about ten.

As she reached them, Sarah stopped and bent over the child, tucking a grubby, threadbare blanket very carefully around her legs. Watching, Tess noticed her unhealthy pallor, the painful cough and the narrow, rounded shoulders.

'Milly's really been lookin' forward to today, haven't you, me love?' Sarah asked her sister tenderly, brushing the hair back from her small, peaky face.

Milly nodded her head with a vigour Tess wouldn't have thought her capable of. 'Are we really going to a bluebell wood?' she asked.

'Course, we are,' her sister assured her. She looked at Tess. 'You're takin' us there, ain't you, Tess?'

By now Tess knew the general direction of the forest, but not its exact position. The thing to do was keep walking, she felt. Bluebells were another matter, of course, but she was without the courage to say so.

Never having travelled more than a mile or two in any direction from her home, distance had little meaning for Tess and she expected, at every turn in the road, to see a great swaying forest rise up in front of them. But it was just more houses – and a dusty road. They took it in turns pushing Milly and as they did they sang music-hall songs they'd picked up from the girls at work. And as they sang, they pumped the carriage up and down which delighted Milly, who laughed and coughed until two bright red spots appeared on her cheeks. Looking at her, Tess felt pleased. The fresh air's really doing her good, she thought.

But as the sun climbed in the sky and it became increasingly hot, so Tom started to complain. Finally, tired of his constant 'How much further, Tess, how much further?' she decided they might as well stop for a while. The previous evening, in a moment of rare generosity, Florence had given her tuppence to spend and the coppers were now burning a hole in her pocket. But what should they spend it on? It was a big decision to make.

Across the road were a few shops, and dragging the pram over, they stood gazing in at a baker's window full of lardy cakes and spiced buns. Next door was an equally tempting sweet shop, displaying in its window jars of boiled sweets whose deep, vibrant colours seemed to glow like the crown jewels.

They darted indecisively from window to window and were still agonizing when they heard, 'Ices . . . ices . . . all flavours . . . chocolate . . . vanilla . . . strawberry . . .' They looked at each other for a moment.

'Well, what's it to be?' said Tess.

'Ice cream!' the others said in one voice, and they began to hurry after the swarthy man pushing a canopied cart.

'Four halfpenny 'okeys, please,' said Tom importantly, when they finally caught up with him. They watched in silent anticipation as he scooped ice cream into cornets and handed one to each impatient child in turn.

Nothing . . . nothing has ever tasted like this, thought Tess, closing her eyes with delight as her tongue lapped at the cold, soft mixture.

The dark man smiled. 'You lika?' he asked.

'Mmm,' they murmured through mouthfuls of the dissolving cream, then, quite unable to believe their good fortune, watched as he pressed another scoop on to their half-eaten cornets.

Suddenly Tess remembered her manners and she nudged the others in turn. 'Say thank you,' she muttered.

'Thank you, mister,' they chorused happily, licking their fingers as the mixture began to melt and drip on to their clothes.

'I lika the bambini, I got fourteen at home.'

With that many mouths to feed, Tess didn't think he should be giving ice cream away. But they thanked him again for his generosity and then the vendor trundled off, singing happily to himself in a foreign tongue.

Finding some shade they went and sat down, none of them talking until the last mouthful was gone.

Tom was the first to speak. 'Coo, that was lovely,' he said, wiping his hands down the front of his shirt.

'You'll get lovely, if you go home with a filthy shirt,' Tess warned him, although she knew it was her who would get the clout if Tom was dirty.

When they were all finished they moved on. Their shadows were short now on the dusty road and their pale cheeks had begun to redden and freckle in the hot sun. Although the houses were thinning out and being replaced by hedges and wild flowers, still the forest seemed no nearer. She was beginning to doubt its existence and wish they'd gone to Victoria Park instead, when suddenly there they were, trees, lots of them. There was no hiding her sense of relief.

'There it is!' she shouted excitedly and in a final burst of energy they surged forward into the forest.

The brother and sister immediately flung themselves down on the ground where they lay with their arms spreadeagled, panting loudly. But Sarah's first thought was for Milly and she spread the blanket out on the ground before lifting her carefully out of the pram. Tess tried hard not to stare, tried hard not to notice how deformed Milly's legs were, how stunted and thin. Rickety and crippled children were a common enough sight but what Tess found moving was Sarah's loving concern for her young sister, which showed an entirely different aspect of her character.

They were all so hot and tired that no one spoke for a while. But Tom – Florence always said he had buttons on his bottom – soon began to wriggle like a worm.

'Sit still,' said Tess, 'you make me feel hot just looking at you.'

'I'm hungry, I want me dinner,' he complained.

Knowing there'd be no peace until he devoured his share of the meal, Tess undid the cloth and carefully divided the bread and cheese in two. But she made sure she had first drink out of the bottle, for once Tom got his hands on it, she knew he would drink it dry.

But even after they'd eaten, Tom was still restless. 'I'm gonna explore,' he announced, picking up a large stick. 'And this is in case I have to fight off any bears,' he informed them bravely, waving the stick above his head.

'Just see you don't get lost, that's all,' answered Tess, lying back on the dry peaty earth and stretching lazily as she gazed up at the large smooth-barked, arching trees. Sharp green leaves were just uncurling from buds that looked like small brown cigars, and a stippled lacy light filtered through the network of branches. She gave a small sigh of pleasure. If only . . . if only she didn't have to go back to that place tomorrow. The thought of it almost marred her pleasure of the day.

She rolled over on to her stomach and poked Sarah with a sharp twig. 'Hey, Sarah, wake up, I want to ask you something.'

Sarah stirred drowsily. 'What's that?'

'Are you gonna stay in that factory all your life?'

'Did you wake me up just to ask me a silly question like that? How should I know? It's a job. Beats dying of starvation

30

any day. You've got a mum and dad, me and Milly 'ave only got each other and beggars can't be choosers.'

'Starvation or phossy jaw, what a choice,' said Tess bitterly, marvelling at Sarah's resignation. 'I was good at me lessons at school, you know, I could probably do something a lot better.'

'Such as?'

'Such as work in one of them big shops up West. Or maybe train to be a milliner.' But these were pipe dreams, of course. Where would she – or her mum – get the money to pay for an apprenticeship?

Just then Tom returned. 'Can't see no bluebells,' he informed them.

Milly's face dropped. 'But you promised me, Tess. You said we'd get some, didn't you?'

'Course we'll get some,' Tess assured her, glaring at Tom. 'Come on, let's get going.'

Milly was dumped back into the perambulator and they pushed on, deeper into the forest. But the ground was quite soft and extruding roots lay in wait, ready to trip unwary city children. And it was steep in parts too, making it heavy going with the pram. But it was Milly who urged them on all the time and with an energy Tess wouldn't have thought her capable of.

She was just beginning to worry about getting lost when suddenly, like questing pilgrims, their patience was rewarded. Reaching the brow of a steep embankment they stopped to draw breath and suddenly there they were, bluebells, thousands of them, stretching into the distance, a misty ocean of blue.

'Crumbs,' said Tom in awe.

'Oh look,' said Milly with a squeal of delight, then like an invading army, they rushed forward into the fragile blooms. But just then a pram wheel caught in the root of a tree and it was wrenched from Sarah's hands. They watched in frozen horror as it went hurtling down the slope, flinging its tiny occupant into the bright flowers where she lay like a crumpled, broken doll.

Sarah clapped her hands to her mouth, otherwise nobody dared move. Then to their intense relief Milly opened her eyes, gazed around her in blinking surprise for a second then, laughing wildly, started to roll over and over in the blue flowers. With a whoop of delight Tom galloped down the hill to join her, then Sarah. Only Tess hesitated, considering herself too old for such childish goings-on.

But then Tom yelled, 'Come on, Tess,' and forgetting any inhibitions, she plunged into the sea of flowers. Laughing wildly they rolled in the bluebells and pawed the air like boisterous puppies, crushing the tall, elegant stems under the weight of their young bodies.

Suddenly Tom sat up, looking very pale. 'I feel sick,' he announced, and to emphasize his point vomited down the front of his breeches. The effect was dramatic and sobering.

Tess regarded her brother with a rising sense of panic. There was no doubt about it, Tom looked a mess. Apart from the darkening vomit stain, twigs and leaves clung to his hair and a slimy deposit of sap snailed across his clothes. Already she could hear her mother's angry voice. Picking some leaves from a tree, she wiped at the vomit on his trousers with a notable lack of success. She then noticed a small hollow with some murky-looking water in it. Dipping the corner of her apron in it she attempted to dab away the worst effects of their day out. When she'd finished she stood back to judge the effect. He looked awful.

'I think we'd better go,' she said.

Nobody felt like arguing with her so Milly was returned to the baby carriage, bluebells were hurriedly picked and piled on top of her, and the long walk home began.

And it seemed interminable. All of them were tired and when Tom started to grizzle and drag on her hand, Tess's temper flared and she gave him a sharp clout across the head. He started to bawl then, very loudly. Tess felt like shaking him but she didn't have the energy. Instead she contented herself with giving him another cuff round the ear and he snivelled noisily all the way up the Bow Road.

32

Tess noticed too that the flowers, which such a short time ago had stood so tall and proud, now hung limp and lifeless over the perambulator, their heads fallen as if in sorrow.

The sky to the east was almost dark when, tired and bedraggled, they finally trudged up the Mile End Road, past the Salvation Army banging out with evangelical zeal the hymn 'Soldiers of Christ Arise'. Savings souls was their task. But they were wasting their time and Tess could have told them so.

Outside the Wesleyan Chapel the friends separated and as Tess scooped up an armful of the wilting flowers she saw that Milly was deeply and contentedly asleep. Pausing for a moment she stared down at the small, deformed body and her heart gave a lurch of pity. The day had been worth it, she thought, if only for the brief taste of freedom it had given Milly.

'See you tomorrow, then,' called Sarah and with a wave of her hand was gone.

In spite of the gift of flowers, Tess approached Golden Court in some trepidation. Tom looked like one of the guttersnipes Florence so abhorred, and Tess's appearance was hardly better. Her apron was none too clean and her gypsy curls, which were such a trial to her mother, had detached themselves from hairpins and ribbon and fell on to her shoulders in frightful disarray.

It had taken Tess a long time to realize it, but her strong resemblance to her father was a constant, bitter reminder to Florence of her own lapse. To feel the full weight of Florence's disapproval was a terrifying experience, and dreading her wounding tongue, the nearer Tess came to Golden Court, the more her feet dragged.

The sounds of violence reached them from some way off. Their father's curses, their mother's screams. Forgetting her own fears and with Tom close behind her, Tess picked up her skirts and started to run, scattering the fading bluebells in her wake.

With Tom clinging to her skirts, Tess flung open the door and strode fearlessly into the room.

Patrick Kelly had his wife down on the bed and was sitting astride her, systematically punching her in the ribs and face while roaring, 'You're me wife, you'll not refuse me, woman.'

Florence's skirt had been savagely ripped and exposed thin, pale legs latticed with swollen blue veins. She was making a desperate attempt to protect herself against the violent onslaught but there was little she could do. Already her lip was split and bleeding, her face and eyes yellowing and bruised.

All Tess's anger erupted at this not uncommon sight and she picked up the first thing that came to hand. Then swiftly, hardly knowing what she was doing, she turned to the bed and lifting both hands high above her head and with all the force of her strong young body, she brought the heavy coal shovel down, with a fearsome crack, upon her father's head.

He gave a grunt of surprise, stood up and spun drunkenly round to face his terrified daughter. Then, to her utter relief, his legs suddenly buckled under him, his eyes closed and he fell heavily to the floor.

It was very quiet in the room. Shaking violently, Tess gazed in horror at the blood trickling through the thick thatch of hair. Her eyes were large, the pupils dilated with terror, when she finally spoke. 'Is 'e dead, Mum?'

Florence eased herself painfully off the bed and as she tried to adjust her torn clothing, stared down with hatred at her inert husband. 'Not a chance,' she said grimly. 'His skull's too thick for that. Better have a listen, though.' Bending, she put her ear to Patrick's heart. 'Still beating, more's the pity.'

Tess let out a slow silent breath of relief and then watched as with practised ease, Florence went through her husband's pockets. Standing up she then counted out the pickings and gave a whistle of surprise. 'There's nearly five pounds here, and all in florins. Now I wonder where he got all that from?' she mused. She counted it again, slipped three pounds into her apron pocket and returned the rest to her husband's jacket. She was wise enough never to strip him of all his assets.

34

'Now let's get him outside,' Florence said. 'Tom, you open the door, Tess, you grab hold of his legs and I'll take his arms. He belongs in the gutter and that's where he's going tonight. He'll remember none of this in the morning,' she assured her children as they shuffled the body across the floor, 'he was too drunk. He'll just think he fell.'

Patrick Kelly was a large man and getting him out of the house was no easy task but a small group of interested neighbours, attracted by the sound of a domestic dispute, had gathered outside.

'Here, we'll give a hand with the bugger,' one of the women said and, united now against a common enemy – husbands – two of them helped Patrick Kelly's family to drag him through Golden Court and out on to the street.

But looking at him as he lay inert among the debris of the gutter, Tess felt a twinge of remorse. 'Will 'e be arright, Mum?'

'Course he will. The devil looks after his own, doesn't he? God, how I hate him,' she said bitterly, giving him a sharp kick with the toe of her boot. Then to emphasize her point, she slowly, and very deliberately, spat upon his upturned face. 'That bolt's going on the door tonight . . . just in case.'

But Tess was too weary to care now. 'Come on, Mum, your face needs attending to.' Taking her arm, she led her mother back to the house where she sat her down in a chair. Pouring water into a bowl, she carefully bathed the split lip and bruised face. And as she tried to repair the damage and saw the extensive bruising, all the old hatred for her father returned.

'I'll swing for 'im one day, I really will,' she muttered through clenched teeth.

'Don't let him get at you, Tess. It'll only destroy you.'

'I can't understand anyone marrying, just to be treated like this.'

'Not all men are like your father, although it might seem like it round here. My father never once struck Mother.'

'Well, I'm not even going to try and find out, cos I shall never marry.' Tess stood up and surveyed her mother's bruised face. 'I've tidied you up a bit, but you're gonna look awful in the morning.'

'You're a good girl, Tess,' Florence said, clasping her daughter's hand, and there was actually a note of tenderness in her voice.

But then Mrs Kelly turned to Tom, who had been frightened into silence by the whole incident. 'You all right, my little man?' And the undiluted love in her voice tore at Tess's heart.

Tom nodded and then ran to her, burying his head in her lap. Florence nursed him for a moment, stroking his hair gently, then easing him away from her, she plunged her hand into her apron pocket. 'After what's happened tonight I think we all deserve a bit of relish. Go and get some jellied eels, Tom, a few whelks and a bottle of sarsaparilla.'

This was indeed a rare treat, and Tom went quickly before Florence could change her mind.

Patrick Kelly didn't come thundering on the door in the middle of the night as Florence had feared, neither did he show up the day after, and it wasn't long before they knew why. He was in prison awaiting trial on a charge of dealing in counterfeit coins. Found in the gutter by two Peelers, apparently blind drunk, he'd been carted off to a police cell for the night. It was here that the florins in his pocket were discovered to be counterfeit.

It was a serious crime and the evidence was damning, although he swore at his trial he knew nothing of the money. Because he had no previous criminal record the sentence was comparatively light; seven years' penal servitude. And it was Patrick Kelly's even greater tragedy that not one member of his family cared.

36

3

Patrick Kelly's departure to Her Majesty's prison had one adverse effect on the family: it upset the fragile household economy. Like everyone else in the neighbourhood they lived on a knife edge of poverty, so that without his meagre contribution the situation became desperate, no matter how many floors Florence scrubbed or extra washing she took in.

It was finally decided they would have to take in a lodger, although Florence didn't care for strangers in the house. She'd had them in the past and they'd proved to be more trouble than they were worth, often proving to be feckless and dishonest.

But in the end, with the spectre of Parish Relief hanging over them, she had to accept defeat and that was how Mr Appleby came to stay with them.

Mr Appleby was, like his name, small, round and rosy-cheeked, and even by Florence's high standards was judged respectable. For he had a job, was clean in his habits and paid his rent without prompting.

He bought and sold things, he told Mrs Kelly when she inquired as to his business.

'What sort of things?' asked Florence.

'Oh, this and that,' he answered vaguely, adding that it would often take him around the country. And this suited Florence quite well, just as long as he continued to pay his rent.

Pip, as the children were soon calling him, was a Devon man and a spinner of yarns. In his soft west country voice he would tell them stories of wreckers and smugglers and of outwitting the Excise men. He would talk too of his days at sea and, chins cupped in hands, Tess and Tom would sit entranced as he told them of the great tea clippers and of the races to India and China and back, sometimes in under a hundred days.

Listening to him sometimes, Florence would smile and think to herself that some of his tales sounded as tall as the masts of those great ships in which he'd once sailed.

But as well as his stories, he brought books and an optimistic energy into the house, and Tess and Tom adored him.

He was sitting with them in the kitchen one evening as Tess and Tom stood folding sheets for Mrs Kelly to iron. Florence worked with two large flat irons, heating each one in turn and then spitting on the base to check that the temperature was right.

Bored with this job, Tom said to Mr Appleby, 'You promised to show us your tattoos soon, Pip.'

'I did, didn't I,' replied Mr Appleby, pulling up the sleeve of his shirt. The children, glad of any diversion, stopped what they were doing and stood gazing in admiration at this evidence of the tatooist's art, at the anchor, the dragon and the snake that wound its way up his left arm. On his right arm there was a heart pierced with an arrow and underneath a girl's name: Meg.

'Who's Meg, Mr Appleby?' Tess asked nosily.

'Just a girl, hardly remember myself now.'

'Did you love her?' she pursued.

'A little, perhaps. I loved them all a little. But I only had one true love, my maid, and that was Annie, God rest her soul, and her name is tatooed next to my heart.'

'Can we see it?' asked Tom, jumping up and down with excitement now.

'Why of course you can,' replied Pip and began unbuttoning the front of his shirt.

Mrs Kelly put the iron down with a thud and gazed at Mr Appleby reprovingly. 'I think that will do, Mr Appleby, if you don't mind.'

Mr Appleby quickly rebuttoned his shirt. 'Eh . . . sorry, Mrs Kelly, no offence meant,' and he looked so embarrassed,

Tess had to restrain herself from leaping to his defence and telling her mother not to be such a killjoy.

It was Mr Appleby, too, who encouraged Tess to read the books he brought home, much to her mother's disapproval. Florence considered the reading of novels the most extreme form of idleness. But Tess had a sharp curiosity and the books, and Mr Appleby's stories, began to round out her vision of the world and fill in many of the gaps in her scanty schoolgirl knowledge.

As well as reading everything he brought home, she also questioned him eagerly and even dared to argue with him on certain points.

'My, she's a bright one, this daughter of yours, Mrs K.,' Pip would say admiringly when Tess had scored a point in some argument.

'Impertinent is the word I would use,' replied Florence sharply. Then to Tess: 'You're over-reaching yourself, my girl, arguing with your elders and betters like that, so watch your step,' she added warningly.

But even Florence began to mellow as the months passed. Although she was still rigorously self-disciplined, she became less acid-tongued and tense, the bitter lines round her mouth began to fade and the bony hollows of her slight frame to flesh out into a more comfortable shape.

But if home life improved, conditions at the factory remained much as always, with the same petty restrictions which were so numerous Tess found it difficult to remember most of them. Often, though, a lighter pay packet at the end of the week was a painful reminder that the pockmarked Bert Higgins had caught her talking or found her work bench untidy.

Tess tried her best to avoid him but this wasn't easy for he had a peculiarly silent crab-like walk and he would sneak up on the girls when they least expected it.

Tess considered him a foul-mouthed pig but she noticed that some of the other women seemed to relish his coarse, offensive remarks and were quite his equal in crudity and suggestiveness. Listening to these exchanges sometimes,

Tess would feel herself blush with shame for her own sex in allowing a man to talk to them in such a familiar way. He'd tried it on her. But only once. For when he saw the contempt in her grey eyes the words had died on his lips and from then on he'd tended to leave her alone.

Sarah, however, was less fortunate. Working alongside her now, Tess began to understand why her friend was always anxious not to upset him. She couldn't afford trouble, because all the two sisters had in the world was what Sarah earned each week. But Bert, knowing a victim when he saw one, had it in for her, although he had little opportunity. She was a good worker, kept her mouth shut while he was around and was never late for work. But unfortunately she'd once made the mistake of publicly humiliating him.

He'd come up behind Sarah, as he often did with some of the other women, and clasping her around the waist had pressed himself against her, making appreciative grunts at the same time. Sarah's face, always pale, had taken on a chalky hue and even her lips seemed to drain of colour. She'd endured his fumblings for about ten seconds only and then she gave him an almighty shove with her behind. 'Ger orf, you dirty sod,' she spat at him, her eyes ablaze with hatred and contempt.

Taken by surprise, the foreman stumbled back and Sarah turned on him then with a further shove against the chest which sent him staggering across the room, where he finally came to a halt against a pillar. Every woman in the immediate area stopped work and waited. There was a small snigger, then another, a bit louder this time, until finally the whole room erupted into loud, derisive laughter.

'Shurrup!' Bert roared, his face red, his fists clenched.

As quickly as it had started, the laughter ceased. But it was Sarah's undoing and from that moment it became Bert Higgins's sole intention to make Sarah's working hours as unbearable as possible.

One morning, when she'd accidentally spilt a tray of matches, he fined her sixpence. Sarah didn't say a word, but as she bent to pick them up, Tess could see that she was in tears. Choking back her anger, Tess crouched down beside her.

'That tanner would 'ave bought me and Milly enough food for three days,' Sarah sobbed.

Peering under the benches, Tess saw heavy boots approaching and quickly put out a hand to comfort her friend. 'Don't worry,' she muttered, 'I'll get him for this one day, I promise,' and then stood up again, glowering at Bert Higgins with murder in her heart.

Although Tess plotted various slow, painful deaths for the chargehand, she knew that even though it was a very large factory, employing over a thousand women, they were yoked to the place by poverty. There was nothing any of them could do about the iniquitous fines except seethe inwardly. It was only in the dinner hour, well away from the ears of those in charge, that the women dared to voice their grievances more loudly.

And even though cowed by foreman and backbreaking hours of work, the women still managed to let off steam on a Friday night when, with full pay packets, they made for the nearest pub. Lizzie Cakebread was always trying to persuade Tess to join them.

'Go on, let your hair down a bit,' she would urge.

But Tess always shook her head. If her mother smelt drink on her breath she was quite likely to knock her daughter to the ground.

But life did have its better moments. She now subscribed three pence a week to a boot and dress fund run by a woman in her section. For the first time in her life Tess experienced the pleasure of wearing a dress that wasn't second hand, picked up off a market stall and smelling of someone else's sweat.

She began to get more than a passing glance from the opposite sex, too, for although her face still had the fresh roundness of youth, at fifteen Tess was a striking girl with firm, high breasts and slender waist. But her thick curly hair, now worn up, was still a source of some despair because it seemed to defy the restrictions of either comb or pin and would often tumble childishly around her shoulders.

Still, Mrs Chadwick obviously considered her a young lady, for these days when they called, although Tom was given ginger beer, Tess was offered a sherry. Not that she liked it particularly but it did make her feel very grown up drinking from the fragile, long-stemmed glasses. Also to be actively defying her mother by drinking alcohol was a pleasure in itself.

'Liking the job any better these days?' Mrs Chadwick asked, as she refilled all their glasses.

'Not really,' replied Tess glumly. 'But I've got no choice, have I?'

'Why not? I told you a long time ago you could come and work for me. You'd do well here, a smart girl like you.'

Too embarrassed to answer, Tess sipped the sweet, sticky liquid. 'Mum says I've got to stay where I am,' she mumbled at last, and to her relief Mrs Chadwick pursued the matter no further.

But it still rankled, her mother's attitude, and as she and Tom walked home she felt the old resentment simmering again. 'I don't see why I can't work for Mrs Chadwick, Mum knows how much I hate working at that rat 'ole of a factory.' Tess thought for a moment. 'It's spite, I reckon.'

'Well, I'm glad I'm not going there,' answered Tom feelingly.

Tess stopped and stared at her brother. 'Since when?' she asked. She assumed the time could be reckoned in weeks now when Tom would join her at work and see for himself the horrors she so graphically described.

Looking jaunty, Tom tipped his cap forward so that the peak nearly covered his eyes. 'Since last week. Didn't you know? I'm gonna be a stable boy way out in the country in a big 'ouse. Maybe even learn to be a jockey.'

This statement was such utter nonsense that Tess waited for her brother's face to break into its mischievous smile. Then with a little shove he would say, as he often did, that he was only teasing her.

But it was apparent Tom was taking himself seriously. 'It was Pip's idea. He knows someone who could get me into a racing stable. Seems I've got the right build.'

Well no one could argue with that. Tom hadn't matched her own spectacular growth and at thirteen he was as small and wiry as his mother.

Nonplussed, but with a slightly sick, anxious feeling that Tom might be speaking the truth after all, Tess took refuge in derision. 'But you don't know one end of an 'oss from the other.'

'It don't matter, I can soon learn,' Tom answered defensively, sensing his news wasn't being too well received.

'And what does Mum say?' Florence, surely, would not be parted from her beloved son.

'She thinks it's too good a chance to miss.'

Tess stopped and stared fiercely at her brother. 'It's always the way, ain't it? Mum lets you have anything you want. But what about me, eh? Don't my feelings count at all? Sometimes I think she really hates me.'

Tom put out a hand, anxious to placate his sister. 'No she don't, Tess.'

'Why can't I work for Mrs Chadwick, then?'

Tom puzzled over this for a moment. 'I dunno, Tess, I really don't. But it ain't *my* fault, you know.'

Tess lifted her shoulders in a movement of resignation. 'No, you're right, Tom, it's mine for being born a woman.'

But she felt a keen sense of betrayal. Pip encouraged her to have an independent mind, to think for herself, and yet it was Tom's future he was making secure, not hers. But she wasn't going to let the hurt she felt go unsaid, although she was wise enough to make sure her mother was out of the way before tackling him on the subject.

As usual when a ship arrived from the Far East, Pip had been down at the docks all day and Tess watched him as he carefully unwrapped some small, carved ornaments and set them down on the table.

'Nice pieces these, should get a good price for them,'

he said with some satisfaction. He picked up one of the ornaments, a figure of an old man. 'Look at this detail, princess. Exquisite, isn't it? And all carved by hand.'

Tess gave an uncommunicative grunt and gazed at the figure indifferently. There were more pressing matters to be discussed. 'Pip, how'd you manage to get Tommy that job? In the stables.'

'Ah, bit o' luck that. I had these oriental rugs, was down in Suffolk and Lord Petrie got to hear about them. He bought them off me, he did. Afterwards I was shown round his stables, got talking to someone there and thought I'd put in a good word for Tom while I was about it. It was as easy as that.'

'But what about me? Why didn't you find me a job?'

Pip laughed. 'What, as a stable boy?'

'There are other jobs in big houses.'

'True enough. But I think your mum would like you here for a while now that's she losing Tom.' He began re-wrapping the ornaments, then picked up his hat. 'Now, young lady, I've got a little business to attend to. Tell your mum I'll be back about ten. And Tess . . .'

'What?' Her mouth had a sullen, downward droop.

Pip patted her gently on the cheek. 'Come on now, it's not like you, try and be glad for Tom.'

And that was that. But she really did try, over the next few weeks, to hide her deepening sense of envy as letters arranging Tom's future flew between Golden Court and Suffolk. Tess even tried not to feel a guilty delight when there was a hiccup in the proceedings and Pip had to rush off down to Suffolk bearing a fine-looking vase. After this, though, events really gathered momentum. Finally Tom's future was settled to everyone's satisfaction, his few things were tied in a bundle and he was waiting for one of the Great Eastern trains which would carry him off to his new life on a grand Suffolk estate.

They looked an awkward little group as they stood on the platform, uncomfortable with each other now that departure was near.

Mr Appleby ruffled Tom's hair. 'Now don't worry, son, you're going to be all right. Famous, even.'

Tom didn't answer, just swallowed hard and looked miserable. When the train drew in he kissed his mother and Tess goodbye shyly, then shook hands with Pip, nervous and ill at ease in his new role. Getting into the carriage he pulled down the window. The guard waved his green flag and the train began to lurch and shudder down the platform.

Suddenly there were a thousand things Tess needed to say to her brother, advice she wanted to give. Clutching the brass door handle, she ran along beside him, but as the great engine began to build up speed, Tess found she couldn't hold on. Letting go, she cupped her hands to her mouth. 'Don't forget to change at Cambridge,' she called but her instructions were lost in the hiss of steam and the plaint of metal wheels. In the end all she could do was stand at the end of the platform and wave frantically as Tom's small, sad face became a blur and the tail of the train disappeared round a curve in the track.

With a lump in her throat Tess walked back down the platform and saw that her mother's face had disintegrated into grief. Knowing she'd just been robbed of the one person she held dear, Tess felt a terrible pity for Florence and longed to offer solace, to put an arm round her and comfort her. But there had never been an easy affection between them and such display of emotion would have discomforted them both, so the moment passed.

In an effort to cheer them both up Mr Appleby said breezily, 'You know, he's going to one of the best stables in England. And Lord Petrie looks after his servants. Tom will have clean country air and more than enough to eat. Why, you won't recognize him next time he comes home. And wait until he's riding that Derby winner, you'll be proud of him then.'

But none of this sounded very convincing, even to Mr Appleby himself, and it was a sad and silent little trio who walked down the steps and into the street.

It was the same on the omnibus going home. Pip gave up trying to sound cheerful, Florence dabbed at her eyes and Tess felt the familiar dissatisfaction return. Florence was forever complaining that it was a man's world, and then proved it by favouring Tom.

If I'd been born a man, Tess thought fiercely, I could have done anything. Anything. The possibilities were limitless. But she was shackled by her femininity. Never had Tess felt life to be so unfair.

The house, with Tom gone, was very quiet and even Florence, never one to sit with idle hands, briefly stirred the fire and then sat gazing into it with a listless, dejected air.

But Mr Appleby wasn't a person to mope for long and the gloomy atmosphere began to get on his nerves. 'Tell you what,' he said, jumping up from his chair, 'why don't we all go to a music hall?'

Florence Kelly looked profoundly shocked. 'Mr Appleby, whatever are you suggesting?' she said in her most intimidating voice.

But Pip ploughed bravely on. 'You'd think we'd all been to a wake, not seeing Tom off to a new life. A night out would do us all good.'

Like most pleasurable things in life, Florence disapproved strongly of music halls. Dens of iniquity, she called them. 'I have never, Mr Appleby, visited a music hall in my life,' she declared with some pride.

'About time you did then, old girl, do you a power of good.'

That was it, thought Tess. Old girl. He'd put his foot in it this time. She'd never go now. But if she was shocked by such familiarity, she said nothing.

'Go on, girls,' Mr Appleby urged, 'best bib and tucker on and we'll have a night on the tiles. How about it, Mrs K.? A music hall and a bite of supper afterwards. It's what we all need.'

It sounded a marvellous idea to Tess and she held her breath as she waited for her mother's reply. Several emotions crossed Florence's face before it cleared.

'Well, just this once then.'

Tess let out a whoop of delight and danced round the room.

'And you can calm yourself down, my girl, or you won't be going anywhere,' Florence warned.

But Tess didn't really believe her and she tore over to the corner of the room and opened a small chest. Pulling out a dark blue serge skirt and a white frilled blouse, she quickly heated the iron. Meanwhile Florence changed into a dark dress that only saw the light of day on very special occasions, usually funerals.

Mr Appleby traded in 'Oriental Curiosities', and for her last birthday he had given Florence a lovely fringed black silk shawl decorated with pink roses, large as cabbages. Although it was her most prized possession she had never worn it and it lay, wrapped in tissue, in the bottom of a chest of drawers. But tonight, for the first time, she got it out and draped it round her shoulders.

'How do I look? Not too gaudy, is it?' she asked doubtfully.

'It looks lovely, Mum, it really does,' said Tess truthfully, and she realized that Florence, with her fine bones, must have been a remarkably pretty young woman.

Just then Mr Appleby came back downstairs, his shoes buffed to a shiny perfection and his brown derby set at a jaunty angle. 'Right then, off we go.' And taking each of them by the arm, he marched them out of the house.

Tess knew that she looked her best that evening and she was also aware of the admiring glances of men. But her own gaze remained aloof and unwavering as she steadfastly refused to meet any young buck's eye.

At the end of the street Mr Appleby hailed a cab and they made their way to the Paragon in great style.

Pip got them very good seats in the front row of the dress circle and Tess could see that her mother was in her element as she gazed disdainfully down at the totters and rag pickers in the pit and up at the domestic servants in the gods. She should have been born a lady, my mum, thought Tess, smiling to herself.

Tess, who had never been inside a theatre before, had an immediate impression of gold paintwork and red plush seats and curtains. She was also quickly caught up in the excitement of the crowd and as she waited with some impatience for the heavy safety curtain to rise, she studied the adverts, silently mocking the claims that Snowdrift Flour would make her pastry the envy of her neighbours or that Dr Tibbald's Blood Mixture could cure anything from bad breath to gout.

Finally the lights dimmed and the orchestra scraped out an overture. As the curtains rose, Tess sat forward in her seat, unwilling to miss one single moment of the unfolding spectacle. The first act was a juggler, but he was so incompetent, balls fell from his hands and plates crashed in pieces at his feet. The audience responded with catcalls and whistles and the poor man had to duck to avoid airborne apple cores and orange peel. Completely demoralized, the juggler picked up his props and sidled off the stage to a slow hand clap.

The next act was a man with dogs who did tricks and after this, two dancing sisters. But it was Miss Fanny Baxter everyone was waiting for.

She wasn't very old, perhaps twenty, and neither her singing nor her dancing amounted to much, but she had a stage presence which defied these failings and a repertoire of saucy songs. And she could put all the innuendo in the world into a wink and a swish of her skirts, and the audience, loving it, roared their approval.

Mr Appleby was thoroughly enjoying himself, slapping his thighs with delight and tapping his feet in time with the music. But one glimpse of her mother's grim profile told Tess she wasn't sharing Pip's enthusiasm.

After several encores the audience finally let Fanny go and the curtain came down for the first interval.

Florence stood up. 'I think that's quite enough for one evening,' she said firmly.

Mr Appleby looked very taken aback. 'Aren't you enjoying yourself then, Mrs Kelly?'

'I certainly am not,' replied Florence, managing to express moral outrage in the merest twitch of her shawl. 'I can't stand smut, nor the spectacle of that woman showing all her legs. You can stay, if you like, but I'm . . . we're going. Come along, Teresa,' she ordered imperiously.

Pip was speechless now and Tess could do nothing but trail after Florence, although at that moment she could have cheerfully throttled her. Why did she have to be so self-righteous all the time? Why couldn't she enjoy herself, just once, particularly when Pip had spent all that money on seats for them?

With dragging feet she followed her mother down the broad steps and into the main foyer where the interval crowd were milling around, gossiping, drinking and smoking. She was standing on the bottom step when she saw Mrs Chadwick. She caught her mother's arm. 'Look, Mum, there's Mrs Chadwick, give her a wave.'

Florence shook her arm free. 'I'll do nothing of the sort.' And then without even bothering to glance in Mrs Chadwick's direction, she swept out of the theatre and into the street.

Prepared now to defy her mother, Tess was just about to cross over and speak to Mrs Chadwick when she noticed that she was deep in conversation with a gentleman. Tess's nerve deserted her then and she hurried to catch up with her mother.

They were a few yards from the theatre when Mr Appleby overtook them, panting noisily. Mrs Kelly stopped and gazed at him stonily. 'I thought you were enjoying that cavorting woman too much to want to leave.'

'So I was and what's the harm in it?' Pip answered good-naturedly. 'And you enjoyed it too, didn't you, princess? Go on, I saw you laugh, admit it.' He gave Tess a sly wink.

'I did, I really enjoyed myself, and thanks for taking us both,' Tess said courageously, refusing to meet her mother's eye.

'Well, we'll let bygones be bygones then and get a bite to eat. Are you two ladies hungry?'

'I could probably manage something,' said Florence, unbending slightly.

'Good. There's a pie and eel shop down the road, we'll go there.'

But not before Florence had first of all peered in through the window to see if the tables and floor satisfied her stringent requirements. Only when it had been thoroughly inspected were they allowed to go in.

They sat in a high-backed wooden booth. Mr Appleby ordered jellied eels but Tess and her mother had pie and mash which came covered in a greenish substance called 'licker'. As Tess cut through the crisp brown pastry a delicious aroma arose from the gravy and chunks of meat. She was less sure about the 'licker', but she ate it anyway, not wanting to offend Mr Appleby any more that day.

While her mother was in the privy and before he went up to bed, Tess thanked Pip again.

Lying in bed later she remembered Mrs Chadwick – one of her mother's best customers and yet she'd chosen to ignore her. It was hard to understand her mother sometimes. In fact she often wondered if it wouldn't be better if she just gave up trying.

4

Although she occasionally harassed her mother about it, Tess was still at the factory almost three years later when Elsie Leggatt died, and as she and Sarah moved with the other workers towards the gates that evening, they talked about it in hushed, frightened voices. The cold January air seemed charged with unrest and fear and the thought was in everyone's mind: whose turn next?

She had been a bully, Elsie, and Tess had never forgotten that first bewildering day at work when the woman struck her. But she could feel nothing but pity when, after developing a cold, she began to complain about toothache and went absent from work. Then the rumours began, with the dreaded words 'phossy jaw' being whispered up and down the benches and quickly spreading unimpeded through the factory.

Nerving herself, Tess had gone with Lizzie to visit Elsie in Bethnal Green Infirmary. By then, the disease was at its tertiary stage, her teeth gone and her face heavily swathed in bandages. Tess knew enough to guess that the suppurating abscesses and insidious poisons had already eaten into the jawbone, facial tissue and throat. Even if she survived, the young woman would be hideously deformed for life. Elsie couldn't speak to them, only the eyes revealed her hopeless terror. It was a look which would haunt Tess for the rest of her life and it needed every ounce of self-control she possessed not to flee from the hospital ward and Elsie's affliction and despair.

She remembered again, how afterwards she'd left Lizzie to rush home and scrub ferociously at her own strong teeth, convinced her gums would soon be a soft, oozing sponge of pus.

That dread had never left her, and was reinforced today by the news of Elsie's death.

Utterly convinced now of her own fate, she turned to Sarah with a shiver of fear. 'We'll all get it in the end, you know that, don't you?'

But Sarah treated such things more lightly than Tess. 'Course we won't. You just have to make sure you wash your hands properly before you eats your dinner and see that you get rid of all the phosphorus, that's all.'

If only it was as simple as that, thought Tess. Just then the low keening sound of a foghorn came from the river, its baleful message seeming to echo her own sense of helplessness, and she shivered again.

The month of December had been bitter. For weeks snow had lain piled in heaps on the side of the road, solid and immovable. Water in standpipes froze and the death rate soared. Hunger and pneumonia carried off many, while the stiffened bodies of those sleeping rough had to be collected each morning for burial in paupers' graves.

But finally the thaw had set in and the snow had melted into a black slush. Walking home, the girls were constantly splashed by the wheels of passing traffic. Soon the hems of their skirts were wet and dirty, their feet, in cheap boots, soaking.

The foghorn sounded again and Sarah said, 'There's fog coming in, do you want to leave it? We could be in for a real pea souper.'

Tess had noticed too that fog was curling in from the river and she hesitated for a moment. She always spent Tuesday evening with Sarah and her sister. If she went home now it would mean disappointing Milly, who looked forward all week to her visit.

'I think I'll risk it. Pip bought me a book of short stories to read to Milly.'

'Let's hurry, then,' said Sarah and picking up their skirts, the girls scurried towards the market. Knowing there wouldn't be much more business that night, most of the costers had packed up and gone home. Those left were selling goods off cheaply and at an offal stall they bought a pound of chitterlings and a lump of pork

52

fat. With the money over they still had enough for a loaf and sugar and tea. After this they scuffed around in the rotting vegetables until they found enough wood for a decent fire.

The sign that swung above the rabbit warren of a house where Sarah lived read 'Logins' and it was peopled for the most part with thieves, pimps, prostitutes and just a few respectable people down on their luck. It was on the somewhat lackadaisical charity of these people that Sarah depended to see that Milly was all right during the day.

Tess often wondered what would happen if Sarah fell ill, for the sisters were quite alone in the world and there was nothing between them and the Union.

Now that they were home Sarah, anxious as always about her sister, hurried on up the dark, crumbling staircase. Tess followed, passing shadowy, ragged figures already roosting for the night and huddled together for the only warmth they would get.

Tess was standing behind Sarah as she opened the door and by the dim light from the window she could just discern the outline of a small bundle on the bed. If Sarah had left a fire that day it had long since gone out, and the room was bitterly cold. Dropping her things, Sarah hurried over to the bed.

She dropped to her knees and asked, her voice tight with anxiety, 'Milly, you arright?'

'Yeah, I'm fine,' Milly wheezed. 'Bit cold, though, the fire's gorn out.'

Tess lit the lamp and as she drew a thin piece of material across the window, noticed a broken pane of glass stuffed with rag. She sighed, wishing there was more she could do for her friends.

With the wood they had collected and some coal, she got the fire going and in the warm light it was possible to ignore the damp, evil-smelling black mould on the walls and the cracks large enough to accommodate a fist.

'What we got to eat then, Tess?' asked Milly as her sister propped her up in a chair.

Tess pretended to look thoughtful. 'Well . . . let me see now. To start with there's hasty pie, then for afters . . . a run round the table and a kick at the cat.'

Milly laughed. 'No, go on, tell me what you've really got,' she urged. There was always a treat on Tuesday.

'Wait and see, young lady,' replied Tess, and bending over the fire she soon had the chitterlings sizzling in the pork fat. When they were crisp and brown, three slices of bread followed to soak up the fat.

'Mmmm, that smells really good,' said Milly when Tess finally put the plate down in front of her and Sarah fussed around making sure she was quite comfortable before she ate.

It always seemed to Tess that Sarah's devotion to Milly was one of those rare miracles. At work Sarah wasn't too popular for she had a surly manner and sharp tongue, and Tess's friendship with her seemed to puzzle some of the other girls.

'Don't know 'ow you puts up wiv 'er, sour-faced cow,' Lizzie Cakebread had grumbled one day after she'd received the short end of Sarah's tongue for no particular reason.

Tess shrugged. She wondered why herself sometimes. 'Life's hard for her, you know.'

'It's bleedin' hard for all of us, duckie,' Lizzie replied with some feeling.

'Yeah, I know, but she worries all the time she's away from Milly, 'specially when her cough's bad.'

'If Sarah talked about it, mebbe we could help.'

'She wouldn't take charity, you know that, she's too proud.'

As always Lizzie's reply was tart and to the point. 'Bugger pride.'

But after this conversation things would sometimes arrive unannounced at the girls' room: a sack of coal, a rabbit to cook or some fruit and vegetables. Obviously there had been a whip round, although Sarah never mentioned it or bothered to thank anyone either.

After the three of them had finished their small meal, tea was made and Sarah and Milly settled back to hear Tess read. This was the best part of the best day of the week for them both.

The book Pip had bought her was entitled *Life and Adventure for Girls*. It was second hand and its spine was broken but there was promise of great riches between its battered covers.

Clearing her throat, Tess opened the book, turned to the first page and started to read, enunciating each word carefully and using her voice to good dramatic effect.

Spellbound the sisters sat and listened as young ladies went on tiger hunts, shot over rapids or solved crimes that had baffled the best minds at Scotland Yard. She was beginning the third story when she realized that the fog must have thickened for it had begun to seep through the broken window pane into the room.

Tess got up and lifted the curtains. The fog was a thick, dense yellow.

She pulled on her coat and hurriedly buttoned it up. 'I'll have to go, it's really bad out there.'

'Don't go yet, Tess,' Milly pleaded, 'read us one more story.'

Tess bent over and gave the small, frail body a quick hug. 'I must, my love, but I'll stay longer next week, I promise.'

Sarah saw Tess to the door and she made her way quickly down the dark staircase, past the formless, crouching bundles and into the street. Once outside, however, she stopped. She could see nothing, and apart from the foghorns everything was silent. There was no traffic, no people, not even a stray dog. The world seemed as flat and dense as cotton wool.

Covering her mouth with her shawl, Tess inched her way gingerly forward, confident that she knew the district too well to get lost and reassured by the occasional pale beacon of light from an ale house. She moved steadily, looking for familiar landmarks and determined not to lose her nerve.

It was some time before she would admit that she was lost. In fact, not until she realized she was in an area of tall, shuttered warehouses and empty factories.

Trying not to panic, she stopped. It was then she heard a muffled footfall. She took several steps forward and then stopped again, her head cocked for any sound, her heart thumping uncomfortably. There it was again, one step, stealthy and threatening, then silence.

Remembering those huddled figures on the stairs, a blind terror seized her. Less fearful now of what lay ahead than the evil that stalked behind, she stumbled blindly forward, her arms outstretched, her breath coming in painful, rasping sobs, her lungs at bursting point.

Tess didn't see the dim light above the glass-panelled door until she was practically on top of it, then, not caring, she flung herself against it and was propelled by her own momentum down several stone steps and into the arms of a young man.

Tall, fair and well dressed, the young man looked only slightly surprised by her somewhat unorthodox entrance.

'Good evening,' he said, as Tess fell against him, panting wildly and trying to steady the terrifying beating of her heart.

Tess, with no breath in her to answer, just stared at him. Balancing her gingerly, he went on, 'Take your time, get your breath back.' He consulted a gold hunter from his waistcoat pocket. 'There's no rush, Mr Jenkins doesn't start for another five minutes. It was good of you to come on a night like this anyway. Now, if you feel up to it, perhaps you'd like to follow me.'

Utterly bewildered, Tess just did as he said and followed him down a rather dim corridor. When they reached some swing doors he held one open to allow her to pass through. She entered uncertainly and found herself in a largish room with several rows of chairs. There was also a magic lantern and against a wall a white screen. Seated in the chairs were not more than half a dozen people, who all turned to stare as she entered.

'Perhaps you'd like to sit here,' said the young man, offering her a seat. Nervously Tess sat down on the edge of the chair, prepared for flight at any moment.

The man went and stood in front of the sparse audience. 'I'm very grateful to you all for coming out on such a dreadful night to hear Mr Jenkins give his talk and show his slides of the pygmy tribes of Equatorial Africa. I'm sure you will all find it a most enlightening experience. Thank you.'

There were a couple of desultory claps and a man sitting in the front row stood up. Mr Jenkins was a tall, nervous-looking man with wispy ginger hair and a prominent adam's apple which leapt up and down as he spoke. Shuffling some papers he said, 'You will realize of course, that pygmies are not like us, but are a primitive people and, naturally, heathens.'

Tess knew nothing at all about pygmies so she decided to settle down and enjoy her enforced lecture. But she'd reckoned without Mr Jenkins, who unfortunately had a dull, sonorous voice and equally dull, grainy slides, only slightly less murky than the fog. One third of his audience was soon asleep and during a brief hiatus in his ramblings there came a loud, contented snore. Tess giggled nervously, and someone sitting further along leaned forward and seemed to glare at her disapprovingly. This only made matters worse and she giggled again, only more audibly this time.

Poor Mr Jenkins, by now thoroughly demoralized, faltered in mid sentence, uhmmed and aahed ineffectually several times and then ground to a halt.

There was some coughing and shuffling of feet and then the gentleman organizing the proceedings, realizing perhaps that Mr Jenkins didn't have the full attention of his audience, stood up.

'Thank you, Mr Jenkins, for your most illuminating and entertaining discussion. I'm sure everyone here will wish to express their appreciation of your efforts.' The meagre audience, knowing what was expected of them, clapped obediently. He waited for them to finish and then went on, 'Now if you'd all like to come through' – there was a quick scraping of chairs and a rapid movement towards the exit – 'tea and cake are being served next door,' he concluded to an empty room.

A much larger audience must have been expected there that night because a long trestle table was set with a dozen or more cups and a plate was piled high with slabs of fruit cake. The cake, Tess noticed, was vanishing rapidly, almost before the young man had time to pour the tea.

As she stood waiting, Tess had time to study the other people in the room. It seemed fairly obvious that several of them, who were elderly and poorly dressed, had come to the meeting only to keep warm and get something to eat.

But one person did interest her. He was perhaps two or three years older than herself and was dressed in the clothes of a working man: corduroy trousers, muffler and heavy boots. The thick, springy brown hair, the broad shoulders and blue eyes also declared his origins even before she heard someone call him Liam.

The superior young man, for that was how she already compared them, finished pouring the tea and, balancing two cups and some cake, brought them over to where Tess stood feeling very awkward and wishing she knew where she was.

He handed her a cup of tea and in his beautifully modulated voice said, 'By the way, I'm David St Clair, I help to run the Settlement.'

'Oh,' replied Tess, who was still no clearer in her mind where she was.

There was an embarrassed silence then the young man asked politely, 'May I know your name?'

'Oh . . . yes,' she stammered, 'Teresa Kelly, but everyone calls me Tess.'

'Well, I shall call you Teresa if I may. Anyway, can I ask you what you thought of Mr Jenkins's talk? Did you find it interesting?'

Tess had a sudden and overwhelming desire to please Mr St Clair. But she also had a strong respect for the truth, for it was something which had been dinned into her at a very early age by her mother. For a few moments she had a silent struggle with her conscience and her eyes wandered vainly round the room seeking guidance. Honesty might have won if she hadn't happened to glance over to where Liam was standing pouring tea into his saucer and, she noticed, blowing on it.

It was obvious he'd been listening to their conversation, for he emptied the saucer in one gulp and then over its rim gave her a conspiratorial wink.

That was it! With a flash of annoyance, both at his lack of manners and his familiarity, she turned back to Mr St Clair. Speaking in her most refined voice, the one she kept for special occasions, she answered, 'Pygmies is very interestin'.'

He seemed pleased by her answer. 'Good, then you must come again. Everything here is completely free, there is always something going on at the Settlement and young ladies are very welcome.'

No one had ever called her a young lady before and she began to feel very warmly disposed towards Mr St Clair – and the idea of returning to the Settlement.

'Have a look on the notice board, there are a variety of classes and we are open every evening.'

Tess saw by the wall clock that it had now gone ten. If she wasn't home soon her mother would start worrying. She put her cup down on the table and then wishing Mr St Clair goodnight, hurried out of the room.

But she stopped to study the notice board in the corridor, reading down the list and hoping to find something that might interest her.

At first glance, with subjects like Greek and Latin, it all seemed way beyond her. Then there was a lecture on Socrates. What was that? Another language? She'd gone right to the bottom of the list before she saw what she wanted; it was a reading party taken each Wednesday night by Mr St Clair. That would do nicely, she thought with a quiet sense of satisfaction, she would join Mr St Clair's class.

She was pushing open the main door, when someone called her. 'Hey, hang on.' She didn't have to turn, she knew it was the young man called Liam.

'Which way you going?' he asked as he caught up with her.

She gave him a brief glance. 'Golden Court.'

'I'll walk with you if you like.' He spoke as if bestowing a great favour.

On any other night Tess might have turned up her nose at such an offer but the fog was still thick and after her earlier fright she was nervous about venturing out alone.

'You're Patrick Kelly's girl, aren't you?' he asked, when they were outside and starting to make their way forward, keeping close to the wall.

Irritated at being reminded of her father, Tess stopped. 'How do you know?' she asked aggressively.

'Well, for a start you're the image of him and for another your old man and my old man worked in the docks together.'

'What's your name then?'

'Liam O'Sullivan.'

And that's not a name to brag about either, thought Tess, for in an area tolerant of most behaviour, Liam's family must have been one of the most notorious. Both his parents drank heavily and fought publicly, and the younger kids, all of them boys, were snotty-nosed little street urchins with hardly a pair of shoes between them. He would know that her own father was in prison but Liam's father had been in and out several times too, which Tess felt put them about on an equal footing and would stop him getting above himself.

The fog began to lift enough for them to walk side by side. 'What did you think of it back there tonight?' Liam asked.

'I thought it was all right. I'm thinking of joining the literature class actually, the one Mr St Clair takes.' She enjoyed saying his name, it sounded so aristocratic.

'Literature.' Liam gave a puff of contempt.

'And what's wrong with that?' asked Tess, not liking his tone.

'Well, it's not actually going to change the world, is it?' He sounded very superior.

'And you are, I suppose?'

'Not just yet, but later on, perhaps.'

'How?'

60

'By going into politics. That's why I'm studying political economy and trade unionism at the Settlement, which is much more important stuff than literature.'

Tess was getting very rattled. 'People like us don't go in for politics. That's for rich folk. Anyway, my mum says that all politicians do is shout their mouths off and line their pockets.'

'I shall be different.' He spoke with a certitude that began to tire and bore her and she was glad to see that they had reached home.

Liam lived further on than her and as he swaggered off down the street he called over his shoulder, 'I'll see you around, I expect.'

'Not if I see you first,' Tess muttered. She watched him for a moment. All mouth and trousers, that one, she thought disparagingly. And not a bit like Mr St Clair. Now there was a real toff!

5

Even to herself Tess couldn't quite admit that what drew her to the Settlement was David St Clair. A little learning was what she was after, that was all. However, with some discreet (or so she thought) questioning she found out from Liam that David was twenty-two, well connected, had been up to Oxford and, it was said, wanted to enter the Church. In the meantime he spent most of his spare time helping to run the Settlement, a very worthy cause.

Tess had never before met anyone quite like David and she would sit gazing at him dreamily, her mind only half on the text they were discussing in class, hypnotized by the beautifully modulated voice, the high noble forehead and the long slender fingers that he pressed together as he spoke.

And he was such a gentleman, too. Not like her dad, or Liam or any other man she'd ever known, coarse and uneducated. But then Mr St Clair came from a world quite different from hers; a world without brutality, a world of refinement and good manners.

Although she was often tongue-tied in his presence, this didn't stop her looking for opportunities to be alone with him. One evening, deciding that she had something of great importance to ask him, she waited a little nervously for the classroom to empty, then took a book of poetry up to his desk.

'Thank you, Teresa.' He gave her one of his vague, sweet smiles and went on packing books into a large black bag.

He'll be gone in a minute, she thought, and yet she couldn't think of a word that would delay his departure.

But he suddenly seemed to realize she was still there. 'Was there something you wanted, Teresa?'

She cleared her throat. 'Could I ask you something, Mr St Clair?' she said in a rush.

'Why of course you can, that's what I'm here for. By the way, I thought you read that sonnet most beautifully this evening. You seem to enjoy poetry.'

Tess blushed with pleasure. 'Oh I do, but I don't always understand what they're getting at.'

'Never mind, that will come,' he assured her. 'After all, that's what this class is for, to acquire an appreciation of our rich cultural heritage.'

Tess gazed at him in admiration. She really loved it when he spoke like that, used long words she hardly understood.

'You know,' he went on, 'the Settlement has a lot to offer an intelligent girl like you. Have you ever thought of taking advantage of some of the other classes on offer here?'

'Yes, I have. But I'm not sure what to take. I just know I want to better meself . . . myself. So that I can get away from that factory.'

'What about shorthand, then? And we've recently acquired one of those type-writing machines people are beginning to use. Just think what a help you would be to us here if you could master those two skills.'

'Would I?' Tess's face lit up.

'You most certainly would.' David moved towards the door, holding it open for her, and although she longed to delay him a little longer she could see that he was impatient to be gone.

But his words had given her hope and she even dared to form pictures in her mind. She saw herself, hair neat for once, in a plain dark dress with starched white collar and cuffs, tremendously competent and quite invaluable to David. But then doubt seized her and her steps faltered. She had so little education it would take years to master skills like shorthand and type-writing. Then she gave herself a mental shake. For heaven's sake have faith in yourself, Teresa Kelly. Liam was no better than she was and yet look at the confidence he had. Even saw himself in Parliament. All I want to do is work in an office. Surely that's not beyond anyone. Besides, it might be her one chance of escape. If she didn't grab it she deserved to spend the rest of her days in the lucifer factory where the simmering discontent now voiced itself occasionally in outbreaks of mindless vandalism.

But there was something that did briefly lighten the lives of everyone that summer and that was when Queen Victoria, who was so old and who had reigned for so long, had her Golden Jubilee. There was to be a holiday for everyone, the Queen would ride in an open carriage from the Palace to Westminster Abbey and the whole country had been invited to celebrate. However, since Mrs Kelly's only acknowledgement of the event was some red, white and blue ribbon pinned to the Queen's portrait and Mr Appleby, who might have taken them somewhere, was away on 'business', Tess had made no particular plans for the day.

After finishing work early one Saturday, Tess and Sarah were on their way home when they were diverted by a small crowd and stopped to watch with interest as an escapologist, bound in heavy chains, prepared to extricate himself from a sack bound in even more chains. But then his partner began to move amongst them, jingling coins hopefully in his cap and the girls decided it was time to move on.

They were just walking away when Sarah gave Tess a nudge. 'Don't look now,' she muttered, 'but that Liam O'Sullivan's just behind us.'

Tess gave a hiss of exasperation. 'Pretend you haven't seen him.' She grabbed Sarah's arm. 'Come on, let's go.'

Like her mother's, Tess's tolerance wasn't limitless, and Liam had a knack of materializing from nowhere. He didn't seem to suffer the uncertainty or doubts of other people and her indifference to his undoubted good looks didn't deter him in the slightest. Pleased at having outwitted him, the two friends hurried away, giggling conspiratorially. Before parting they stood for a moment discussing what they would do that afternoon and decided that if the rain held off, they would take Milly to the park. As they separated, Tess felt a spot of rain. Anxiously she scanned the grey swollen clouds, turned a corner and cannoned straight into Liam.

'Ah, just the girl I wanted to see,' he said with a broad grin.

'Sorry, I'm in a hurry, can't stop.' Tess tried to dodge round his large frame.

'I'll walk with you then.'

'It's a free country,' she answered indifferently. They walked in silence for a few yards then Liam began to whistle through his teeth.

'Do you have to make that noise?' she asked crossly.

'Nope,' he answered cheerfully and resumed his tuneless dirge.

Knowing he was trying to provoke her, Tess refused to take up the bait. Instead she found solace in the dissection of his character, deciding quickly that he would probably make an extremely good politician, since he was equipped with both insensitivity and the hide of a rhinoceros. She tried to hurry on, to leave him behind, but his long legs could easily match her stride even when she almost broke into a run. Finally, seeing there was only one way she would get rid of him, she stopped to draw breath. 'What was it you wanted to see me about?'

Liam gazed intently at the bright shine of his boots and shrugged. 'I don't suppose you'd be very interested.'

Aggravated beyond endurance and remembering his well-earned reputation for messing girls about, Tess glared at him ferociously. 'Liam O'Sullivan, you are being very childish.'

'Sorry. It's nothing much really, just that I might take myself up West to see the Jubilee and wondered if you'd like to tag along.'

Tess smiled sweetly but the sarcasm came undiluted. 'Going to see the Queen, Liam, a good socialist like you? I am surprised.'

For a second he looked slightly discomforted but quickly recovered. 'Well, you have got to admit it, Tess, they are a load of parasites. What makes them entitled to lead lives of idleness while the rest of us spill our guts out for a pittance? Doesn't that strike you as wrong?'

''Course it does, but I don't keep on about it like you. And if you've got principles, you should stick to them.'

'I thought I'd better take a look at them while they're still around.'

'What do you mean?' she asked suspiciously.

'Well, come the revolution it will be off with their heads, like in France.' He demonstrated by drawing a forefinger menacingly across his throat, and Tess shuddered. 'The whole blinkin' lot of them would go, even your precious Mr St Clair.' As he spoke, Liam watched her face closely for some reaction.

'Why, what harm has he ever done you?' she demanded indignantly.

'Ah, I knew you had a soft spot for him,' Liam jeered.

'Watch it,' Tess warned, but felt angry with herself at allowing her feelings for David to become so transparently obvious that even Liam had noticed. 'Anyway, it wouldn't hurt if you showed a bit of gratitude, instead of talking like that. You would if you had any sense.' Then deciding his spiteful remark about David called for a few home truths, she went on, 'But then that's not something you've got much of, is it, Liam? Common sense. Fact is, I sometimes think all your brains are in those big feet of yours.' And Tess watched with a guilty feeling of pleasure as she saw a flicker of hurt in the blue eyes.

She walked on then but as always, when her quick tongue got the better of her, she began to feel slightly ashamed and when Liam called out persistently, 'So you're not coming then?' she stopped and waited for him to catch up with her.

'I'm not saying I will definitely, but just supposing I do, will you go on about socialism and unions all day?'

'Course I won't.'

'And what about money? How much is it all going to cost?'

Liam waved his hand airily. 'I'll take care of that.'

'Right,' said Tess, 'I'll come on two conditions, no politics and I pay for myself. I like to be independent.'

'Done,' said Liam and as he threw back his head and laughed, Tess noticed the strong, muscular neck and the powerfully built workman's shoulders. Making a comparison then between Liam and David's almost fragile slimness, she still knew which of the men she preferred.

In spite of herself, Tess couldn't help feeling excited as Jubilee day approached. There was such a feeling in the air it picked her up and carried her along. And it might be her one chance of seeing the Queen, an old lady now but who, when she'd come to the throne fifty years previously, had been a shy young girl, hardly older than Tess herself.

The day started dull with a slight mist which didn't fool anyone. For this was 'Queen's weather' and later on it would get very hot. Tess had scrubbed herself pink in the zinc bath the night before and a new dress, purchased through the club, lay waiting to be put on. It was a fresh blue and white striped cotton with a wide belt that flattered her trim waist, and she knew she looked good in it. To complete the ensemble there was a straw boater trimmed with cornflowers which reflected in her rather serious grey eyes and turned them to blue.

When the dress was on, Florence stood back and regarded her daughter in silence. Her mother's gaze could always induce unease in Tess and she fidgeted with her hat, waiting for the criticism to come.

'Do you know,' said Florence at last, 'you're not a bad-looking girl, Tess.' She sounded surprised, as if making some momentous discovery. 'And it'll be wasted on that Liam O'Sullivan. He's never going to appreciate you, coming from a tribe of Irish good for nothings like that.'

I'm Irish too, Tess was tempted to say, although it would have been unwise, since any reminder of Patrick Kelly brought an instant darkening of her mother's mood.

Only a week before, a letter had come from the prison governor, informing Florence in unemotional official language which gave no hint of any suffering, that her husband's left hand, badly crushed in a brawl, had since had to be amputated. Florence read the letter without a flicker of feeling and then handed it to Tess. She scanned the note, thinking to herself, this was surely her mother's chance to forgive, to be magnanimous towards a man who had seen none of his family since he entered gaol.

'Will you go and visit him now, Mum?' she asked.

'Certainly not,' Florence replied and to make her intentions quite clear, she committed the letter to the flames.

A semi-illiterate scrawl from Patrick followed. It was a letter from a sick and lonely man, and in it he pleaded with his wife to visit him. This letter was torn into small angry shreds and Tess, who found her mother's steely indifference somewhat inhuman, became quite eloquent on her father's behalf.

'But you must go and see him, Mum, he's ill.'

'I'll do nothing of the sort. I never want to set eyes on that man again!' she'd answered venomously, and had put paid to any further argument by disappearing into the wash house.

Today, though, her mother was in a light-hearted frame of mind and Tess didn't want to spoil it. Moving over to the mirror, she pinned her hat into place. 'You don't have to worry, there's nothing between Liam and me,' Tess said, addressing her mother's reflection. 'Besides, he's not like his ma and pa, he wants to do something with his life.' She pushed the last pin into place and turned round. 'Well, how do I look?'

'Fit for the Prince of Wales himself,' her mother said proudly. She took two florins from her pocket and thrust them awkwardly into Tess's hand. 'Enjoy yourself and tell me all about it when you get back.'

'Thanks, Mum.' Tess gave her stiff-backed unyielding mother a quick hug.

Florence watched Tess with a melancholy expression as she picked her way carefully through the debris of Golden Court. She's like a butterfly on a dung heap, she thought. Please God, spare her a life like mine. Tess reached the corner and turned and waved. Florence waved back, stood there for a moment longer, then with a sigh went back into the house and closed the door.

Liam was waiting for her on the corner, imprisoned in a stiff white collar, his wiry hair supporting a smartly rolled brown derby that aged him by several years. His eyes lit up with pleasure when he saw Tess. 'Turn round and let me have a good look at you.'

Pleased, but self-conscious at the same time, Tess did as he said.

'My, it's a real lady I'm taking out today, that's for sure.'

But Tess hadn't quite reached the age where she could accept compliments graciously from a man. 'Less of the blarney,' she said briskly, 'and let's go.'

'Well, it's true. You and me, Tess, are wasted in a midden like this.' He waved an arm to encompass the whole of the East End of London.

'There's nothing we can do about it, though, is there?' said Tess fatalistically. 'We're stuck, just like our parents are, and theirs before them.'

'You don't want to take that attitude, you know,' said Liam severely.

But Tess, who was regarding her new white shoes with some concern and wondering if they would be quite as pristine by the time they reached the main road, was hardly listening. 'Can we hurry?' she said. 'My shoes are getting mucky.'

Deaf to her pleas, Liam went on, 'I shall go abroad, of course, make a lot of money, come back . . .'

'Yeah, I know, and change the world.' The white shoes began to tap impatiently on the pavement. 'I hope you've said as much as you're going to say about politics for one day, because if you haven't, let me know and I can go now.'

Liam looked sulky. 'If you want to remain one of the downtrodden masses that's your concern.'

'Liam . . .' Trying to silence him her voice held a warning note – although she had no intention of going home, she'd gone to too much trouble and expense for that and was vain enough to want to be seen.

He laughed then and held up his hands in surrender. 'All right, not another word.' And clasping her arm, he plunged into the confusion of Mile End Road.

Everyone today was in their Sunday best and in a carefree, holiday mood. Buildings and shops had been decked out in red, white and blue, and down side streets Tess could see trestle tables being set up for street parties later in the day when there would be games and dancing, too much drinking and a few bloodied noses, and where every child would receive a jubilee mug.

After a long wait and with much pushing and shoving, Tess and Liam were eventually able to struggle on to a very crowded bus.

Liam got them a seat upstairs. The greyness had cleared and it was now hot, and they had a perfect view from the open-decked bus of everything that was going on.

Slowly the horses made their way through the packed streets, past the rounded dome of St Paul's Cathedral and up Fleet Street. But by this time the crowds had brought everything to a halt. Clambering down the stairs and on to the pavement, they were lifted up by the great swell of people and carried along the Strand.

Terrified that she would be swept away by the great tidal wave of humanity, knocked down and crushed to death by a million stampeding feet, Tess clung to Liam for dear life. And as her hat was knocked sideways and her white shoes trampled on by heavy boots, she began to wish she hadn't come. But they were hemmed in by a wall of people and there was nothing they could do but move with the crowd. Trafalgar Square was identified to her by Nelson's Column and here Tess stopped, straightened her hat and announced firmly, 'I'm not moving a step further.'

'Yes you are, we're nearly in Whitehall.' Grabbing her hand and using his powerful frame as a battering ram, Liam ploughed on through the crowds, undeterred by oaths or the threats of violence to his person that followed them. Tripping and stumbling behind him, Tess felt as if her arm was being wrenched from its socket. Just when she thought they had stopped, Liam would change his mind and move on again, so that when they did eventually come to a halt, Tess's head was spinning with heat and exhaustion and all she could see was the rear end of a very large horse.

'I told you I'd get us a good spot, didn't I?' declared Liam triumphantly.

'You did indeed, Liam,' Tess answered, with only a trace of irony. After all, he had done his best and if she stood on tiptoe and craned her neck there was a chance she might see something of the procession. Nevertheless, she couldn't help casting envious glances towards those rich enough to afford a seat in the stands or even at people perched precariously on roofs or leaning from upstairs windows.

'How long do you think we'll have to wait?' Tess asked, wincing as she felt a sharp elbow in the small of her back.

'Not long, she's at her service of thanksgiving. We'll see her on the way back.' But Tess was beginning not to care. The sun, high in the sky, beat down on them mercilessly, she was perspiring freely and longed only for shade and a gallon of cold water.

They heard the music first, then the words, like an excited refrain, 'She's coming! She's coming!' At that precise moment the mounted guard in front of Tess moved just enough to give her a clear view down Whitehall to six elaborately harnessed white horses pulling an open landau and followed by an escort of Indian Cavalry. There was a spontaneous, triumphant roar and every man, even the republican Liam, lifted his hat in salute.

As the landau drew level Tess was disappointed to see how plainly dressed the Queen was. She wore no ceremonial robes, no crown, just a dark dress with a rather strange, white-plumed bonnet tied under her chin with lace. She looked so ordinary, so tiny it was hard to believe she ruled over a great empire and had weathered periods of unpopularity and gossip. After her beloved Albert died she'd become almost reclusive. Then again there had been the speculation over her relationship with one of her servants, a Scottish ghillie, John Brown. But there was no hint of this today, just a triumphant reaffirmation of the esteem in which her subjects held her.

71

With her in the carriage was her daughter, Vicky, Crown Princess of Germany, and the Princess of Wales. The ladies smiled and waved and bowed and Tess waved back frantically, hoping to gain the Queen's attention. But the coach passed and was followed by the male members of her family, sons, sons-in-law and grandsons, resplendent in their uniforms, creating a dazzling, golden splendour. After this came the princes and kings and queens of Europe and the East, and the crowds roared themselves hoarse until the last soldier had disappeared from view. Not satisfied, they then broke up and started to surge towards Buckingham Palace where they could cheer some more.

In the excitement, Tess had forgotten her thirst and discomfort but as Whitehall emptied of people there appeared, as if from nowhere, a solitary figure trundling in front of him a tea stall bearing the inscription Temperance Society.

For Tess it was like an oasis in the desert. She grabbed Liam's hand. 'Come on, I'm thirsty,' she said and hurried him towards it.

It was tea strong enough to stand a spoon in, but it was hot and sweet and reviving, and after two cups they both felt sufficiently restored to go and look for some shade. St James's Park was thronging with picnicking families but eventually they found a spot under a tree and near the lake. Flopping down, Liam stretched himself out on the grass, closed his eyes and soon appeared to be fast asleep. Leaning against a tree, Tess resisted the urge to remove her shoes, but instead allowed herself to make a cool assessment of Liam, noticing the thick curling lashes and the taut strength of his thighs that seemed to strain against the material of his suit. That came with working in the docks, of course, it made men hard and strong.

He wasn't a bad-looking chap really, she thought. In fact most girls would be, were, glad to have his attention, but her own preference was for slim, fair men, men of refinement and good manners, and Liam would never do for her.

Just then he opened one eye. 'Will I do?' he asked with a smile.

Disconcerted Tess stared back at him blankly. 'I don't know what you mean,' she said distantly.

Turning on to his side he rested his head on his hand and gazed up at her. 'Come on, admit it, you've been looking me over for the past five minutes.'

Nettled at being caught out, she answered, 'Do you really want to know?'

He gave her a confident smile. 'Course I do.'

'All right. But you asked for it, remember,' she warned. 'Personally I think you've got too big an opinion of yourself, without good cause.' Tess hadn't intended being quite so harsh in her judgement but as she'd started to speak, he'd reached up and rather familiarly smoothed a stray curl behind her ear.

His fingers lingered but as she pushed them away, she saw his expression change and understood for the first time that in spite of the brash exterior Liam was as sensitive to criticism as anyone. 'I'm sorry, Liam, that was unkind. But you do ask for it, you know. Anyway, what do you expect me to say, that I find you irresistible?'

'I wish you did.'

'And be treated like all the other women in your life? No fear.' She'd heard gossip about Liam at the factory, some of it fairly unsavoury, and although it might have become exaggerated in the telling, she knew at least one girl who'd been very badly hurt indeed.

'I'd treat you like a queen,' he said, gazing at her earnestly.

'No you wouldn't. In time you'd treat me exactly as you treat all women, badly.' To put an end to the conversation, Tess stood up, adjusting her hat and smoothing her dress.

Liam sighed audibly and stood up too. 'I give up. Come on, let's go and find something to eat.'

Neither of them had eaten all day and they were both starving. But down on the Embankment they found a coffee stall and here they gorged themselves on hot sausage sandwiches and small pastry tarts filled with jam and sponge and topped with pieces of coconut. Coffee followed after which they felt ready for anything and set off towards Piccadilly and the illuminations.

Every street, every building and lamp post was garlanded with flowers and banners. Triumphal arches spanned the streets proclaiming: Victoria, All Nations Salute You. Shop windows had been lavishly illuminated, and as it grew dark and fireworks soared into the dark sky, exploding and dropping in a waterfall of colour, the dirt and squalor of London were forgotten and the town took on a magical quality.

For most of the day the crowds had been good-natured and well-behaved, but then people started getting drunk, youths became boisterous and pockets were picked. And Tess could no longer ignore her aching feet, nor the painful blister on her heel. By the time they climbed on the right omnibus, she was limping badly and when they got off at the other end, she was glad to take Liam's arm for support.

They'd reached Golden Court and she was about to thank him with a carefully prepared small speech for her day out when he suddenly slipped his arm around her waist and pulled her close.

She'd been taken unawares but she knew exactly what he had in mind. 'Let me go, please.' She spoke very quietly, and unfortunately for Liam he couldn't see the thunderous look in her grey eyes.

'It's arright, I'm not going to do anything,' he said with a laugh, although he sounded a little uncertain.

'Get your hands off me, this minute, or you'll live to regret it,' she threatened through clenched teeth. She tried to wriggle free then but he was too strong for her.

Pinning her arms to her side, he said, 'For Christ's sake, Tess, I'm not gonna rape you, all I want is a kiss. Like this,' and before she could protest any further, he bent his head to her mouth. It was a brief kiss, gentle as summer rain, and then he let go of her.

Her breasts heaving with indignation, Tess took a step back and wiped her hand across her mouth in a deliberate movement of disgust. Then she lifted her foot and delivered a sharp kick upon Liam's right shin.

'Ouch, what you wanna do that for?' he yelled, clutching his leg and hopping around in an exaggerated dance of pain.

'I'm not one of your tuppenny ha'penny tarts. A day out doesn't buy me. Be on your way, Liam O'Sullivan,' she ordered imperiously. 'And don't ever bother to ask me out again.'

Liam watched her as she hobbled with blistered heel up the narrow alleyway to her house. Then with a resigned shrug he too limped off into the night, bearing with him a bruised shin and somewhat injured pride.

Tess's fury lasted until the door of her house. Here she was brought up short by the sound of laughter from within. It was a rare enough sound for Tess to stop for a moment and peer in through the window. Sitting at the table were her mother, Mr Appleby and Tom. With a cry of delight Tess almost fell into the small room as she rushed to embrace her brother.

'Why didn't you tell me you were coming?' she asked. 'I wouldn't have bothered to go out.' Already she was regretting the wasted hours with Liam.

'I didn't know, did I?' Tom replied. 'Pip just turned up, had a word in the Guv's ear, and here I am. I've got three whole days off.'

Tom might have grown an inch or two, but it didn't seem like it to Tess. But his lack of height didn't seem to bother him. 'I'm an apprentice jockey now, Tess, I daren't carry too much weight.'

For Tess it was a marvellous end to a mixed day and as soon as she had taken off her shoes and bathed her sore feet they sat down to a table laden with pickles, cheese and cold meats.

They wanted to hear about the Jubilee procession in every minute detail. What the Queen wore, the uniforms of the soldiers, who was in the carriage with her. And as they sat listening, Tess saw that Florence, surrounded by her family, wore an expression of rare contentment. She also noticed, once and very briefly, Mr Appleby cover Florence's hand with his. It was a small, almost casual gesture but since her mother never encouraged intimacy of any sort, it took Tess completely by surprise.

Oh, thought Tess, and studied her mother's features more closely. That happy glow wasn't entirely due to Tom's presence, then. Still it was nice to think she and Mr Appleby were fond of each other. Not that it could go any further. Florence had a husband, *and* a rigid moral code.

6

Although she felt very tired from her exhausting day and late night Tess managed somehow to be at her work bench on time the following morning. But as the hand on the large wall clock began to move inexorably from six thirty to twenty to seven, Tess began to glance anxiously round for Sarah. Where was she? Then to her relief she saw her friend, discarding hat and shawl as she came panting down the centre aisle of the shed, between rows of working girls, empty trays and barrels and all the debris of factory life.

But as Sarah tried to slip in unnoticed beside her, Tess heard with a sinking heart Bert Higgins's voice.

'Decided to work part time, 'ave you?' he bawled across the floor, pleased that nothing escaped his sharp eyes.

Sarah gave a nervous look in his direction and then, hoping to avoid any further confrontation or sarcasm, hung up her shawl and hat and began rapidly filling boxes.

But he never allowed Sarah to get away with anything now, not since the day of his very public humiliation, and Tess watched with a deep loathing as he moved in on his helpless prey. He pushed between them and, ignoring Tess, spoke to Sarah in a low, threatening snarl.

'I'm asking you a question, Atkins, and you'd better bloody answer.'

'Me sister's been took ill, I just couldn't leave her,' Sarah explained in a troubled voice.

He shouldered his way nearer and Tess noticed with disgust the crust of spittle that encircled his loose mouth. Just looking at him made her flesh crawl.

'Well now, that's just too bad, hain't it, cos we hain't running no charity 'ere. We expect a day's work out of you, me girl, not half a day.'

'I was only ten minutes late ... I'll work through the dinner hour,' Sarah offered, but without much hope.

'Oh no you won't.'

'But you let some of the other girls ...' Sarah protested, with a break in her voice.

He nodded in evident satisfaction. 'That's right, I do, but not you, you little madam. It's comin' out of yer wages, see, and count yerself lucky you hain't been sent 'ome.'

'But you can't do that,' she cried desperately, 'you knows 'ow much I needs the money. Me sister's got to have medicine.'

'Too bad.' Jostling them roughly, he turned to walk away.

Sarah stopped pleading then and her voice went hard. 'Course there's some who gets away with murder here, ain't there? Them who goes behind the sheds with you, for instance and do you little favours. We all know about them, don't we, girls?' She turned to her workmates seeking affirmation. A few of them looked shifty and bent their heads to their work, but others murmured bravely in assent, Tess the loudest of all.

Higgins turned round to face Sarah again, his fists clenched like cannonballs, his eyes bulging. 'I've 'ad enough of your lip ...' He lifted his fist threateningly.

But Sarah didn't budge. 'Touch me and I'm warning you, you'll live to regret it ...' and before she'd finished his hand came up and dealt her a swinging blow across the face.

Slightly stunned by the impact, Sarah stood for a moment trying to fight back the tears, the impression of his fingers already showing red on her ashen skin. Then in an unexpected movement she leapt towards the chargehand like a tigress, claws out and pulling them down the length of his face, scoring it with blood. She was going for his eyes when Tess grabbed her. But fury had given Sarah a superhuman strength and she managed to wrench herself from Tess's grasp, shrieking, 'I'll kill 'im, I'll kill 'im.'

As Tess caught hold of her again, she felt the violent tremors in Sarah's body and in that instant would have gladly done the deed on her behalf. But for Sarah's good she had to control her own venom, that was vital if she was to salvage anything out of the incident, to save her friend's job. Restraining her struggling friend with difficulty, Tess said quietly, 'Calm down, Sarah. Can't you see it's what he wants?'

Her reply was a wild, hysterical laugh. 'I don't care, the old fart can do what he likes.'

'Right, I will. Out! Now!' Bert Higgins roared, dabbing gingerly at his wounds with a piece of dirty rag. 'And don't bother to come back.'

'You lousy sod!' Tess spat at him, unable to curb her anger any longer.

'S'right. But I've got a job and she hasn't. And neither will you 'ave if you don't watch yer tongue. Go on, Atkins, bugger off before I kick you up the arse.'

The other women had watched this drama in total silence, none of them daring to express their support in case the foreman turned on them too. But as Sarah gathered her few things together and walked past them, her thin shoulders sagging in defeat, there were defiant murmurs of sympathy.

Although she was on piece work, Tess didn't work well that day. The empty space beside her was a constant reminder of Sarah's humiliation, and Tess had so much anger locked inside her, she thought she might be sick.

All that day Bert Higgins watched her, daring her to put a foot wrong. Tess longed to wipe the gloating, pleased expression from his stupid face with some terrible act of violence and as she brought the razor sharp blade down on the lucifers, she took a ferocious delight in imagining it was the foreman's neck that was being bloodily severed in two.

She was so anxious about Sarah that she grabbed her coat before the hooter had sounded its final blast. This gave Bert his chance.

'What's yer hurry? I'll tell you when you can go. And get that bench tidied up first.' Tess took a deep breath, clenched her teeth and waited. As soon as the foreman had gone and she was on her own, she went over to his bench and kneeling down scrawled defiantly in large letters on the

79

dusty floor, 'We'll get you, Bert Higgins, one day.' Standing up again she wiped her hands down her apron and surveyed her work with some pride. Even if he half guessed, there was no way he could prove absolutely who it was had done it.

But even this didn't rid Tess of her anger. It was still with her when she walked through one of the workshops where the noisy, dangerous box-making machinery, capable of slicing a finger off, now stood silent. On either side of the workshop and running its length were two shafts fitted with pulleys. From these pulleys a leather drive belt ran down to each machine. How easy it would be, thought Tess, to put them all out of order. Just one sharp knife. She could smuggle it in under her coat. But she knew she wasn't capable of such a wilful act of destruction, and it would put girls out of work who could ill afford it.

Frightened by her own dark thoughts, Tess hurried out of the gloomy building. When she heard someone behind her call 'Hey' the hairs on the back of her neck prickled with fear. She didn't dare look around and it wasn't until she'd almost reached the gates that Lizzie Cakebread caught up with her.

'What's wrong with you? You were moving so fast I thought you had the devil on your tail.' Puffing from her exertions, Lizzie limped along beside her.

Tess's body sagged with relief. 'I'm on my way to see Sarah and Milly. I haven't been able to stop worrying about them. That sod Bert Higgins wouldn't care if they died of starvation.'

'Perhaps this will help a bit then.' Lizzie pressed some silver and copper coins into Tess's hands and she stared at them in surprise. There was almost five shillings in the palm of her hand and she knew there was no way Lizzie could afford to part with that amount of money.

'Where did you get this from?' Tessa asked, trying not to sound suspicious.

'The girls 'ad a whip round. Everyone gave something. Tell Sarah she's to take the little 'un to see the quack or get some medicine.'

Tess was so overwrought by the events of the day that this surprising act of kindness brought tears to her eyes. She was a real rough diamond, was Lizzie: plain, with a deformed foot and a fondness for gin but with a tender heart. Tess squeezed the girl's hand in gratitude and blinked back the tears. 'Thanks, Lizzie.'

Deeply embarrassed, Lizzie spoke roughly. 'Go on, don't 'ang about.'

Tess thanked her again and then taking her advice, hurried on in front, cheered slightly by the gift of money for Sarah and Milly.

The harsh coughing reached her while she was still only halfway up the stairs. As soon as she opened the door, heard the shallow, laboured breathing and saw the bleak, stricken look in Sarah's eyes, Tess knew Milly was in a bad way. She didn't waste any time.

'I'm gonna get some medicine for you, Milly, something that'll make you well again,' she promised, and driven by a sense of urgency she recklessly took the dark stairs two at a time in her hurry to get to the market.

She knew exactly where the medicine man's stall was but as she threaded her way through the crowds of bargain hunters she fretted that he might have already gone, But he was still there, working busily on the corns of a perspiring, elderly gentleman, wielding an evil-looking knife and with a small boy as an interested spectator.

Seeing a potential customer, the medicine man left off sawing at his patient's toes and began rearranging bottles and packets hopefully on his barrow. Wisely the old man chose this moment to slip his feet back into his shoes and creep furtively away.

'What can I do for you, luv?' the stallholder asked as Tess studied the ointments, powders and personal testimonials of satisfied customers, seemingly cured of such diverse ailments as abscesses, dropsy, consumption and morbidity.

'I want something for a cough.'

'I've got just the thing,' he said, lifting his index finger. Then diving under the counter he produced a thick, muddy-looking substance which he shook vigorously and then offered for her inspection.

Tess gazed at the bottle doubtfully. 'How much is it?' she asked.

'To you, luv, three pence.'

'I'll take it,' she said, handing over three coppers and deciding that anything so unpalatable-looking would have to do the trick. Then with the medicine man's assurances of its restorative powers ringing in her ears, Tess hastened back to Sarah and Milly.

By now Milly's coughing had eased slightly and some of her old spirit had returned. 'I'm not taking none of that stuff,' she declared, eyeing the brown liquid suspiciously.

'But you've got to,' Tess urged, holding the spoon to Milly's compressed lips. 'It'll make you better.'

'Are you sure?'

'Course I am,' Tess lied.

'Well . . . arright then.' Reluctantly Milly allowed Tess to spoon the mixture into her mouth and then gave a shudder of disgust. 'Ugh, it's 'orrible,' she announced, which didn't surprise Tess in the slightest, although its beneficial qualities soon became apparent when Milly quickly became drowsy and then fell into a deep, exhausted sleep. Sarah covered her carefully with a thin blanket and as they both stood looking down at her and Tess saw the bruised eye sockets, the bloodless lips, she began to understand better some of Liam's arguments and the need for change. None of us deserve this, she thought bitterly, least of all Milly.

Satisfied that her sister was comfortable, Sarah put on the kettle. 'I can't afford it, but let's have a cup of tea anyway.'

Remembering the money in her pocket, Tess drew it out and handed it to Sarah, who stared at it in disbelief.

'What's this, then?'

'It's for you.'

'Me?' She held the coins gingerly as if they might burn her. 'But where'd you get all this from?'

'Don't worry, I haven't robbed anyone. Lizzie had a whip round, said you were to get medicine for Milly.' Persuading

Sarah to take charity without damaging her pride was always a tricky business.

Without a word, not even a murmur of thanks, Sarah put the money in a jar on the mantelpiece and then poured water on to some well-stewed tea leaves. As they sat drinking the tea with its bitter, tannin flavour, they discussed Sarah's future, talking in low voices so as not to disturb Milly.

'I'll find something, and nearer home this time so that I can look in on Milly in me dinner hour,' Sarah said optimistically. 'They need a hand at Blackstone's. I saw a card in their window this morning. If I goes round first thing, they'll probably take me on right away.'

Walking home later that evening, Tess wondered if Sarah had been a bit over-optimistic, for she had a good look in the jam factory window and she saw no card there.

Sarah eventually ended up sewing trousers in a crowded, ill-ventilated attic room where the hours were longer and the wages lower even than at the lucifer factory. Hardly robust, she seemed almost as fragile as Milly at times. And as the winter drew in and the fogs came so Milly's cough worsened.

One day when Tess arrived at their room Sarah was taking down the jar from the mantelpiece and counting out a few coppers, probably the last she had.

'I'm taking Milly to the quack.' She looked up from counting the money. 'Sixpence, do you think that will be enough?'

'We'll soon find out,' answered Tess as she helped Sarah to lift her sister into the perambulator and struggle with it down the steep stairs. They wheeled her round to the hospital and then waited for a long time in a cold, dimly lit corridor with malingerers, the sick and the dying.

Eventually a young doctor examined Milly and, looking very serious, diagnosed inflamed lungs. 'Your sister should be in hospital,' he told Sarah as he removed the stethoscope from his ears.

'But how can she? I've only got sixpence.' Sarah held out the money to the doctor, her face tense with worry.

The young doctor took her hand and closed her fingers over the coins. 'It won't be necessary for you to pay anything, this hospital has a charity ward,' he explained patiently.

Milly, who had been listening intently to this exchange with frightened eyes, began to sob. 'I don't want to go in no 'orspital,' she protested, clutching at Sarah's hand.

The tired doctor was now looking over Sarah's shoulder at the long line of patients still waiting to be seen. 'Well, of course, I can't force you . . .'

'She'll go,' said Sarah quickly. Then to Milly who had started to wail again: 'Shut up, it's for your own good.' Very much against her will, Milly was trundled off to the charity ward and Sarah stood listening with a distressed expression until her sister's wild protestations gradually subsided and could be heard no more.

'We've never been parted before,' she said gruffly, trying to explain her own tears away as she and Tess pushed the empty pram back home.

'She'll get better in there,' said Tess gently, trying to find comforting words. 'She'll have proper medicines, doctors and nurses to keep an eye on her, why, you won't know her in a few days' time.'

And Milly's health did seem to improve even though she complained bitterly, every time Sarah and Tess visited her, of the strict regime and bossy nurses, and fretted to be home with her sister.

During Milly's stay in hospital and until she was well enough to go home again, Tess found it difficult to get to her classes and she missed them. Missed David and the young men and women like herself she met there and with whom she had long heated discussions in the canteen while her tea grew cold. In their company she began to formulate concepts and opinions for herself and to learn respect for other people's views, sometimes even listening to Liam's.

Along with the others she took her turn in the canteen but her main pleasure was helping David in the office, even though her mother complained that he made use of Tess.

'He should pay you for what you do,' said Florence, who considered any labourer worthy of his hire.

'Most people work there for nothing. David ... Mr St Clair,' she quickly amended when she saw her mother's cool glance, 'doesn't get paid.'

'I should think not, with all the money he's got,' said Florence indignantly. 'Besides, if you've got so much time and energy, you should be here, helping me.'

Tess felt very cold. If her mother stopped her going to the Settlement now, she might as well die, she thought dramatically. There would be nothing left worth living for. 'I'm repaying him for all the help he's given me, that's all,' she hurried to explain.

Florence snorted down her nose at such idealist nonsense, but to her daughter's intense relief she said no more. Tess was well aware of the hopelessness of her feelings for David and the great divide of money, background and breeding. But she was able to accept this; just as long as she could be near him there was little more she asked for in life.

Things might have been different, she often thought, if she could have been like the beautiful, upper-class young ladies who, wearing exquisite diamond watches pinned to fashionably bustled gowns, appeared to assist David at the Settlement. Young women who hung on his every word and who would, a trifle condescendingly, agree to help out in the canteen. When David introduced them to Tess, they would make a swift assessment of where she came in the social scale, realize she was of no importance and so offered no threat, and thereafter pretend she didn't exist.

But they never stayed long. Neither did the young men who appeared from time to time. Tess, who was as quick as anyone in making social distinctions, guessed by their shabby clothes and genteel accents that they were probably city clerks, although they tried to disguise this by acting over-familiarly with David.

They did have one thing in common, though, these young men and women: they were unreliable to a fault. Left in the lurch, Tess was alone one evening in the canteen when Liam came in and leaned over the counter. Tess went on pouring milk into cups, pretending she hadn't seen him.

'What about a cup of tea, then?' he said at last.

Tess poured a cup and handed it to him silently, making it clear he still hadn't been forgiven for his caddish behaviour on Jubilee day.

'Aren't you going to talk to me?'

'What would you like to talk about?' she asked primly as she sliced slab cake into fingers.

'Us. I want you to be my girl.' His voice was earnest.

The cake knife poised in mid-air, Tess looked at Liam for the first time. 'And what about Maisie Lewis? She probably thinks she's your girl.' Maisie was a young woman Tess had seen Liam with on a number of occasions during the past weeks.

'Oh her, she's nothing,' he said indifferently and confirming what she'd already guessed: if Tess had been more readily available, Liam wouldn't pursue her with such persistence.

'I'm sorry, Liam, I'm prepared to be your friend, but that's all.' She felt that in the circumstances this was a very generous offer.

'I don't know what's wrong with you, Tess.'

Her grey eyes glinted dangerously. 'Oh, there's something wrong with me, is there, because I don't happen to swoon at your charms?'

Just then, behind him, Liam heard the swing doors open and shut and footsteps cross the wooden floor. But he didn't have to look round, he knew who it was by the way Tess lifted her head and smiled and by the sudden rosy tint of her skin. Liam sighed then, pitying Tess for the hopelessness of her love and pitying himself, too, because he knew there was no way he could compete.

But David was in a hurry and didn't stop. He gave a smile Tess felt sure he reserved especially for her. 'Teresa, be a dear and bring a couple of cups of tea and some cake round to my office, will you?' he asked and was quickly gone again.

Eagerly she set about putting cups and cakes on a tray, while Liam watched silently. Outside the office door she put the tray down briefly, pinched her cheeks and pressed her lips together to give them colour, tried to pat her hair into order and then knocked lightly on the door. When she entered David was deep in conversation with a young soldier who looked up with a hostile stare. Nobody spoke and no introductions were made so Tess swiftly left, thinking as she closed the door that the young soldier must be one of the 'lame ducks', as David called them, who turned up so frequently at the Settlement.

When she returned to the canteen the classes had finished and she was kept so busy serving tea she had no time to think of Liam. It was with a flash of annoyance then, when after washing up and pulling down the shutters, she saw he was still there. She buttoned up her coat and pinned on her hat very slowly, then, ignoring him, crossed to the swing doors.

He almost skidded across the floor. 'Allow me,' he said with a courtly bow, holding the door open for her.

She paused only long enough to glare at him. 'Are you trying to be funny?'

'I know you have a preference for gentlemen, so I'm just trying to behave like one.'

'Oh, go to hell.' And with a lofty toss of her head she flounced out of the building.

He watched her stiff-backed departure. Hoity-toity madam, he thought as he began to follow her. He often wondered why he bothered. After all, there were plenty more fish in the sea, many of them willing to be netted. And Tess wouldn't be every man's taste, she was too tall, too strongly built and with too much to say for herself. But she was intelligent and that, of course, was what he liked about her. He played around a bit at the moment but one day he'd be looking for a wife and a smart one at that, for he was going places. How old was Tess? Not eighteen yet, he guessed. There was plenty of time then, she was bound to come to her senses eventually, he thought, his natural confidence reasserting itself. He lengthened his stride. He couldn't see

87

her now but that didn't matter, for he knew that if he hurried he would soon catch up with her.

It should have been a good Christmas. There was a party at the Settlement with dancing and games. Tess helped to decorate the hall with holly and mistletoe, then, knowing David was bound to ask her to dance, spent ages practising the waltz with Mr Appleby. They'd push back the tables and chairs in the small room and Pip, amazingly light on his feet in spite of his plumpness, would whirl her effortlessly around the room. Then letting go of Tess he would grab Florence.

'I can't, Mr Appleby,' she would protest as he dragged her to her feet, but delighted at the same time.

'Of course you can, Mrs K., everyone can dance.'

They'd do a couple of turns, then he'd sit her down with a courteous little bow, and although Florence, quite out of breath, would declare that he'd be the death of her, she said it with a sparkle in her eyes.

In spite of all her preparations, when David did lead her on to the floor, Tessa's mouth was dry with terror. She held herself stiffly, stumbled over his feet and spent her time miserably apologizing.

'One two three. One two three,' he murmured quietly in her ear and as she felt the pressure of his hand on her back, Tess began to relax and move to the rhythm of the music.

David was wearing a white carnation in the buttonhole of his evening jacket, his fair hair, which he wore rather long, flopped boyishly over his forehead, and Tess thought how exotic he looked against Liam and all the other men in their dull best suits. She prayed he would stay and that the evening clothes weren't an indication that he would be moving on somewhere else. And he did, joining in the games and finally taking over the piano. They finished the evening singing sentimental ballads, which induced in Tess such feelings of longing and sadness she felt herself grow misty eyed.

As David said goodnight and wished her a happy Christmas, he kissed her under the mistletoe, then spoilt it all for Tess by kissing every other girl as well.

On Christmas day itself, Tom got home in time for the rich meal of chicken and plum pudding so generously provided by Pip. Mrs Kelly had invited Milly and Sarah to dinner and although they all pretended until the last minute, Tess knew that moving Milly was out of the question.

After her short stay in hospital she'd improved slightly but Tess recognized that she was slowly slipping away from them. Her lungs were so congested she had to fight for every painful breath, and the cough that shook her frail body brought up a thick yellow phlegm ominously tinged with blood. The pain had extinguished her once vibrant personality, her face was gaunt, her eyes feverishly bright.

Because of Milly's health and her erratic time-keeping, Sarah lost various jobs. In desperation she applied for out-door relief. She was called to appear before the Board of Guardians one bleak Monday morning in January. The faces of these philanthropic gentlemen, as Sarah stood defiantly before them, were almost as chilly as the feelings they nursed towards the needy of that parish. They saw little deserving about the poor, particularly if their relief had to come out of the rates. And as for those expecting charity, a proper and obsequious manner was recommended, otherwise that pumping, beating organ that passed for a heart could easily turn to ice.

And unfortunately Sarah, with her surly manner, did not put her case well, nor did she treat her 'betters' with due respect. Making notes, the Guardians questioned her for a long time before one of them, a clergyman, informed her that an overseer would be round to see whether she and Milly were really in need of the two shillings a week the Guardians so generously planned to allow them.

At this final insult to her dignity, Sarah snapped. She turned on the clergyman and in a glorious outpouring of pent-up fury, screamed at him, 'I don't want your charity, you stupid old bugger. And as for your measly two bob, you know what you can do with that, stick it up that tight arse of yours, if it'll go.' Then with a curious feeling of elation, Sarah turned on her heel and swept out of the room.

But pride is no hedge against hunger and the two sisters might have starved if it hadn't been for the true charity of friends who helped where and when they could; the girls at the factory with weekly contributions and Florence with her nourishing bowls of broth and stew.

All Tess could give them was her time and she gave it unstintingly, sitting with the two girls often until it was so late her eyes would drop in fatigue. And sometimes when she was there Milly would even rally slightly.

'Will . . . you . . . read . . . me a . . . story . . . Tess,' she would ask at these times, each word exhaled on a barely audible gasp. And it was then that a brief hope would flicker in Sarah's eyes and was so profoundly disturbing that Tess found it almost impossible to bear.

She saved her own tears until she was on her own, though, and walking home. Then she would lift her fists to the sky, raging against the unfairness of life and an indifferent God. They had so little, Milly and Sarah, just each other, and yet God, in his infinite wisdom, had seen fit to cast them asunder like an ailing branch from a sturdy tree.

A cold stinging rain, which froze her fingers and chilled the hot dish of stew she was carrying, made her keep her head down and hurry to reach Sarah's and Milly's a couple of nights later. It was Irish stew, a mixture of potatoes, carrots, turnips and scrag end of mutton, and a favourite of Milly's. But now there was a coagulating layer of fat on its surface and she wanted to get it to the girls before it was too cold for them to enjoy.

Tess was so glad to reach somewhere dry that for once she didn't even notice the filth and degradation that seemed to seep through the very walls of the tenement.

Clutching the stew, she made her way up the dark staircase, stepping over drunks sleeping off hangovers, and nudged open the door of the sisters' room. At first she thought it was empty for there wasn't even a glimmer of light from a fire and there was a tomb-like chill to the room.

As Tess fumbled her way towards the table her eyes adjusted slightly to the gloom and she saw that Sarah was sitting on the bed nursing a small bundle in her arms. Tess's throat went dry and she pressed her knuckles against the table until they hurt. This was a moment she had never been able to prepare herself for. At last she found the courage to speak.

'Sarah . . .' she called softly, her heart fluttering with anxiety.

Sarah didn't answer, instead she began rocking the bundle backwards and forwards, crooning to it like a baby. As Tess went to her, Sarah's features distorted into a terrible mask of grief.

'She's gone, my darling Milly's gone,' she cried and then throwing back her head she let out a wail, a high, keening, almost inhuman sound and one of total despair.

There are no appropriate words that can be offered in comfort when confronted with such pain, and Tess didn't even try. Over the past weeks she had prayed every night for a small miracle, and while Milly was alive, against all the odds she'd allowed herself to hope. Witnessing her friend's torment, fragments of a biblical text came to her. 'For he that hath . . .' How did it go? . . . 'For he that hath . . . to him shall be given and he that hath not, from him shall be taken . . . even that which he hath.' And remembering these words she suddenly perceived the futility of those prayers. Her own tears came then and, filled with a need to express her own sorrow, she sat down on the bed and pulling Sarah towards her in an embrace, joined her in her grief.

Tess knew she would have to make all the arrangements for Milly's funeral. Sarah was in no state to do anything and her sister's body still lay in the small room they once shared. And it would have to be a pauper's grave, too, unless money could be found from somewhere.

But somehow, by the following evening, everyone in the tall, gloomy house had donated something even if it was only a farthing, and the small coffin that was lowered into the ground a few days later was made of oak and all the mourners wore black crape.

Sarah stood white and motionless, her eyes fixed unseeingly in the distance. But as the priest chanted his prayers for the dead and sprinkled soil symbolically on to the coffin, she moved forward with a single arum lily. But then she started to sway and Tess quickly caught her arm. Her grasp seemed to give Sarah some strength but as the flower fell, a dusting of yellow pollen tarnishing its white purity, Tess felt as if they were both poised on the edge of a precipice rather than a narrow grave.

In the weeks following Milly's death, Tess really began to fear for her friend's sanity. She worked only spasmodically and ate nothing, and sleep had become such a drug for her that some days she didn't even bother to get out of bed. Sarah had never troubled a great deal about her personal appearance but now her hair was lank and greasy and she seemed to live, and sleep, in the same filthy blouse and skirt.

Tess felt she might be heading for the lunatic asylum unless something was dome. And then she hit on a rather brilliant idea, although as she rang Mrs Chadwick's doorbell, her idea had lost something of its original glow. Supposing Mrs Chadwick just thought she had a lot of cheek?

Mrs Chadwick answered the door dressed to go out for the evening and seemed rather surprised to see Tess. 'What can I do for you, lovey?' she asked, smoothing long white gloves over her fingers.

Quickly Tess tried to think of a reason for being there. 'I've . . . come for a washing,' she finally spluttered.

'Not on a Saturday, surely, dear.'

'Oh . . . oh . . . is it Saturday?' Tess laughed weakly. 'I've got my days mixed up, I thought it was Friday.'

'No, it's Saturday all day today.' Mrs Chadwick stared at Tess curiously and then with a shrewd sense that something was amiss, she opened the door a bit wider. 'You'd better come in for a minute and tell me all about it.'

Standing in the hall Tess felt even more at a loss for words.

'Well, it's obviously not the washing you've come for, so out with it,' Mrs Chadwick said a trifle impatiently as she clipped a long blue velvet cloak over her shoulders.

'It's . . . not about . . . me . . .' Tess stuttered. 'It's about me friend, Sarah, you know, the one whose sister died.'

'Poor wee mite, yes I remember,' Mrs Chadwick clucked sympathetically.

Gathering all her courage up in one breath, Tess plunged recklessly in at the deep end. 'Well, it's like this, you see, she's in a real bad way and she needs a job and I know you offered me one once so I thought . . .' Her voice trailed away.

'You thought I might take her on,' Mrs Chadwick finished for her.

Tess nodded her head.

There was a bang on the front door and Mrs Chadwick picked up her evening bag. 'This is all a bit sudden and that's my cab. Tell you what, why don't you bring your friend for tea tomorrow afternoon? But I'm not promising anything, mind. I'll have to like the girl. I'm particular too, so she'll have to look presentable if she wants to be my maid.'

Well, the last thing Sarah could be called was presentable, and Tess had a strong feeling that the next few hours weren't going to be easy, either in cleaning up Sarah or in persuading her she actually wanted the job.

Sarah's reaction was just as expected. 'Why should she want to offer me a job? She doesn't even know me,' she said, eyeing Tess suspiciously through a curtain of lank hair.

'But she knows me, doesn't she, and I've put in a good word for you. Anyway, you haven't got the job yet, she just wants to see you.' Tess gazed round the squalid room. 'Wouldn't you like to get out of this hole, make a fresh start?'

'S'ppose so,' admitted Sarah reluctantly.

'If you got the job you'd have a room to yourself, a nice uniform. Gosh, I'd give anything to work there, except Mum won't let me,' she said in an aggrieved voice and thinking to herself that if Sarah let this opportunity pass she would take her by the shoulders and shake her.

Suddenly Sarah seemed to stir from her apathy. 'But what would I wear?'

'Well, you'd have to smarten yourself up a bit if you want to make a good impression,' said Tess, studying her friend critically. 'I might be able to get hold of one of Mum's dresses, you're about the same size. And you'll have to wash your hair. Go and get some water and I'll do it for you now.' Picking up a jug, she handed it to Sarah and gave her a shove towards the door before she lost interest again.

Sarah was gone for several minutes for there was only one tap to serve the whole building and this was down in the back yard. When she returned she filled a saucepan and put it on the fire to heat.

Holding her head over a bowl, Tess washed Sarah's hair until it was squeaky clean and her colourless locks became strands of dark blonde silk. Then, instead of the normal tight bun, she arranged it into a more becoming style on top of Sarah's head and pinned a fringe of curls across her forehead with the instruction to keep them in all night.

Sarah giggled self-consciously as she preened herself in the piece of cracked glass balanced on the mantelpiece, but nonetheless Tess knew she was pleased with what she saw.

Getting the dress she promised to lend Sarah was more of a problem. She didn't want to tell her mother that Sarah was going after a job with Mrs Chadwick, neither did she plan to tell her she was borrowing her best dress. Tess hung around impatiently until her mother went upstairs to make Mr Appleby's bed, then she grabbed the dress and, stuffing it under her coat, made a dash for the door, praying fervently that its absence wouldn't be discovered.

By the time she got it round to Sarah's some creases had to be shaken out before she could try it on. Apart from her bony wrists sticking out from too short sleeves the dress, of dark grey cotton, fitted her quite well.

'How do I look?' Sarah asked a little uncertainly when she was finally buttoned into place.

Tess stood back and surveyed her friend with a cool, dispassionate eye. 'You look really nice.'

'Honestly?'

'Honestly,' repeated Tess, just as astonished as Sarah by the transformation.

All she has to do now, thought Tess, as they were walking round to Mrs Chadwick's, was make a good impression. For Sarah, unfortunately, with her lack of charm, wasn't everyone's cup of tea.

But Mrs Chadwick's smile, when she opened the door, was welcoming. 'Come along in, girls,' she said and Tess managed quite well to hide her surprise and slight sense of awe when she led them into her front parlour where a table was set for tea and a silver kettle boiled on a small spirit stove.

But Sarah stood in the middle of the room gazing around at the deep, comfortable chairs, the coloured glass and pieces of silver, with such a look of terror that for a moment Tess thought she might actually make a bolt for it.

Sensing the girl's unease Mrs Chadwick said kindly, 'Sit down, Sarah.'

Gingerly Sarah lowered herself down on to the very edge of the chair and Tess could see that fear had made her face go flat and sullen. It was a bad sign.

As Mrs Chadwick made the tea, Tess eyed the tiny, daintily cut sandwiches and plum cake hungrily. Mrs Chadwick would have prepared it all, she knew, for she'd once confided in Tess that before her days on the stage she'd been a cook in a large country house.

Pouring tea, she handed a cup to Sarah who took it without a word of thanks. Irritated by her friend's lack of manners, Tess gave her a sharp kick in the ankle and Sarah gave such a yelp of surprise that half the tea shot out of her cup and on to her lap. There was a moment's silence then Sarah's eyes began to fill with tears. Mrs Chadwick stood up.

'I'll fetch something to clean that up,' she said, and hurried out of the room.

Sarah turned on Tess then. 'What you wanna do that for?' she demanded with a resentful sniff.

'Because you forgot your manners, that's why. You want to make a good impression, don't you?' Tess hissed back at her.

95

'No I don't and I'm going.' She stood up and Tess saw with alarm a dark stain down the front of her mother's dress.

Anxious equally about the dress and what Mrs Chadwick would say when she returned and found Sarah gone, Tess darted across the room in front of her and held her arms out, blocking her path. 'You can't go now.'

'Yes I can.' Sarah tried to duck under the bridge of her arm just as Mrs Chadwick returned with a bowl of hot water and a towel and Tess knew it would take more courage than Sarah had to walk out then.

Making light of the incident, Mrs Chadwick sponged the dress down and then advised Sarah to sit near the fire so that she could dry herself off.

And gradually, as Sarah drank her tea and munched sandwiches and cake, she began to relax. But wisely, Mrs Chadwick waited until she'd finished eating before turning to more important matters.

'I hear you're looking for a position, Sarah,' she said, watching with a mild irritation as the girl flicked crumbs off her skirt on to the dark red carpet.

'Yes, mum,' answered Sarah, remembering her manners now.

'What I'm looking for is someone to answer the door, clean out the fires and do a bit of cooking.'

Overwhelmed at the thought of such responsibilities, Sarah answered in a small, frightened voice, 'Oh I've never done nuffink like that before.'

'Well, I don't imagine it's something you're going to take long to learn,' declared Mrs Chadwick firmly, and feeling green with envy, Tess realized she must have decided to take Sarah on.

'When would you like to start, Sarah?'

Looking quite bemused now, Sarah didn't answer. 'She can start tomorrow. Can't you?' Tess said, turning to her friend who somehow managed to nod in agreement.

'Tomorrow it is then,' said Mrs Chadwick, standing up. 'And once you're settled in we'll have you measured up for a nice uniform.'

'I wish it was me,' said Tess, feeling slightly disgruntled at her friend's sudden good fortune, as later they walked home together.

But if it was gratitude she was expecting, she had another think coming. Never the most optimistic of people, Sarah did nothing but moan. She'd never learn to cook properly, and what would she say to people when she answered the door? The complaints went on and on.

In the end Tess snapped, 'For God's sake stop moaning, Sarah, you'll be living like a toff, what more do you want? I'd change jobs with you any time.'

Sarah stopped and gripped Tess's arm. 'Oh, you will come and see me, won't you, Tess?' Her voice wobbled with uncertainty and Tess realized with a sudden insight that although her friend's life could do nothing but improve, she was beset with fear and anxiety.

'Course I will, you idiot.'

'You'll not forget me, then?'

'Chance would be a fine thing,' Tess mocked, and they both laughed then.

After work the next day she walked round to Sarah's lodgings to see if she needed any help with moving. But Sarah and her few belongings had already gone and the door clattered to and fro on a rusting hinge.

There was nothing left now of those evenings the three of them had spent together, just ghosts. For some reason, Tess felt unutterably lonely and it was with a lump in her throat that she turned and walked down the dark, rickety stairs for the very last time.

7

It astonished Tess just how quickly Sarah adapted to her new life. Aided and abetted by Mrs Chadwick's excellent cooking, her angular, half-starved frame began to mature and develop some unexpected and pleasing curves. Even her teeth, in the past always discoloured and stained, now had the milky white lustre of pearls, so that it hardly seemed to matter that several were already missing. Her complexion improved dramatically, too, although studying her friend more closely one day, Tess realized with a slight sense of shock that it was a bloom that could only come out of a pot.

Enviously she relayed the news of Sarah's good fortune to her mother. But Florence was unimpressed.

'No good will come of it,' she muttered enigmatically, and refused to be drawn any further on the subject.

Although Sarah was always delighted to see her, Tess began to sense that her friend needed her less now. She'd expected that there would be some severing of ties as Sarah made her break with the old life, but it saddened Tess just the same. However, she was soon to be caught up in matters and events that would change their lives, and leave her little time to mope.

For some weeks rumours had been circulating that a group of men and women who ran a small socialist newspaper were showing a keen interest in conditions at the factory and were stopping and questioning workers. Poking their noses into matters that didn't concern them, was how Bert Higgins put it, and warned that anyone seen talking to these people would be sacked immediately.

Oh yeah, thought Tess, and resolved then to tell these mysterious people everything the moment she set eyes on them. For she was in no doubt about who was responsible for Milly's death and she nursed a strong desire for revenge, to see Bert Higgins brought down and humiliated. If she could just do that, getting the sack would be a small price to pay.

So she took to hanging around outside the factory gates after work and as she waited she rehearsed what she would say, listing in her mind her employers' transgressions, the dirt, the dangers and their servitude. She thought of Milly and Sarah and the poor doomed Elsie and was filled with such a bitter, passionate sense of injustice and loathing, she kicked viciously at an empty can, imagining it was Bert Higgins's head. Oh yes, she had plenty to tell these folks all right, enough to fill a book.

Tess kept us this vigil, with remarkable lack of success, for several evenings until a nightwatchman, catching sight of her on his rounds, came up and glowered at her suspiciously through the railings. 'Ain't you got no 'ome to go to, then?'

Muttering something noncommittal, Tess hurried away from the gates and the nightwatchman's ill-tempered gaze, realizing that in future she would have to make herself a little less conspicuous. However, she was beginning to suspect she might be wasting her time, that these so-called meetings were nothing more than a figment of someone's over fertile imagination. She was so depressed by this thought that she couldn't even summon up the energy to dodge out of Liam's way.

She saw him while he was still some way off, dressed to kill and obviously on his way to meet a girl. 'Seen anyone, then?' he asked as they drew level.

For a second, Tess was tempted to lie. In the past, Liam had berated her for their lack of guts and organization at the factory, so she longed to boast of imaginary accomplishments, to see the reluctant admiration in his eyes. But then, of course, he would start to cross-examine her and the pathetic little falsehoods would be revealed for what they were. 'No, I haven't,' she answered finally and reluctantly.

'Never mind, they'll be back.'

'If there is anyone. Anyway, who's going to be interested in a load of factory girls or their problems?' She had been marking out a pattern in the dust with the toe of her boot, but now she looked up at Liam, challenging him to deny this remark.

'People *are* getting interested. Things have got to change, Tess, conditions improved, otherwise . . .' Here he paused to allow Tess to get the full impact of his weighty pronouncement. '. . . Otherwise the proletariat will rise up against their masters eventually.'

Tess groaned inwardly. She'd really let herself in for it this time, and steeled herself for a sermon she knew would be liberally peppered with the preachings of a man called Karl Marx. She allowed Liam to ramble on for only a short while before interrupting. 'Weren't you on your way somewhere?'

Liam, who didn't like interruptions when he was airing his views, looked slightly annoyed. 'Yes . . . I suppose I was,' he admitted grumpily.

'Well you'd better go then, it never does to keep a lady waiting.' And as he sped off, Tess amused herself by thinking that if it was Maisie Lewis he was still seeing, by no stretch of the imagination could she be called a lady. And she doubted if the evening would be wasted discussing revolution, which Tess herself often wondered was really quite as imminent as Liam supposed. Oh, she'd heard people voicing their discontent often enough against the government, constantly rising prices and low wages, but most of them looked too apathetic and ill-fed to run a whelk stall, let alone start an uprising. Besides, if it involved the wholesale slaughter Liam threatened, she certainly wanted no part of it. Justice yes, but bloodshed no.

It was over a week later and Tess had almost given up hope when she saw the small knot of girls and heard the excited buzz of conversation as they pressed in on someone, gesticulating wildly to make a point.

Unable to believe her luck, Tess gripped Lizzie's arm and started to pull her towards the group, craning her neck and bobbing between the girls to see who it was they were speaking to. What Tess eventually saw was a striking, auburn-haired woman of about forty, and although she had never seen the lady in her life before, her heart gave a thump, almost of recognition.

Her whole manner, the proud lift of her head, her speech, her clothes spoke of breeding. With notebook and pencil poised, she was questioning the girls intently, although Tess noticed that a few of them, terrified of the consequences, were already slipping away. But Tess was in her element, and still holding on to Lizzie she pushed her way to the front of the small crowd.

'Now tell me about these fines,' the lady said and licked the end of her pencil.

She looked directly at Tess, who suddenly felt so shy and awkward that all her carefully prepared phrases vanished like the swallows in autumn. But Lizzie obviously felt less inhibited by the grand lady, for she launched into a graphic account of how they could be fined three pence for talking and even as much as a shilling for leaving spent matches on a bench.

'This,' she finished aggrievedly, 'sometimes out of a wage of only four shillings a week.'

'And if we're late they sometimes shuts us out and then we ain't paid at all,' continued another girl.

'Really!' the lady exclaimed, and with her finely arched brows drawn together in a frown she noted it down in her book.

Still too nervous to speak up, Tess nudged a girl standing beside her. 'What's her name?'

'Mrs Besant.'

'Lizzie,' Tess hissed, 'tell Mrs Besant how the foremen knock us about too.'

'Tell 'er yerself, you've got a tongue in yer 'ead and you've bin going on about it long enough, what you're gonna say an' everything, and so far you ain't said a word.'

Tess ran her tongue over her dry lips and cleared her throat. Lizzie was right, she'd have to say something, she owed it to Milly and Sarah, and she might never get another chance. Finding her voice at last she called over the shoulder of a large woman almost blocking her view, 'They hits us sometimes, too.'

Mrs Besant looked horrified. 'Hit you?'

'That's nothing,' declared another girl, and Mrs Besant's eyes widened in disgust as the girl gave her a fairly graphic account of the sexual abuse many of them had to endure from foremen. Dangerous machinery that could slice a finger off paled into insignificance beside this.

Once the girls got going it was hard to stop them and once or twice and with a laugh, Mrs Besant had to hold up her hand and tell them to slow down so that she could get it all down in her book.

But they saved the real horror story until the last. 'And do you know about the jaw disease, Missis?' Tess asked. Having lost her nervousness completely now she wanted the woman to know everything. Nothing might be done about it but at least she would have got it off her chest.

Mrs Besant paused in her scribbling. 'Jaw disease?'

'Come here, Ada.' Tess turned and beckoned to a girl hanging around on the fringe of the crowd. The other women made a pathway for her and she came shuffling forward, head down.

'Let the lady see you, then,' Tess said gently, for the girl's chin was still burrowed in her chest.

Reluctantly Ada lifted her head, revealing a jaw ravaged and misshapen by phosphorus necrosis. Part of the bone had been sloughed away, her teeth were gone and her face so grotesquely disfigured that puckered skin pulled on the lid of one eye, causing it to water continuously.

Watching Mrs Besant closely, Tess saw the instinctive look of revulsion quickly replaced by pity at the girl's terrible deformity. 'Poor child,' she said, her voice aching with pity, 'whatever has happened to you?'

'She had phossy jaw, she got it from the compo ... phosphorus, what they make the matches with,' Tess explained, for Ada herself spoke only with great difficulty.

102

'And we could all get it,' she added, voicing a fear that never left her.

Tess could see that the sight of the poor, unfortunate Ada had roused Mrs Besant to real anger.

'This is monstrous,' she exclaimed, 'and it must be stopped. These people are nothing more than criminals, subjecting you girls to such dangers.' Raising her voice so that she could be heard at the back of the growing crowd, she called, 'My name is Mrs Besant and I'd like to know if you'd be prepared to repeat these allegations to a factory inspector.'

Well, this was altogether a different matter, of course, and for a moment there was some low, nervous mumblings and furtive shuffling of feet in the dust. But then Lizzie spoke up. 'Well, I've got nothing to lose, only me job,' she said with a bitter laugh. 'Let 'im ask me anything he likes.' Encouraged by this short speech there were murmurs of assent from the other women, although they all knew by now what the cost might be.

After checking a few more facts and with an assurance of her support, Mrs Besant left them. But with her went some of their newfound confidence, and on the way home there was a great deal of earnest discussion. That is, until they reached the Kentish Drovers.

Here Lizzie decided she needed to fortify herself with a glass of Old Tom and she called to the others, 'Come on, girls, let's go and drown our sorrows.'

Her suggestion was greeted with enthusiasm and they all crowded in through the bar door, chattering noisily as a flock of starlings. Tess made a brief excuse and walked on, but envying them slightly nevertheless. A couple of gins, she knew, would cheer them up no end, a few more and their confidence would be restored completely.

Tess's own thoughts were in a ferment and, indifferent to the jostling crowds, she walked home in a state of euphoria, remembering every single word Mrs Besant had spoken and bursting to talk about her to somebody.

She'd hardly closed the door behind her when she started,

103

tripping over her tongue in her eagerness to describe every detail of her newfound heroine to her mother. She told her what she'd said, what she'd worn, even the colour of her hair.

Florence, busy at the mangle, stopped what she was doing and rested soda-roughened hands on her hips. The look she gave her daughter was one almost of pity.

'She'll be one of those socialists, come to stir up trouble, I suppose.' Accompanying these words was a contemptuous sniff that quickly put paid to further discussion.

But nothing could dampen Tess's sense of elation that day. Besides, she knew someone she was sure would be very interested to hear her news.

When she got to the Settlement, though, David was giving a lecture and she waited with a barely concealed impatience for him to finish.

When she saw him going to his office she rushed after him. The door was open and she tapped lightly to gain his attention for he was sorting through papers and seemed somewhat preoccupied.

He looked up at her knock. 'Hello, Teresa,' he said but without that special smile that sent the blood rushing to her cheeks.

'Are you busy?' she asked hesitantly.

'A little. I've got that wayward brother of mine coming shortly. There's a family matter to be discussed and these papers need sorting before he arrives.' The thought of his brother seemed to irritate him for there was now a slight frown between his blue eyes. It was strange, but until that moment, she'd never known he had a brother.

'I'll go then.'

But he obviously heard the disappointment in her voice because he stopped what he was doing, patted a chair and said kindly, 'But come and sit down anyway.'

David listened intently while she told him about Mrs Besant and when she'd finished he said thoughtfully, 'Mrs Besant is casting her net very wide these days.'

Tess leaned forward eagerly in her chair. 'Do you know her then?'

David laughed. 'Not personally, but I've heard a lot about her and she's a very formidable lady, by all accounts. Apparently she was once married to a vicar, lost her faith and left him. Whether that was a brave or foolhardy thing to do, I'm not sure, but it certainly got her talked about, as have some of the other things she's got up to since. I imagine she'd be quite a determined lady, so you girls had better consider just how far you want this thing to go, because if she starts something, I'm sure she finishes it, whatever the cost.' He started shuffling the papers again and Tess knew she was being told to go.

Even so, she was too excited to want to go home again, but the building seemed deserted. However, discussions started in the canteen were often carried on outside on the pavement and as she stepped out into a warm, light evening Tess noticed a group of men and girls laughing and arguing together further on down the street. Liam's voice called to her from the crowd and she was just walking towards them when, suddenly, two drunks, their arms entwined for support, lurched against her, forcing her into the gutter.

It all happened in an instant. A horse shied, she felt the wheels of a cab shave her face and heard a rough male voice swear vehemently. Then someone else yelled, 'Look out!' and strong arms lifted her bodily back on to the pavement. Her face was now buried in an enormous chest and she was aware of the pervasive smell of expensive soap and cigars. Then slowly she was lowered to the ground and she found herself looking a long way up into a pair of very knowing dark eyes. As she hurriedly adjusted her blouse and skirt she could see that her rescuer was dressed unmistakably in the clothes of a gentleman.

'That was a close one,' he said in a deep cultured voice, appraising her with some interest.

Still dazed, Tess could only nod her head.

'But you're all right?'

Again she shook her head.

'I'll bid you good night, then.' He briefly lifted his hat and then turned and disappeared through the doors of the Settlement.

Bemused now, Tess stared after him.

Just then her friends came running towards her and Liam asked anxiously, 'You're not hurt, are you, Tess?' He tried to take her hand but she pulled it away.

'Who was that?' she asked.

'Oh, don't you know? That's Sir Rupert,' Liam replied, 'Mr St Clair's older brother.'

'*Sir* Rupert,' she repeated stupidly, aware suddenly that she was shaking violently.

'I hear you nearly had a nasty accident last night. Scooped up from under the wheels of a hansom by that feckless brother of mine.'

For the second time she noticed David's disparaging references to his brother. This surprised her, for David rarely spoke ill of anyone, although it was reassuring in a way to know that the rich had their jealousies and feuds just like anyone else. Of course, there were bound to be differences between them, she thought. They appeared to be so completely dissimilar and against David's slender build, Rupert must appear massive and somewhat threatening. Almost against her will she found herself remembering the all-enveloping embrace of those powerful arms, the warmth of his body, the steady heart beat and the insolent, compelling look in the night-black eyes.

With a guilty start she realized that David was speaking to her . . . 'Eh . . . eh . . . what did you say?'

David laughed. 'You were miles away then.'

'Was I?' she said lamely.

'To get back to what I was saying. I shall have to be away from the Settlement for a few days, Teresa, there's something of a family crisis and various matters will have to be sorted out with a solicitor.'

'Oh,' said Tess, wondering curiously who was responsible for this crisis. Was it Rupert? Was he the black sheep every

106

rich family was supposed to have? He'd certainly fit the role perfectly.

David went on, 'You know the ropes here, Teresa, so do you think you might be able to look after things here in the office until I get back?' He gave her one of his irresistible smiles but this time Tess hardened her heart. There were a few things she wanted to get settled, and now was as good a time as any.

That early promise of working with David was what sustained her through the dreary days at the factory and why she worked so doggedly at learning to use the type-writer and struggling to decipher shorthand. But Tess was beginning to feel she was wasting her time. Only once had there been mention of a job, and she'd been patient long enough. She could see he was waiting for an answer and expecting an eager affirmative, and there was a certain pleasure in knowing she was going to surprise him.

'Mr St Clair, will there ever be a paid position for me here?'

He seemed somewhat taken aback by her forthright question but then he shook his head sorrowfully. 'I doubt it. I would love to give you a job here, Teresa, and you'd be worth every penny you earned. But as you know, there's very little money and the Settlement only just manages to remain solvent.'

There was no arguing with this but her disappointment was so acute she thought she might break down and cry. Tess wished now she'd never asked, never had her hopes dashed, never had to face the prospect of the bleak years stretching out in front of her, on and on into eternity.

David, seeing her crestfallen face and the grey eyes fighting back tears, squeezed her hand sympathetically. 'Come on, cheer up. I know how much you hate it at that factory, but remember, Teresa, learning is never wasted and something might turn up, it often does – and when you least expect it.'

'What, for instance?' Tess didn't feel inclined to be fobbed off today.

David looked thoughtful. 'Well, I have to admit there's nothing comes to mind at this moment. But I'll keep my eyes and ears open and ask around among my friends.'

'Promise?'

'I promise.' Amused by her tenacity, David smiled.

And Tess knew she would have to be satisfied with this. Besides, if he was having problems with his brother, she shouldn't be adding to them by making a fuss. David had done so much for her already, and he couldn't perform miracles.

'You'll help me out, then?'

In spite of her resolutions, Tess felt herself surrendering to that quiet, persuasive charm. 'Of course I will. I'll come in straight from work.'

A few days later at work Tess had good reason to remember David's warning words about Mrs Besant when a girl standing next to her muttered out of the corner of her mouth, 'We're to meet outside in the timber yard at dinner time. Pass it on.' Tess repeated the message, which was carried on down the line of benches, and then she spent a frustrating two hours trying to work out what the baffling message could mean.

She didn't feel much more enlightened when a large group of them finally gathered, well away from prying, suspicious eyes, between rows of timber piled high as a cathedral.

Lizzie, her expression a mixture of excitement and apprehension, pulled a newspaper from under her apron and thrust it at Tess. 'Here, you reads best, tell us what it says.'

Puzzled, Tess stared down at the halfpenny journal. 'What's this, then?'

'What's it look like? It's a bloody newspaper, of course. Mrs Besant 'as writ about us in it.'

'Where?' More interested now, Tess smoothed out the crumpled flimsy sheets.

'Come on, Tess, for heaven's sake put us out of our misery and tell us what it says,' shouted an impatient girl.

Tess cleared her throat. 'Arright. Well it's called "The Link",' she explained, waving the paper at the expectant faces now clustering around her. But as she went on, reading out the heading 'White Slavery in London', and then giving details of shares and dividends paid by the company, the girls' expressions turned to puzzlement.

'What's all this got to do with us?' several of them interrupted in disgruntled voices.

'If you hold your jaw, you'll hear in a minute,' interjected Lizzie.

Anxious to placate them, Tessa skimmed the paper looking for more interesting bits. 'Hey, this'll be you, Florrie,' she called. '". . . One girl was fined a shilling for letting the web twist round a machine in the endeavour to save her fingers from being cut and was sharply told to take care of the machine, never mind your fingers . . ."'

Florrie giggled. 'That's me all right.'

'And listen to this, she must be talking about Bert Higgins: ". . . a foreman; one, who appears to be a gentleman of variable temper, clouts them when he is mad . . ."'

The girls hooted in derision. 'Him . . . a gentleman!'

But as Tess read on to the end and the article described in detail wages, conditions and the host of other complaints they'd made, the laughter died and she was aware of nervous shuffling and murmured, 'Did we say that?' She finished the article to silence, and when she looked up she saw the early elation had given way to panic, and intermingled with the resinous smell of wood was the odour of fear. She could guess what they were thinking: they shouldn't have let their tongues run away with them like that. But it was that Mrs Besant who'd encouraged them and then written it down, in black print, their accusations for the whole world to see, directors, foremen . . . Guessing the consequences, the gathering began to melt quietly away.

And retribution was swift. A day or so later Tess heard that three girls had been sacked. Then Bert, his face like thunder, came up to them while they were sitting eating their dinner, brandishing a sheet of paper. Glowering at them in an intimidating manner, he flung it down on the bench in front of Tess.

'Read that, all of you, then sign it,' he bellowed, and stomped off.

With a dismissive sweep of the hand, Tess pushed the document away and as it fluttered to the floor, she stood up and deliberately punctured the thin paper with the heel of her boot. The other girls went on eating their dinner in a silence which showed a remarkable restraint. Tess could see by their faces they were bursting with curiosity.

Lizzie was the first to speak. 'I wonder what it says.'

With a slight air of resignation, Tess bent and picked up the torn, dirty scrap of paper. And as she read it, with Lizzie peering over her shoulder, her expression hardened and the grey eyes took on a dark turbulent quality: Tess was ready for a fight. She thrust the notice at Lizzie. 'You can do what you like, but I'm not signing that.'

It took Lizzie rather longer to decipher the words, but when she had she flung it back down on the bench and walked away. 'Neither am I,' she said and her tone was just as decisive as Tess's.

Some of the women who could neither read nor write now began plucking at Tess's sleeve. 'What does it say? What does it say?' they queried in troubled voices, because the thought uppermost in everyone's mind was the sacking of the three girls, and they knew they could be next.

Tess picked up the paper again. 'I'll tell you. It says we are contented and well treated and what Mrs Besant wrote about us is a pack of lies.' She looked around at the group of girls, searching for traitors. 'Now does anyone want to sign such tripe? I'm warning you, though, if you do we'll be back where we started. I can't see anyone else taking an interest in us like Mrs Besant does. We might all end up out of work, but this will be our only chance. Are you all ready to take the risk?'

It was a question that didn't need any thinking about. 'Yes,' they roared in one voice, for Tess's short speech had inspired in them the confidence they so badly needed.

'Good, I'll put it back then.' With a smile of quiet satisfaction, Tess put the unsigned sheet on Bert's desk and then they all scurried back to their places and waited, in a high state of tension, for him to return.

They didn't have to wait long and a couple of nervous titters accompanied him back to his desk. He stared down at the paper, devoid of even a cross, and then slowly lifted his head. His small, evil eyes were suffused with hate.

'What's the meanin' of this insubordination, then?' he snarled. There was the rumble and clack of machinery in other sheds but in the immediate vicinity all labour ceased. The atmosphere oozed unease. 'You'll sign this, the lot of you, or you'll be out.' He brought his fist down so loudly on the bench that they all jumped in fright.

But although every woman in that room had good reason to fear his wrath and the power he wielded, Tess was gratified to see that not one of them budged, and she silently applauded them for their bravery.

'Right, you haven't heard the last of this.' His head swung slowly round, glaring threateningly at each girl in turn. Some wilted under his gaze and their hands shook, but although her heart thumped violently, Tess held herself with a stiff-backed pride and her own gaze was steady and unflinching. 'And don't think I don't know who the ringleaders are.' Snatching up the paper he marched off while the women, throwing up a cloud of dust that made them cough and sneeze, executed an exuberant dance around the factory floor.

But their gaiety was checked by the foreman's return a short while later. As they rushed back to their machines, Tess saw him go over and speak to Lizzie. She didn't hear what Bert said, but she certainly heard Lizzie's reply, which was explosive. 'Bleedin' hell, I ain't done nuffink, what you sacking me for?'

'You spell trouble, that's why,' the foreman replied, more pleased with himself than he had been for several days. 'I've 'ad my eye on you for a long time and I know you're one of the bloody ringleaders.'

111

Recklessly Tess sprang to Lizzie's defence. 'No she isn't, we're all in this together, so you'd better take her back if you know what's good for you.'

The top lip curled back in a sneer, then he spat, aiming deliberately at Tess's boots, although she refused to yield an inch. 'And what if I don't, madam?'

Arms akimbo, Tess threw back her head in a defiant gesture. 'You'll see soon enough,' she warned.

'Is that a threat?'

'If you like.' The blood of Celtic princes ran through Tess's veins and as she turned to the girls she was an impetuous, fearless chieftain calling his clan to arms. 'Are we staying to put up with this bullying or do we go?'

'We're going,' they yelled back and then in those first heady moments of revolt, they whistled, shouted and leapt up and down with joy. Then, with Lizzie and Tess at their head, the great mass of women began to move through the building, calling, urging girls on upper floors and in other sheds to join them. This was their hour, they knew that, and their faces shone with hope and courage, so that by the time they reached the gates they were a triumphant cavalcade of a thousand girls or more.

Outside the gates, stunned by the noise and her own impulsive actions, Tess stared at Lizzie with a bewildered expression. The feeling was growing in her by the minute that events would now move forward under their own impetus and it scared her just what she had set in motion.

But the women were exhibiting a reckless indifference to their fate. Elated by the stand they had taken against their masters they were in no mood to go home, and the noise and clamour continued for a good hour. No longer were they the downtrodden, the despised. Within them grew a burgeoning sense of their own worth and the knowledge that they could be a power to be reckoned with. However there was a small, dissenting group at the edge of the crowd who didn't share in the mood of euphoria and one of them, a pugnacious widow woman with six children, approached Tess and Lizzie after a short while with an accusing look.

'You two 'ave really started something, ain't you?'

'It wasn't just us and nobody 'ad to come if they didn't want to. Go on, go back in, we won't stop you,' replied Lizzie, and she thrust her head forward so belligerently the widow had to step back off the pavement.

'I can't . . . you know that, not today, but I will tomorrow if they don't lock us out. It's arright for you two, you ain't got six hungry mouths to feed.'

'And I don't know what me old man'll say, going 'ome this early,' a woman standing beside her interjected.

'He'll probably belt you one,' answered the widow, who liked to stir things up.

Tess felt more than a passing sympathy with the women because, although she didn't have six kids or a violent husband, she did have her mother to face. 'What do you think will happen now, Lizzie?' Tess asked as the two women, still grumbling, drifted away.

'Mrs Besant will think of something, don't worry,' replied Lizzie confidently.

'I suppose we're on strike now,' said Tess as she watched the crowds disperse, home either to be applauded for their actions or thumped for their imbecility.

'I suppose we are,' agreed Lizzie with unabated cheerfulness.

But Tess's earlier certainties and convictions were deserting her and as she and Lizzie parted company her stomach began to churn unpleasantly and her footsteps faltered. She dreaded facing her mother and although she rehearsed several short speeches, she knew logical argument and debate would be wasted on Florence. And indeed this proved to be a very accurate assessment.

Florence was darning a pair of black stockings and she looked up with a frown as Tess opened the door. 'What are you doing home at this time of day?' she asked and then glanced rather pointedly at the nickel clock on the mantelpiece.

Tess cleared her throat nervously. In some ways she felt she'd rather face up to Bert Higgins than her mother. 'We've

113

stopped . . . work,' she explained, annoyed with herself that her voice faltered when she spoke.

'What do you mean, stopped work?' Eyeing her coldly, Florence bit through the black cotton she was using, rolled up the stocking and put it back in her work basket.

'Gone . . . on . . . s . . . strike.' Try as she might, she couldn't stop the wobble in her voice.

Florence stood up and advanced on Tess, a dangerous glint in her eyes. 'Gone on strike. You?'

'Not . . . just . . . me,' she stuttered, and backing away from her mother's raised hand she pressed herself defensively against the door. But Florence grabbed her by both arms and proceeded to shake her violently.

'I knew this would happen, listening to that woman's socialist claptrap,' she shrieked, her voice on a rising pitch of hysteria. 'But it'll get you nowhere. Those bosses of yours will grind your faces in the mud and laugh while they're doing it.' She shook Tess again and her nails bit painfully into the flesh of her upper arm.

'Let go, you're hurting me,' Tess protested tearfully, trying to wrench herself from her mother's surprisingly strong grip.

The grip tightened. 'When I've finished. Don't think I haven't seen it all before, this half-baked poppycock. They'll see you starve to death rather than give in. You watch, in a few days you'll go crawling back with your begging bowls. Hah, they must be laughing their heads off. And what does this . . . this Annie Besant woman intend to do? Tell me that?' Florence shook Tess again, knocking her head so violently against the door, she saw an explosion of stars in front of her eyes. 'Is she going to pay your wages? Course not. It's just a game for her and she'll have forgotten you tomorrow.'

Dizzy and confused as she felt, Tess still wasn't going to allow Florence to take her heroine's name in vain any longer. 'No she won't,' she shot back with as much spirit as she could muster, and attempted again to twist herself free.

Florence was drawing breath to continue with her diatribe when the door handle rattled and they heard Mr Appleby's voice calling, 'Anyone there?' Reluctantly, Florence let go of her daughter and Tess moved away from the door, rubbing very pointedly at the painful weals already rising on her arm and glaring ferociously at her mother.

Mr Appleby took one look at Tess's tearstained, darkly mutinous countenance and Mrs Kelly's red-blotched neck, and quickly tried to diffuse the highly volatile atmosphere. 'Everything all right, ladies?' he asked cheerfully.

Mrs Kelly gave him a withering look. 'No it isn't. Lady Muck here has seen fit to go on strike.'

'Me and a thousand others,' Tess threw back at her.

'Shut up,' Florence snapped.

'Well, I can't say I'm surprised, the way they treat you there,' answered Mr Appleby, bravely allying himself to Tess.

Florence swung round so sharply then that Tess thought she might actually strike Mr Appleby. 'I'll thank you not to interfere, sir. My daughter has had her head stuffed with enough rubbish, she doesn't need any encouragement from you. Ideals are all right for those that can afford it. This family can't.'

'You won't starve, Mrs Kelly, you know that, not while I'm around,' Pip assured her.

'I'm not looking for charity, thank you, just for my daughter to do an honest day's work and get paid for it.'

Tess glared at her mother provocatively. 'Why didn't you let me go and work for Mrs Chadwick? I wouldn't be on strike now if you had. Would I? I hate that factory and always will, it's a prison.' She stamped her foot angrily, for it still rankled that Sarah had the job she'd so desperately wanted.

'You've said enough, my girl,' her mother warned, controlling herself with considerable effort. 'Another word from you and you'll feel my hand across your face, whether Mr Appleby's here or not.'

'You wouldn't dare.' And then as Tess saw her mother's hand lift warningly, she quickly opened the door and fled.

As she trudged the streets, Tess tried to brush away the angry tears with the sleeve of her blouse. But even as she did it, more came, blurring her eyes and making her unaware of the sympathetic glances of passers-by.

A coster, setting up his stall, stopped polishing a sweet red apple on his trouser leg, and as she approached, pressed it into her hand. 'Cheer up, duckie, pretty girl like you shouldn't be crying.'

Tess gave him a tremulous smile but felt too choked up to speak. The man watched her slow progress down the street, admiring the glossy dark curls, the straight back and slim waist. Then with a sight of regret, he turned back to his work, wishing briefly that he was twenty years younger.

Meanwhile Tess, totally unaware of the effect she was having on one ageing heart, railed inwardly against her uncompromising mother. Florence always had to be right, she thought bitterly, sinking her white teeth into the apple. Why was it she could never unbend enough to see someone else's point of view? Sometimes, and guiltily, she actually found herself hating Florence for her narrow vision of the world, where the only virtues seemed to be respectability and unremitting toil. But as Tess's temper cooled, common sense began to tell her that this was her mother's only way of coping with the world and what she saw as a rising tide of barbarism that threatened to swamp her and those she loved.

Sitting down on a low wall Tess threw her apple core into an oily-looking stream that meandered sluggishly down to the Thames. She watched as it hit a rusty can, then a pile of refuse. It had just managed to release itself and was bobbing away to freedom when a water rat swam out, caught it between whiskered jaws and devoured it in one go.

That's me, she thought, caught and with no means of escape. She felt self-pity welling up inside her and as she remembered how twice her hopes of a new life had been dashed, it threatened to overwhelm her. She still found it difficult to comprehend that in spite of her office skills there was never going to be a paid job for her at the Settlement. It was a dream she'd nursed for so long, working beside David, that without it life seemed totally meaningless and grey.

In spite of the recently consumed apple, Tess was now beginning to feel very hungry. However, facing her mother would have taken more courage than she had at that moment. It was then that she noticed from a street sign that she wasn't very far from where Mrs Chadwick lived. Jumping down off the wall she straightened her skirt, flicked some dust off the toes of her boots and decided to go and see Sarah. Immediately she began to feel a bit more cheerful as she anticipated Sarah's joyful reaction to the news that they were all out on strike. She wouldn't think they were crazy, no fear, wouldn't say that what they were doing was a waste of time. Sarah would be behind them one hundred per cent.

As Tess turned into the road leading to Mrs Chadwick's house she was once again struck by its respectable air. Here no children played in the gutter and the only discordant sound was the tuneless whistle of an errand boy. Geranium-filled window boxes and neatly cut hedges gave it almost a country air, and Tess knew with the utmost certainty that if she could live in a road like this she would have achieved her heart's desire.

She was a few yards away from Mrs Chadwick's when her front door opened and a gentleman appeared on the top step. Just behind him stood Sarah, looking exceedingly trim in a brown uniform with a cream frilled apron and cap.

Tess stopped, and almost obscured by a thick privet hedge, waited for the visitor to go. But then something so unusual happened, Tess's mouth dropped open in surprise. For the gentleman had turned, and lifting his hand, he very gently stroked Sarah's cheek. He then bent and whispered something in her ear and she giggled, loud enough for Tess to hear. He spoke to her again and as Sarah nodded, carried on a light breeze Tess heard the words, 'Thursday, then,' and lifting his hat in a farewell salute, he ran down the steps.

His cane swinging, he approached Tess at a brisk pace and she saw that he was a tall, middle-aged man with a ruddy complexion and grey hair and almost, but not quite, a gentleman. But he looked very pleased with life and was humming quietly to himself as he passed Tess, who stared after him curiously as he continued on down the street.

Tess was so astounded by Sarah's uncharacteristic behaviour that, hardly knowing what she was doing, she started to walk away from the house, but had just turned the corner when she bumped straight into Mrs Chadwick.

'Well bless my soul, what are you doing here at this time of the day?' asked Mrs Chadwick, who looked extremely fashionable in a grey silk dress and large hat plumed with ostrich feathers.

Thinking of the gentleman caller, Tess wanted to ask the same thing except that it would have sounded impertinent. Instead she said brightly, 'Oh, haven't you heard? We've gone on strike.'

'Who'd have thought it?' Mrs Chadwick gazed at Tess reflectively. 'Brave of you, but I don't know that it'll get you anywhere. It didn't when they tried before.'

'It'll be different this time,' said Tess confidently, wondering why it was people only saw defeat for them.

Mrs Chadwick had started to walk on again but she obviously expected Tess to follow her for she called over her shoulder, 'You'd better come and tell Sarah, she'll be dying to hear all about it.'

But Tess felt a sudden strange reluctance to meet her friend, so making a vague excuse to Mrs Chadwick about having to get home she hurried off, her dark brows drawn together in a perplexed frown as she tried to unravel the mystery of Sarah's visitor.

Tess hadn't intended going straight home but as her empty stomach began to protest violently she saw she had only two choices. She could spend an uncomfortable night sleeping under the stars or she could face her mother's wrath. As an alternative it held little charm but she *was* hungry. The nearer she got to Golden Court the more her feet dragged. She would have felt better if she could have been assured of Mr Appleby's presence, for Florence would at least try to exercise some control over her temper if he was there.

She was still a few hundred yards from home when she heard it, the sweet and unfamiliar sound of her mother singing. She hadn't heard the song for years and yet she recognized it immediately. It was 'The Last Rose of Summer', and as she stopped for a moment, listening to its plaintive, elegiac theme, she remembered how, when they were children, Florence would sing to Tom and her almost every night. But gradually the singing had stopped. She couldn't remember exactly when, perhaps after the death of one more tiny thing after only a few hours' life, perhaps after one of Patrick Kelly's more violent drunken bouts when she and Tom had crouched terrified in the corner of the room while he pummelled Florence's body like a punch bag.

Her mother rarely spoke of her dead parents so it wasn't until the day Florence told her she'd learnt to play the piano as a child that Tess began to understand the social sacrifice she had made by marrying Patrick Kelly.

Strange, but she could never think of her mother as being young, wilful and carefree and so much in love that she was willing to flout the wishes of her stern, God-fearing parents. Patrick Kelly must once have had something more than a glib tongue to bewitch the young Florence. Once, too, they must have been happy together.

And yet, as with her parents, Florence never mentioned her husband either. Since his imprisonment he'd been banished from her life; she never visited him, never even wrote him a letter, not even after the amputation of his hand. But always, uneasily at the back of Tess's mind was the thought that one day her father would be released. And what would happen then? She shivered as if someone had walked over her grave.

The singing was weaving its magic now, and completely forgetting her earlier confrontation with her mother, Tess rushed eagerly forward, expecting to be gathered up, like a child, into her mother's arms.

But almost in mid sentence the singing stopped, as soon as she opened the door.

Her mother, who, was, as usual, ironing, looked up with a blank unwelcoming expression. 'Oh, it's you,' she said and the magic was gone.

The room was full of the smell of damp washing, a smell Tess hated. But there was also something cooking. She went over to the small oil stove her mother used to cook on in summer and lifted the lid of the pot. Closing her eyes she sniffed and knew it was oxtail stew. 'Is this for me?' she asked hopefully, for she was now so hungry she could have devoured the ox as well as its tail.

'Help yourself,' her mother replied, but in a tone of voice that warned her she hadn't been forgiven yet.

So Tess moved around the room quietly, getting herself a mug and plate and anxious not to ignite her mother to anger.

Florence went on ironing the nurses' goffered caps from the infirmary in silence, and while Tess was eating her meal she noticed a letter on the table addressed to her mother. Squinting at it she recognized Tom's handwriting.

Tess looked up at her mother. 'So you've heard from Tom?' Tom, to Florence's great disappointment, was a very sporadic letter writer.

Florence's face suddenly lit up in an unexpected smile. 'Yes, and he's coming home for a few days' holiday,' she replied and Tess understood then the reason for the song.

8

For Tess, her brother's presence around the house proved to be a godsend. Florence stopped concerning herself with what Tess was getting up to and began to cluck over Tom like a broody hen instead.

'What on earth are they doing to you down there? You're wasting away, son,' said Florence as she stood gazing at Tom with a worried frown after their first brief, almost awkward greeting.

And it was true. Tom, with the same bird-thin bones as his mother, didn't carry an ounce of spare flesh.

Tom smiled tolerantly at his mother but his tone was dismissive. 'Course I'm not, Mum. Jockeys have to keep their weight down if they want to ride a few winners, and I want to ride more than a few. I want to be the best jockey in England and if that means eating less than I want to, well . . .' and here he shrugged.

'Your health comes first,' said Florence decisively.

'But I am healthy.' He went over and put a reassuring arm around his mother's shoulder, pulling her to him. 'And I'm going to make a lot of money one day and when I do, guess what the first thing is I'm going to do?'

'Tell me.' Florence gazed up at Tom adoringly and watching them together Tess's heart contracted with pain, even though she knew that by now she should have accepted that her mother loved her rather less than she loved Tom.

'I'm going to buy a certain someone a cottage in the country.'

Humouring him, Florence replied, 'Now wouldn't that be just the ticket. Not too far in the country . . . just far enough to get away from this hell hole . . .' In spite of herself, her eyes went dreamy.

'And you'll have a garden, grow vegetables, keep chickens,' Tom continued, piling dream upon dream.

'But who would dig the garden?' the practical Florence asked.

'Why, Mr Appleby, of course.'

Tess saw her mother turn slightly pink. 'Oh, I don't know that he'd be coming with me,' she answered, as if the cottage was an established fact. 'You must remember, he's only the lodger. Besides, it wouldn't be proper,' she added, almost as an afterthought.

Listening to her, Tess wondered if, wherever he was, Mr Appleby's ears were burning at that moment.

Tess had wasted no time in telling Liam what was happening at the factory, if only to impress him with their organizing skills and ability to convince a disparate group of women that they were fighting for a common cause.

It had gratified her to see the look of reluctant admiration in his eyes too, for she sensed – and perhaps he was right – that he considered women cared little for politics.

'I take my hat off to you girls, I really do,' Liam had said, 'and I wish you luck. It's about time we dockers got ourselves organized and followed your example. We have to fight for work at the dock gates and they treat us no better than animals.'

Later she would tell him about the great crush of women and girls who had turned up at the factory gates the following morning, jubilant, argumentative and uncertain what to do next. But as they milled around, their opinions were sought by scribbling reporters from national newspapers. As she passed, one of them grabbed Tess.

'Is it true what Mrs Besant has written about you?' he asked.

Tess glared at him indignantly, not caring for his smart-aleck manner. 'Course it is. What do you take us for, a load of liars?'

'I was just checking the facts,' said the young man uncertainly and hurried away to find more malleable prey. And as

Tess watched him accost another girl, questioning her and scribbling at the same time, she realized with a growing sense of importance that they were probably about to achieve a certain notoriety.

But then the reporters, with their copy to get in, left and the early euphoria once again gave way to uncertainty, argument and doubt.

'I'm going home,' said one woman. 'We're not doing any good standing around here.' She walked away, then several of her friends followed and Tess saw that if the momentum of the strike was to be maintained something definite needed to be done. In that same instant she saw one of the older women, a Mrs Naulls, being helped up on to a wall.

'Wait! Wait!' Mrs Naulls shouted, and as the departing women paused, gestured for silence. 'Look, why don't we go and see Mrs Besant? She'll tell us what to do,' she called over a sea of lifted expectant faces.

Here was the positive suggestion they needed and once again in complete accord there was prolonged cheering and waving. A short time later Tess found herself with a hundred or so other women as they threaded their way through the squalor of the East End, up into the City – the financial heart of the empire – and down Ludgate Hill. Some of the girls had produced makeshift banners and as they walked, singing, chanting and laughing, Tess felt a great surge of energy and excitement. Never in her life had she felt so alive, so charged with optimism, so sure that she could control her own destiny instead of passively accepting anything ladled out to her.

Tess guessed that with their shabby clothes and battered hats they must look a strange sight and this was soon confirmed, for when they reached the City, windows shot up as they passed, heads were thrust out and cat calls and whistles followed them down the street. Children too found the marchers an agreeable diversion, either to skip alongside or to heave missiles at. Even a black mongrel dog fell in beside them and bounded around under their feet, its long bushy tail waving like a flag.

But whether the attention was friendly or hostile, Tess

didn't care, her step was buoyant and her face glowed with pleasure. She waved to everyone, friend and foe alike.

Further on pedestrians stopped to gape but, being in the range of reprisals, their comments were more circumspect, just a few shouts of 'good luck, girls' although Tess doubted whether any of them had any idea where they came from or where they might be going.

Come to that, neither did she, and when she saw Lizzie some way behind, limping badly and struggling to keep up, Tess fell back and waited for her.

'Where we going, Lizzie, do you know?'

'Lord only knows,' Lizzie replied in a tired voice, and stopped to rest for a moment, panting slightly.

It was a warm, sultry day and there were dark patches of sweat under the arms of her dress and lines of pain etched around her mouth. Tess doubted whether Lizzie was capable of going much further, although she knew nothing on earth would induce her to admit this.

'Well, I think I've had enough, anyway,' Tess lied. 'Let's stop here and get an omnibus back.'

'Not on your life,' replied Lizzie, rallying suddenly. 'Something is happening today that I don't want to miss.'

But by now they were walking up Fleet Street anyway and shortly afterwards the procession turned into Bouverie Street and halted. Then someone saw a photograph of Mrs Besant in a window and as everyone crowded round, realizing they had finally reached the office from where the *Link* newspaper was run, a wild cheer went up.

The narrow, cavernous street was completely blocked, traffic was at a standstill and once again, attracted by the noise, curious heads appeared at windows. In spite of all the hubbub, though, there was no sign of Mrs Besant.

Trying to hide her disappointment, Tess looked at Lizzie. 'What do you think's going to happen now?'

Lizzie looked uncertain. 'Nothing much by the look of it.'

Tess remembered her mother's words then with a sinking heart. Perhaps she was right after all and Mrs Besant had already lost interest in them. She was reflecting on this perfidy when, over the heads of the crowd, she saw a thin man with large ears and a heavy moustache come out on to the office steps. He lifted his hands for silence but even so, amongst all the babble, Tess and those standing at the back could hear nothing.

Eventually, by word of mouth, his message was relayed back to them: they were blocking the thoroughfare and must move on. Thoroughly disgruntled, the girls broke rank. Her mother's prediction was right, thought Tess bitterly, they'd just been used for political reasons. Never, she felt, would she put her trust in anyone again.

As the crowd began to disperse, Lizzie scanned the street. 'Tell you what,' she said, not seeming the least put out by what had just happened, 'I could do with something to wet me whistle.'

'You go, I'm off home,' replied Tess, who now felt so completely demoralized she only wanted to be on her own.

But Lizzie took hold of her arm. 'You're not, you're coming with me. We both need cheering up.' And Tess found herself being propelled in the direction of the nearest pub. She detested spirits of any kind but when Lizzie came back with a shandy she realized just how thirsty she was and drank it gratefully.

Sipping her gin, Lizzie nodded in the direction of a group of girls sitting on the other side of the pub. 'I've just had a word with them, it's not as bad as we thought. Seems there's three women in with Mrs Besant at this moment. All she had room for, apparently.'

'Thank God for that.' Tess sighed with relief, for try as she might, she couldn't reconcile herself to the fact that the dazzling Mrs Besant might have feet of clay. Her faith in human nature restored, she finished the shandy in one gulp and stood up. 'I'm going to wait outside those offices. I want to see them when they come out.'

'Hey, hang on,' called Lizzie, downing her gin, 'I'm coming with you.'

The flow of traffic was back to normal so the two girls were able to take up a position right opposite the *Link* offices, where there was a steady stream of activity, both in and out. Men, looking deeply serious, rushed down the steps with files tucked under their arms, easily distracted office boys delivered messages and occasionally even a young lady would appear, looking smart and self-assured in a well-cut suit.

'That's what I should be doing, working in an office,' said Tess to Lizzie and they both watched enviously as one young woman was met by a suitor, who lifted his hat politely and then helped her into a cab.

Across in the Link office an occasional figure would come to the window and peer down into the street. Once Tess even saw Mrs Besant but it was no more than a fleeting glimpse and then she was gone.

After a while, Lizzie began to move impatiently from foot to foot. 'I could have had four gins while I was standing here.' She gazed longingly at the pub door.

Nearby a church clock struck four. 'We'll give it ten minutes and then go,' Tess promised. Five slow minutes passed and then three women stepped into the street looking fairly pleased with themselves.

'There they are! Let's find out what happened.' Tess urged Lizzie across the road, the questions already forming in her mind. 'What happened, Mrs Naulls, what did Mrs Besant say?' The words tumbled out of her in an excess of zeal.

Mrs Naulls swished her skirt importantly and her voice took on an edge of refinement. 'Talked about everything under the sun, we did.'

'About the form they wanted us to sign?'

'Of course.'

'And what did she say?' asked Lizzie.

'Said we did the right thing not signing it. And she says she's going to get a strike fund going for us. Empty bellies – stomachs – never won a strike, she says.'

A strike fund. That was the best news yet, for there wasn't one woman, or man, who could afford to lose even a few days' pay. The money might even pacify her mother, thought Tess practically.

'There's to be a meeting on Mile End Waste on Sunday and lots of important people are coming to give their support, so see that you go,' Mrs Naulls ordered.

'Oh we'll go all right,' Lizzie promised.

'We explained about the pennies, too,' Mrs Naulls went on, 'told her we've made it clear to the bosses they're part of our wages and we're staying out until we've got them back.'

Pennies. These had long been a bone of contention and the source of great bitterness between the women and management. Talking it over on the bus going home, Tess and Lizzie between them decided that it wasn't a problem which would be easily resolved and the strike could go on for a long time.

After she left Lizzie to walk on home, Tess remembered the importance of those pennies in her early days at work. For they'd been the only wages she'd earned and were deducted from those women for whom she carried trays. Now there were no girls doing that particular job but still a penny in every shilling was taken and was manifestly unjust, as any reasonable person must see – which, of course, excluded their employers. Still, it would be interesting to see if, as Mrs Naulls promised, those few coppers could actually bring them to their knees.

There was a huge crowd on Mile End Waste the following Sunday. Not just striking men and girls but whole families, for it was a warm July morning and they were treating the event as a day out. Street vendors and entertainers hoping to reap some profit from the occasion arrived too, and Tess watched as a shellfish stall was set up. The stallholder then laid out black and pink shrimps, saucers of cockles and whelks and quivering bowls of jellied eels. As an accompaniment there were bottles of malt vinegar and hunks of white bread. Very soon he was doing a brisk trade and the ground was spattered with shells and vertebrae.

All this was too much for Tess's empty stomach and she moved away through the jostling crowd and past an elderly

127

tramp playing a few tuneless airs on a penny whistle. His music, however, was soon drowned by the more insistent noise of a hurdy-gurdy, and unable to face such fearsome competition, the tramp picked up his empty cap and shuffled off, cursing darkly under his breath.

A small monkey with an old man's face and wearing a red fez was perched on top of the hurdy-gurdy. As Tess passed, it seemed to fix its gaze on her and she had to turn away from the recrimination in his sad brown eyes.

At the bottom end of the Waste a makeshift platform had been erected in the dust. Tess wandered across quite prepared for a long wait, just as long as she had an uninterrupted view of her heroine and determined not to budge, even when she found herself being pressed against the platform by a swaying, pushing crowd.

The end of her vigil was signalled by a rustle of excitement through the audience. Mrs Besant strode confidently on to the platform, accompanied by several colleagues, and was so close that Tess could have touched the hem of her skirt.

Mrs Besant introduced each of her friends in turn. Tess only recognized one of them, a Mr Herbert Burrows, who she'd last seen standing on the steps of the *Link* office. There was also a clergyman and a rather haughty lady called Mrs Clementina Black. But the name which caused the greatest flurry of interest when he was introduced was Mr Cunninghame Graham's, for he was a Member of Parliament, no less.

Some newspapers supported their cause, others like *The Times* predicted defeat, and Tess's own swings of mood were just as extreme as the opinions of the press. At one moment she was quietly confident of victory and the next she saw only destitution and the workhouse.

But now, with the powerful support of an MP, how could they possibly lose, thought Tess with a rising optimism which even the several dull speeches that followed couldn't quite quench. She tried hard to look interested and keep her expression bright and alert, just in case Mrs Besant was watching her, but on several occasions her mind wandered and she had to stifle a yawn. As soon as Mrs Besant stood up to speak, though, there was no need for pretence, for the air was charged with her personal magnetism and even the unruly in the crowd became quiet and attentive.

Noting her every movement, the way she used her hands to argue a point and the confident, easy way in which she tackled hecklers, all increased Tess's deep admiration and aroused in her a desire to model herself on this shining example of womanhood.

She kept her speech short and to the point, urging them to hold out until their demands were met and suggesting some of them form themselves into a strike committee for the purpose of negotiation. Finally she spoke of the strike fund, urging the crowd to dig deep into their pockets, then sat down to wild applause and the clink of coins into collection boxes.

After this the crowd began to break up and as they milled around, gossiping with friends or hunting for lost children, Tess thought she saw Liam talking to someone. But the throng, like a shaken kaleidoscope, arranged itself into a different pattern and he was lost to her again.

She was about to walk away when the crowd parted – just, Tess thought, as the Red Sea must have done for Moses and the children of Israel – and a clear path led her to Liam and David.

With a nervous fluttering in her throat she pushed her way forward before they disappeared again. The two men were deep in earnest conversation and, feeling slightly breathless, Tess stopped to adjust her hat which had been knocked slightly askew in the crush of people.

'Hello,' she said, when she finally reached them, and as they turned it was impossible to ignore the open admiration in Liam's eyes or the curiously blank expression in David's. Tess studied his face with concern. He looked so tired and preoccupied. Was he having trouble with that older brother of his again? Speaking directly to David, she said, 'What did you think of Mrs Besant? Wasn't she marvellous?'

129

'I'm impressed, I must say. A brilliant speaker and prepared to get things done.'

'Do you know she's arranged for some of us to go to the House of Commons?' Tess said with shining eyes.

'Good for her,' exclaimed David admiringly.

Seeing he was deliberately being excluded from this conversation, Liam decided to interrupt. 'Will you go, Tess?'

Now this was a delicate subject and one which, at that moment, Tess had no wish to pursue. She gave Liam a brief, indifferent glance. 'I don't know . . . it depends . . .' Depended, of course, on whether she was picked to be part of the delegation and depended even more on her mother who was daily becoming more intolerant of the strike.

David consulted his pocket watch. 'Well, you must tell me all about it but I'd better get back to the Settlement now, I've a lot of catching up to do and there's a speaker coming this evening to lecture on the antiquities of Greece. It should be very interesting.' He looked from one to the other. 'Shall you both be coming?'

'Yes, I will,' said Tess quickly.

'And you, Liam?'

'Probably,' he replied, with a glance at Tess.

'I'll see you both later, then.'

Tess watched as he was swallowed up in the crowd, realizing rather miserably that he had neither thanked her nor made any mention of the office work she'd done while he was away. But, perking up, she thought, he's bound to thank me later – and with an irritable frown at Liam – when we're alone. Something else occurred to her then and her frown deepened.

'How long have you been interested in Greek antiquities, Liam?'

'For just about as long as you have,' was his swift reply.

'And where do you think you're going, madam?'

'To a meeting.' It was a brave admission.

'You are doing nothing of the sort. Today you'll stay here and help me.'

'But Mrs Besant . . .' Tess didn't finish the sentence.

'Mrs Besant nothing, I'm tired of hearing that woman's name. It's about time you began to earn your keep. You've done enough gallivanting around for the time being, so get your coat off and get started on that washing in there.' Thin-lipped, Florence pointed to the wash house. 'There's enough to keep you out of mischief for a fortnight.'

'But, Mum,' Tess protested frantically, 'I've got to go, some girls are going to be picked to go to the Houses of Parliament and I could be one.'

'Too bad,' Florence snapped, and picking up a broom began to sweep the floor furiously. 'Out of my way,' she ordered, pushing the broom against Tess's shoes. Knowing the futility of arguing with her mother in such a mood, Tess went into the wash house, rolled up her sleeves and wept silently into the soapy washing. Why, she thought, as she stopped to blow her nose and wipe the sweat from her face, did Tom have to choose yesterday to return to Suffolk? Her mother had been churlish ever since.

True to her word, Florence kept her daughter at the wash tub with hardly a break: lighting the copper, filling it with water, pushing in linen sheets then heaving them out again for a final blue-bag rinse in the brown stone sink. Steam rolled in clouds round the cramped outbuilding, sweat dripped from her body and as Tess fell exhausted into bed, she tried not to think that this was what her mother did several times a week.

It wasn't until the following day, when Lizzie called round, that Tess got to hear any news.

'Where'd you get to yesterday?' Lizzie asked, when Tess opened the door.

'Shut up,' Tess mouthed with a furtive glance over her shoulder at her mother, who sat turning sheets and listening to every word.

Understanding, Lizzie nodded her head and kept her voice low. 'I've got heaps to tell you.'

'Let's sit out here, then.' Tess pulled the door closed behind her. Since the previous day she'd managed to maintain a mutinous, unforgiving silence and wasn't going to let her mother in on any of the gossip now. They made themselves as comfortable as they could on the hard step. 'Now,' said Tess, folding her arms, 'I want to hear everything.'

Lizzie put her head on one side and looked thoughtful. 'Now where shall I start?'

'You could try the beginning,' suggested Tess.

Lizzie gave her a swift glance. 'You trying to be funny?'

'No I'm not, just get on with it,' replied Tess impatiently.

'Well, about fifty of us went in the end, as well as Mrs Besant and Mr Burrows. It wasn't half a long walk. My feet were killing me by the time we got to the 'ouse of Commons and there were extra policemen there to see we didn't get out of control. That was a laugh, I can tell you, we didn't have the energy to heave a brick even.'

'What was Mrs Besant wearing?'

Lizzie looked at Tess with a puzzled frown. 'How should I know?'

'Well, you were there, weren't you?'

'Course I was, but I had more important things to worry about. I think it was a striped dress,' she lied. 'Do you want to hear any more or not? If you keep interrupting I lose me thread. Now where was I?'

'At the House of Commons.'

'Oh yeah. Well, only twelve of us were allowed in there. Me, I wasn't one of the lucky ones. Mind you they told us all about it afterwards. They were asked lots of questions.'

'What sort of questions?'

'You know, the usual ones about stoppages and would we go back if they gave us our pennies.'

'What was the answer to that?'

'Said they'd go back, of course. And you know that little girl? The one who lost her hair through carrying them boxes on her head?' Tess nodded. 'They took one look at her and were really upset.'

'I should jolly well think so,' said Tess indignantly, remembering how frightened she'd been in her early days at work that she might lose her own dark curls. 'It's a bloomin' disgrace.' She was silent for a moment. 'Is that all, then?'

'Just about.'

'I wish I'd been there,' said Tess enviously. She lowered her voice. 'But you know how it is with Mum sometimes . . .' Her voice trailed away as the subject under discussion opened the door.

'I've just made a pot of tea, do you girls want some?' Although the tone was brusque, Tess could see that an olive branch was being proffered. She stood up, pulling Lizzie to her feet as well. When she saw the best cups and saucers laid out and a plate of biscuits on the table, she knew a truce had been called.

Mrs Kelly poured the tea, handed the plate of biscuits round and then sat down, stirring her tea thoughtfully. Tess suspected now there was a motive in her mother's invitation. At last Florence spoke. 'Do you know something? You girls don't know when you're well off.' And Tess guessed that Florence might have had her ear to the door, listening to their conversation.

Lizzie looked astonished at Florence's remark. 'Mrs Kelly, even if we got a full wage packet every week, which we don't, we still wouldn't be well off.'

'You still work for a better firm than most. I can remember when I was a young woman and just married I cleaned at a house where they had a lucifer manufactory which was little more than a shed in the back garden.'

Lizzie leaned forward on the table, her expression alert. 'A shed?'

'Yes, and I've never forgotten it, it was a dreadful place. Do you know, this man had half-starved little children, boys and girls working there who couldn't have been more than seven or eight. He used to put them to stirring the composition. You could see the vapour rising, their faces were right in it and they used to cough their little lungs out. He was a brute that man, didn't care if they got burnt, sometimes he didn't even pay them. But what could they do? They were so ignorant, so unschooled, they hardly knew how old they were.

133

In the end I got so angry about it I had a stand-up fight with him and got the sack.'

'Good for you, Mum.'

Florence looked at her daughter. 'It didn't do those kids any good, though, did it? It still haunts me, that place. I often wonder what happened to them, poor little souls.'

'I should imagine they're six feet under by now, working in those conditions,' answered Lizzie somewhat brutally.

Florence sighed. 'You're probably right. You can see why I think you're making a fuss about nothing, though.'

But Lizzie was prepared to pursue this argument. 'No, I can't. There's not just us, you know. What about the out-workers, the women who make matchboxes at home? They're on starvation wages, have to pay for their own paste and brushes and their little ones are there with them, working all the hours God sent. It's a crying shame.' Indignation had brought a flush to Lizzie's cheeks. 'Anyway, we're staying out until our demands are met, aren't we, Tess?'

Tess gave her mother a fearful sideways glance and then nodded her head silently.

Florence's expression darkened ominously. 'So in the meantime we live on fresh air, do we?'

Sensing trouble might be brewing, Lizzie quickly interjected. 'No, Mrs Kelly, didn't you know? On Saturday we get our first strike pay.'

When Tess arrived at the Assembly Hall on the Saturday morning where they were to collect their strike pay, Mr Burrows was already there, rather officiously sorting the girls into orderly groups and making sure they each had a numbered ticket which corresponded to their names on the strike register. 'Hold on to that piece of paper, girls, without it there'll be no money,' he warned.

Clutching hers as if her life depended on it, Tess went and sat down, glancing along the row to see if there was anyone she knew. Although some of the women on strike had gone fruit picking, the hall was still very crowded and Tess began to worry that there might not be enough money to go round.

And it certainly had to be earned, for there were several dull speeches to sit through although Mr Burrows did tell them that the London Trades Council had agreed to arbitrate on their behalf and that any settlement would have to go before them and their own strike committee.

He finished to polite applause and then Mrs Besant stood up, looking like a princess. Immediately everyone in the hall was alert.

'You'll stand together, won't you, girls? You'll not let them intimidate you, will you? A settlement must be acceptable to you all.'

The applause was resounding when she sat down and the girls stamped, waved, cheered and whistled in unrestrained good humour.

But Tess just sat there spellbound by her magnetism, wishing desperately she could be one of that select group of girls who formed the strike committee. They went everywhere with Mrs Besant and recently had developed very superior airs.

Then with a flutter of excitement she thought: But what's to stop me? After all, if you wanted something in this world, it had to be asked for – although, even then you didn't always get it, she reminded herself, thinking of David. Perhaps it will be different with Mrs Besant, she thought as she was directed to the line of girls waiting for their strike pay. Perhaps she'll be a bit more appreciative of my skills.

Impatiently she shuffled along in the line, and reached the platform where Mrs Besant sat only to find her wits had deserted her. But Mrs Besant took the ticket from her with such a warm, encouraging smile that Tess's tongue managed to dislodge itself from her palate. Leaning over, she clasped Mrs Besant's hand tightly, her eyes shining with fervour. In a rush, before her nerve went, she blurted out, 'My name's Teresa Kelly . . . if you ever want any help . . .' Behind her someone pushed impatiently. '. . . and thank you . . . dear lady, for everything . . .' Her face was now a deep poppy red, and embarrassed by her audacious behaviour, she turned and fled from the hall, not realizing until she was outside that she was clutching two florins and a shilling in her hand.

The strike gathered momentum. Mrs Besant's partisan articles in support of the girls enraged the factory directors who threatened her with libel action; questions were asked in Parliament; and Tess waited with diminishing hope to be drawn into Mrs Besant's small, charmed circle. Finally she had to accept that she'd been relegated to the sideline of events, but since things were going their way she didn't feel entitled to be too depressed about this.

The public, alerted by letters in newspapers, were now sympathetic to their cause and seemed quite willing to turn out their pockets in order to keep the strike fund solvent. Also the London Trades Council, a power to be reckoned with, had become interested in their plight and had offered to arbitrate on the girls' behalf.

Imperceptibly the bullish stance of the company became more conciliatory. Finally, amid a great buzz of excitement, Tess learned they had agreed to see a deputation from the London Trades Council as well as the women on the strike committee.

All day Tess hung around the factory waiting to hear the outcome, and at four a notice was pinned up outside announcing: Meeting in the Great Assembly Hall, Mile End Road at six o'clock. As she'd promised to, she hurried round to collect Lizzie. The packed hall was hot and stuffy and redolent of sweat and unwashed clothes. Tess and Lizzie manoeuvred themselves to the front, competing with girls standing on chairs or sitting on window sills to get the best view of the proceedings. Although she was hoping for the best, Tess couldn't help feeling anxious about the outcome today.

'I hope to God they've reached an agreement,' she said. 'Life's not worth living at home. Strike money doesn't satisfy Mum and it's nag, nag, nag. I never thought I'd look forward to going back to work.'

'I'm with you there,' answered Lizzie. 'I 'aven't had a tot of gin or a glass of stout pass me lips in a fortnight. If we 'ave won, I promise you I'll get drunk as Davy's sow tonight.'

Tess's attitude to drink was almost as missionary as her mother's and she would have dearly loved to bring about a conversion to abstinence in Lizzie. But to say anything would have been a waste of breath. And besides, who was she anyway to deny Lizzie a brief hiatus in a fairly desolate existence?

Unable to conceal a certain strutting air of self-importance, a middle-aged man had now appeared on the stage and the girls turned expectantly towards him like flowers to the sun. Rather unnecessarily he clapped his hands for silence then indulged in such a lengthy scrutiny of his notes an audible dissatisfied murmur began to percolate through the hall.

Scratching an armpit and surveying them as if they were a class of rebellious children, he began to speak. 'My name is Shipton and I must tell you that we 'ave been most courteously received by your directors and they have made a number of concessions with a view to improving conditions. I'll read them out and then it's up to you to decide whether you want to accept them or not.'

The mood in the hall was charged and turbulent, Tess could feel it. Heaven help Mr Shipton, she thought, if the outcome isn't favourable, he might find himself at the mercy of a thousand angry women.

But she had no need to worry. As soon as Mr Shipton announced that all fines would be abolished and their pennies restored to their pay packets, pandemonium broke loose. He had a job after this making himself heard but went on just the same, explaining that a separate dining room had been procured for them and that the directors had even suggested they form themselves into a trade union, so that in future any grievances could be dealt with by the heads of the firm and not foremen. Not many of the other women were even bothering to listen now but through the general mayhem, Tess did hear, with a feeling of extreme relief, that no girl would be singled out or discharged for her part in the strike. This was good news for Lizzie – except that she had disappeared. Tess looked round for her but she could guess where she was, in the Kentish Drovers enjoying a celebratory drink.

Mrs Besant had now come on to the stage and with a mere lift of the hand gained the girls' absolute attention. 'These terms far exceed my expectations and I think you would do well to accept them, don't you agree?'

If there was any opposition to these proposals, Tess didn't hear it. An exultant 'We've won! We've won!' reverberated round the hall and was then carried out into the street as the hall began to empty of women still slightly dazed by what they had achieved.

Tess, bringing up the rear, followed them feeling slightly empty and deflated now that it was all over. Her mother had given no encouragement and she herself had often wavered between great optimism and sloughs of despair. Only Liam had been absolutely confident and she had to concede that what he said was right. Given the right leader, even the oppressed and unregarded of this world could achieve something, and small miracles like today were just a beginning. Never again would she be entirely dismissive of Liam's ideas or views.

In this magnanimous frame of mind she set off for the Settlement, knowing this was where she would probably find him. Her mother could wait, Liam would be the first to hear of their triumph.

She found him in the corner of the canteen, flirting outrageously with an insipid-looking girl Tess had never seen before. He looked up, gave her a cheerful wave and then returned to his wooing.

Feeling piqued, Tess took herself off to David's office which she found firmly locked although she was certain she heard movement inside. She rattled the handle and called, but there was no reply. Almost bursting with her news she went back to the canteen and was nearly sent flying by Liam's lady friend, who rushed out of the building obviously distraught and biting her lip tearfully.

In the canteen, looking bored, Liam was ordering a cup of tea.

'What have you done to that poor girl? She was almost in tears.'

'Serves her right,' said Liam brutally. 'I can't stand stupid women.' Then: 'Do you want a cup of tea?'

'Yes, please,' she answered, curbing her curiosity. Liam's complicated love life was really no concern of hers. She took a sip of tea. 'Do you know what has just happened?' Tess spoke casually, trying to keep the excitement out of her voice.

'You decided you couldn't live without me.'

Tess sighed audibly. 'Do you want to know or not?'

'Course I do m'darling.' He put an arm across her shoulder but Tess shook it off, refusing to be irritated only because of her riveting news.

Watching him closely to see how he'd react, she said in a level voice, 'We've won the strike.'

Slowly he replaced the cup in its saucer and as he swung round to face her, Tess was gratified to see that he was flabbergasted. Here was a person too, she realized, who in spite of his apparent confidence, had been as uncertain about the outcome as anyone.

'When did this happen?'

'About an hour ago,' she answered and only then was it truly brought home to her that powerful men had been outmanoeuvred by the likes of her – Teresa Kelly. She laughed exultantly at their audacity, their breathtaking nerve, and waved her hands in the air like victory pennants. Quite spontaneously she then grabbed Liam and together they executed a dance around the floor so that when he picked her up, spun her round and kissed her firmly on the mouth she was too out of breath to protest.

'That's bloody marvellous!' Liam exclaimed as he put her down. 'I knew you'd do it.'

Everyone else in the canteen seemed to be of the same opinion and they formed a circle round her, pumping her hand up and down so vigorously it began to ache. For these were politically motivated men and women and this was their victory as well. That day, they knew, democracy had taken a tentative step forward, to the ultimate good of every working man, woman and child.

'We're forming a union, too,' Tess announced, wallowing in the warm glow of their approval and esteem.

'Are you now?' There was a respect in Liam's eyes which was even more gratifying. 'Didn't I always say the likes of you and me could change the world?'

Nourished by victory, Tess smiled happily.

'I'll tell you something else as well. What you girls have done today will go into the history books,' Liam prophesied, and for once in her life, Tess didn't feel inclined to disagree with him.

9

They'd been ideal copy for the newspapers. That unique combination of poverty and youth, the drama of David against Goliath had proved irresistible and ensured them a place on the front page of most papers for the duration of the strike. The press had rejoiced with them, too, when it was over. A Great and Noble Victory, was how the *Pall Mall Gazette* described it and then had promptly forgotten about them, not even warranting them the occasional paragraph on the back page.

But then, of course, Tess mused, they had more gruesome copy these days as a newsboy was now horribly reminding her.

'Read all about it! Read all about it!' he exhorted in her ear. 'Jack the Ripper strikes again!' Enjoying the brief glory these grisly details brought him, the barefoot boy ran along beside Tess, flapping the newspaper under her nose. 'Go on, buy one, Missus,' he urged. 'Tells you 'ow 'e done it in there.'

With a shiver of apprehension, Tess pushed him away, then glancing fearfully over her shoulder, hurried to the sanctuary of home. Jack the Ripper. It was a name that struck terror in the heart of every woman living in or near Whitechapel. So far, his victims had been prostitutes, all of them had been brutally murdered and mutilated in a way that suggested the killer was either a surgeon or butcher by trade.

Recently he'd embarked upon a cat and mouse game with the police, and bloodstained cards and letters, boasting of the murders, were received daily at police stations and newspaper offices. Rewards were offered, copies of the letters appeared on hoardings in the hope that someone might be able to identify the handwriting, but still the Ripper went free.

His latest ravings had been in a letter sent to the factory. Whether it was a hoax or not no one could guess, but every chilling word was etched on Tess's brain: 'I hereby notify that I am going to pay your girls a visit. I hear that they are beginning to say what they will do with me. I am going to see what a few of them have in their stomachs . . .' The signature had been: John Ripper.

In spite of a Vigilance Committee, respectable women were terrified to go out after dark and Tess never left the safety of home now, not even to deliver laundry to Mrs Chadwick or visit the Settlement.

In fact she felt more hemmed in by life than ever. Although conditions had improved at work, wage packets were bulkier and Bert Higgins had been sent packing, the deadly yellow phosphorus was still being used in preference to the safer but more expensive red phosphorus. In spite of regular dental inspection their lives were still at risk. But worst of all for Tess was the drudgery and monotony of the work. She missed the excitement of the strike, the extra dimension it had brought to her life, the tantalizing glimpse of something better. She often wondered if people could actually die of boredom. She sometimes thought she would, slowly, imperceptibly . . . and nobody even noticing.

It was a chill autumn evening and when Tess finally reached it the house was dark. Lighting the lamp, she saw that the fire would have to be coaxed into life before she could cook supper. With a rattle of the poker against bars, she emptied the grate of ash, applied the bellows and as the coal began to glow, improvidently threw on a handful of sugar. It sizzled on the hot coal, a weak blue flame fluttered briefly and the smell of burnt sugar filled the room. Tess dashed for the door, fanning it open and shut, at the same time peering into the dim passage, hoping her mother would delay her return for ten minutes or so.

The fire was now going well, so pushing back her sleeves in a businesslike manner and balancing the frying pan over the flames, Tess cut a thick wedge out of a bowl of dripping. She waited for the fat to spit and frizzle, then dropped in three mutton chops. Leaving them to cook, she laid three places and was slicing some bread when her eyes were drawn to a book, one of Pip's probably, lying open on a chair. The written word was irresistible to Tess so she picked up the book and was immediately engrossed in the life of Nicholas Nickleby. It was the smell of overdone meat which finally alerted her. 'O Lor',' she exclaimed and throwing down the novel, made a dive for the frying pan, rashly adding another generous dollop of dripping in an attempt to rescue their supper. She was bent over the hot range, poking desperately at the chops now swimming in fat and deciding that perhaps they didn't look too bad on one side, when she heard the door click shut behind her. 'Sit down, Mum, supper's nearly ready,' she called brightly over her shoulder but with the fervent wish that Florence's sensitive nostrils hadn't caught the whiff of charred meat.

But there was no reply, no scraping of a chair as her mother eased her weary body into it, just silence.

Tess cocked her head, straightened and with a faint stirring of unease, turned, still clasping the frying pan in her hand. In the half light by the door was the figure of a man. The Ripper! Tess let out a primeval shriek of pure terror, and the pan slipped from her fingers and clattered noisily on the floor. Paralysed with fear, she stood there in a pool of congealing fat, waiting almost fatalistically for the lunging blade of steel she knew would disembowel her.

But then the huge, shambling figure moved out of the shadow and although the hair was close cropped and the features blurred by a heavy growth of grey stubble, Tess gave a gasp of recognition and relief flooded through her numbed body.

'Dad,' she managed to croak, not even stopping to wonder why he was there.

'Yes, it's your dad right enough. Surprised yer, did I?' He advanced towards her and she tried not to recoil from the putrefying stench of him and the clothes, ragged as a scarecrow's, hanging from his emaciated frame.

143

Hardly an inch separated them now but if Tess had moved she would have been in the fire.

'Got a kiss for your old man, then?' he cajoled.

Unable to hide her revulsion, Tess arched her neck away from him and averted her face.

'Something wrong?' The tone exuded such menace, Tess felt an edgy sense of disquiet.

'N . . . n . . . no,' she stuttered unconvincingly.

'A kiss, I said,' and Tess gave a gasp of fascinated horror as a metal claw shot out from a ragged sleeve and she felt its sharp, cold point biting painfully into the soft flesh of her neck. Then the man she called her father pulled her towards him like a hooked fish. 'Frightens yer, does it? Me 'ook. And so it ought.' With his good hand he grabbed her hair, yanking her head back with such spine-breaking force, she was unable to utter a word.

He studied her for a moment. ''Andsome little bitch, ain't yer?' he said grudgingly. 'But we'll soon put that right. No man will look at you again by the time I've done.' With a gloating sense of power, he drew the curved point slowly down her cheek. 'This was your fault. You and the old woman's. It was you two 'ad me sent down and then left me to rot. Not even a letter or a visit. But you're gonna pay for it now. I've spent many an hour relishin' what I'd do to the pair of you when I got out.'

His threats managed to jerk Tess out of her trance-like state of terror. Finding some inner strength and with a sudden quick twist of her body, she fought to free herself.

But although her father was thin, Tess was still no match for him and as she struggled and her feet slipped helplessly in the viscous mutton fat, Patrick Kelly's arm came down around his daughter's throat in a vice-like grip. The more she struggled, the more his grip tightened against her windpipe, depriving her lungs of air. There was an explosive buzzing in her ears, her vision became blurred and reality began to recede. Lifting her, Patrick Kelly dragged her forcibly to the fire and thrust his hook into the red-hot coals. Knowing her father was about to disfigure her, Tess tried to speak, to plead but there were only strange frantic gurgles in her throat. Weakly she tried to grapple with him but her strength had gone and she watched stupefied as her father pulled the fired metal from the glowing coal and then very deliberately brought it down on her bare forearm, holding it there so that it seared her flesh like a branding iron. In a convulsive movement of torment, Tess flung out her blistered arm and as her torturer momentarily loosened his grip, she let out a wild, agonized scream of pain. Then, though she fought desperately against it, the sickening smell of her own burnt flesh put her briefly beyond consciousness. But he wasn't finished with her yet. Again the hook was thrust into the flames, held there, then waved, like a wand, about an inch from her face. As she shrank from its heat, the primitive instinct of self-preservation took hold of her and she began to plead with her father, still unable to accept totally that he was irredeemably evil.

'Please, Dad, don't . . . not that,' she whimpered and then started to shake uncontrollably.

'I'm showing you no pity, you showed me none,' he snarled back at her. 'Tell you what, though, I'll make it a nice fancy pattern to go with that pretty little face of yours, and you can choose which side.' He shook her roughly. 'Which side? Quickly now or I'll mark you good and proper on both sides.'

Tess attempted to speak. 'I . . . I . . . I . . .' But reason had abandoned her. In her confused mind the hot scarring talon had already scored the tender flesh of her cheeks, a crucifying pain assaulted her body and she longed for an oblivion which would free her from her father's savagery. But then, suddenly, Patrick Kelly gave a great bellow of outrage, the life-denying lock upon her neck was loosened and as he swung away from her, Tess had a confused impression of blood splattering her apron, a knife and of her mother standing somewhere in the room.

'Mum . . .' she sobbed. Delirious with pain, and holding out her injured arm she stumbled towards her mother. Then, mercifully, the room darkened, her knees buckled and Tess slowly crumpled to the floor in a dead faint.

Tess had the muzzy impression she was floating on a soft, downy cloud of feathers. It was such a warm delightful sensation she wanted to abandon herself to it, and only with some reluctance did she open her eyes. A splinter of light filtered through drawn curtains and as her drugged gaze moved slowly round the half-darkened room, she saw the blurred outline of heavy, unfamiliar furniture. Puzzled, Tess stretched out her leg, feeling her way round the bed with her toes. It was very large, that was certain, twice the size of the one she shared with her mother. And it was canopied, with pretty lace curtains looped up to the brass bed head. She lifted her head stiffly from the pillows. What was her arm doing, heavily bandaged like that? Clumsily she tried to move it and winced as it began to throb painfully. Something had happened to her, an accident of some sort. Closing her eyes again she forced herself to remember, and frightening images were just infiltrating her anaesthetized brain when the door opened and there was the rustling of starch as someone came into the room and stood over her. Tess opened her eyes. 'So you're awake,' the woman said, and going to the window drew back the heavy curtains, letting in a dull afternoon light.

Tess watched her with a slightly befuddled curiosity as she came to stand by the bed again, noticing the multitude of keys that jangled at her waist and the pince-nez that clung precariously to her sharp nose.

'And how are you, young woman?' she inquired briskly.

Bewildered and still only half awake, Tess said hoarsely, 'Who are you?'

'I'm Mrs Bradshaw, the housekeeper.'

Tess was totally at a loss now. 'Housekeeper?'

'To Sir Rupert, Mr David and Miss Virginia.'

Tess was so startled by this information that she managed to lever herself up in bed. 'I'm in Mr David St Clair's house?'

'Yes, and I hope you'll remember what a privilege that is, know your place and show a proper respect for your betters,' Mrs Bradshaw lectured coldly.

Too confused and exhausted to think straight, Tess sank back on to the pillows. 'But how did I get here?'

'I'm sure I don't know, you'll have to ask Mr David.' Her expression was as starchy as her apron and by her tone it was becoming evident to Tess that Mrs Bradshaw didn't exactly warm to her. Studying the prim, humourless features covertly, Tess decided the antagonism was going to be mutual.

'Perhaps you could tell me the time, then.'

The housekeeper peered at a small timepiece pinned to her grey dress. 'It's two o'clock.'

'Two o'clock? In the afternoon?' Tess was horrified. 'I've got to get home, me mum will be worried sick.' She struggled to get out of bed.

'You'll stay right where you are.' Mrs Bradshaw spoke sharply. 'My instructions are that you stay in bed until the doctor calls again tomorrow. You've had strong, pain-killing medicines and are in no state to go anywhere.'

Tess found she was in no position to argue. The sudden movement as she tried to get out of bed had made her head swim and sent needle-sharp spasms shooting through her arm. For the time being, anyway, she would do as she was told, even though she resented deeply being ordered about by a toffee-nosed housekeeper.

'I'll arrange for something to be sent up on a tray and hot water for you to wash. You'll have to look a bit presentable when Mr David and Miss Virginia visit you later on.' Mrs Bradshaw studied her critically for a moment. 'And see you brush your hair, it looks a proper mess.'

When she had gone, Tess lay gazing up at the moulded ceiling. In Mr David's house? It was unbelievable. But why? She rubbed her forehead crossly. If only she could think straight and her head didn't feel so fuzzy. Her injured arm had something to do with her being here, but what else . . .? Tess closed her eyes and tried hard to concentrate. Her father . . . of course. Slowly her mind made the connection and with a fearful clarity she saw him, felt the hot white metal against her cheek. Tensing herself and with a sick

147

apprehension, Tess lifted her hand and gingerly touched her face, searching for the disfiguring burns. Only half believing her skin was unblemished, her fingers checked again and again. And yet he'd been so near. It was the knife that had stopped him in his tracks, the one her mother was holding, and there'd been blood, she could remember that. Supposing he was dead? Her father. The implications of that were so disturbing, Tess shuddered with a sense of dread.

A tap on the door diverted Tess from her troubled thoughts and a girl of about her own age and wearing a maid's uniform came into the room carrying a large tray. Without a word she laid it across the bed, where it balanced on four legs. The girl then gave Tess a quick, sly look and before she could even thank her, she'd scurried from the room.

Sitting up, Tess surveyed the tray with some interest. The cloth was fine linen, beautifully embroidered and set with translucent china. Two boiled eggs were balanced in silver cups, and fanned out on a plate were slivers of bread and butter with the crusts removed.

With the use of only one arm, Tess felt awkward and clumsy and worried she might tip the contents of the tray over the bed. Then she thought seditiously, oh what the hell, enjoy yourself, my girl, such unashamed luxury might never come your way again.

The tea was pale, slightly scented and quite different from the tarry brew at home. Although she sipped it carefully, the first mouthful hurt, for her throat was raw and bruised, but she was so thirsty she drank it anyway and afterwards the two boiled eggs slipped down almost painlessly.

Tess had just finished and was patting her mouth with a napkin in what she felt was the prescribed manner, when Mrs Bradshaw returned with a large jug of water, which she placed on the wash stand. She then went to a chest of drawers and from it pulled a white garment, laying it on the bed.

'Mr David and Miss Virginia are coming up to see you in about an hour, so get yourself tidied up. And put that on.' She indicated the garment on the bed, a dressing gown of broderie anglaise, threaded with blue ribbons and about the prettiest thing Tess had ever seen. But she didn't dare say so, in case Mrs Bradshaw, seeing her delight, took it away from her.

She waited until the housekeeper had gone and then she tried to get out of bed. But as she swung her feet to the floor and stood up, the room started to tilt alarmingly. Hanging on to the brass bed rail for support and trying not to panic, she closed her eyes and took several deep breaths.

She opened them again very cautiously and only when the furniture remained solidly in place did she venture to edge her way towards the dressing table which stood between two long windows.

Although she'd thought herself prepared, Tess was profoundly shocked by the plum-coloured bruises and ugly red weals on her neck. Scrutinizing them, she knew it was the work of an unhinged mind. For surely no sane man would almost throttle his daughter then deliberately set out to scar her for life. She stared at herself fretfully. If only David would come, there was so much she needed to know. Not that he'd be very impressed by her unkempt appearance. Quickly she picked up a silver-backed hair brush and tried to pull it through her hair. Failing to make much of an incursion into the thick tangle, she slapped the brush down in disgust. Her mother was right, she thought despairingly, she did look like a tinker. There was a row of tiny cut-glass bottles lined up in front of her with silver filigree stoppers. Lifting one she sniffed appreciatively and was about to put a dab of scent behind her ear when she remembered Mrs Bradshaw and quickly returned the bottle to its place.

A wash was what she really needed. The water was now tepid but she managed to pour some into a bowl then struggled to remove her nightdress. But the wound began to throb and she had to settle for a quick wash of her hands and face, but enjoying the sensual pleasure of fragrant soap and huge fluffy white towels.

The most gratifying experience, though, was slipping into the dressing gown and admiring herself in the mirror. It was so pretty, so feminine, and the frills concealed the bruising on

149

her neck. Nothing could hide her startling pallor, though, nor the dilated pupils, which made her eyes look almost black.

Would it be proper, David seeing her like this, only half dressed and with her hair hanging down her back? Probably not, she decided, and quickly scrambled back into bed, pulling the sheets up round her ears and glancing nervously at the door from time to time. But no one appeared and after a while she relaxed and gazed round the room, making a full inventory of her surroundings. The floor was wooden, highly polished and scattered with expensive-looking rugs. Across the bottom of her bed was another day bed and in a recessed corner by the fireplace, a writing desk. The room was lit by gas and Tess realized with a growing sense of awe that at that moment she was enjoying the life of the very rich.

A jangle of keys and a crackle of starch announced Mrs Bradshaw's return. Looking prim and censorious she pulled the sheet down from around Tess's chin, leaving her feeling naked and vulnerable. 'Sit up,' she ordered, 'Mr David and Miss Virginia will be here in a minute, so see you attend to what they are saying and watch your Ps and Qs.'

From her prone position Tess felt at a distinct disadvantage, but as the housekeeper bustled about tidying an already immaculate room, her dislike for the woman grew. Her colourless features reminded Tess of the caged ferrets she had seen in markets, sharp and with a tendency to twitch.

Answering the light tap on the door, Mrs Bradshaw turned just in time to see the way Tess's face lit up when David entered the room. Huh, like that, is it? she thought with a sniff and then went out, closing the door rather loudly behind her.

With David was a young woman and as he pulled two chairs up to the bed, Tess saw that she was tall and slim with a long bony face and dark intelligent eyes. She also had an abundance of straight hair which was looped untidily on top of her head, and wore a plain loose dress of indeterminate line.

'This is my sister, Virginia,' said David as they both sat down.

'Hello, Teresa.' Virginia's smile was friendly and sympathetic, and in the lift of the mouth Tess caught a resemblance between her and David.

'How'd you do, ma'am,' Tess answered politely, remembering to watch her manners.

'I do hope you're feeling a little better, my dear,' Virginia went on, and Tess knew by the tone of her voice that there was nothing forced about her concern.

'Yes, you've been through the most terrible ordeal imaginable,' David interrupted and his voice, usually so gentle, sounded deeply angry. 'That father of yours is a monster. How he could contemplate doing such a thing, and to his own flesh and blood, is beyond me.'

Tess shivered and Virginia placed a warning hand on her brother's arm. 'Perhaps we should come back later when you're feeling more up to it.'

'No, no, don't go.' Tess knew that only by talking about her horrific experience could she exorcize it and the healing process take place. Besides, she wanted to know about her mother, who was her main concern.

Virginia looked uncertainly at David. 'Are you quite sure?' he asked.

'Positive.'

David squeezed her hand. 'Good girl. But as soon as you've had enough, say. We don't want the doctor accusing us of ill treating his patient. Take it slowly and tell us what you remember.'

Tess licked her lips. 'I . . . I . . . was . . .' But she couldn't go on. Her temples began to throb and she sank back on the pillows. 'Dad . . . is he dead?' She felt she hardly dare ask the question.

'No, but wounded, highly dangerous and on the run.'

'Will they put Mum in prison?'

'It's hardly likely under the circumstances. If your mother hadn't intervened your father might have killed you.'

'I must go to her,' Tess announced and sat up again.

Virginia's voice was gentle but firm. 'I'm afraid that's out of the question at the moment, Teresa. It would be

151

unsafe. Your father had broken out of gaol, so the police were after him anyway. He knows his way around the docks so they think he might try to get on a ship and that's where they're concentrating their search. It would be most unwise to go home.'

'But there's nowhere else for me to go, and Mum needs me more than ever now.'

'You will be staying here for the time being,' said David. 'Remember that promise I made to you? Well Ginny and I have had a little talk and we wondered if you'd like to help her with her work. When you've fully recovered, of course.'

'Yes, I'm desperately in need of assistance in my office and you've been highly recommended,' Virginia added.

Knowing she wasn't hearing correctly, Tess gazed at David, then Virginia.

Perplexed by her silence, David made haste to explain. 'Ginny's campaigning for votes for women, I'm sure you'd find the work extremely interesting.'

For a second Tess allowed herself a swift surge of hope, then the reality of the situation asserted itself. 'Mum would never allow it,' she answered glumly.

'I think you'll find she will. Your mother is very concerned for your safety and she knows your father would never come looking for you here.'

'And I won't have to go back to that factory?' Tess asked warily.

'No.'

'Never?'

'Never,' Virginia confirmed and then laughed. But Tess contained herself until the brother and sister had gone. Then disregarding her affliction she gave full rein to her elation by bouncing up and down on the bed in joy. It was only when she heard footsteps outside that she lay back feigning sleep.

The doctor came the following day and Tess winced with pain as he dressed the raw, angry wound and applied a salve. She could see that even when it healed there would be an unsightly scar.

With her resilient nature, within a few days Tess was feeling a lot better, but the doctor insisted she continue to rest. She managed a letter to her mother, though, which David was to take with him when he went to collect her belongings from home.

In it she made no mention of her father's outrages against her. Instead she asked Florence not to worry and said she would arrange to send some money home each week. Tess had never written to her mother before and she sat chewing her pencil thoughtfully before she signed it. Finally coming to a decision, she wrote carefully: 'Your loving and obedient daughter, Teresa'. Then she folded it and put it in a thick vellum envelope ready for David to take with him to Golden Court.

10

Number fifteen Lennox Street was a tall, narrow house, one in a row of equally elegant dwellings, surrounded by iron railings and with a basement area leading directly into the kitchens. Wide steps led up to a white-painted front door with a crescented fanlight and a decorative brass door knocker in the shape of a dolphin. Even after two weeks, Tess hadn't accustomed herself to the fact that she was living on so grand a scale.

Meals were taken with Mrs Bradshaw. These tended to be silent, uncomfortable affairs, heavy with disapproval since the housekeeper made no secret of her feeling that Tess's rightful place was below stairs and not sharing a sitting room with her.

Tess had no wish to return to her old life for she'd quickly become accustomed to all the things which make life pleasant: hot baths, clean clothes and decent food. But she desperately missed her mother, Lizzie and Sarah and the companionship of the girls at work, and fought a constant battle against loneliness. At Lennox Street, she felt, she was neither fish, flesh, fowl nor good red herring and the mutual dislike between her and Mrs Bradshaw did little to alleviate her sense of isolation.

But whether she disliked her or not there were things to be learnt from the housekeeper. At her first meal Tess had been thrown into a blind panic by the bewildering array of cutlery. To have asked which she should use for her soup would only confirm Mrs Bradshaw's opinion that she was a little ignoramus, so she just sat staring at the silver with a dry mouth and mounting terror.

Across the table Mrs Bradshaw lifted her hand to her mouth, coughed delicately and then without a word picked up a spoon and dipped it into her soup. Gratefully Tess followed suit and this was how the meal proceeded until she felt she was handling the various pieces of cutlery with all the aplomb of a duchess.

Tess rarely ventured an opinion. She had once, and had her head snapped off in no uncertain manner. Now she left it to Mrs Bradshaw to speak first and sometimes a whole meal would pass where the only sound was the clicking of Mrs Bradshaw's jawbone as she laboriously chewed every morsel of food thirty times.

But she did have her more expansive moods and then Tess would be treated to a detailed history of the St Clair family. And it soon became apparent that they were Mrs Bradshaw's whole life. She had been with them since she was a girl of twelve, first as a nursery maid, then a nanny and finally, when the children had all grown up, as their housekeeper in London. It was during one of these monologues – for Tess was given little opportunity to express a view – that she heard about the family house in Sussex, Elms Court.

'Of course, that house had been in the family for generations. They're such an old family, the St Clairs,' the housekeeper informed Tess as she delicately cut her meat into minute squares.

Tess looked puzzled. 'How do you mean, old?'

Mrs Bradshaw, who had finally managed to spike a piece of meat, paused with her fork in mid air and gazed at Tess through her pince-nez as if she were an imbecile. 'I mean the family tree can be traced back to William the Conqueror.'

The significance of this was lost on Tess who replied cheerfully, 'Well, I expect I could trace mine back too, if I took the trouble.'

The housekeeper's cold, grey eyes glinted maliciously. 'I doubt it, not with a name like Kelly,' and the inflection in her voice made a perfectly ordinary name sound like a rather nasty disease.

It was a deliberate slight and Tess could feel her anger rising. She held her tongue, but only with great difficulty. There was nothing to be gained from crossing swords with someone who wielded as much power in the household as

Mrs Bradshaw. Instead, Tess satisfied herself with glowering at her from underneath her eyelashes and muttering with some venom, 'Starchy-faced old bitch!'

As soon as she could, she escaped to her own room where she found a letter waiting for her. Although she recognized Sarah's handwriting and expected little news, she pounced on it eagerly and slit it open. Sarah wrote with great difficulty, her handwriting was large and unformed, the spelling poor, but as Tess scanned the awkwardly penned letter, her face lit up.

Deer Tess, Sarah wrote, *do yu have a afternoon of if yu hav we cud meat and hav tea mi afternoon of is satday plees rite hoping this leeves yu as it leeves me yor luving frend Sarah. we cud meat up west. xxxx*

Delighted at the thought of seeing Sarah again, Tess sat down at her desk and replied immediately.

Dear Sarah, I would love to see you for tea. How about next Saturday afternoon? Meet me outside Swan and Edgar's department store in Piccadilly Circus at three o'clock. I've got such a lot to tell you and I'm dying to see you again, your loving friend, Tess.

Although it was only Tuesday Tess wanted to give Sarah plenty of time in which to reply, so as soon as the letter was sealed, she rushed downstairs to catch the post on the corner. Feeling extremely light-hearted at the prospect of seeing her old friend again, Tess took the front steps two at a time and in a fairly unladylike manner. She reached the pavement just as a cab moved away and not paying much attention to where she was going, suddenly collided with an object of some substance.

'Ouch,' she gasped, winded by the collision.

'Hello,' said a masculine voice, equally surprised, and as he steadied her she found herself being regarded with considerable interest by Sir Rupert St Clair. 'Don't I know you?' he asked.

Rupert wasn't in residence at Lennox Street but had his own chambers in Eaton Square, and so as far as she knew he had only ever set eyes on her once in his life before. But

Tess knew she had no wish for him to make any connection between that East End girl he'd rescued from under the wheels of a cab and the smartly dressed young woman who now stood before him.

'No, Sir Rupert, I don't think so,' she answered, surprised at the ease with which the lie slipped from her tongue.

'You seem to know who I am, though.'

Caught, she could only stutter lamely, 'Ye . . . es, you see I'm Miss Virginia's secretary.'

The corner of his mouth went up in a slight smile. 'Ah, I see, my sister's little helpmeet. I've heard all about you.'

Tess wondered what he had heard, for he was studying her even more intently now. But, determined not to flinch from his appraisal, she returned his gaze, noticing that although with his dark colouring, he bore more than a passing resemblance to Virginia and the features were handsome, it was also a face that had done a fair amount of living – and drinking.

As the silence lengthened Tess began to feel uncomfortable. 'If you'll excuse me, sir . . . I'd better post this.' She waved the envelope uncertainly.

'Of course.' He lifted his hat. 'I'll bid you good day Miss . . .?' The question hung in the air.

'My name's Teresa. Teresa Kelly.'

'Good afternoon, Miss Kelly, and I do hope I might have the pleasure of bumping into you again.' The corner of his mouth lifted again in an odd, quirky smile.

'Good afternoon, sir,' Tess replied, and knowing he was watching her, walked straight-backed down the road, trying hard not to hurry from his scrutiny. By the time she reached the post box he had gone but she was careful when she returned to the house to pause and listen outside Virginia's office before cautiously opening the door.

Virginia looked up with a smile when she entered. 'Hello, Teresa, I hear you met my brother Rupert on one of his whirlwind visits.'

'Yes,' said Tess, and turned anxiously in case he might suddenly appear.

'Don't worry, he's gone. I only see him when he wants something.' Virginia laughed tolerantly.

Probably money, thought Tess knowingly as she sat down at her type-writer. For she was thoroughly steeped in the literature of the ne'er do well son who wasn't content until the last of the family silver had been pawned to pay his gambling debts. And certainly Rupert would gamble. She began to feel sorry for David and Virginia.

But Virginia, unaware of Tess's concern, was making a frantic search amongst an untidy heap of papers. Then exasperated and impatient, she threw up her hands in despair. 'Where on earth did I put that speech? I must get it done for my meeting on Friday evening.'

Tess stopped her type-writing and thought for a moment. 'Try the left-hand drawer in your desk,' she suggested.

Opening the drawer, Virginia pulled out a sheaf of papers. 'Phew, thank heavens for that, I really thought I'd lost them that time. Miss Carr and Miss Robinson are coming to tea this afternoon and there'll be nothing done once they arrive.'

Like Virginia, the two ladies were suffragists and as Tess had discovered through the speeches and articles she typed, they were agitating for votes for women. It was something Tess had never even considered before, the possibility of women voting. However, the more involved she became with the movement's aspirations, the more she realized how unjust the parliamentary system was: a club devised by men exclusively for men. But not for long if the indomitable women Tess now met in Virginia's study were anything to go by. And persistence could win, the strike had taught her that, so she read everything she could lay her hands on with a burgeoning political awareness. Besides, Virginia was a woman she instinctively admired, like Mrs Besant in a way, determined, outspoken, hardworking and intelligent. She was also desperately untidy and when Tess first moved in papers spilled out of drawers or lay gathering dust on window sills. Books were piled on chairs and when visitors called, Virginia just swept them to the floor, which only added to the general confusion. Matters weren't helped either by Virginia's King Charles spaniel, Snuffy, who had a predilection for paper – the more important, the greater his pleasure in tearing it to shreds.

But it hadn't taken Tess long to get the study organized because, like her mother, she had a quick, neat mind. Soon books were back in bookcases, letters and articles were sorted and filed away, magazines stacked in an orderly pile.

'However did I manage without you, Teresa?' Virginia exclaimed when she saw the transformation for the first time. Although Tess had felt a glow of pleasure at the compliment she also had a sense of her own worth and an inner confidence that she could do her new job well. She also had every intention of making herself indispensable.

Dead on the stroke of four, Miss Carr and Miss Robinson arrived. Tea was served, very informally, in the study for all three ladies were addressing a meeting in Manchester on the Friday evening and many final details still had to be discussed.

Miss Carr, who looked about twenty-five, was small and quiet and Tess found it difficult to imagine her standing up in a crowded hall delivering a rousing speech. Miss Robinson was quite the opposite, a large, well-corseted lady with a booming voice that sent Snuffy rushing for cover under the table, his paws over his ears.

At these regular afternoon teas Tess said little but managed to make herself useful handing round plates of sandwiches and cakes, and all the time listening intently.

With her loud, imperious voice Miss Robinson had little difficulty in dominating the conversation, which she did, in between hearty mouthfuls of cake. 'It's a disgrace to think that any man, no matter how ignorant and unlettered, who hardly knows where to put his cross on the ballot paper, can now vote if he is a householder, whereas no woman, whatever her intellectual powers, has any say in the running of this country. That, my dear Miss St Clair, is the theme I shall pursue on Friday.' Lifting her plate, she bit decisively into her third cream horn.

'I intend to talk about the role of the working woman,' Virginia said, in the lull allowed by Miss Robinson's ingestion of food. 'It's no good just confining our activities to the middle and upper classes. The woman in the mill, in the factory must become involved too, if we are to succeed in our struggle. Don't you agree, Teresa?'

Startled at having her opinion sought, Tess cleared her throat as three pairs of eyes gazed at her expectantly. 'Well, Mrs Besant managed to get us organized at the lucifer factory and look what happened there. I'm sure there are lots of women where I come from, especially those who earn half what men do for the same job, would be interested in what you have to say.'

'Where is it you come from, my dear?' asked Miss Robinson.

'Bethnal Green way.'

'We must arrange something down there, then. Whatever our class, we women must stand together. Men get away with far too much.' Here the feathers in her hat quivered with indignation, and so did several of her chins.

Not long ago Tess would have said that these well-to-do ladies nursed hopeless dreams and were only trying to fill their empty hours. But not any longer. Now she knew that with determination and organization even the impossible could be achieved, and she supported them every step of the way.

Virginia left for Manchester on the Thursday. There was a great flurry of activity as notes and speeches were gathered up in an untidy bundle, then with Snuffy tucked firmly under her arm, she departed leaving the study in complete turmoil. Glad to have something to do, Tess cleared away the debris of departure and then a silence descended upon the house.

It was at these times, when Virginia was away, that Tess felt her loneliness most acutely. With little to do she would wander from room to room like a lost soul. Sometimes, hearing laughter from behind the green baize door that led to the kitchens, she longed to push it open and join in the fun. But the uncertainty of her position prevented her, as did the imagined comments of Mrs Bradshaw if she found her there.

So she filled the empty hours with books. Virginia belonged to Mr Mudie's lending library and from here Tess obtained a constant supply of new novels. When she tired of these there was the library at Lennox Street, stacked from floor to ceiling with books on politics, history and travel, all books to plunder for ideas.

The reply from Sarah she'd been waiting so impatiently for didn't come until Friday afternoon, and she held herself in readiness to be disappointed when she opened it. But as she scanned the few words quickly, her face broke into a smile:

Deer Tess yes I can meat yu where you sed on Satday luv Sarah.

It seemed such a long time since she'd seen Sarah, seen anyone in fact, although it was still only a month since her father's attack on her. Shortly after her arrival at Lennox Street a policeman had called and probed her gently about her ordeal, warning her not to go near Golden Court until her father was finally recaptured. He was now, they explained, extremely violent and had been since the prison fight in which he'd lost his hand.

Tess needed no reminding of his violence, she saw it for herself every time she undressed. The burns themselves had healed well but the scars, which would remain with her for life, like the mark of Cain, had darkened and puckered the white skin of her forearm.

Tess was so hungry for news of her mother and friends that she turned up at Swan and Edgar's half an hour early. And even when Sarah came walking towards her she hardly recognized the confident young lady in the dark red velvet coat and fur-trimmed muff and hat.

The two friends stood gazing at each other shyly for a moment, at a loss for words. It was Sarah who broke the ice. 'Well, who'd 'ave thought it, a couple of bleedin' ladies.' They both laughed immoderately then, and linking arms walked up into Soho to find a quiet café where they could have a good gossip and tea.

'What do you think of me outfit, then?' Sarah asked as they waited for their order to come.

'You look smart as threepence, you really do,' said Tess generously. Although she herself was wearing a well-cut woollen coat, she wasn't a patch on Sarah for style that day.

'It's not rabbit, you know,' said Sarah, stroking the expensive-looking fur muff.

'I can see that. Did Mrs Chadwick give it to you?' Tess knew there was no way a maid's wages would pay for the outfit Sarah was wearing.

'Coo luv a duck, no. Everything I've got on me back I paid for meself.'

Tess, who was now pouring the tea, tried not to look astonished. 'It must have taken a long time.'

Sarah lifted a cup to her mouth, sipped thoughtfully and then put it down again. 'Tess, have you any idea what Mrs Chadwick's line of business is?'

'She's an actress, of course.'

Sarah seemed to find this extremely funny and for several moments she couldn't speak. 'Oh don't make me laugh, Tess, or I'll choke on me sandwich,' she said finally, wiping her eyes with a handkerchief.

Tess felt slightly irritated. 'Tell me the joke, then I can share it.'

'It's just that you're such an innocent,' said Sarah indulgently. 'I'll let you into a little secret, though. Mrs Chadwick entertains gentlemen . . . for a price.'

'What *are* you talking about . . .?' Tess felt reluctant to grasp what Sarah was telling her. 'You mean . . . she's . . . a . . . prostitute?' Even as she spoke the words she knew it couldn't possibly be true.

'You can call her that if you like, it's what you'll have to call me too, I suppose,' Sarah replied coolly.

Tess felt as if she'd been punched violently in the stomach. 'You? I don't believe it!' she shrieked and so loudly several people in the café turned to stare.

Sarah giggled. 'Sssh, I don't want the whole world to know. Girls like us don't get fur-trimmed muffs for nothing,

162

they have to be worked for. Whoever said virtue was its own reward was talking a load of rot. People who make those remarks have never lived in one stinking room or shared a privy with ten other families.'

Tess was so stunned she fell silent. It was uncomfortable information to digest. Then something occurred to her more frightening than ever. 'Mrs Chadwick . . . did she force you to . . . to . . .?'

'Course not. Everything I've done has been of my own free will. And I'll tell you something else.' Sarah leaned over the table confidentially, lowering her voice. 'It's the easiest work I've ever done. All you do is lie there with your legs open. It's the blokes who does all the work. Get themselves into a real muck sweat they do, makes me laugh sometimes. And I'll tell you something else, too, it beats making bloody matches . . . and the pay's better. Don't worry, Tess,' she said when she saw her friend's horror-struck expression, 'Mrs Chadwick's pretty choosy, we only 'ave regulars, not any old Tom, Dick or Harry.'

Tess was now beginning to feel she bore some responsibility for Sarah's downfall. After all, she'd got her the job. 'You've got to give up this life, Sarah,' she said urgently, clasping her friend's sleeves. 'Now, before it's too late.'

'No fear. Anyway, where would I go? I'm very comfortable where I am, thank you.' Then seeing she had in no way reassured Tess, she went on, 'I'm all right, really. When I do leave it will be to a place of me own. One of my gentlemen has said he'll set me up in a nice little place in St John's Wood. It's very posh there, he took me to have a look one day. I'm thinking about it carefully.' Sarah paused and her eyes clouded. 'Do you know, there's only one thing I regret and that's that Milly isn't here to share all this with me. If only it had come a bit sooner.' Her lower lip trembled. 'I could have given her such a lot.'

Sarah's candour had left a dry, sour taste in Tess's mouth and she felt she wanted to get up and walk away from its implications. But to have done so would have been deeply hurtful to her friend, so taking a quick gulp of cold tea she

163

decided the only thing to do was change the subject. 'Have you seen Lizzie or any of the girls from the factory lately?'

'I've seen Liam.'

'Where was that?' asked Tess, more eagerly than she'd intended.

'At the Paragon. With a girl, of course.'

'Tell him he can write to me if you see him again.' Her tone was casual.

Sarah looked amused. 'And after all you've said about him, too. Have you suddenly gone soft on him? I think you're wasting your time at the moment, he's been going out with this latest girl for about a month and that's a long time for Liam. She's very pretty, too,' she added unnecessarily.

'It's only a letter I want from him, not a proposal of marriage. I like to hear from friends,' Tess replied, wondering why she should have to justify herself and knowing too that she was speaking to Sarah more sharply than was necessary. But her friend's revelations had cast a pall over their old easy relationship and Tess was glad when Sarah said she would have to go.

Walking to the bus stop, Sarah, knowing her confessions had hit Tess hard, tried to reassure her. 'You mustn't worry about me, you know, Tess. I can look after meself, honest. And men don't amount to a great deal, you know. They've got these things called cocks and it seems to me they spend a lot of time thinking how they can get them up and keep them up. And if they're prepared to pay for it, well, it suits me,' she said with a shrug.

Tess wondered if she was going to cry. 'You will look after yourself, won't you, Sarah? And we mustn't lose touch,' she called as Sarah jumped on to a bus. 'I'll write to you every week and you must answer. Promise.'

'I promise,' Sarah shouted back and with a wave disappeared inside the bus.

Tess waited until it was out of sight then she turned and started to walk down Piccadilly. She kept her head well down because it was a cold November day with a gritty wind that blew particles of dust into her eyes and made even young faces look pinched and aged. Discarded newspapers, whipped into a whirlwind of activity, danced down the street and wrapped themselves around the ankles of people hurrying to the comfort and warmth of their fires. Grey clouds scudded across a darkening sky and, pulling up the collar of her coat, Tess began to hurry too, her heart heavy as she thought of Mrs Chadwick's house and what went on there.

And all the time she believed Mrs Chadwick was an actress ... Well, she'd certainly been good enough to fool her, even though it was all going on under her nose ... That man saying goodbye to Sarah on the front step, the soiled linen, and of course her mother's attitude to Mrs Chadwick. Florence should have told her, warned her when Sarah went to work there. Surely at eighteen she was old enough to know these things, she thought bitterly.

But how could Sarah ... and with all those men? Tess gave a shudder of disgust. And how did she manage to avoid getting pregnant? Although she had no knowledge of sex herself, after several years in a factory Tess was fairly familiar with the mechanics of it. And one thing she'd understood very quickly, there was little joy in it for women. It had to be endured, of course, once married, because that was a husband's inalienable right. After that it was fingers crossed until the end of the month. For the unlucky, various concoctions such as pennyroyal and slippery-elm bark would be purchased from a quack. Failing that, the more desperate women would resort to knitting needles, often with deadly results.

Sustained by a steady diet of romantic fiction, Tess could in no way equate her own unfulfilled, intensely romantic yearnings for David with the brutal act of sex. Love, sex, in her mind the two things remained entirely separate.

As she left the main thoroughfare she passed a young prostitute lounging against some railings and jangling her door keys impatiently. Like Sarah, she was young, her body was firm, her skin unlined, and men would pay gladly for her services. But as she got older, what then? London was full

165

of women willing to take her place. She would move East perhaps, ending up down at the docks waiting for a ship to come in, glad of a few coppers and prey to disease and maniacs like the Ripper. Was that to be Sarah's end, too? Her throat cut in some dark alley? Tess shuddered and realized what Virginia said was true: there was something basically rotten about a society where men made all the rules and thousands of women were forced to sell their bodies, merely to survive.

When she reached Lennox Street and saw that lights were on in the drawing room her gloom lifted slightly. Someone was home. Virginia perhaps, or even David. She sprinted up the stairs to the first floor but was pulled up short by the sound of male voices, arguing violently. Curious and thinking it must be Rupert and David in brotherly conflict, she approached the drawing room cautiously and through the open door saw David, with his back to her, conducting a very heated exchange with a shabbily dressed young man Tess had never seen before. She was about to tiptoe away when she heard David say, his voice loud and unrecognizably harsh, 'Go on, get out!'

A moment later the young man, oblivious to Tess, went rushing down the hall, calling back over his shoulder, 'You'll pay for this, you'll see.'

David pursued him into the hall. 'Don't you threaten me,' he shouted after him, and then saw Tess. 'Oh . . .' he faltered, 'it's you, Teresa. I thought you were out.'

'I've . . . only just got in this minute,' Tess stuttered, feeling she'd been caught eavesdropping.

Noticing her coat and hat David looked relieved, while downstairs a door banged angrily. 'That was just some scrounger trying to get money out of me. As you can see, I showed him the door.'

'You should put the police on to him, coming here and speaking to you like that,' said Tess indignantly.

'Oh . . . no . . . I couldn't do that. He's very poor, you see.'

Tess, who couldn't see the reasoning of this, said nothing.

'And Teresa . . .'

'Yes?'

'I'd rather you didn't mention this incident to Virginia, it would only upset her.'

'Oh, I won't,' she promised, happy to be sharing a secret with David. He hovered uncertainly for a moment. 'Well, I'd better cut along and get dressed, I'm going to the theatre tonight.'

If only I could go with him, she thought longingly. Share a box and afterwards have supper together. Instead, she would be eating supper with Mrs Bradshaw, possibly in silence. As Tess went to her room to change, depression descended again like a damp, dark cloud.

She was right about the silence and it continued through the meal well into the evening, broken only by the small chiming clock striking the hour. Tess, glad that she was able to lose herself in a book, sat on one side of the fireplace. Mrs Bradshaw, embroidering a tray cloth, sat opposite.

At about nine o'clock there was a sudden commotion downstairs. Mrs Bradshaw, her needle poised in mid air, cocked her head on one side and listened. Unexpectedly, her eyes lit up and putting down her sewing, she went to the door, pulling it slightly ajar. The hubbub downstairs seemed to fill the small room. She stood listening attentively for a few minutes and then closed the door carefully. Putting her hands to her head, she smoothed back her hair into its tight bun and then tweaked fussily at the cuffs of her dress.

'As I thought,' she said, a smile animating her usually stern expression, 'Sir Rupert's here. He'll be up in a moment, you'll see. He never misses a chance to see his old nanny.' Her plain, sharp features softened. 'He was always my favourite, the scamp, could wrap me around his little finger.' Her tone was extremely indulgent.

Well, who'd have thought it, mused Tess, gazing at the housekeeper in surprise. Fancy old sour face going gaga over Sir Rupert. What qualities did he have, she wondered, to inspire such devotion.

But although even Tess would have welcomed the diversion of Sir Rupert's presence that evening, the sitting room door remained firmly shut. Watching covertly over her book as Mrs Bradshaw stabbed dejectedly at her sewing, Tess began to feel sorry for the housekeeper. Why couldn't the beastly man come and visit her, if only for a minute?

At nine thirty Tess decided she'd had enough for one day. Closing her book, she put her hand to her mouth and yawned. She stood up. 'Good night, Mrs Bradshaw.'

The housekeeper didn't look up. 'Good night,' she replied tonelessly.

The housekeeper's downcast expression pulled at Tess's heart strings. Not daring to say anything, she cursed the man under her breath for his insensitivity and indifference.

Going to her room, she heard the voices again, slightly drunken male laughter and a smothered giggle or two. She imagined the ladies being helped into fur wraps and men clipping on black cloaks. There was a draught of cold air up the stairs as the front door opened and shut, the sound of carriages moving away, and then the house settled down again to an uninterrupted silence.

11

Tess just knew she was going to enjoy Christmas. For a start she had more money than ever before in her life and the sovereigns felt reassuringly heavy as she wandered down Regent Street and in and out of brilliantly decorated department stores, choosing presents for her family.

And she enjoyed the deference her newfound prosperity brought, the fussing shop assistants, the proffered chair. She inspected gloves, critically assessed the stitching on fine lawn handkerchiefs and after a great deal of consultation and indecision, finally bought a warm tweed coat for her mother – something that would last for years – a silk cravat for Tom and a leather-bound book of poetry for Mr Appleby.

Although there was no question of her spending Christmas with her family she did persuade Florence to make the journey to Lennox Street one afternoon to collect the presents. When she arrived, her mother stood gazing around the sitting room Tess shared with Mrs Bradshaw, looking small, shabby and ill at ease.

'Here, let me take your coat, Mum,' said Tess, holding out her hand. Reluctantly, Florence parted with the coat and then sat down, but bolt upright and clutching her handbag like a drowning woman. She still hadn't spoken when the maid brought in tea.

Tess handed her mother a dish of hot muffins. 'Go on, Mum, have one,' she urged, 'they're very nice.' Now that she was here, she wanted her mother to really enjoy herself.

Florence regarded the muffins uncertainly and then took one. It was easy to see she approved of the tea service though. She handled the cup almost reverently, holding it up to the

169

light, admiring its translucence, the gold rim and delicate tracing of flowers and leaves.

Speaking for the first time she declared, 'My mother had a service just like this.'

Having some idea of its worth, Tess looked doubtful. 'Exactly like it?'

'We ... ll, perhaps *not exactly*, but something like it,' replied Florence, who had a profound regard for the truth. 'Your grandparents weren't riffraff, you know, they kept a shop and were God-fearing, clean-living folk.'

Yes, and unforgiving, too, Tess wanted to say, but wisely held her tongue.

'And that's what you always want to remember,' her mother continued, 'one side of your family's respectable anyway.'

It was one of her mother's great fears, often openly expressed in the past, that along with his looks, Tess might also have inherited her father's vicious character. But as Florence relaxed and gazed around the well-appointed room Tess could see that she no longer considered this a particular worry; her daughter had achieved a respectability beyond her wildest dreams.

At ease now she went on, 'And wanting to better yourself, you get that from my side. Tom's doing very well and so are you.'

'How is Tom? It seems ages since I saw him.' She felt a sudden sick longing to be with her family again. 'Oh, Mum, let me come home for Christmas, please.'

'We daren't risk it. Your father's a dangerous man, Tess. He was always violent, particularly after a drink, but to brand you, like a beast in the field ... well.' Lost for words, she shook her head in disbelief.

'You went for him, didn't you? With a knife?'

'I did,' replied Florence matter of factly, 'and I'd do it again if I had the chance. I only injured him. I wish I'd killed him.' Her face had gone white and hard.

Tess shivered. 'Don't say that, Mum. He blames us for what happened. Going to prison, losing his hand.'

'The only thing to blame is booze, it's addled his brain.'

Tess thought there was more to it than that and sometimes she even found herself trying to make excuses for her father's attack on her. For if he was wholly evil then she might indeed be tainted with the same blood, as her mother feared. Might herself in future be afflicted with the same madness. If his assault on her could be justified it might lessen the terror which often overcame her.

'Perhaps it was the fight in prison, that could have affected his brain.'

'Perhaps.'

'Anyway, you're no safer than I am,' Tess argued. 'He said he was going to get both of us.'

'I can look after myself and I've got Mr Appleby there, remember.'

Tess almost laughed. 'But Mr Appleby's half Dad's size.'

Florence looked wise. 'Ah, but you'd be surprised what he can do. He learnt some very strange tricks on his travels in the Far East. Seems he can fell a man like a tree in one swift movement.'

'Where do you think Dad is now?'

'There's been absolutely no trace of him, so let's hope he got on a ship like the police said he might do. He won't trouble us any more then.'

'So I could come home for Christmas.'

'Certainly not.' Her mother spoke sharply, and then more gently when she saw her daughter's downcast face. 'It's for the best.'

Defeated, Tess sighed. 'I suppose you're right. But I probably won't even have Mrs Bradshaw for company, she's spending Christmas day with her sister in Peckham.'

'That will be no great loss, from what you've said.' Her mother's tone was brisk and Tess could see that she wasn't going to be allowed to indulge in self-pity.

'By the way, I was talking to that Liam O'Sullivan the other day,' said Florence. 'Said he's been writing to you.'

'I've had a couple of letters,' replied Tess casually.

'Well, don't get too involved. One drunk Irishman in the family is enough.'

This was a slur on Liam's character and it brought Tess quickly to his defence. 'Oh, Mum,' she protested, 'Liam hardly drinks at all.'

'His parents more than make up for it, then.'

'That's not his fault you can't choose your parents,' said Tess, thinking of her own father.

'No, I suppose not. Just the same, don't get too involved. I don't want you ending up back in Bethnal Green with a load of kids. You've got away, make sure you stay away. A chance like this will only come once in a lifetime.'

'Don't worry, I've no intention of marrying, Liam or anyone else, for that matter. Only stupid girls think that's all there is in life. And Miss Virginia seems very happy in her single state.'

'Money makes a difference, you know.'

'Perhaps. Anyway I don't want to talk about men, or marriage. I've got something for you, which is far more important.' Diving behind a chair Tess struggled with a large parcel, which she dropped on to her mother's lap. 'Happy Christmas, Mum.'

'My word, what is it?' asked Florence as she surveyed the bulky gift.

'Open it and see,' Tess urged, anticipating her mother's delight when she saw what it was.

But Florence wouldn't be hurried, each knot in the string had to be carefully untied, each piece of paper smoothed out and folded for future use. By the time she reached the tissue, Tess was almost jumping up and down with impatience.

'Well, well,' Florence exclaimed when she finally lifted the coat from its box. She always kept a tight rein on emotion but as she fingered the soft wool and held the coat up, admiring its subtle autumn colours, Tess saw her mother's features relax into undisguised pleasure.

'Do you like it, Mum? It's tweed and very warm.'

'It's lovely,' she breathed. Then doubtfully, looking at her daughter, 'But it must have cost the earth.'

'I could afford it and I wanted you to have something nice for a change, instead of someone else's hand-me-downs.

172

It's what you deserve. Think how long it will last, too.' By appealing to her mother's sense of economy, Tess knew she could dispel any lingering doubts. 'Try it on.' She took the coat from her mother and held it so that Florence could slip her arms into the sleeves.

It was a perfect fit and Tess led Florence along to her bedroom so that she could admire herself at leisure in the long cheval mirror. 'Now see that you wear it. I don't want it kept for high days and holidays.'

'I get few enough of those,' Florence answered, studying herself from every angle and finding no fault with what she saw. 'Shall I keep it on to go home in?' she asked, excited and uncertain as a young girl as she turned to face her daughter.

'Of course you must.'

She looked at herself again. 'I wonder what Mr Appleby will say when he sees me in it.'

'He'll fall head over heels in love,' replied Tess flippantly, and was startled to see her mother blush.

After a great deal of uncertainty Florence's old, frayed jacket was parcelled up, and laden with gifts she departed in a hansom. There was a tightness in her throat as Tess said goodbye to her mother but she managed to control her tears until she was back upstairs where, overcome with homesickness, she wept quietly into her handkerchief.

Tess didn't hear the tap on the sitting room door, nor the rustle of skirts across the floor.

'Teresa, what is the matter, my dear?'

At the sound of Virginia's voice, Tess gave a guilty start, blew her nose violently and dabbed ineffectually at brimming eyes. 'It's nothing,' she mumbled unconvincingly.

Virginia sat down beside her. 'It's your mother, you miss her, don't you?'

Tess nodded and crumpled her handkerchief into a damp ball. Then thinking this might be taken for ingratitude, she looked up and said quickly, 'But don't think I don't like it here, because I do. It's just that I would have liked to have gone home for Christmas.'

Virginia's dark eyes were sympathetic. 'Of course you would, it's only natural you should want to be with your family. But it wouldn't be safe at present.' She looked thoughtful for a moment. 'I know it wouldn't be quite the same, but how would you like to have Christmas dinner with us? It'll be a very quiet affair, just Rupert, David and myself, but it would be better than being on your own.'

At this staggering suggestion Tess blinked back her tears and gazed at Virginia in wide-eyed astonishment.

Misinterpreting the lengthening silence, Virginia went on uncertainly, 'Of course, you might find it a little dull.'

'Oh no I wouldn't, I'd love to come,' Tess interjected quickly in case Virginia changed her mind. With a growing excitement she did some quick mental arithmetic, wondering if she had enough money for a new dress because she'd spent rather lavishly on Christmas presents.

'We have dinner at one,' Virginia explained. 'That gives the servants a chance to spend the rest of the day with their families. And we start the celebration with a glass of champagne in the drawing room at twelve thirty.'

Listening to all this, Tess's initial excitement began to ebb, as did her confidence. She'd never be able to cope, she'd make a fool of herself in front of David, commit all sorts of social gaffs which they would titter over together afterwards. It was an evening cast over with doubt – she wanted desperately to go, but dreaded it too. So the following day, on her way to buy a dress, she went into a bookshop and when she came out, looking well pleased with herself, she was carrying a small book entitled *A Society Lady's Book of Etiquette*, with the assurance on the fly leaf that its authoress, Mrs F.W. Elgin, moved only in the highest social circles.

By the time she'd read it, Tess knew she'd be well equipped to deal with any pitfalls. More relaxed now she went to hunt for a suitable dress. With only ten shillings and sixpence left in her purse Tess decided it would be a waste of time even looking in the window of Peter Robinson's or any other large department store. Instead she plunged into the back streets and the smaller shops of Soho.

By craning her neck she could see that the label said ten shillings. It was dark red wool and she sensed immediately that it was her dress. As she paid for it and waited for it to be packed, she wondered a little wistfully if David would notice how flattering the rich colour was against her dark hair and how smoothly the bodice moulded itself to her body, emphasizing the rounded curve of her breasts and neat waist. Well, with only three days to go, I'll soon find out, she thought.

It was Christmas eve and the house seemed to be full of green and gold and light. Holly and ivy festooned the walls, candles lit up dark corners and a huge Christmas tree brought up from Elms Court stood in the hall glowing with gold and silver decorations and with presents piled high beneath its fanning branches.

Tess, gazing down at this scene, was so keyed up that her hands trembled as she clutched the banisters. She'd only ever read about Christmases like this in the novels of Charles Dickens. In less than half an hour, Virginia, David and Rupert would gather in the hall, all the servants would file in, hot punch would be served after which Rupert, as the eldest, would distribute presents to each and every member of the staff.

At half past seven Virginia and David appeared and Tess and Mrs Bradshaw followed them downstairs where they all took up a position by the Christmas tree.

Virginia, who was a member of the Rational Dress Society, rarely dressed elaborately, but tonight she was wearing a low-cut, very beautiful dress of dark blue silk and her bare arms, her hair and neck glittered with sapphires and diamonds. Beside her, Tess felt shabby and insignificant and she began to wish she'd worn her new dress instead of saving it for Christmas day.

At a quarter to eight the steaming, spicy punch was carried in followed by the servants, looking slightly self-conscious and wearing their best clothes for the party that would follow below stairs after the distribution of gifts. Soon everyone had arrived except Rupert.

David began to look tight-lipped. He leaned across to Virginia. 'We'll just have to start without him.'

'Oh, I'm sure he'll be here in a moment. This is an occasion Rupert never misses. He knows how much store everyone sets by it, and it's so traditional.'

'We are not waiting all night for my brother.' He strode over to the footman. 'Serve the punch immediately, will you, Hawkins.'

'But Sir Rupert's not here yet, sir,' replied Hawkins.

'We are starting without him,' David said and there was no mistaking the grim satisfaction in his voice.

Looking unhappy the footman began to fill glasses and hand them round. David waited until everyone was served and then lifted his glass.

'Happy . . .' He didn't finish. There was a loud commotion at the door and everyone's eyes turned expectantly as Hawkins hurried to open it, letting in a cold night air and a slightly swaying Rupert.

He held out his hand. 'A drink, Hawkins,' he ordered and then as a hush fell on the room he made his way unsteadily towards the small group standing by the tree.

David's face was thunderous. 'You're drunk,' he muttered accusingly through clenched teeth.

'Am I?' Rupert slurred, managing to look surprised. 'But isn't it a time of good cheer, after all?' He gazed blearily at David for a moment. 'Except that you don't look very cheerful, old chap.'

'Must you make an exhibition of yourself in front of the servants?' David hissed, his eyes darting around the room.

Rupert stopped swaying and looked very sober. Stabbing at David's chest with his index finger, he said, 'I'll do exactly as I please, little brother.'

'Rupert,' Virginia interjected, for the staff were now looking extremely interested. Here was enough gossip to last for several days. 'Aren't you going to wish me a happy Christmas?' She offered her cheek to be kissed.

Immediately Rupert turned away from David and enfolded her in his arms. 'Happy Christmas, darling,' he said and kissed her on both cheeks. Then he turned to Mrs Bradshaw. 'Hello, Nanny,' he said fondly and bent to kiss her papery cheeks, too.

Mrs Bradshaw went pink with happiness. 'Happy Christmas, Mr Rupert,' she replied with a small curtsey.

When he reached Tess he gazed at her uncertainly for a moment with unfocused eyes. 'Ah, I remember now, Miss Kelly.'

Following Mrs Bradshaw's lead, she gave a small curtsey and when he held out his hand she placed hers in it, expecting it to be shaken. Instead, startlingly, he lifted her hand to his lips, holding it there for just a fraction too long. Shocked and embarrassed, Tess wanted to pull her hand away, but this couldn't have been achieved without a tussle, for his grip was firm.

David's face was white with a barely suppressed rage. He thrust a parcel at Rupert. 'You'd better see to these – if you're capable, that is. The staff want to get away.'

Rupert turned to the silent, attentive audience. 'Right,' he called, 'another drink for everyone, Hawkins, including me.' He started to read out the names on each gift then, beginning with the lowly tweeny who scrubbed the stairs, and finishing with Tess and Mrs Bradshaw.

Later, as she undressed for bed, Tess wondered what it was that caused such tension between the two brothers. All right, Rupert had had a bit too much to drink, but David had certainly overreacted, and in turn Rupert had deliberately behaved even more outrageously than he might ordinarily have done. Kissing her hand, for instance, that had only been done to irritate David. Sitting up in bed reading Mrs Elgin's book on manners for the last time, she wished the good lady had some advice on how to deal with situations like that. She'd felt uncomfortable and used. And there was still tomorrow and a whole meal to sit through with the warring brothers. Tess began to worry less about how she would conduct herself than how they might. She felt sorry for Virginia, too. How must she have felt, watching two grown men behaving like that in front of the servants? Tess knew what her mother would have said: They need their heads knocking together to bring them to their senses. Tess felt her mother was right.

Out of habit, Tess rose early on Christmas morning and as she lay stretched out in the hot scented tub, she thought of the zinc bath, the draughty scullery and rapidly cooling water at home, and decided that no matter how homesick she felt, she had no wish to give all this up.

A fire had been lit while she was out of the bedroom and as she sat in front of it, drying her thick hair, she opened her presents.

From Mr Appleby there was a fine Kashmir shawl in a swirling pattern of red and green which would go well with her new frock. Her mother had sent handkerchiefs and Tommy a small leather purse. Tess had deliberately kept her present from the St Clairs until last, and before she opened it she fingered and prodded the small parcel, trying to imagine what it was. But she soon gave up trying and as she tore impatiently at the wrapping paper and saw a small leather box embossed with the address of a very exclusive Bond Street jeweller, she held her breath and slowly lifted the lid. Lying on a cushion of blue velvet was a gold, pearl-encrusted brooch. Any jewellery Tess possessed amounted to no more than a few cheap trinkets bought from a market stall, and as she turned the delicate star-shaped brooch over and over in her hand she marvelled at its fragile beauty.

Gosh, they must think something of me, buying me this, Tess thought and felt deeply reassured, for it was an indication of her worth in the family's eyes. If they were thinking of getting rid of me they wouldn't have been quite so generous. There was a certain insecurity about her position, so that the gift seemed, somehow, like a seal of approval. Replacing it in the box and taking no chances, she put it in her desk and turned the key. Later it would adorn her new dress.

Even after a leisurely breakfast, Tess still had a few hours to fill before The Dinner. A walk, she decided, would fulfil several purposes – it would calm her nerves, pass the time and sharpen her appetite.

Pulling on a heavy coat, she set off for Hyde Park, walking briskly through deserted streets. During the night there had been a hard frost but although it was still bitterly cold, the sky was a bright enamel blue. In the park a hoar frost had turned the natural world prematurely white, each twig, branch and blade of glass a filament of frozen mist.

It was busier in the park than Tess had imagined it would be, and as she wandered along beside the Serpentine, several men in bathing costumes made half-hearted attempts at breaking the ice for a swim. Their lack of success didn't worry them unduly and Tess noticed that they were easily consoled by a hip flask passed round among the group.

On Rotten Row there was even more activity, with people riding off the effects of the previous night or in anticipation of the feast to come.

Tess was just about to turn and strike off across the park when she saw Rupert. He was riding along beside an imperious-looking, fair-haired beauty and his head was bent attentively, listening to every word she said. As they cantered past, the woman's voice, with its ringing, aristocratic tones, was carried, like a bell, over the still, frosty air. 'Of course, Rudolph said ...' What the gentleman said Tess never heard, for a carriage passed and the voice was drowned by the crunch of wheels on stone.

With a worried frown Tess made for home. Would that young woman be joining them today? She fervently hoped not, she had enough to cope with and she could just imagine her supercilious amusement at finding herself sharing a table with a humble secretary.

Modest though it was, when she'd changed into her new dress and pinned the pearl brooch to her throat, Tess felt better. Her hair shone, her skin glowed from the walk and she was now, thanks to Mrs Elgin, well schooled in the ways of the nobility. She could do no more. Pausing at her bedroom door, she took a deep breath, smoothed away an imaginary crease from her dress then, seeing it had gone

179

half past twelve, hurried along to the drawing room. But it was still empty and she hovered uncertainly on the threshold, wondering what to do. She lacked the courage to stand there on her own and she'd just decided to return to her room when a deep voice behind her said, 'Come on, let's have a glass before the others arrive.' Tess found her elbow being taken and she was propelled across the room by Rupert to where a champagne bottle stood in a bucket.

Lifting the dark green bottle, Rupert eased the cork out expertly with a slight pop and filled two glasses. It looks just like ginger beer, Tess thought as he handed her a glass and she watched as the bubbles rose quickly to the top. Feeling now like the conspirator in some crime, she whispered nervously, 'Shouldn't we wait for the others, sir?'

'What, and waste good drinking time? Certainly not.' He lifted his glass. 'Now, what's the toast to be?' He appraised her familiarly for a moment. 'I know, let's make it to a very beautiful young lady in a red dress.'

Tess, whose face was now the colour of her dress, took a frantic sip of her drink, hiccuped loudly, put her hand to her mouth briefly in shame and then giggled with embarrassment.

Rupert laughed too. 'See, it's doing you good already.' He lifted the bottle and gazed at it reflectively. 'With a bit of luck it might even put David in a good mood.' He slopped some more carelessly into his own glass and Tess, feeling more relaxed by the minute and deciding that indeed, champagne was no more harmful than ginger beer, held hers out to be refilled as well.

She'd just put the glass to her lips when David and Virginia entered the room. Filling two more glasses, Rupert handed them one each, saying casually, 'Hope you didn't mind this young lady and me starting without you but I was desperately in need of liquid refreshment after my ride this morning. Hair of the dog, you know.'

One glance at David's face told Tess that he did indeed mind and was holding his tongue only with great difficulty.

Oh Lor', she thought, had she overstepped the bounds of propriety already? Mrs Elgin had slipped up again.

'Of course we don't mind you starting, darling,' Virginia interceded quickly. 'It's Christmas day, we want everyone, particularly Tess, to enjoy themselves, don't we, David?'

'Ah . . . eh . . . yes . . . of course,' answered David uncertainly.

'Good, then we'll drink to that, shall we? Happy Christmas everyone.'

'Happy Christmas,' the brothers and Tess answered obediently, and then she thanked them all, slightly shyly and clumsily, for her present.

Virginia took her hand. 'Well, it's certainly no more than you deserve. I don't know how I ever managed without you.'

Rupert came and stood close to her, peering with some interest at the brooch. Tess began to feel rather hot. 'So we bought you that pretty little bauble, did we?'

'Yes, you did, sir,' Tess replied, not in the least surprised he'd played no part in its selection. The brooch had been purchased with some care and bore all the trademarks of Virginia's thoughtfulness rather than of her brothers'.

At one o'clock the gong in the hall announced dinner. David lifted his arm. 'If you'll allow me, Teresa.' Straightening her back and lifting her chin, Tess slipped her hand through the proffered arm, flexing her fingers pleasurably against the green velvet jacket David was wearing. This is it, she thought as they followed Rupert and Virginia downstairs to the dining room.

It was a dark room at the back of the house overlooking a winter-dead garden. Today, however, hot-house plants and greenery were arranged the length of the snowy white napery, slim candles stood in tall candelabra, their golden flame enhancing the antique sheen of silver and the cool brilliance of cut glass. Entranced, Tess clasped her hands in front of her all pretence at sophistication gone. 'It's . . . it's all so lovely,' she breathed.

Somehow her simple pleasure had a unifying effect on the two brothers and they became quite civil to one another. David held her chair for her as she sat down then a large succulent roast goose was brought to the table. Sharpening a knife, Rupert gazed at it doubtfully then rather ineptly began to carve and the hilarity this induced broke down any lingering sense of reserve Tess still felt.

Sipping a sweet liqueur at the end of the meal, Tess gazed round the table in a state of happy euphoria. They were a handsome trio and it was nice seeing them happy in each other's company, differences resolved. The rich quarrelled, and made up, just like ordinary families, Tess thought benignly. But of course, Virginia and David had social consciences, Rupert didn't and that could cause some dissent. All the same she couldn't help warming to him in spite of his obvious faults. The line of the mouth was humorous and that slightly rakish air undeniably attractive . . .

Rupert looked up, caught her rather intent scrutiny and, obviously amused, raised a questioning eyebrow.

. . . And knows it too, thought Tess, and with women galore no doubt. Turning her attention to David, she allowed him to refill her glass. Then with a glow of pride she sat back and thought to herself: if only Mrs Elgin could see me now.

It was nearly four when they finally rose from the table. Rupert was off to Essex for the Boxing Day Meet, David and Virginia visiting friends.

As she went up to her room, Tess heard the servants leaving, shouting greetings to each other as they parted at the top of the area steps. They were just starting their Christmas, joining their families for cold ham, trifle and games. Hers had already ended, not that she minded, there couldn't be too many people who'd had a better day than she had.

12

Early in the new year Rupert left for Italy and the house settled down again into its normal routine. David, always more relaxed when his brother wasn't around, came and went regularly and as Virginia darted about all over the country, Tess was kept busy organizing her affairs. She was daily becoming more and more immersed in Virginia's work and the ideals of the movement, and longed to take a more active part. So she dropped several hints that she would like to attend some meetings and waited for Virginia to take up the challenge.

What she hadn't bargained for, though, was Bermondsey on a wet March night. Tess had seen herself in exciting far-away cities like Manchester and Leeds, not south-east London. But Virginia was carrying through her plan to reach working-class women, and as the carriage swayed and bumped over pot-holed streets and Tess saw the miserable housing, the drunks and bands of marauding children, she began to wish she'd stayed at home. And would they get any support? The meeting had been well advertised on posters but that didn't mean anyone would turn up. Tess glanced sideways at Virginia who was busy scribbling amendments to her notes. Perhaps she ought to say something. Prepare her . . . just in case. But having heard Tess's version of the strike, Virginia had convinced herself that in the working-class woman their movement had a vast untapped reservoir of support.

But they were all such well-meaning women, Virginia and her friends, even though they had little idea of how their 'working-class sisters', as they liked to call them, lived, or the sheer drudgery of their everyday lives. Tess just hoped they wouldn't be too disappointed by the meagre turnout tonight.

Standing a little later on the platform peering down into the dim, cold reaches of the hall, Tess realized that if she had voiced her fears she would now be eating her words. The hall was well over half full and apart from a sprinkling of men, the rest of the audience was women, some busily knitting, others nursing babies, and only Tess knew the effort that must have gone into dragging their tired bodies out on a wet night like this.

Before the meeting commenced she moved amongst the audience distributing leaflets. When one young man very pointedly crumpled his into a ball and threw it to the floor, Tess knew they had a heckler on their hands.

It was decided, after an extremely polite debate amongst the ladies, that Virginia should speak first. With her thick pelt of hair looped untidily under a large hat and her dark, expressive eyes lit with an inner fervour, she leaned over the lectern, inviting the rows of women into her confidence. She spoke clearly and simply and in a voice that carried effortlessly to the back of the gloomy hall, but in no way did she talk down to her audience.

'As you will know, ladies, only our menfolk have the right to vote in parliamentary elections, so that means half the adult population of this country has no proper representation in Parliament – and that is unjust. There are enlightened men in, and outside government, who support our petitions. Unfortunately there are also ignorant and ill-formed forces lined up against us, not just men, but women too. These people class us along with imbeciles and children and consider us incapable of casting a vote.'

She paused briefly to make her point and in the hiatus a male voice shouted provocatively from the back of the hall: 'So you are. Lady, there's only one thing wimmin is capable of . . .' But he never finished, for the women who had a moment earlier been sitting in docile silence, rounded on him, abusing him with a richness of vocabulary that sent the young chap scurrying from the hall in fear of his manhood.

Virginia waited until the door banged shut behind him, then she said quietly, 'There goes one of our intellectual superiors,' whereupon the whole room erupted with laughter and by the end of the evening the movement had several dozen new recruits to their cause.

When the meeting finished several young women came up to the platform with questions for the committee. Tess knew their queries had to be answered, but there was also an impatient caretaker anxious to lock up and get home. Collecting Virginia's notes together, Tess stuffed them into a large canvas bag her employer carried everywhere with her.

A slight disturbance and a woman's voice complaining 'Watch where yer goin', can't yer?' made Tess look up and she saw a man pushing his way down the centre aisle, against the stream of women making for the door. The lighting was so poor, she thought at first it must be the abusive heckler returning and she was just about to warn Virginia, when she saw that it was Liam.

'Good heavens, I didn't know you were here,' she said. Then she saw that he must have just arrived because the strongly curling hair had been flattened and darkened by the heavy rain and he was panting slightly from his exertions.

'Phew,' he said at last, 'I thought I'd never make it.'

'You're too late for the meeting, we've just finished.'

'It's you I came to see.'

'Why didn't you come earlier, then? We're just going home.'

'I would if I could have found the bloomin' place. I've searched all evening for this hall, and all for you, Miss Teresa Kelly.'

'Nobody asked you to,' replied Tess, bristling slightly.

'That's true. I thought you might like to see an old friend, just the same.'

'Oh, I am pleased to see you,' Tess assured him. The hall was empty now, Virginia had gone to the carriage and the caretaker was standing by the door jangling his keys impatiently. Tess jumped down from the platform. 'Come on, we'll have to go.'

Outside, the rain fell straight as rods of steel. Behind them was the sound of bolts being shot and there was no shelter of any kind. A few feet away stood Virginia's carriage. 'I'm sorry, Liam, but I'll have to go.' She pulled up her collar, ready to make a dart for it.

'And after I've come all this way,' Liam complained.

Tess started to run. 'When can I see you then?' he called after her.

Feeling sorry for him, she shouted back through the rain, 'Write and we'll arrange something.' She jumped into the carriage and sank down beside Virginia panting. The horse was just moving away at a brisk pace when she noticed Liam running along beside them, mouthing something through the closed window. Embarrassed, she turned, and stared straight in front of her but as the horse left him behind she thought she heard him say faintly, 'I might be going away . . .'

Startled, then obviously amused by Liam's face at the window, Virginia said, 'Well, well, who was that? An admirer?'

Nettled, Tess replied, 'No, just a friend, someone I knew at the Settlement.'

'Don't tell me it was devotion to our cause that brought him all this way tonight.' Her voice still held a hint of laughter.

Tess felt it was incumbent upon her to clarify her relationship with Liam immediately. 'Liam fancies himself as a lady-killer. Likes collecting trophies, and I don't intend being one.'

'Pity,' mused Virginia, 'he seemed a nice-looking young man.'

Liam *was* going away, to South Africa. It said so in his letter, and in less than a month. To accustom herself to this unsettling news, Tess sat down at the desk and began, absentmindedly, to stroke Misty, a small tortoiseshell of unknown parentage and with a split ear, who'd somehow managed to work her way up from the kitchens and into Virginia's heart. At ease with the world in spite of her unkempt appearance, she sat on an important pile of documents, fastidiously manicuring her nails. She and Misty, Tess often felt, had quite a lot in common.

More disturbed than she would have wished by Liam's letter, Tess drew a world atlas from the bookshelf and opened it at the map of Africa. Two things were noticeable about the place: it was very big and a long way from England. Picking up his letter she read it again . . . *You said you'd come out with me and since it's likely to be for the last time, how about a trip to Brighton?* The study looked out over the back garden where a pink cherry tree was in full bloom. After a cold, wet March, late April had turned unseasonably warm. A day at the seaside might not be a bad idea, it could do no harm and Liam was going away. Besides she had never seen the sea.

It seemed to Tess that the whole of London must be taking the excursion train to Brighton that Sunday. Victoria station overflowed with jostling, shoving families and she and Liam found there was stiff competition for a seat from buckets, spades, rugs, picnic hampers and all the paraphernalia of a day out at the seaside. For several minutes they darted up and down the platform, peering into carriages to see if they could find two seats together. When Tess saw the porter striding towards them, slamming doors, she began to panic.

'There's one seat 'ere,' the porter offered, holding open a door. 'I should 'op on, miss, if you want to reach Brighton today. There's one for you, sir, two carriages down.'

Before Tess could think, Liam had pushed her into the carriage. 'I'll see you in Brighton,' he called and she watched anxiously from the window as he tore down the platform and into a carriage barely a second before the porter waved his green flag.

With a jolt the great black and golden-yellow engine moved out of the station. Tess found herself wedged uncomfortably between a large, well-corseted lady dressed entirely in black and a small, restless girl who chewed noisily on a bag of boiled sweets. With a dizzying energy the child leapt to her feet at every stop. 'Are we there? At the seaside yet, Ma?' she would ask expectantly as she clambered over legs, bruising ankles and shins in her eagerness to reach the window. Soon the tolerant smiles of the other passengers became rather more fixed, while the lady in black fairly oozed disapproval. Finally the child's exasperated mother slapped her but this only produced a fury of sound which lasted until the train reached Brighton. Tess watched with a feeling of relief as the girl, still wailing, was hauled off down the platform. Her sticky fingers had taken their toll on Tess's pale green lawn dress, and she scrutinized herself carefully in the oval carriage mirror to see whether any smudges of soot had done the same to her complexion.

Liam caught her spitting on to her hankerchief and vigorously rubbing her chin. 'Stop admiring yourself, you look lovely.'

'I'm tidying myself up, if you must know,' she countered tartly.

'And missing the best part of the day. Come on.' He took her hand and helped her down to the platform, then tucked her hand through his arm. 'Now listen, young lady, before we start, let's call a truce, no arguing today.'

'You're the one who argues.'

'Tess . . .' Liam wagged a warning finger at her and she had the grace to laugh.

'Well, perhaps I do go on a bit at times,' she admitted as they walked from the vaulted cool of the station into a squinting brightness of hot streets and melting tar.

Here, long lines of people waited patiently for buses to the front. 'Do you want to wait or shall we walk?' Liam asked.

The road to the front was steep and through a breach between buildings, Tess caught her first glimpse of the sea. Pip had fed her imagination with his tales of the sea but she'd never thought it would be quite like this, so vast and deep and moving like molten silver. She caught a whiff of salty air and in no mood now to stand in line, she pulled on Liam's arm. 'We'll walk, of course,' she answered promptly and, almost as excited as the small girl on the train, she dragged him down the hill to the front.

Here it was as crowded as Petticoat Lane on a Saturday night and people were spending as freely too. Ice cream, lemonade, paper windmills for the children, donkey rides, boat trips were there for anyone with the money to pay for them. And today, in true London fashion, everyone was determined to enjoy themselves, tomorrow could take care of itself.

Liam wanted to stop and watch a Punch and Judy show. Tess endured it uneasily for a moment and then pulled him away. As a child she had found Punch, with his large nose and humped back, grotesque and frightening, and she had never outgrown her dislike of the puppet. Also the spectacle of him beating up Judy and the baby carried with it uncomfortable echoes of her own father's brutality, which was the last thing she wanted or needed today.

But like everyone else in the audience, Liam laughed loudly when Punch laid about him, and he moved away from the narrow booth very reluctantly. 'I was just beginning to enjoy that,' he complained.

Tess shivered. 'He's horrible, that Punch.'

Liam gave her a quick, perceptive glance and took her hand. 'You're absolutely right. He's a nasty old man and we shouldn't be wasting time here when we could be on the beach.'

Tess had imagined that the beach would be a wide strand of golden sand. What she hadn't bargained for was a high tide and dark grey shingle, which was very hard on the bottom, as she discovered when they sat down.

'Let's go for a paddle,' said Liam, unlacing his boots.

'Oh, I couldn't go in the water.'

Liam looked slightly surprised. 'Why ever not?'

Tess flapped her hand at the crowded beach. 'I can't take my shoes and stockings off here, not in front of all these people.'

'Nobody will even bother to look at you and I'll turn my head away, I promise.'

Just then, her mother's prim, disapproving features rose in front of her. Tess could almost hear the reprimand on her lips. She shook her head. 'I'm sorry, I just can't.'

Liam began to look slightly exasperated. 'For heaven's sake, Tess, don't be so prudish. Let your hair down for

189

once in your life. Look at those girls, they're really enjoying themselves.' He indicated two young women who were splashing around in the shallows, laughing rather shrilly and showing, Tess thought, far too much leg.

'And making an exhibition of themselves,' she retorted acidly, then thought: Oh Lor', I sound just like my mother, and was so appalled she stood up and scanned the beach. Just behind them, pulled well up on to the pebbles, was a rowing boat. 'I'll be back in a moment,' she said and set off with a determined look. Tess glanced cautiously around her, then crouching behind the boat and feeling rather wanton, removed her garters. It took a little longer to roll down her stockings, so it was with a great sense of achievement that she stuffed them into her shoes and, wincing with pain, hobbled to where Liam stood on the edge of the water. Bunching up her dress, she edged her way forward. Small waves lapped around her feet, frothy and cold as champagne. 'It's freezing!' she exclaimed, with a sharp intake of breath.

Liam laughed. 'Yes, but think of the good it's doing you.'

But in no time it seemed quite warm and Tess began to enjoy the sensation of shifting sand and pebbles through her toes and the ebb and flow of the tide under her feet. She closed her eyes and lifted her face to the sun. She was thinking to herself: I'll get freckles, I suppose, when her gentle reverie was interrupted by the two young women as they went shrieking past, displacing a great deal of water and closely pursued by two young men.

Tess gave an exclamation of annoyance and glared after them. 'Look at my dress, it's soaking.'

'Never mind, it'll soon dry in the sun. Come and sit down, then we'll take a turn along the pier.'

'If it's all the same to you, I'd rather go and see the pavilion,' she answered as she dusted sand from between her toes.

'It's just a prince's extravagant whim, what do you want to see that for?'

But Tess was fascinated by the story of poor, neglected Mrs Fitzherbert and her somewhat irregular union with

George IV, and she wasn't leaving Brighton without visiting the pavilion. She stood up, trying to smooth the creases out of her still damp dress. 'You don't need to come, I can go on my own.'

'Well, if you are determined . . .' Reluctantly, Liam stood up too.

They passed the two young women on the way up the beach, stretched out on the shingle and already on very familiar terms with the young men they had just met.

Tess and Liam exchanged amused glances. 'It just shows you what a bit of sea air can do,' said Liam in an aside. This set them both giggling and they had to hurry in case the embracing couples heard them.

'A monument to one man's greed,' intoned Liam rather pompously, when a short time later they stood staring up at the onion-shaped cupolas and moorish arches of the pavilion. But Tess was fascinated, it was so exotic, so out of keeping with the restraint and elegance of the other houses in the town.

'I can just imagine Prinny in there with his cohorts, drinking, gambling and whoring while his subjects starved. There was a revolution going on in France and yet he had the nerve to build that extravagance. It should be razed to the ground.' Liam sounded very censorious. He began to tug on her arm. 'Come on, I can't look at that excrescence any longer, it makes me angry. Let's go and get some dinner.'

Tess went reluctantly. She could understand Liam's disapproval but she still thought the building beautiful and, with its whiff of the Orient, alien and thrilling too.

The fish restaurant where they had dinner was rather more commonplace, but it served the best fish and chips in town. Splashing her plateful liberally with vinegar, Tess ate hungrily.

'It seems ages since I had fish and chips.'

'I expect it is.' Liam looked gloomy. 'You don't do much mixing with the hoi polloi these days, do you, Tess? You're a lady now, you dress like one, you even talk like one.'

191

Pleased and flattered by Liam's observations, Tess helped herself to some bread and butter. She worked hard on erasing her cockney vowels, it was reassuring to know she wasn't wasting her time.

Swinging back on the legs of his chair, Liam surveyed the noisy café with an air of dissatisfaction. 'I wish I could have taken you to one of those posh hotels along the front, instead of here. Still, when I come back from South Africa I'll be rich as Croesus, we'll go anywhere you like then, Paris, Vienna . . .'

'Why do you want to go to South Africa?' Tess interrupted. 'What's wrong with England?'

Liam straightened his chair. 'I'll tell you what's wrong with England,' he answered angrily, stabbing the air with his fork. 'Five pence a bloody hour is what's wrong with England. The dockers have asked for a tanner and they won't give it to us. I'm lucky, I suppose, I'm young and strong and there's plenty of work for me. It's the older ones I feel sorry for and the casual labourers scratching and fighting for a couple of hours' work and treated worse than animals. It can't go on, though, there'll be a strike soon, you'll see, everyone's had enough.'

'After all you've said you should be staying then, not gallivanting off halfway round the world.'

'I didn't know there was going to be a strike when Uncle Josh wrote, did I?' Liam sounded a bit on the defensive. 'At the time there didn't seem much to keep me here and there are opportunities out there if you're prepared to work. My uncle's done very well. Anyway, it's too late now, he's paying my fare, my passage is booked to Durban and I sail in two weeks' time.'

'As soon as that?' Tess pushed her plate away, her appetite gone. Her time with Liam would now have to be counted out in minutes and hours, rather than days or weeks. Strange how you squandered time and then suddenly it became precious.

'Will you miss me?' he asked.

She gave a small, sad sigh and picked at the tablecloth. 'Probably.'

Hope flared in Liam's blue eyes. 'You could always marry me.'

'I can't marry you, Liam.'

'Why not?'

'Because I don't love you,' she answered simply.

'Not like you love David St Clair, eh?' He gave her a sly, knowing grin and Tess felt herself going red to the roots of her hair. She compressed her lips into a taut, angry line.

'Don't be ridiculous,' she snapped, hating him for his callous indifference to her feelings.

But Liam ploughed tactlessly on. 'The upper classes only marry their own kind, you ought to know that.'

She tried to freeze him into silence with a look. 'Say one more word and I'm leaving this restaurant.' She began gathering her things together.

A family of four at the next table had ceased their stolid chomping and, their jaws hung slack, were listening to every word.

Liam glowered at them. 'Something wrong?' he asked and Tess felt so embarrassed on their behalf that she rose from the table and strode out of the restaurant.

'Wait,' she heard Liam call. Knowing he still had the bill to pay and hoping to confuse him, Tess felt a certain delight in turning east along the esplanade, away from the main part of the town and the station. I'll give him a run for his money, she thought grimly. She hated it when he made personal remarks about her and David, for they left her feeling exposed and vulnerable. It was none of his business, although it obviously irked that she preferred someone else to him. But then his vanity knew no bounds. Tess could hear him panting some way behind her but she kept up her brisk pace. I hope he's sweating, she thought vindictively, it'll serve him jolly well right.

When Liam finally caught up with her he put out a restraining hand but she shook it off irritably. 'I thought I'd . . . lost . . . you. Can . . . you . . . wait . . . a bit, Tess, I'm out of breath . . . and I've got a stitch . . . in my side.'

She deliberately increased her speed, her heels tapping indignantly on the pavement. 'Serves you right,' she snapped unsympathetically.

'Look, I'm sorry, I really am.'

She gazed at him with distaste. 'Why do you try to cheapen everything?'

'Because I'm jealous, I suppose,' he replied, humbled at last. Liam watched Tess's profile closely then, saw several emotions cross her face but searched in vain for forgiveness. Why can't I hold my tongue? he thought. It got him into so much trouble with Tess, he ought to have learnt by now. His real trouble, of course, was that his love for Tess ran as deep and strong as a subterranean stream and caused him to say things he was bound to regret. No girl had ever caught his imagination like Tess and no girl had spurned his advances as she had, and sometimes he set out to hurt her for the unwitting hurt she caused him. But he would have her one day, he was confident about that, when he had money and position she would come to him then. David St Clair offered no real threat, and in a way, while she hankered after him she was safe from other men. And absence did make the heart grow fonder . . . so perhaps while he was away . . .

A bus trundled past and stopped a few yards further on. Suddenly Tess picked up her skirts and ran, jumping on to the platform just as it moved off. Liam stared after her in surprise.

'Hey, where are you going?' he yelled, and then with a run, leapt on after her.

'Where to, Guv?' the conductor asked as they took their seats.

'Aah . . . uhm . . . I'm not sure . . .' Liam looked at Tess for guidance, but she averted her face and stared out of the window, enjoying his discomfiture.

The conductor began to look suspicious. 'This gentleman bothering you, lady?' he asked in a loud voice, and every passenger on the lower deck turned and stared at him accusingly. Liam ran his finger nervously round the edge of

194

his collar, wondering if he should cut his losses and make a bolt for it.

Relenting not a moment too soon, Tess came to his rescue. 'It's all right, we are together. How far do you go?' She offered the conductor a smile of great sweetness.

'Rottingdean, lady.' He jingled his change impatiently.

Liam fumbled around in his pocket and drew out some coppers. 'Two to Rottingdean then, please.' The rest of the bus, satisfied now there was no impropriety, returned to contemplating the passing scene.

At the terminus the bus emptied and, still ignoring Liam, Tess started to walk up through the village towards a windmill that stood high on the Downs. Very soon it was behind them and they were following an ancient chalk path, the turf eroded by generations of cattle and wayfarers, and now lying exposed like the spine of some long-dead beast. Tess was soon hot and exhausted from the exertion of the climb, so unpinning her hat she flung it down on the short, springy turf and then sank down beside it. Drawing up her legs, she rested her chin on her knees and gazed out to sea at the small fishing boats, the coal-carrying sailing barges and the pleasure steamers dotted, like a morse code, along the horizon. The air was fragrant with wild thyme and the only sound was a slight susurration of grasses and harebells as a gentle breeze moved over the Downs. Tess's irritation began to ebb away and with a sigh of contentment, she lay back on the grass. Stretching her arms languidly above her head she watched as a skylark sang its way to the heavens, then through half-closed eyes studied Liam's sulky profile. A moment later she was asleep.

She was awakened by grass tickling her cheek, and opening her eyes found Liam leaning over her and so close she could see that the long thick lashes were tipped with gold and that his blue eyes were full of love. Without knowing why, she lifted her arms and wrapping them around his neck, pulled him down towards her.

There was no gentleness in Liam as he lay claim to her lips and although a warning pulse beat in her head, her own

195

response to the hungry, insistent pressure of his mouth and the caressing movement of his hands upon her breasts was swift. Imprisoned by the weight of his body, she felt him fumble impatiently with the unyielding buttons of her dress and then move down and pull at the hem. With a quick intake of breath, she closed her eyes and abandoned herself to the pleasure of fingers gently stroking the soft warm flesh of her thighs. But then the fingers began to search and probe and Tess, with a sudden fright, found the strength to push him away from her and sit up.

Trembling slightly and ashamed of her own lack of control, she spoke sharply, 'That's quite enough of that, I'm not one of your little tarts, you know.' She straightened her dress and pinned her hat back on, to emphasize the point.

Defeated, Liam ran his hands through his hair in a distracted manner. 'I'm sorry, Tess, I went too far, I know, but I love you, I can't help it. Sometimes I wish I didn't. Love only enslaves you. So what am I going to do, eh?' He turned on her almost angrily as if it were her fault.

In control of the situation again and believing it to be true, Tess answered matter of factly, 'By the time you reach South Africa you'll have forgotten all about me.'

Liam gazed at her, his blue eyes intense and unflinching. 'How can you say such a thing? Knowing how I feel about you. And I will marry you. I promise you that.'

Tess laughed. 'What, with me here and you in Africa?'

'I'll be back, don't you worry, just as soon as I've made my pile.'

That day, Tess would have liked to believe him, for she felt herself to be half in love with him, which, of course, was very foolish indeed, she told herself sternly. Perhaps sentiment and a sense of loss were clouding her judgement, for Liam's departure would leave a significant gap in her life, although she couldn't bring herself to tell him so. A sudden breeze blew in from the sea, chilling the air, and she shivered.

Liam held out his hand and pulled her to her feet. 'Come on, let's go and get a cup of tea in the village.' Glad that the conversation had taken a less serious turn, Tess followed him down the path, past the windmill and into a café that sold cream teas.

By the time they returned to Brighton the sun was low in the sky and the crowds were leaving the beach and streaming up the hill to the station. Tired children were being carried aloft on their fathers' shoulders, while smaller ones were already asleep in their mothers' arms. Equally tired, Tess and Liam were trudging up the hill with the crowd when Liam suddenly stopped in front of a photographer's window.

'I want a picture of you to take with me to Africa.'

'What, looking like this, with my hair a mess and my dress all crumpled?'

'It's exactly how I want to remember you, freckled and untidy.'

'Oh, no,' Tess moaned, rubbing ineffectually at her nose, 'I haven't really got freckles, have I?'

He kissed the end of her nose. 'You certainly have and they look adorable. Now come on.' Taking her hand he pulled her towards the door at the same time as the owner materialized to turn the card from open to shut.

'We're too late,' said Tess with relief.

'Don't you believe it,' said Liam, banging loudly on the door and gesticulating for the man to open.

Eventually, through a chink, the man called, 'Sorry, sir, I've closed for the day.'

Liam lowered his voice confidentially. 'But this is a very important and happy occasion for me and my young lady. You see we've just become engaged and a photograph would be a record of the happy event.'

What lies, thought Tess, too astonished to say anything. The door had now opened wide enough for two people to squeeze through and, wasting no time, Liam took her hand and pulled her into the shop. Leading them through the darkened shop the photographer drew back some red chenille curtains on a small studio containing equipment and painted cloth scenery. The man, who had thin strands of hair plastered to a pink scalp, stood studying them with his head on one side.

197

'Now let me see, the rose arbour, I think,' he said and pushed some wobbling scenery into place. 'If you'd just stand there please … No, not like that,' he exclaimed fussily as Liam and Tess stood self-conscious and stiff as two soldiers on parade. 'Relax, please, and if you'd take your fiancé's arm, miss …' He disappeared under a dark cloth. 'Keep very still,' came his muffled voice and as he reappeared Tess was startled by a loud flash.

'Lovely, lovely,' the photographer exclaimed, carefully re-arranging his hair. 'I think you'll both be very pleased with the results.' As Liam paid, he wrote down their addresses. 'They'll be about a week,' he said as he showed them to the door. Here he took Tess's hand in his, his dark eyes moistly sentimental. 'And I hope you'll both be very happy, my dears.'

'Oh, we will,' answered Liam with the utmost certainty.

They contained themselves until they were outside and then dissolved into a rib-aching explosion of laughter. 'That poor man, how could you tell him such lies, Liam?' Tess asked as she wiped her eyes.

'It was a very small lie. Anyway, we will be engaged one day.'

'You're very certain of yourself, aren't you?'

'Not really,' he answered with disarming honesty. 'Often I'm just whistling in the dark to keep my spirits up.'

She gazed at him affectionately, feeling closer to him than she ever had before. 'Liam O'Sullivan, you really are impossible,' she said, then took his arm as they joined the mass of people moving slowly towards the station. By some miracle they managed to get seats together. There was no chance to talk though, because they shared the carriage with a group of rowdy young men, all rather the worse for drink, who insisted on singing their entire repertoire of music-hall songs all the way to Victoria. When the smell of fish no longer fresh began to waft through the carriages, Tess's temples started to throb and it was with a feeling of relief that she saw the train pull into the station.

198

Liam wanted to see her home, but she didn't want to prolong the painful goodbyes. She stood very close to him, gazing up at his sombre face.

'I shall miss you, Liam.' The words were dragged from her almost reluctantly. Then angrily: 'But why do you have to go so far away?'

But Liam had a solid lump of misery in his throat and couldn't trust himself to speak; to say it was all for her. She kissed him lightly and gently on the lips, then turning away, jumped on to a bus. As it drew away she waved and called out to him, 'Write to me, won't you?'

But Liam's eyes were full of tears and all he could do was nod his head.

13

Liam wrote every day before he sailed, pouring out his love for her in a torrent of words and solemn pledges of constancy. Tess read each letter several times, tried to keep her replies noncommittal, but bound the first love letters she'd ever received in a length of blue ribbon and then secreted them at the back of her bureau.

About a week later the photograph came. She studied the serious young man and woman intently, for already that day had become wrapped in an aura of nostalgia and happiness as she recalled sea, sunshine and that afternoon with Liam on the Downs. With a shiver she remembered his rather forceful ardour and her own quick arousal and response, the urgent feeling within her of wanting to let go; that brief denial of common sense. But thank God she'd found the will to resist, for that was the path to damnation and everlasting shame. She stood the photograph in a prominent position on her desk then, deciding it would only encourage questions, took it down and tucked it away with Liam's letters.

On the day Liam was due to sail, Tess fell into an acute state of depression. Her movements were so slothful, her work so erratic even Virginia was moved to comment. 'My dear Tess, whatever is the matter?' she asked as she handed back a letter to be altered for the third time.

'Nothing much,' answered Tess listlessly, then disproved this remark by sighing deeply.

'I've never known you like this before. Are you ill?'

'No, just a bit downcast, I suppose. A friend of mine's just gone off to South Africa. He sails today.' Tess's body seemed to sag, even as she spoke.

'It wouldn't be that young man we saw in Bermondsey?' said Virginia perceptively.

Tess looked up in surprise. 'How did you know?'

Virginia laughed. 'It didn't take too much working out, and I think you're fonder of him than you'll admit.'

'There's absolutely nothing between us, we're good friends, that's all,' Tess assured her, conveniently forgetting the afternoon on the Downs. 'It's just . . . well . . . I suppose I never thought he'd go.'

'Will he be away for long?'

'For as long as it takes to get some money together. Liam's got an uncle out there and he's done quite well. It was his idea that Liam should go.'

'Well let's hope he strikes rich then he can come home and marry you.'

Tess ground her teeth in annoyance. Did anyone ever listen to her? 'I shan't marry Liam, or anyone else for that matter. I've seen what marriage does to women, seen my father beat my mother to pulp, give her endless dead babies and then leave us all to starve while he spent the money on booze.' She shook her head. 'No thanks, that's not what I want and I'd be a fool to change the life I've got: independence, money of my own and freedom. What married woman ever had that?'

'You're quite right, Tess, although it's not a popular thing to say. The view in my circle is that if you're not married it's because you can't get a man, not that you don't want one. Marriage and a husband would hamper my ambitions, it would be a rare husband who would support our cause. So we'll stay happy spinsters together, shall we? Grow old and strange together.' And in the first flush of youth they both laughed, for neither of them could imagine themselves strange or, indeed, even old.

In late May two things happened. The first was a letter from Liam, posted from Gibralter and complaining of seasickness, the confined conditions and rotten food of the cargo ship. In fact he couldn't wait to reach Durban, he said.

The second thing, quite out of the blue, was Virginia's decision to desert London for Elms Court and, Tess was relieved to hear, taking her. For the next few days it was sheer pandemonium as trunks were packed and sent off and books and journals sorted through. Being in the country, Virginia informed Tess as she struggled with piles of dusty papers, was no excuse for being idle.

The relationship between Tess and Mrs Bradshaw remained uneasy, and she knew the older woman resented her growing friendship with Virginia. It was a relief, therefore, to discover that the housekeeper wouldn't be accompanying them to Sussex but staying behind to supervise the annual Lennox Street spring clean.

Just before they were due to leave a letter came from Sarah with a new address in St John's Wood and an invitation to visit her. Tess hastily scribbled a reply saying she would be out of London for a few weeks but would visit as soon as she got back. And I wonder who's paying for that, she thought as she wrote out the rather good address on the envelope before posting it.

As she had done on that day with Liam, Tess – with Virginia, Snuffy and an assortment of hat boxes and books – left London from Victoria station. The big difference was that they travelled first class and there were no sticky-fingered children or drunken louts to disturb their comfort. The train steamed through lush green countryside and meadows thick with golden buttercups, where black and white cows stood ankle deep in streams, and children waved from crossing gates.

Virginia was soon engrossed in a book but Tess felt too excited to read. Having heard so much about Elms Court from Mrs Bradshaw, she envisaged a house of vast proportions, something approaching the size of Buckingham Palace, and she was impatient to see it.

But the train seemed to stop at every station and halt. Nothing happened, though, and it would stand huffing quietly to itself, waiting for passengers who never came. After a long-drawn-out journey they finally reached their destination, Arun Halt, where carefully tended flowerbeds lay torpid in the summer sun. Virginia and Tess were the only people to alight but they'd hardly stepped down from the train when a porter came scuttling along the platform, doffing his cap deferentially and clutching it to his chest.

'How do, ma'am,' he said to Virginia and the words came rolling out on one long extended syllable. He lifted some of the boxes out of the carriage. 'Mr Johnson's outside, I'll go and get 'im.'

'If you would be so kind, Sowerby,' replied Virginia graciously, and the man departed backwards down the platform as if in the presence of royalty.

In the meantime Tess, who was holding Snuffy's lead, found herself being pulled down the platform by a dog anxious to relieve himself, which he finally did over Mr Sowerby's marigolds.

Just then a tall, burly man in brown livery appeared, saw Virginia standing by the luggage and strode towards her.

'Hello, Johnson,' Tess heard Virginia say.

The coachman picked up the remaining pieces. 'Afternoon, Miss Virginia.' His voice was courteous but not, like the porter's, deferential.

Tess waited for them and as they caught up with her Virginia said, 'Johnson, this is my secretary, Miss Teresa Kelly.'

He touched his cap and his look, as he sized her up, was direct and friendly. 'Pleased ter meet you, miss.'

Tess returned his greeting, liking his face, red-hued like his hair, but cheerful.

Outside the station a brougham was waiting for them. Johnson, with the help of Sowerby, stowed everything away and then helped Virginia and Tess into the carriage. Driving along, Tess could see they were in the heart of the South Downs and in many places it was a hard slog for the horse, through lanes cut deep into chalky soil and kept cool by large, overhanging trees. By the time they came to tall, wrought-iron gates and a lodge, the ground had levelled out. Here the going was easier and the horse trotted along a drive bordered by tall elms with a great sweep of parkland on either side. By contrast the house seemed disappointingly small and plain and not at all what she'd expected. In fact, although Tess didn't realize it, she was looking at a house built on strict classical lines by Inigo Jones and perfect in its symmetry.

As the carriage came to a halt in the gravel drive the front door opened and footmen and servants came hurrying down the curved steps to greet them. Overcome by all this activity, Snuffy began to rush around, yelping noisily and entangling himself in everyone's feet.

Feeling she'd shrunk to the size of a pea amidst all this commotion, Tess followed Virginia uncertainly into the house. The hall was a chequerboard of black and white tiles and around the pale green walls hung dark oil paintings of pompous men, insipid-looking women and handsome horses.

Never had she seen such grandeur and as she stood in the middle of the hall gazing in awe at the exquisitely moulded ceiling and the carved wooden staircase, Tess felt the veneer of confidence she'd acquired with such effort over the months quietly crumble.

Virginia had been called away to deal with some small domestic crisis and without her as a prop these surfacing doubts were already rendering Tess, in her own eyes, insignificant and shabby. She was certain too she had been scrutinized by the servants and found wanting: a charlatan and impostor with no right to be there. With every fibre of her being, Tess wanted to turn tail, make a bolt for it through the door and catch the first train back to London. But a small boy was picking up the valise she'd brought with her as hand luggage and it seemed she had no choice but to follow him. Tess inhaled deeply, threw back her shoulders and, even though her legs quaked, ascended the wide staircase to the manner born.

On the first floor the lad opened a door and Tess found she was in a large airy bedroom, with two elegant windows reaching almost to the floor. When the boy had gone, Tess sped to an open window and looked out. Directly beneath her was a terrace running the length of the house. Steps led down to a formal garden of geometrically designed box hedges at the centre of which stood an ornately carved stone fountain where water spouted from the mouths of large fish. Beyond this was a smooth lawn and wide herbaceous borders, then parkland, punctuated with sheep, deer, a small lake and an infinite variety of trees through which Tess could just see the steeple of a church.

It was idyllic but it did cause Tess to wonder why one family should have so much. No doubt Liam would have told her – and how they should be relieved of it. Kindly disposed as Virginia and David were, they probably still thought it was their inalienable right to own this vast estate.

Hearing a sound, Tess leaned out a bit and saw that the lad who had helped her with her luggage was now sweeping the terrace. After a short while he paused in his labours, glanced furtively about him, then from his waistcoat pocket drew the flattened stub of a cigarette. Lighting it, he inhaled deeply and with obvious pleasure. Unable to contain her amusement, Tess giggled and the boy froze like a garden statue. Quickly Tess withdrew before he could see who had caught him out in this small transgression.

Her main luggage had been sent on along with Virginia's and this had already been unpacked. Soon so was the valise she'd brought with her. Taking her time she washed and changed into a clean dress then stood in the middle of the room wondering what on earth she should do. Tess had so looked forward to coming to Elms Court she hadn't stopped to consider whether she might actually enjoy it. After all, there was no lending library here, no department stores in which to while away the odd hour, just solitude, an abundance of it, in fact enough to send her barmy.

With a yearning to be back in the noise and dirt of London, Tess began pacing the room, wondering how she could fill her time until dinner. Dare she walk down those stairs, cross the hall and let herself out into the garden? No. What could she do then? Well, she could write to her mother, to Sarah, to Tom or even Liam. Sitting down at her desk she stared at the blank sheets of writing paper, picked up a pen and put it down again. She'd just opened a book without much hope of being able to concentrate on it when there was a tap on the door. 'Come in,' she called eagerly. Even if it was only one of the servants at least it would be someone to talk to. But it was Virginia's head that appeared round the door.

'Like to take a look round the grounds?' she asked. Tess didn't even reply, just leapt out of the chair and followed Virginia down the stairs with the joy of a caged bird set free.

The sheds full of farm machinery didn't interest Tess a great deal but the long greenhouse with its huge vine, which in late September would hang heavy with black grapes, did. So did the walled kitchen garden of mellow crumbling brick which gave support to peach, apricot and pear trees, as well as clematis with purple flowers as large as saucers, and sweetly scented climbing roses already in bloom. In its enclosed warmth the air was fragrant and there was the faint buzz of industrious bees. A place to linger in. But Virginia was anxious to show Tess the stables – and the horses, which were her pride and joy.

The same young lad Tess had seen earlier was now cleaning tack, and as she and Virginia crossed the stableyard, he swept off his cap in acknowledgement. 'Hello, Billy,' Virginia called, then in an aside to Tess, 'You have to watch your step in here. This is Johnson's domain and he rules it like some eastern potentate,' and she laughed almost apologetically.

Glad that Johnson wasn't around, Tess followed Virginia over to where a sleek chestnut horse was noisily trying to gain their attention.

'This is Poppy,' said Virginia, searching around in her pocket, while Poppy waited with a barely concealed impatience for her treat of sugar cubes. As she munched, Virginia stroked her muzzle fondly. 'Here, you give her one,' said Virginia, for the horse was nosing around in the hope of extra treats. Taking a lump of sugar from Virginia, Tess regarded the large animal uncertainly.

'Give it to her on the flat of your hand, she's very gentle and won't bite.'

Cautiously Tess held out her hand and the horse sucked the sugar daintily into her mouth. Relieved to see she was still in possession of her fingers, Tess even managed to pat the mare.

'Do you fancy having a ride on her?'

Tess backed away in alarm. 'Oh no, I could never ride a horse.'

'Yes you could, Johnson would teach you. Isn't that right, Johnson?' She called to the coachman who had just come into the yard and was striding towards them.

'What's that, Miss Virginia?'

'You could teach Miss Kelly to ride.'

'Yes, if she's prepared to do as I tell her,' he answered bluntly.

'That's very kind of you, Mr Johnson, but if it's all the same to you, I don't think I'll bother.' Tess had the panicky feeling that at any minute she might find herself astride a horse.

Johnson shrugged and gave her a pitying look. 'It's up to you, miss, but you're denying yourself a great experience.' He turned away then, dismissing her as someone of no consequence, which Tess resented deeply. While Johnson had been talking to them, half his attention had been on the stable boy, who obviously did something to incur his wrath. 'You good for nothing imbecile, what do you think you're doing?' he roared, then, hardly moving, reached out and cuffed the boy across the head, not hard, but enough to turn him bright red with humiliation. Tess waited for Virginia to remonstrate with Johnson but instead she took her arm.

'Come on, I think we're in the way here.' She drew her out of the yard.

But Tess felt angry on the boy's behalf. 'Why did you let Johnson get away with that?'

'As I said, I don't interfere in the stables.'

'But he hit the boy!' It astounded Tess that anyone as strong as Virginia could be intimidated by a servant.

'He probably has to put up with far worse at home,' replied Virginia philosophically. 'Johnson has a hasty temper but he'll make it up to the boy in his own way. And he won't get better training anywhere else. Johnson knows more about horses than anyone I know, that's why you should get him to teach you to ride. There's not much else to do down here and I've got a riding habit you could borrow, we're about the same size.'

It was obvious Virginia couldn't understand her timidity but the fact was, all Tess had ever seen of horses was the broken-down old nags of the London streets, a step away from the glue factory and so ill-fed and badly treated they often collapsed in harness. These glossy thoroughbreds, with their high-stepping beauty and confident air, were a different matter altogether. But although she was slightly in awe of them, Tess felt drawn too.

Even so, she felt slightly disconcerted when she found herself back in the stableyard rather early the following morning after she'd been given raucous proof by the dawn chorus that it wasn't always quiet in the country. Stretching and yawning she'd gone to the window and pulled back the curtains. In London she never noticed the sky but here it was impossible to ignore and as the sun, unimpeded by buildings, moved up over the lip of the earth, the dove grey clouds became streaked with a golden light. On a pane of glass a spider had laboriously spun its intricate configuration, and as it lay in wait for its prey, tiny crystalline beads of dew were caught in the fiery rays of the sun. Beauty and death, thought Tess, in nature they always seemed to go hand in hand. In the midst of seeming perfection there always lurked cruelty. Briefly she was tempted to put out her hand and destroy the web.

Instead she got back into bed, wishing she felt less hungry because breakfast was unlikely to appear until half past eight. Hoping to pass the time she tried to sleep but it was hopeless, so she got out of bed again and dressed. Obsessed now by the idea of food, she decided to raid the kitchen before anyone else was up. Creeping quietly down the stairs, she tiptoed across the wide expanse of hall, pushed open the kitchen door and nearly tripped over a little skivvy of no more than twelve, down on her hands and knees, scrubbing the flagstoned passage. The two girls stared at each other in surprise.

'Sorry, wrong door,' muttered Tess, feeling rather foolish and, backing out of the door, let herself out into the garden instead.

She got the whiff of frying bacon immediately. Crossing the dew-wet grass, her nose led her unerringly to the stables and tack room where Johnson and the stable boy were preparing breakfast over a small stove.

Tess hovered uncertainly at the door, her stomach rumbling audibly.

'Morning, miss,' said Johnson, turning a rasher over in the fat.

'Morning, Mr Johnson. That smells good,' Tess ventured hopefully.

'Fancy a bit, do you?' He lifted a piece on the end of a fork.

Tess moved forward into the tack room. 'Yes please,' she said, without pride. Laying several rashers between thick slices of bread, Johnson handed it to Tess.

'Sit yerself down.' He indicated an upturned box. 'Cup o'char?'

Tess bit into the sandwich and nodded. Mr Johnson turned to the boy. 'Billy, pour the lady a mug of tea.'

Sitting around in a circle the three of them ate and drank in companionable silence. When he'd finished, Johnson sucked his teeth reflectively, then drew out a red-spotted handkerchief and wiped his moustache free of crumbs.

'Now, young lady,' he said at last, 'have you thought any more about learning to ride?'

Having just accepted his hospitality, Tess decided to tread carefully. 'Yes, I have thought about it.'

He studied her for a moment. 'You're frightened of 'osses, ain't yer?'

'No I'm not,' she flashed back at him.

'There's no need to be, just as long as you let them know who's in charge. Excuse me asking, but would you perhaps have a bit of Irish blood in you?'

'More than a bit, but why do you ask?'

'Well, I've never met an Irishman, or woman, yet who wasn't mad about horseflesh, so I don't suppose you'll be the exception.'

'My brother Tommy's a jockey,' Tess volunteered.

Johnson looked pleased with himself. 'What did I tell you, it's in the blood. I bet you'd make a splendid horsewoman.'

'Do you really think so?' said Tess, warming to his flattery.

Johnson turned to the boy. 'Billy, go and get Poppy, bring her out into the yard.' Tess had sugar ready for her this time and she enjoyed the mare's warm breath as she nuzzled her hand.

'Now who could be frightened of this lady, she's as gentle as a lamb.' Johnson's tone was very persuasive.

A sudden thought occurred to Tess. 'Does Mr David ride?'

'Why bless me, of course he does, although Sir Rupert's the real horseman. Lives and breathes them, he does. Some people would say he's far too keen on the gee-gees, especially when it comes to gambling.'

As the indiscretions came tripping off Johnson's tongue, Tess pricked up her ears, although they only confirmed what she'd long suspected.

But Johnson was now saddling Poppy and seemed unaware of her heightened interest. 'Him and his cronies will be down here soon for Goodwood. It'll be bedlam then.' Tightening a strap, he caught a glimpse of Tess's face, silent and attentive. Realizing he'd perhaps said more than he should, he swung himself up on to the mare's back. 'Well, I can't stand around gossiping to young ladies all day, I've got work to do.' As Poppy moved out of the yard he turned in his saddle. 'Now see you come properly dressed next time and I'll give you a lesson.'

It was the tantalizing vision of herself and David galloping recklessly over the Downs together that finally persuaded Tess she should learn to ride. But she felt diffident about asking Virginia for a loan of her riding habit. It seemed such a cheek somehow. However this problem was solved when Virginia brought it along to Tess's room herself.

'See how it fits you,' she said, laying the claret-coloured outfit down on the bed. 'I've got another one so if it is the right size you can keep it.'

Tess thanked her gratefully but waited until she had gone before picking up each garment individually and examining it carefully. What did interest her were the trousers, made of a soft chamois leather round the seat and top half of the legs, and woollen down at the bottom. Curious, Tess took off her dress and slipped into them. What a sight! she thought, gazing at herself in the mirror. She looked better when the skirt was on and by the time she buttoned up the tight-fitting jacket and pressed the bowler hat, trimmed with silk ribbon, on to her head she was beginning to feel well pleased with herself. Lor' luv a duck, what would they think at the factory if they could see me now? But it was all pose, she knew that, deep inside she still felt a fraud, knowing that really she should be down on her hands and knees like the little skivvy, scrubbing the black and white tiles.

Still, now I've got it on I might as well keep it on, she thought, regarding herself from every angle in the mirror. Then with a self-conscious giggle she ran down the stairs, glad there was no one about to see her.

'So you've come,' said Johnson, scanning her with a professional eye. 'Come on, let's go and get Poppy, then you can have a gentle saunter around the yard and get to know each other. Now, you're not to be nervous. I'll try and explain as much as possible before you get on.'

'And how do I do that?'

'You stand on that mounting block over there.'

Tess didn't think there was the slightest possibility of her getting on a horse without falling face first into the stableyard mire. But honour was at stake here: if she backed down now, she would stand for ever condemned as a coward in Johnson's eyes.

'And you'll be riding side saddle,' Mr Johnson continued. 'These 'ere things are called pommels, you hook your right leg over the top one and fit your left leg under the lower one

211

and your foot goes in the stirrup. Think you can manage that?'

Tess nodded uncertainly, walked to the mounting block and with a good deal of assistance from Johnson, found herself on Poppy's back and a long way from the ground. Terrified, she clung to the reins tightly.

'Don't clutch them like that, you'll hurt her mouth. Relax.'

She wished she could and she wanted to scream – let me down, let me down – but pride wouldn't let her.

'Sit up straight, elbows in, and if you're ready we'll take a turn round the yard.'

When they moved off Tess was so amazed to find she was still affixed to the seat that she began to feel less tense, and listened to Johnson's instructions on how she should use her legs, seat, hands and voice to control the horse. In a very short while she was even enjoying herself, her only worry being how she should dismount. She eventually achieved this small hurdle rather clumsily but with assistance again from Johnson. By the time she was lying in her bath, she was feeling rather pleased with herself. She would certainly go again.

'How am I doing, Mr Johnson?' Tess asked, when after a few days he let her out into the park.

'Don't let it go to your head, but you're quite good.' When he was sufficiently confident of her prowess to allow her to handle Poppy alone he rode a large horse called Hector, which, Johnson explained, belonged to Sir Rupert. It soon became a habit for them to ride together every morning. Tess enjoyed these gentle canters, and not entirely for the riding. Johnson was delightfully indiscreet and he saw the family with a slightly more jaundiced eye than did Mrs Bradshaw. Tess listened to it all with a guilty pleasure.

'Excuse my French,' he said one morning as they trotted across the park, 'but they're bloody lucky to have this.' With a sweep of his arm, he indicated the house and grounds. 'Most of the male members of the family have been drinking and gambling away the fortune for centuries. See that church

212

spire over there?' Tess nodded. 'Well, their land extended far beyond that village. Fortunately, the old man, Sir Percy, did one sensible thing in his life, he married money. Thought he was marrying beneath him, mind you. Considered the money to be tainted by trade: coal and railways. It saved Elms Court, though, mortgaged up to the eyebrows, they were. The St Clair men have always been a lot better at spending money than making it.'

'How long have you worked here, Mr Johnson?' Tess asked, wondering how far back his knowledge of the family extended.

'Since I was twelve, and my dad before that. There have been Johnsons here as long as the St Clairs.'

'What was Sir Percy's wife like?'

'Lady Cynthia? Oh she was a good sort, down to earth and sensible. Miss Virginia's just like her. The women have got all the brains in this family, the men pickle theirs in brandy at a very early age.'

'Not Mr David, he's not like that,' Tess protested.

Mr Johnson seemed to consider this. 'No he's not, but he's an exception. Must take after his mother, she was forever doing good works. I expect that's why Miss Virginia's into this suffragist thing. She's not prepared to sit around on her bottom doing nowt. Not like some of these other upper-class twits.' To Tess this irreverence was refreshing after Mrs Bradshaw's hushed eulogies, and egging him on a bit she said, 'So you don't think much of the aristocracy, then, Mr Johnson?'

'Not a lot. I've seen enough of their goings on to fill several books. Things I could tell you.' He shook his head sadly. 'My 'osses knows 'ow to behave better than some o' them lot. Sooner we get rid o' them the better. Still, I'd better keep me political opinions to meself or I might be out of a job. Least said, best mended.' Then having said more than enough, he tapped his nose meaningfully.

In one of the fields, farm labourers had stopped to have breakfast. 'Is that the time already?' said Johnson. 'Come on,

213

we'd better be getting back, I'm picking Mr David up at the station this morning.'

Until Johnson told her, Tess had no idea that David was coming down and she wondered why Virginia hadn't mentioned it. Not that Tess saw anything of him: as the weekend progressed, she began to feel he was deliberately avoiding her. Which was a stupid thing to think, she told herself, for why ever should he want to do that?

Still, when Sunday came and she still hadn't set eyes on him, she did find it rather curious.

The few words she did finally have with him were quite by chance and in the library where she'd gone in search of information for Virginia. She was just reaching up for a heavy, leather-bound political biography which, judging by the dust, hadn't been opened for several decades, when the door opened. Tess turned to see who it was, caught a glimpse of David and was so flustered that the book slipped from her grasp and landed with a heavy thud at her feet, making her leap back in fright.

Immediately David was at her side and, picking up the book, laid it on the desk. 'That might have broken a bone in your foot.'

Making light of it, Tess laughed. 'Judging by the cobwebs, that's the greatest impact the author of that tome is likely to have on anyone.' She thought David would share her amusement but he was hardly listening to her. Instead, his fingers tapped nervously on the desk and he gazed out of the window as if she weren't there. Scrutinizing the beloved features, Tess was shocked by his changed appearance, for he looked quite ill. David always had a pale, fragile quality about him, and that was what drew her. But now the blue eyes had a haunted look and deep lines of anxiety were etched the length of his jaw.

Tess longed to take him in her arms and comfort him; to smooth away his cares with soft words and loving gestures, to scare away the devils she sensed were snapping at his heels. But the social divide was too great and she could

214

only stand there helplessly, her heart aching with pity and love.

The drumming stopped and he began to pace up and down the room. But his movements were jerky and dislocated like a string-puppet. Wanting to share his agony, Tess went towards him, her arms outstretched. 'David, please, what's wrong?' she cried, her voice hoarse with emotion.

But as she approached David seemed to shrink from her in fear and he stared round the room as if seeking escape. 'I must go,' he muttered, and fled from the room. Tess's arms dropped to her sides in defeat and, filled with the pain of rejection, she stared after him, her eyes brimming with tears.

Trying to collect herself, she started turning over the pages of the book but the words blurred in front of her eyes. She squeezed them shut and the tears ran unheeded down her cheeks and on to the dusty pages. Some of the tears were for David but mainly they were for herself, because in those few moments she'd just spent with him, that small fluttering thing called hope, and nurtured only by dreams, had finally died.

14

When she thought about it afterwards, Tess was glad that David had returned to London immediately. She'd always tried to keep a guard on her feelings for him, but his distress had made her careless and she sensed she'd badly damaged that special friendship they enjoyed.

It astonished Tess, though, when Virginia, who openly expressed her dislike of London in the hot summer months, decided to follow David.

Still, thought Tess with a shrug, she wasn't paid to question her employer's actions but to get on with the job in hand. 'So what are we taking back with us?' she asked, eyeing with little enthusiasm the books and journals that would have to be re-packed.

'Oh, I won't be taking any of this. And there's no need for you to come, my dear, I shall keep my visit as short as possible.'

Tess was pleased to be spared the burden of re-packing and she wasn't unhappy to stay on at Elms Court. She'd quickly overcome early reservations about rural life and looked forward with real pleasure to some rides with Johnson while Virginia was away.

Although she was curious about the London trip, Tess was no wiser by the time Virginia left. Not that Tess had time to speculate, Virginia had left her too much work for that. But one hot afternoon when three letters came for her in the late post, one of them bearing a South African stamp, Tess decided to call it a day and sit out on the terrace.

With a sense of anticipation she opened Liam's letter first. He'd have so much to tell her. *My darling Tess*, she read. *Well here I am in Durban, on terra firma at last, thank God, and with no plans to join the navy. Judging by the house and servants, my uncle seems to have done quite well for himself, so perhaps the luck will hold out for me too. There's a lot of gold prospecting going on up country and that's where the fortunes are to be made. I'm moving on from here soon to see what's happening, so you might not hear from me for long stretches at a time. But it doesn't mean I'm not thinking of you, because I am, every minute of the day. And all this is for you, remember. You deserve only the best, my darling. Take care of yourself. I love you, Liam. PS Write to me at my uncle's address for the time being.*

Tess sighed when she came to the end of the letter as she felt the burden of being loved. She had come near to returning Liam's love that day in Brighton but he was so far away now the memory was already fading. Anyway, the first pretty face and Liam would have forgotten about her. Love had to be nourished, and they might not meet for several years.

Turning to the second letter, she slit it open. This was from Sarah. Her delight in her new house had made her spelling worse than ever, but the descriptions of each room ran to several pages. Although a 'gentleman friend' had set her up in this establishment, Tess realized that to sit in judgement would be pointless and sanctimonious. What were the alternatives for Sarah after all? They could both probably count themselves lucky to have got away from the lucifer factory and possibly an early death from phossy jaw. As Sarah had said, a life of sin was preferable to that any day. Tess's own escape had been a mere fluke, and just supposing their positions had been reversed, what would she be doing now? Why, perhaps having a house bought for her in St John's Wood. And returning Sarah's letter to its envelope, Tess laughed out loud at such a preposterous idea.

Her mother's letter Tess read last, preparing herself even before she opened it for the homilies that accompanied any correspondence from Florence. But today as she quickly scanned the page, her heart gave a lurch of fear and her fingers began to shake uncontrollably against the paper. There had been a definite sighting of her father in Canning Town, her mother wrote, and the police had stepped up their hunt for him.

217

For months now Tess had believed her father to be in some foreign country, and as she had tried to put the past behind her the nightmares had gradually subsided. But the stark fact of seeing his name on the paper induced in her such terror that she was sure his malevolent power could reach out and find her, even amid these peaceful, sunlit gardens. Too agitated to read any further, Tess screwed the cheap writing paper into a tight ball and stuffed it into her pocket. Then she began pacing up and down the terrace, gripping her hands tightly in an effort to control their trembling.

She was so overwrought that when she turned at the furthest end of the terrace and, her vision momentarily dazzled by the sun, saw a tall dark figure approaching, Tess let out a shrill cry and backed away, searching frantically for some means of escape. As the man drew nearer, she closed her eyes and clutched at the balustrade, the blood draining from her face.

'Good heavens, what on earth's the matter?' When she heard Rupert's startled voice, Tess opened her eyes, but she couldn't speak because her tongue was welded firmly to the roof of her mouth.

'Here, come and sit down.' Rupert took her hand and led her to a seat. 'Why, your hands are freezing!' he exclaimed, massaging life back into them. 'And you'd have thought I was the ghost of Banquo coming across that terrace.' He studied her pale features for a moment then stood up. 'What you need is a drink.' He disappeared into the house. When he came out again he was carrying two large goblets and he handed one to Tess.

'Drink up,' he urged, 'a brandy will usually put the world to rights. At least that's what I find.' He swirled the golden liquid around in the glass, lifted it to the light and sniffed appreciatively. Only after he had performed this little ritual did he drink. 'Now tell me what's the matter,' he said at last, crossing one long leg over the other.

'Nothing's the matter,' Tess answered, although the spasms in her hand as she lifted the glass to her lips gave lie to this fact.

'Of course there is. I admit to certain failings but I don't usually have such a catastrophic effect on women. Still, it's none of my business and if you don't wish to tell me . . .' He gave an indifferent shrug and took another sip of his drink.

Tess wasn't sure how much Rupert knew about her past or even if he was very interested. But she supposed she owed him some sort of explanation. 'For a moment I thought you were my dad, it frightened me,' she managed to say at last.

Rupert looked thoughtful, then surprised her by saying, 'Ah yes, your papa, rather a beast of a man as I remember.'

Tess took a large gulp of brandy. Then setting down the glass, she rolled back her sleeve. 'How's that for fatherly affection?' she said bitterly as she extended her arm.

Rupert took her wrist, rubbing the scar gently with the ball of his thumb. Tess found it a very agreeable sensation.

'Good God!' Rupert exclaimed as he examined the scar. 'No wonder you're terrified of him.' He continued idly to stroke her arm. 'But you don't have to worry, you know, he won't come here.'

The manipulating pressure of his fingers on her cool skin had a calming effect on Tess and she allowed herself to enjoy it longer than she knew she should. They were strong, those hands, she thought, and skilled . . . skilled in the art of seduction. With a quick, jerky movement she suddenly pulled away from him, rolled down her sleeve and emptied her glass.

Rupert made no comment, didn't even seem surprised, just fetched the brandy decanter and refilled his own glass, then hers. Sipping the brandy and enjoying its fiery warmth, Tess began to relax. Rupert was right, her fears were irrational, her father would never come here, move away from familiar haunts where he might be able to count on some protection from the police. She finished her drink for the second time and the world had now taken on such a rosy hue she hardly noticed when Rupert filled her glass again.

Tess had already lost any sense of time when a footman appeared bearing a telegram for Rupert on a silver salver. Her vision seemed a bit blurred, she noticed, as she watched him scrutinize the brief message and stand up. 'You must excuse me, I have to return to London.'

Tess stood as well, or at least attempted to. For some reason, though, her legs seemed unable to bear her weight and she sat down heavily. She tried again, taking more care and clutching the seat for support. Her head began to swim and she closed her eyes. She felt rather peculiar.

'Hey, don't tell me you're drunk.' Rupert's voice sounded amused as he caught hold of her arm.

'I . . . ss . . . ss . . . ssertainly am not,' Tess replied with great dignity. 'And I can manage quite well on my own.'

'As you wish.' He released his grip on her, and by placing one foot very carefully in front of the other, Tess reached the french windows without mishap. Here she took several deep breaths and grabbed hold of the door. Dear God, don't let me be sick, and in front of Rupert, she prayed.

'Come on, young lady,' said Rupert behind her. 'You need some help, and this is my fault.' Before she could protest, he'd scooped her up in his arms and as he moved swiftly through the house and up the stairs, Tess, her arm around his neck, was dimly aware of the rough texture of his coat against her cheek and the faint scent of sandalwood. In her room he laid her down on the bed where she giggled, broke into brief song and then fell fast asleep.

With a smile on his face, Rupert stood looking down at her, noting the dark lashes against the pale skin and the gentle rise and fall of her breasts. She was quite a beauty, this young secretary of Ginny's, and spirited. She interested him but he must watch his step, he'd always made it a strict rule never to tamper with women out of his own class. Drawing the curtains, he rang for a maid to come and undress her. But returning to his room there came unbidden to Rupert the vision of Tess naked. London could wait, he decided. He would stay here after all.

Tess woke early the next morning and as events from the previous day percolated through her fogged brain she opened one eye and moved her head gingerly from side to side.

Miraculously she had no hangover, although her parched mouth was a shameful reminder of the fool she'd made of herself in front of Rupert. What a relief that he'd gone back to London and she wouldn't have to face him today.

Needing to refresh herself, Tess got up, splashed her face with cold water and rang for tea. While she waited for it to arrive, she retrieved the letters from the pocket of her dress and re-read them. She even managed to read past the first page of her mother's with hardly a tremor. The second page she read with growing excitement: *I don't know how far you are from Goodwood, but Tommy is racing there next week and I wondered if you might be able to get over to see him, as a surprise.*

Resting the letter on her lap, Tess thought hard. She had no idea how she could get to see Tom, only that she would, come hell or high water. She might be able to hire a trap from the village or she could ask Johnson to take her, except that she might not be in his good books, having neglected her riding for the past few mornings. And he was inclined to take things like that a bit personally, Tess thought as she struggled into her riding habit and pinned up her hair. She'd have to butter him up a bit, that was all.

And that proved more difficult than she'd imagined. She'd expected to be treated briskly but not ignored. Johnson was brushing Hector's glossy chestnut coat and when he finally looked up he feigned surprise at seeing her there.

'You're a stranger,' he said at last.

But Tess was quite prepared to eat humble pie to further her cause. 'Yes, I am sorry, Mr Johnson, but with Miss Virginia going away suddenly like that, I had a lot to catch up on and I've really missed my mornings out with you.'

Her efforts at charming him were wasted, though, and with a derisive snort he went back to brushing Hector. But Tess battled on. 'Before she went away, Miss Virginia said you might take me out in the trap some afternoons. Did she happen to mention it to you?'

'She did,' Johnson reluctantly acknowledged.

'There's no chance of a trip to Goodwood next week, is there?' Tess ventured timidly. 'My brother's riding there.'

Johnson's red face appeared briefly over Hector's broad back. 'No chance. Don't you realize, young lady, that next week this house will be filled to overflowing with "our betters"?' He put cynical emphasis on these last two words. 'With every whim needing to be catered for. It'll be bedlam. There won't be time to take you jaunting around the countryside,' he said severely.

Tess's face dropped in sulky disappointment. 'I'll just have to hire a trap from the village then.'

'Seems like it.'

Tess was stumped for a minute. 'But you've got time for a ride this morning, haven't you?' She'd soon sweeten him up once they were out in the park.

'I told you, I'm busy. But don't let me stop you from going.'

'Oh, Mr Johnson, you know I can't go on my own,' she wailed.

Straightening, he gazed at her as if she were a recalcitrant child. 'Yes, you can, there's always got to be a first time for everything, so you might as well start this morning.'

Right, thought Tess crossly, I'll show you. With a haughty toss of her head she marched over to where the stable lad was mucking out. 'Billy,' she commanded, 'saddle Poppy for me.' The boy glanced uncertainly in the direction of Johnson.

'Do as the lady says,' the coachman instructed, and Tess heard him chuckle, which strengthened her resolve to show him what she could do.

With a very determined set to her chin, Tess went to the mounting block and even with Johnson watching her critically she mounted Poppy with a confident ease.

'Now mind you don't go doing anything reckless like breaking into a fast gallop,' Johnson called to her as she moved off out of the stableyard, and then Tess heard him laugh uproariously at his own wit.

In defiance of his instructions, as soon as they were in the park, Tess allowed Poppy a bit of rein and the horse broke into a gentle trot.

A light, gauzy mist still hung in the trees and shy deer lifted startled faces and then frisked away at their approach.

It was on mornings like this that Tess felt the world belonged exclusively to her. Glad to be alive, she breathed deeply, filling her lungs with the pure air and deciding to forget about Johnson and his awkward ways. Feeling confident with the placid Poppy, she decided to ride to the perimeter fence.

When she heard the pounding of hooves behind her, Tess immediately thought Johnson had relented and was now catching up with her. But Hector went flying past, startling Poppy and followed by a few choice expletives from an angry Tess. But there was no mistaking Johnson's ginger mop, and it wasn't him. Some way further on the reckless horseman slowed down and as he turned and cantered towards her, Tess saw that it was Rupert and the prepared reprimand died on her lips. He was the last person she had expected to see.

'Good morning, Miss Kelly,' he called as he approached.

'Good morning, Sir Rupert,' Tess answered stiffly.

'And how are you this morning? Fully recovered, I trust.'

Remembering her rather unladylike lapse, a blush stained the white skin of Tess's throat and travelled up to her cheeks. 'I'm fine, thank you.'

'My, you were in a bad way when I put you to bed.' He shook his head in disbelief, enjoying himself.

Tess, in no doubt now that he was trying to embarrass her, felt her hackles rise in response. It was no way for a gentleman to behave. It was on the tip of her tongue to tell him so too, but he sat astride Hector with such aristocratic arrogance that even her quicksilver tongue was stilled. Here was a man, Tess saw, who was undisputed master of his surroundings. He would not expect to be crossed.

What she didn't have to do was stay and put up with his personal remarks. Mumbling something about it being breakfast time, Tess moved off, assuming Rupert would go his own way. But he fell in beside her, remarking, 'This is much better than London.'

'But shouldn't you be there?' said Tess, remembering the telegram.

'I missed the train,' he lied. 'After that my business didn't seem quite so important. Anyway, only a fool would want to be in Town at this time of the year.'

'Miss Virginia's there at the moment,' Tess reminded him.

'Exactly. My sister's a dear, but anyone who thinks women should have the vote must be a little crazy.'

Tess gritted her teeth. 'That must include me, then.'

He gazed down at her with amused tolerance. 'But you're far too pretty to concern yourself with such matters. It's my considered opinion that only really ugly women take up such causes, to compensate for the fact that no man in his right mind would look at them.'

It was a remark that was both condescending and insulting, and Tess, who'd had enough of his comments for one day, could contain herself no more. 'It seems to me there's a little more to life than worrying about the effect you are likely to have on some man. And it's my opinion, sir, since we are exchanging opinions, that men are nothing but a liability. I would settle for a good cause to support any day. Good morning to you.'

And you can put that in your pipe and smoke it! Tess thought recklessly as she cantered off, although by the sound of the laughter that followed her she'd done nothing to ruffle that air of calm certainty.

By the time Tess reached the stableyard, Rupert had caught up with her again. He quickly dismounted, then came over and held out his hand to her. 'Allow me,' he said and as she slid rather clumsily to the ground, she felt his hands spanning her waist and then the almost imperceptible movement of his fingers against the curve of her breasts. Disturbed, she swallowed nervously and her heart started to race.

At the sound of footsteps on gravel, he released her and as Johnson appeared round the corner of the house, Tess, unable to face him, thrust Poppy's reins at Rupert. 'You see to her,' she said abruptly and then fled, knowing that both men, servant and master, watched her departure with varying degrees of interest.

224

Tess understood what Johnson meant by bedlam when, a few days later, a string of carriages appeared in the drive. Rupert stood waiting on the front steps to greet his friends and Tess watched with inquisitive interest from an upstairs window as men, women, luggage, servants and dogs, spilled from these conveyances.

For a short while it was mayhem as servants scurried around to imperious biddings, and Rupert was greeted with frantic delight. What a fuss, thought Tess slightly tetchily as she saw how Rupert pressed each lady's dainty hand against his mouth, and the simpering pleasure this induced. She could understand it, of course, for there was no denying his power and virility, although he was without David's fine-edged grace. He had no idea he was being observed and as she continued her leisurely inspection of his broad back, Tess recalled how his fingers had so lightly touched her breasts. Had he been trifling with her or was it an accident? Perhaps she'd never know, but the memory of it could still send a pleasurable shiver down her spine. But he was a man approaching thirty with money, looks and rank, so why wasn't he married? A question no doubt these young women were asking themselves as they gazed greedily around and up into the dark, mocking eyes of their host.

As soon as the guests were installed the noise started and never let up. Every entertainment, Tess soon discovered, had to be conducted at a high level of boisterous hilarity, whether it was playing croquet on the lawn or at the card tables late into the night. They drank heavily, too, and from the terrace beneath her window the chink of glasses was accompanied by the sound of rough horseplay and shrill female laughter. Finding it impossible to sleep, Tess would read, but even after they'd made their way upstairs there was still a great deal of opening and shutting of doors, giggles and whispers before the house finally settled down for the night.

Observing their antics, Tess was shocked. Naïvely she'd imagined the rich to be decorous in their behaviour, with a nobility of character befitting their station in life. But instead

225

they swore, gambled, drank and fornicated with all the energy of navvies. Mr Johnson might be a gossip but none of his tales was an exaggeration, they did raise Cain and it was easy to understand his contempt for them.

Hearing Rupert's voice one night, Tess got out of bed and padded to the window. He was leaning against the balustrade, holding a glass and shouting encouragement to a young man swaying drunkenly on the edge of the fountain. A loud splash as he hit the water was greeted with shrieks of delight, then loud clapping as he hauled himself out of the fountain and staggered, dripping wet, up the steps. He was grabbed and debagged by several young bucks, and plied with even more brandy until eventually, too drunk to stand, he crumpled in a senseless heap to the ground while Rupert looked on with amused contempt.

Did Rupert have any moral scruples, she wondered, or was it boredom that drove him on to the endless pursuit of pleasure, the noisy friends, the frequent trips abroad?

Feeling almost sorry for him, Tess returned to bed, covered her head with a blanket and tried to shut out the din from the terrace. But she slept badly and woke late. Virginia had sent down a load of work but it wasn't until the house guests had departed noisily for a picnic that Tess felt able to get down to work with any degree of efficiency.

She was still busy when she heard them return and was down on her hands and knees sorting through some documents, so dusty they made her sneeze, when Rupert wandered into the room.

Feeling discomposed, Tess scrambled to her feet, straightening her skirt and hoping she didn't look too grimy.

Saying nothing, Rupert went to Virginia's desk and flicked indolently through some notes Tess had made. 'So this is where my little sister wastes her time, is it?'

So he was going to start that again, was he? He of all people – who had cultivated doing nothing to a fine art. 'Miss Virginia is planning to write a book. It will be about the oppression of women by the state, church . . . and

226

men.' Tess put deliberate emphasis on the last word. 'Our sex endures many injustices, and will until we get the vote.'

He flapped his hand dismissively. 'That's beside the point. Women will never understand about politics, it's beyond them. They'd only vote as their husbands told them anyway.'

God, him and his arrogant assumptions! What did he know about anything, or the misery of many women's lives? Tess longed to put him in his place with a few carefully chosen words and had to bite on her tongue not to do so. 'I wouldn't,' she stated candidly.

He seemed to consider this point, then the corner of his mouth lifted in a slight smile. 'No, just to aggravate your husband, I don't think you would. But then it's all hypothetical anyway, Parliament will never change its mind.'

Tess could no longer hide her irritation and her voice when she answered was sharp as splintered ice. 'Yes they will, because we'll keep worrying them until they do. We might not, as some men think, have much reasoning power, but we do have patience – in abundance.'

'And what an admirable quality that is,' he answered, and she knew he was ridiculing her. 'But it wasn't my intention to come here and argue but as the bearer of good news, at least I hope so. Johnson tells me you have a brother riding at Goodwood this week.'

'Yes.'

'And you'd like to go?'

Tess nodded, trying not to appear too eager.

'Well Johnson has my permission to take you. It's a busy time for him but I think he can be spared for one afternoon. After all, it is rather a special occasion.'

Tess thanked him formally, determined not to be over-effusive.

But Rupert, treated to one of her rare, glowing smiles, was startled by her beauty. 'You should smile more often, it suits you. You usually look so serious, and men like a woman to smile.'

In a second the smile vanished to be replaced by a frown of impatience. 'I don't consider it my role in life to please men.'

227

'I had rather gathered that.' He walked to the door, not quite sure whether to be amused or irritated by her forthright manner. He turned, deciding to punish her slightly. 'Now see he wins, that brother of yours, I shall be putting my shirt on him.'

'Oh, don't do that, sir,' Tess cried in genuine alarm, 'Tom hasn't done much racing yet.'

'You should have more confidence in your brother. Tom Kelly, mmm, I must remember that name,' he muttered, rather enjoying her glum expression as he closed the door.

There could be no more beautiful place on earth, thought Tess, leaning against a fence and gazing around her with pleasure. High scudding cloud was fashioning an elusive, shifting pattern of light and dark on the fragrant, sheep-cropped grass; on the hollows and folds and sweeping lines of the Downs; on the thick copses of beech and elm.

The sombre clothes of the men added little to the scene but the ladies in their fluttering pastel-shaded dresses looked like fragile, elusive butterflies beside which the jockeys, in their bold primary colours, struck an almost discordant note.

Just in case, Tess had instructed her mother not to mention to Tom that she was coming today, but now she scanned the enclosure, hoping she would catch a glimpse of him.

Johnson, stretched out on the turf and filling his pipe from a pouch, watched her. 'I should wait until he's finished, it might make him nervous if he knows you're here.' He stuck the pipe into his mouth and without bothering to light it, puffed on it strenuously. Tess, who was most anxious that Tom should give a good account of himself, went and sat down beside him, a frown puckering her brow.

'Sir Rupert said he was going to put his shirt on him, do you think he was joking?'

Johnson took the pipe from his mouth and gazed at it thoughtfully. 'Not for a minute.'

'Oh dear. But . . . suppose Tom loses? I warned him he hadn't been racing long.'

'Look, don't worry your head about it. Sir Rupert is always putting his shirt on some nag . . . and losing it. It's a way of life with him. You'd have thought he could spot a winner by now. His trouble is, he's got more money than he knows what to do with.' Johnson stood up. 'Anyway, I think I'll risk a bob each way on that brother of yours. Come on.'

Tom was riding a horse called Warrior King and Johnson whistled when he saw the odds. 'Twenty to one, not bad. I'll risk five bob to win, seeing it's your brother.' He handed two half crowns to the bookmaker.

'I think I will, too,' said Tess recklessly.

'You might be throwing your money away,' Johnson warned her as they walked back to the track.

Tess shrugged philosophically. 'Never mind, Tom's worth it,' she said, and tried not to think what five shillings could have bought.

To get the best possible position, they had to take up their places early at the rails and soon they were completely hemmed in. As people pushed and shoved against them, Tess thought of Rupert and his friends in the grandstand. Life would always be all right for some. And yet they were no more deserving of the privileges they enjoyed than anyone else. They imagined themselves superior, too, but Tess now knew otherwise.

'Look, here they come.' Johnson nudged her to attention as horses and jockeys went trotting past.

'Where are they going?'

'To the starting line.'

Tess gripped Johnson's arm excitedly. 'There's Tom, in the green and white colours.' She longed to call out to him as he cantered past, but under his cap Tom's face looked pale and tense and she didn't want to risk breaking his concentration. After an age, the horses were finally lined up for the starting signal but as they shot forward, Tess felt she hardly dare look. Please win, Tom, she prayed, but less for her five shillings than Rupert's rather expensive shirt.

Mr Johnson handed her his field glasses. 'Here, borrow these and tell me what you see.' At first it was all a blur of colour, then, focusing, she saw with a gulp of disappointment that Warrior King was almost last in the field. Tess lowered the glasses. 'He's right at the back,' she said dejectedly. As far as she was concerned, Tom had already lost.

'Give 'em time, girl, for heaven's sake. It's the last furlong that counts, not the first. Here, let me have a look.' He grabbed the glasses and followed the runners silently round the course. 'He's moving up,' he said at last. Then, 'My God, look at 'im!'

'Let me see! Let me see!' cried Tess, trying to snatch the glasses back. But he pushed her impatiently away as thundering hooves were urged on by cheering punters. Caught up in the excitement, Tess started to cheer too. 'Come on, Warrior King,' she screamed, clenching her fists and leaping up and down. There was a flash of green and Warrior King went pounding by, foam flying from his mouth. Tess fell silent and held her breath as Tom eased the horse into third, then second place. The last furlong was uphill and the tension was almost too much for her as with a final heart-bursting sprint, Tom urged the horse on past the finishing post, a good two lengths in front. The crowd let out a great roar of approval, delighted that a rank outsider had come in first.

On an impulse, Tess unpinned her light straw hat and with a whoop of delight, threw it high into the air. As it came floating down, several young men fought to catch it and as the victor handed it to her, Tess said excitedly, 'That was my brother on Warrior King, and he's *won*!'

'By jove, jolly good show,' said the young man and as he pumped her hand up and down, several other punters, who were now the richer by several pounds, came to shake her hand too. Only those who had lost tore their tickets in half, and with glum expressions sought consolation in the beer tent.

Tess, totally immersed in a sea of good will, was enjoying herself so much Mr Johnson found it difficult to extricate her. Only the threat of not seeing Tom finally got her away.

He was just being led away by the trainer and Lord Petrie, who looked very pleased with life as people pressed in on them, offering their good wishes. But Tess, watching from the edge of the crowd, saw how pale and vulnerable Tom looked. Immediately her protective instincts were aroused and she remembered how, as a small boy when the world turned ugly, he would curl himself up on her lap and suck his thumb for reassurance. She pushed forward, calling his name, not sure if he would even hear her. But he turned immediately, searching for her in the crowd. When he saw her, he waved, and his expression lightened into a broad, happy grin before being claimed by an admiring public again.

'Don't look so down in the mouth, you'll probably see him before the day's out,' Mr Johnson said when he saw her doleful expression. 'Mind you,' he continued with a jocular nudge, 'if he keeps this up, he'll be dining with princes shortly. You won't see him at all then.'

'Tom would never forget his family.' Tess was indignant at such a suggestion.

'You could have a Fred Archer in the family.'

'Fred Archer is dead,' Tess reminded him.

Johnson shook his head in sorrow. 'Bloody marvellous jockey, though. Just think of it, over two thousand winners. I tell you, it would take a lot to be as good as him even if he did mismanage his life a bit.'

To say Fred Archer mismanaged his life *a bit* was, Tess felt, a gross understatement. Even she, who knew nothing of the racing world, had heard of the price he paid for that success; the Turkish baths and the constant doses of castor oil, all to keep his weight down. Then, when his genius had seemed to desert him, despair and death had come at twenty-nine by his own hands. If that was fame she wanted none of it for Tom. She would rather he was an also ran any day, as she pointed out to Johnson in no uncertain terms.

'Don't worry,' he said cheerfully, 'I was only joking, you won't see that sort of genius again in this century. But your brother's won today and that's the main thing. And he's made us both a little bit better off.'

'How much do you reckon it'll be?' Tess asked as they went to collect their winnings.

'By my reckoning, five pounds.'

'Gosh, as much as that!'

'Yes, and if you've got any sense, you'll hang on to it, leastways that's what I'm going to do. Most of these mugs – he indicated the punters lining up for their winnings – 'looking so pleased with life will have lost it all again by five o'clock, you wait and see. A flutter never hurt anyone but I see no point in throwing money around or helping bookies get richer than they already are.'

Tess considered this sound advice, and when she had the money in her hands she counted it carefully and then tucked it away in her purse. You never knew when that rainy day might arrive, and this small windfall would add significantly to her nest egg.

Later on, as she and Mr Johnson drove home through Sussex lanes where swallows swooped and dived over thick green hedgerows and the scent of sweet briar rose and honeysuckle hung on the early evening air, Tess reflected on her day. It had seemed to be going well, what with her win and everything, but the day had darkened after her meeting with Tom. She didn't get to see him until late afternoon and as they greeted each other with a joyous hug, it struck her forcefully how thin he was, nothing more than bones really.

Remembering Fred Archer, Tess had felt frightened and as she gazed at her brother's gaunt face, she spoke more sharply than she intended. 'What do you think you're doing, starving yourself like this?'

His denial was swift. 'No I'm not.'

'Are you happy, then, Tom?' she asked more kindly, recalling how tense he'd looked before the race, almost as if he might be sick, and wondering if the pressures of the racing world were just too much for him.

'You're asking some daft questions, Tess, do you know that?' he'd answered good-naturedly.

'Perhaps. But be sensible, Tom,' Tess urged. 'Nothing's worth ill health. Give it up, do something else if you can't keep your weight down.'

'I'm not trained for anything else,' Tom reminded her practically. 'No, I'll take my chance here, there's good money to be made . . . If I can last the course.'

These were telling words and Tess brooded on them the rest of the way home. And what would she say to Florence when she wrote? She'd just tell her the good bits, she decided. Describe in detail the scene at Goodwood, the women's dresses and how Tom had come from the back to win.

Tess could imagine her mother's expression softening as she read the letter and her heart swelling with pride at her son's achievements, and this helped to deflect her own feelings of unease.

Later in her room, Tess heard Rupert and his guests return. I wonder how much they lost between them today? Still, she thought, even if Rupert had lost his shirt, it was no longer any concern of hers. Tom had seen to that, but at what cost to his health, only time would show.

15

A couple of days after the race meeting it became very hot and oppressive. During the night a wind blew up, doors and shutters banged to and fro and curtains were sucked out through open windows. There were warning rolls of thunder, and lightning cracked open the sky. Then it started to rain and continued for several days so that the river feeding the lake rose up and broke its banks, flooding fields, washing away precious topsoil and bending to its will wheat and barley which then lay flattened and useless on the sodden earth.

Everyone was confined to the house and Tess expected Rupert and his friends to return to the more obvious pleasures of London. But they stayed on, annoying the servants with their continual demands, playing charades or practical jokes, and then when these sports palled, quarrelling like noisy, petulant children.

Tess soon found the atmosphere in the house claustrophobic and in the afternoons, to escape, she would don a weatherproof hooded cloak and overshoes and regardless of the soaking rain, walk the three miles to the village, just to post a letter. She enjoyed these solitary walks along lanes overhung with dripping trees and down which water the colour of cold tea coursed. It gave her time to think and wonder at Rupert's sudden interest in the suffrage movement. She'd hastily dismissed from her mind that it was herself rather than the Cause which motivated him into calling at the office at the most inconvenient of times.

The morning after Tommy's successful race he'd poked his head round the door and, looking rather pleased, said, 'I'll have to keep an eye on that brother of yours. I did very well out of him yesterday. Mind you, I lost it all again at cards the same night,' he added as a careless afterthought.

As the door closed behind him again Tess found herself laughing although she knew she should disapprove of such profligacy. But his pace of living astonished her and she wondered how long he could maintain it without damaging his health. The late nights, the drink, the smoky atmosphere of gaming rooms must surely take their toll. He seemed to thrive on it, though. Perhaps his figure was a little more bulky than it should have been for a man of his age, but that and a slightly heightened colour were the only evidence of a predilection for fast living.

The next morning, with heavy rain beating against the window, Rupert came to the office again. He sat down and, stretching his legs out in front of him, watched her as she worked.

Assuming there was something he wanted to say to her, Tess stopped and waited for him to speak.

'Go on with your work. Bit of a hangover y'know and this is about the quietest place in the house.'

But not that quiet, for outside her door several young bucks were piggybacking each other up and down the corridor in a boisterous game of mock polo. The sound of splintering glass as yet another family heirloom smashed to the ground made him wince slightly but this was his only reaction and Tess wondered, not for the first time, why he put up with such ill-mannered friends. Was the idea of his own company really too much for him? She studied him covertly under her lashes, feeling a sudden, inexplicable pity for him, which was quite ridiculous, she told herself firmly. Trying to ignore the commotion outside the door, Tess fed paper into the type-writer but she was so conscious of his intent scrutiny that her fingers felt as fat as sausages and it took several attempts to get one letter right.

Just when things seemed to have quietened down slightly there was an almighty crash against the door and Tess jumped to her feet in alarm as it swung open and two flailing bodies fell into the room.

At this behaviour even Rupert was moved to protest. He stood up, looking vaguely annoyed. 'I say, what's going on?'

The two young men struggled to their feet, laughing immoderately but offering no apology. 'Just a bit of fun, old chap, why don't you join us, eh?'

Tired of these carryings on, Tess made no effort to hide her contempt and seeing this look, Rupert answered, 'Perhaps I will,' and then mercifully had ushered them out of the room, leaving her to get on with her work.

This afternoon when she'd left the house to walk to the village a blessed calm seemed to have descended although, no doubt, this was merely in preparation for the evening's romp. I wish Virginia would hurry up and come back, Tess thought as she reached the small village of Elmsleigh, she would sort things out. But yesterday she'd had a letter from Virginia saying she was leaving for Paris, for how long or what reason, she didn't make clear.

Waggons trundling through the village sent up great waves of muddy rain water, so after making several purchases in the small general store, Tess started the three-mile walk back to Elms Court. She was less than halfway home when the steady downpour became a deluge and she was forced to find shelter under a tree. But its branches could offer little protection from the drenching rain and she was soon soaked through and shivering with cold.

When a gale blew up, lashing the trees around in fury, dismembering branches and sending them scudding down the lane in a wild dance, Tess began to feel uneasy. Deciding it might be safer if she walked, she leaned forward into the wind, battling doggedly against a turbulent force that lifted her skirt and petticoats, whipped off her hood and sent her cloak billowing out behind her.

Almost blinded by stinging rain, she didn't see the gig until it overtook her and stopped. She recognized the angry voice, though. 'What on earth do you think you are doing, young woman, wandering round the countryside in this weather?' Rupert demanded over the roar of the wind.

Tess was cold, wet and more than a little frightened, the last thing she needed was a lecture from Rupert. She was about to retort bluntly that it was none of his business when there was a loud crack, a harsh splintering sound and a heavy branch fell across the road, not a foot from them. Panicking, Tess shrieked, Rupert swore and the horse shied in fright.

'Whoa there girl, you'll be all right.' Rupert's tone was gentle as he tried to calm the nervous mare. Then more abruptly to Tess and holding out his hand, 'You'd better get in if you don't want to be killed.'

He drove on for about a hundred yards and then turned into a field, where they swayed and jolted over a deeply rutted, waterlogged footpath until they came to a large, flint-stone barn full of rusting farm equipment and bales of hay. 'We'll shelter here,' said Rupert, getting down from the gig and leading the cob into the barn.

With the wind no longer roaring in her ears, it seemed quite peaceful in the barn. 'How long will we have to stay here?' Tess asked, gazing around.

'Until the wind lets up and it's safe to go outside again,' Rupert answered, unbuttoning his heavy tweed coat and spreading it out on the hay. 'I should take your coat off, too,' he advised, 'otherwise you'll be chilled to the bone.'

Tess fumbled at the buttons with cold fingers. 'Here, let me,' he offered coming across.

'I can manage on my own, thank you,' she answered, turning away from him. Then, persistently because it was worrying her, 'How long do you think the storm will last?'

Rupert shrugged. 'Who can say? Gales often blow themselves out at sundown, but it could go on all night.'

Tess swallowed nervously. '. . . All night . . .?' she repeated faintly.

Rupert paused in unhitching the two-wheeled gig and gazed at her coolly. 'Oh I see, you imagine yourself to be in some sort of moral danger. Don't worry, my dear, I don't go in for seducing maidens, at least not against their will. Your chastity is safe with me. I don't know what your opinion is of me, obviously it's not very high, but do you really think I'd compromise you in a situation like this?' His tone was icy.

Not sure how to answer this, Tess went and stood by the barn door, her teeth chattering with nerves and cold. It must be about four o'clock, she thought, watching the grey scudding cloud. There was still time for the weather to clear.

Behind her she could hear Rupert preparing a bed for himself in the straw. 'Good night,' he called and in a few minutes she knew by his regular breathing that he was fast asleep.

She continued to stand by the door, almost enjoying the storm now that she was safe from its destructive force. After about an hour the rain and wind eased off and the thick, grape-coloured clouds began to break for the first time in days. Here and there patches of blue sky appeared, and when finally the sun broke through the English countryside began to steam like a tropical rain forest.

Joyously Tess ran outside, dancing childishly around in puddles then closing her eyes and lifting her face to the warm sun.

Rupert's voice startled her, for she had imagined him to be still asleep. 'Is this a private celebration or can anyone join in?'

'It's just nice to see the sun again, that's all,' Tess mumbled.

'I thought you might be offering up a thanks to the gods for your escape from that fate worse than death,' he said with a wicked grin.

Tess felt her face redden and cursed under her breath, knowing how much he enjoyed seeing her discomposed. 'If you're ready, I'll go and get my coat,' she answered, studiously ignoring his remark.

When she came out again the cob was back between the shafts of the gig. Rupert helped her into the seat and they made the rest of the journey home in total silence, although Tess felt intensely aware of his thigh pressed against hers in the small seat.

It wasn't until they drew up at a door at the side of the house that Rupert spoke. 'I'll drop you off here if you don't mind, Johnson's out and I want to see that the stable boy attends to this mare properly, she'll need a good rub down.'

He jumped down from the vehicle and coming round to Tess's side, held out his hand. Holding it lightly, she reached her foot down for the small metal step but instead caught it in the hem of her dress. As she stumbled forward, Rupert held out his arms to steady her. His grip was firm and he held her hard against him as he lowered her slowly to the ground. He made no attempt to release her and, mesmerized by the pressure of his hands on her back and the naked lust in his dark eyes, she gazed back at him, aware that her body was being assaulted by the same base desires.

Rupert pulled her even closer, completely encircling her in his arms, and the urge to surrender was so compelling that violent tremors shook her whole body. He was bending towards her. In a moment, as his mouth covered hers, there would be no going back. With an anguished 'No! No!' she pushed her hands against his chest and tore herself from the prison of his arms. Throwing herself against the door, she wrenched it open, and as she rushed blindly up the stairs to her room she thought she heard him calling her name.

Still shaken by her own response, Tess stripped off her wet clothes and stood staring in the glass at her defaulting body, at the rosy blotches on her neck and chest, with a sense of shame. Whatever had happened to her? Where was her common sense? Rupert was using her merely as a pleasant diversion, she knew that, and yet he set her body afire just by touching her. Getting into the bath, she scrubbed her body until it hurt, trying to cleanse it of the frightening but compelling need for Rupert that had taken her so unawares.

When she was calm enough to think rationally, although still denying her own aching need, Tess decided she had only one choice and that was to stay out of Rupert's way. He was amusing himself out of boredom. Soon he and his friends would be gone, so until then she would avoid him. And she could work in her room, he would never disturb her there.

But it was too hot to remain indoors all the time so in the afternoons, when the house was quiet, Tess would take a book and rug and stroll to the lake. Fringed with willows, it was a cool spot well away from the house and here, propped against a tree, Tess would feed bread to the ducks, and read. But one afternoon it was so hot even the ducks had lost their appetite and snoozed quietly under a tree. A somnolent heat had descended on everything, even birds and insects had been silenced. Unable to keep her eyes open, Tess let the book fall from her hand but was startled out of her drowsiness by a sound nearby. Not more than a few yards away and riding towards her were Rupert and a young lady. Tess pressed herself against the tree, trying to make herself invisible, for the path ran close to where she sat.

'Come on, Cora,' she heard Rupert say, 'I'll race you to that clump of trees over there.'

The girl called Cora laughed. 'Don't be ridiculous, Rupert, you know I couldn't beat you on Poppy, the poor dear's in her dotage. Besides, as long as women ride side saddle, men will always have an unfair advantage.'

They were almost level with her now and Tess heard every word of Rupert's reply: 'It might be unfair, but you should know by now, m'dear, that there's only one place a lady may open her legs and that is in bed.'

Shocked beyond belief at such direct, coarse language to a young woman, Tess gave a sharp, sympathetic intake of breath, imagining Cora's indignation and waiting for her angry retort. Instead, she gave a deep, throaty chuckle. 'You are incorrigible, Rupert,' she answered by way of a reprimand but as they cantered past and Rupert looked directly at her, Tess knew the words were aimed to shock her rather than the young woman he was with.

If the heat had been stifling during the day it was even worse at night. Tess had a cool bath, put on a light cotton nightdress, brushed her thick black hair a hundred times and then lay on the bed reading a novel by Ouida.

Downstairs a rumbustious party had been going on all evening and seemed to be proceeding to its inevitable drunken conclusion. Gripping as her book was, Tess still couldn't concentrate. Hot and restless, she poured herself a glass of cold water and then went to the window, leaning out to catch a breath of fresh air. The moon had risen, full and pale and so brilliant it cast shadows on the lawn and turned night to day.

As she stood there, a couple, arms entwined, came out on to the terrace. The girl, who Tess recognized as Cora, was wearing a beautiful, low-backed white satin gown and the man started to kiss her hungrily on her face, her shoulders and the curve of her breasts. Cora stood passive for a moment then she grabbed his hair and yanking back his head, pushed him away. With a giggle and swaying slightly, she ran unsteadily down the steps, past the fountain and on to the lawn, her suitor in close pursuit. In her drunken flight, one of Cora's satin slippers came off and as he caught up with her the man reached out and there was the sound of fine satin being ripped in two. Cora shrieked but continued to run and this time the man threw himself upon her and they fell in a jumble of legs and arms.

Vaguely amused, Tess watched their antics as they rolled over and over like a couple of young foals, laughing hysterically. But then it went very quiet. The man started pulling roughly at Cora's dress, lifting it up over her plump legs, throwing off garters and stockings and tearing urgently at her undergarments. With even more urgency he fumbled with his trousers, then lifting himself on to the girl, he began to move up and down on her, the thrust of his body quickly accelerating until there were two thrashing bodies clearly visible in the moonlight. Then the girl let out a long wild cry, and the man rolled away from her and the two of them lay spreadeagled on the grass, gasping audibly. After a moment, and with hardly a glance at the man, Cora stood up, tried to adjust her torn clothing and then hobbled back to the house, casually gathering up discarded garments as she went.

Transfixed, Tess stood watching the coupling, repelled and excited at the same time. A slight movement on the terrace startled her and she gave a small gasp as Rupert stepped out from the shadows and stood staring up at her, leaving Tess in no doubt that he had seen the copulating pair as well.

Agitated, she stepped back from the window and her hands flew to her burning cheeks. Trying to control her trembling limbs and the turbulent beating of her heart, she waited for him. The knock was brief and he entered the room silently, leaning against the closed door, his face half in shadow. Neither of them said a word and Tess stood motionless in the middle of the room in a trance-like state of surrender.

'Do you want me to stay?' he said at last. Tess nodded mutely, too agitated to speak. It was wrong, wicked, she knew that but she felt such a wild, frightening hunger for him it rendered her defenceless.

With a faint smile he came towards her, divesting himself of his clothes, shrugging off his evening coat, unbuttoning the white waistcoat and removing the studs from his starched shirt. When, at last, he stood before her quite naked, Tess didn't flinch, but gazed at him shyly, at the powerful, physical strength of him and the tumescent evidence of his desire for her. When he reached out for her she went willingly, waiting as he swiftly lifted the thin material of her nightdress and pulled it over her head.

Her skin was slightly damp and in the lamp light had the golden sheen of silk, and her heavy hair fell like a dark waterfall over the perfect curve of her breasts. Rupert lifted the thick rope of hair and coiled it round his fingers.

'My God,' he murmured huskily, 'you're even more lovely than I imagined.' Letting the hair fall, he traced a finger along the pure line of her cheekbones and across the full lips. Then his hands were on her shoulders, caressing the smooth skin of her back. Closing her eyes, Tess gave herself up to the exquisite pleasure of his searching hands as they moved to the curve of her waist and then slowly up until they cupped her breasts. Her arms slid round his neck and as his lips came down on hers, hard and demanding, she arched her body into the hardness of his, wanting him with every fibre of her being.

Lifting her up, Rupert carried her to the bed. Hungrily he explored her eager body, his mouth finding the pink, rosebud

242

nipples, his fingers stroking and gently exploring the warm flesh of her thighs. With a moan of pleasure she closed her eyes and when she felt his weight, her sweating body arched with a need that matched his, their juices mingled and he entered her easily and without pain.

Afterwards, though, Tess modestly tried to cover her nakedness with a sheet. Laughing, Rupert pulled it away and cradling her in his arms, he put his mouth to her ear and murmured suggestions that were both ardent and erotic. And all the time he skilfully caressed her, bringing her to such a pitch that this time when he entered her and his thrust became more insistent, she began to move with the same urgency and rhythm until she felt a great shuddering spasm that went on and on and made her cry out with the same wild animal noise as the girl in the garden.

Every night Rupert came to her room. Always he left just as the last stars were fading. Then Tess, her skin rosy with lovemaking, her hair a dark tangle on the pillowcase, would turn over and, flinging her arm across the crumpled bed, fall into a deep exhausted sleep.

And this became the pattern of her life. Outside her nights spent with Rupert, reality ceased to exist. Her whole being was centred on him – work, eating became unimportant. She was no better now than Sarah, Mrs Chadwick or Cora, she knew that, but she didn't care, her obsessive need for Rupert drove out any sense of shame.

Sex, her own passionate response to Rupert had taken Tess unawares, but it gripped her like a fever and brought little happiness. For her one great fear was that, tiring of her, he might no longer come to her room. If he was a few minutes late, she would sit in torment, staring at the door. Then when he did come she would rage at him, tell him how much she hated him and pummel his chest with her fists. Sure of himself, Rupert would smile, grip her wrists and pull her towards him. Locking her hands behind her, he would silence the torrent of angry words with a kiss. Immediately she was aroused, and nightly their lovemaking became more tempestuous and abandoned. But afterwards as Rupert slept, holding her in his arms, Tess would lie crying silently in the dark.

He didn't tell her he was going, didn't even say goodbye. Tess watched, white-faced, from an upstairs window as carriages were piled high with luggage, servants and dogs. Then without even a backward glance, Rupert drove off down the drive with his friends to some other destination of pleasure.

Peace, calm and order once more descended upon the house and Tess felt as if she would die.

16

'I don't know what you've been getting up to while I've been away, Teresa, but you're definitely looking a bit peaky,' said Virginia in a jocular tone.

Tess's heart gave a small thump of fright but she was able to answer calmly, 'It's just the heat in London, I haven't been sleeping well.'

'Well the glass is falling so we should get rain before nightfall.' Virginia studied Tess more closely. 'You look as if you could do with a tonic though.'

'I'm quite all right, really,' Tess lied because there was no cure for her particular malady, which was a sick longing for Rupert. There'd been ample time for regret in those long empty days after he'd left. Stripped of her dignity and self-respect, Tess often asked herself if, given the chance, she would have changed anything. Her truthful answer had always been no. The urgent power of sex, she now realized, made fools of the most sensible people, but she would guard against it in future. It was the casual dismissal of her from his life that had caused the most pain, and even though she'd spun a protective skein around her hurt, she still couldn't forget him.

Virginia arrived back from France in early September and this dissipated some of her unhappiness. But apart from telling Tess that David had gone with her and would remain in Paris, Virginia was rather evasive about her trip.

Tess had been pleased when she heard they were moving back to London. Elms Court had too many unhappy associations and Mr Johnson kept commenting on her pallor. Nothing escaped his sharp eyes and sometimes Tess suspected he had a shrewd idea what had been going on between her and Rupert.

She had hoped that back in London she might forget

Rupert and settle down again in the comfortable routine she and Virginia had established when she'd first begun working at Lennox Street. Just how difficult that was going to be, Tess was already finding out. Suddenly she leapt up from her desk, and clamping her hand over her mouth, rushed out of the room, while an astonished Virginia stared after her. She made it to the bathroom just in time and was heaving and sobbing into the washhand basin and frantically thinking, I can't be, I can't be! when she heard Virginia's voice behind her.

'Here, let me.' Wringing out a face cloth in cold water she carefully wiped the vomit and tears from Tess's face. Feeling truly wretched, Tess closed her eyes. Virginia was bound to guess now, she thought and waited for her to say something.

'You are poorly, aren't you?' Virginia's voice sounded really concerned.

'Yes,' admitted Tess feebly. 'It must have been the fish we had last night, it often upsets me.' The lie tripped unconvincingly off her lips.

'You, young lady, are going to lie down while I sent for the doctor.'

'No, don't. I'll be fine shortly. In fact I feel better already.' Tess smiled weakly to prove her point.

Virginia looked uncertain. 'Well, I insist you rest at least.'

'All right.' She went meekly, lying down on top of the cover while Virginia pulled the curtains, leaving her with a darkened room and her own terrified thoughts. She lay on her side, clutching at the life growing inside her and tears of self-pity coursing down her cheeks. How could she have let things come to this? She, Teresa Kelly, who was always so sensible and level-headed and rather despised those women who weren't?

She'd hardly dared think about the consequences of her first missed monthly, nor the second. It was as if by ignoring her body's rhythms she could make the problem somehow go away. What had been impossible to ignore, however, was the nausea and sickness which left her shaking and exhausted and told her that the life she'd made for herself was in ruins. And there'd be her mother's scorn to face, David's disappointment in her. And Virginia, what would she say? First of all there would be a look of disbelief, then condemnation. Virginia's brown eyes would grow cold and she, Tess, a little nobody, would stand accused of deliberately enticing Rupert. For, whatever their differences, the rich always closed ranks in times of crisis.

But there was no reason why it should be like that. There were numerous ways of getting rid of an unwanted child, women in Bethnal Green managed it every day. Tess sat up in bed and with a sudden resolution wiped her eyes, blew her nose, then went to the door and turned the key in the lock. Opening a drawer in her bureau, she pulled out a small purse and tipped the contents on the bed. She counted the money into piles – gold, silver and copper – and found she had nearly thirty pounds, enough to tide her over for quite some time. Clothes were hastily chucked into a case then, remembering, Tess went to the bureau again. The letters were still in their blue ribbon, the photograph beside them. She hadn't heard from Liam in months, had hardly even thought of him, but now as she studied the photograph she had a sudden longing to turn the clock back to that innocent, chaste girl who stared out of the photograph at her. She was going to throw the letters on to the fire, but she changed her mind, flung them in on top of her clothes and snapped the case shut.

As the barometer had predicted, it had started to rain. Tess buttoned herself into a coat, unlocked the door and scanned the corridor. When she was sure there was no one about, she crept down the back stairs and through a gate in the garden, dragging her suitcase after her. She was now in a quiet back street but she made sure she was well out of sight of the house before she hailed a cab.

Until the driver said. 'Where to, miss?' Tess had no idea of her destination. But she said unhesitatingly, 'Twenty-two Hill Drive, St John's Wood,' and having given these instructions, sat back in the cab feeling a little calmer. Sarah will help me, she thought, she will tell me what to do.

Tess had to admit to being impressed by Hill Drive. It wasn't up to Lennox Street, of course, but if the houses and pretty front gardens were anything to go by a life of sin had certain compensations. Not that she approved of Sarah's way of life, she thought, although she was hardly in a position to censure her friend.

The driver had slowed down to look for the number and he finally called, 'Here we are, miss.' Jumping down, he helped Tess to the front door with her case and after tipping him generously, she pulled the bell. She waited several minutes, rang again and then put her ear against the door, listening for sound. She had just pulled her collar up around her neck and looked disconsolately up at a rain-filled sky when the door slowly opened and a small face appeared.

'Is Miss Atkins in?' Tess called through the crack in the door.

The door opened a fraction wider, revealing a small girl of about twelve dressed in an outsize maid's uniform.

In spite of her troubles, Tess felt a strong desire to giggle. Curbing her mirth she said to the small apparition, 'I'd like to speak to Miss Atkins, please.'

'Who shall I say is calling?' she asked timidly.

'Tell your mistress it's a friend, Miss Teresa Kelly.' With a certain reluctance the girl invited her to step inside and as the door closed, Tess heard Sarah's voice.

'Who is it, Annie?' she called as she came down the hall clad in a thin housecoat and peering slightly in the hall's gloom.

'Hello, Sarah.'

Sarah froze in surprise when she heard Tess's voice and then her face broke into a broad, happy smile. 'Tess! I can't believe it!' She started to fuss, drawing her housecoat self-consciously around her. 'Why didn't you tell me you were coming? You've caught me a little . . . unprepared.' Noticing the suitcase, she asked, 'Are you on your way somewhere?'

'No. The fact is . . .' Tess hesitated then: 'I was wondering if I could stay with you for a few days.'

248

'Of course you can, it'll be lovely to have you. Just like old times. We'll be able to have a real natter, catch up on all the news.' Sarah turned to Annie who had been standing gawping at them both.

'Annie, love, go an' make us both a couple of poached eggs on toast. Lightly done like I've shown you.'

Annie, who reminded Tess of a small furry dormouse, did a quick bob and with a 'Yes mum,' scuttled obediently away to the kitchen.

Taking Tess's arm, Sarah drew her through to the back of the house and into the sitting room which overlooked a rather unkempt garden full of fading summer flowers, although the room itself was furnished in surprisingly good taste.

'Right,' said Sarah, plumping up a cushion, 'sit yourself down and tell me why you're here.' She glanced at the brass-faced grandfather clock in the corner. 'We've got a good two hours, then I've got a gentleman, one of my regulars.'

Being reminded of Sarah's profession made Tess feel slightly uncomfortable and she was glad of the distraction of Annie bringing in the food on a tray.

'What do you think of her?' Sarah asked when the girl had gone.

Tess punctured the soft yolk of her egg and watched it spread over the toast. 'She seems a nice little child,' she answered noncommittally for in truth there was nothing very positive she could say about the girl.

'I got her from an orphanage. I'm training her like Mrs Chadwick did me.'

'Oh, you're not!' exclaimed Tess, half rising from her chair. 'Not that little thing?'

'Not in that way, you idiot. No one would lay a hand on my little Annie. She'll remain respectable, don't worry. I'm training her to cook and keep house and eventually, I hope, she'll meet a nice chap and marry him.' Catching the doubtful look on Tess's face, Sarah became slightly defensive. 'She won't be corrupted here. I know you've never believed me but I wasn't pushed into anything by Mrs

249

Chadwick. I did it of my own free will. And I'll tell you something else, I don't envy anybody. I'm independent and the only difference between me and a married woman, as far as I can see, is that I get paid for my services.'

'Well, you've certainly got a very nice place here,' Tess admitted, wondering who had advised Sarah on the rather good paintings lining the wall.

'I've got a few investments, too. One of my gentlemen advises me. I don't ever intend to be poor again and when I've got enough behind me I shall give all this up and open a shop. I rather fancy a milliner's.'

Tess hoped it would all work out for Sarah and she'd have her shop. The trouble was, fate had a nasty habit of intervening even in the best-laid plans, creating chaos. For instance, if Virginia hadn't taken herself off to London and Paris leaving her alone with Rupert, she wouldn't be sitting here now, her neck stiff with tension and a throbbing pain over her left eye, trying to pluck up enough courage to tell Sarah of her predicament.

'What . . . what . . . would you do if you found yourself in the family way, though?' Tess ventured, twisting her fingers nervously in her lap.

Sarah laughed. 'Oh, I'm too careful for that. Mind you, I thought I was once, phew, it gave me a real fright.' She wiped imaginary sweat from her brow.

Tess leaned forward, her voice urgent. 'But what would you do if you were?'

Sarah's pale eyebrows rose a fraction of an inch at Tess's persistent interrogation. 'Why, I'd get rid of it, of course.'

'You know someone you could go to, then?'

Looking thoughtful, Sarah picked up a poker, swinging it between her fingers. 'No . . . not exactly. But it wouldn't be difficult to find a woman.'

Tess's voice hardly quavered at all as she asked, 'C...ould you find me . . . somebody?'

Sarah, who had been trying to poke some life into a sullen fire, jerked her head up, an uncomprehending look in her eyes. 'What did you say?'

250

Tess's whole body was prickling with embarrassment. She couldn't repeat it, she just couldn't. Unable to meet Sarah's gaze, she stared down at the pattern on the carpet.

There was a very prolonged silence, Sarah gave several more bangs at the coal, then going down on her hands and knees, swept busily around the hearth with a small brush and pan. When this task could occupy her no longer, she rose with a tired, almost old movement and stood facing Tess. 'What are you trying to tell me, that you're expecting a kid?'

Acknowledging her guilt, Tess moved her head slowly up and down.

'Oh ... Tess ... you of all people ...' The disappointment, recrimination and pity in these words was too much for Tess and she finally broke down, rocking backwards and forwards in the chair with loud, heartbreaking sobs.

Kneeling, Sarah clasped Tess against her thin body murmuring angrily, 'It's always the innocent who get caught, always.' She let Tess cry on for a while, then taking her by the shoulders said, 'Tell me who the bugger was so that I can go and personally wring his bleedin' neck.' She gave Tess a small shake. 'Go on, tell me.'

'What's the point, there's ... there's nothing you can do,' Tess sobbed.

But Sarah persisted. 'It was that Liam O'Sullivan, wasn't it? I never thought much of him.'

'Liam's in South Africa.'

'Of course he is.' Sarah thought for a moment. 'Was it one of the servants down at Elms Court, then?'

When Tess shook her head, Sarah looked momentarily baffled, then with sudden suspicion: 'It wasn't ... it couldn't be Mr David.'

Blowing her nose, Tess managed to look indignant. 'You know he's not like that. Mr David's a true gentleman.'

'It's my experience that all men are like it, duckie. I've never had many illusions about them and since I've bin in this line of business I've got even less.'

'Does it really matter whose it is? I've no intention of having it.' Tess sank back in the chair and closed her eyes.

She had a hammering pain in both temples now and needed some quiet. 'But if you really want to know, well, Rupert St Clair's the father.'

'Sir . . . Rupert St Clair?'

'Himself.'

Sarah gave a surprised whistle. 'Cripes! That's a turn-up for the books. Is he married, this Sir Rupert?'

Tess opened her eyes. 'Of course not.'

'Don't you realize then that you're carrying the heir to that pile in Sussex?' Sarah began to sound excited as she saw various possibilities opening up for her friend.

'A child born out of wedlock cannot inherit. Besides it might be a girl.' Tess pressed her fingers against her throbbing temples, she didn't want to talk about the child, give it a sex and human characteristics. She needed to think only of an unwanted mass inside her; something very disposable.

'Does he know about the baby?'

'He didn't stay around long enough to find out.'

'Don't you think he has a right to be told?' Sarah felt she must do something to shift Tess from her trance-like apathy. It was so unlike her, she'd always been a fighter.

Tess managed a weak smile. 'What, so that he can make an honest woman of me? Rupert could take his pick from some of the grandest families in England, he's hardly likely to choose me for his bride.'

Sarah saw the truth of this. 'Still, it wouldn't do any harm to tell him. I think he should be made to face up to his responsibilities. Men, particularly rich ones, always seem to get off scot free.'

'They'd say I was after money,' replied Tess flatly. 'It was all a dreadful mistake but I want to put it all behind me now and make a fresh start. And I need you to help me. You will, won't you, Sarah?' Tess sat forward in her chair, her face tense.

'I . . .' The grandfather clock chose that moment to chime vigorously. Sarah jumped to her feet with an expression of relief. 'Oh Gawd,' she exclaimed, 'is that the time, four

252

o'clock? My client will be here in a minute.' Pulling her wrap around her, she hurried to the door. 'See you in about an hour, this one takes ages,' she called over her shoulder and laughed indecorously.

'But what about me . . .?' Tess called, her voice trailing off as Sarah pulled the door closed. With an unhappy sigh she slumped back in the chair for she had an uncomfortable feeling that Sarah was going to be awkward about helping her. Or perhaps it was her condition making her fanciful. Sarah was her closest friend, she'd do anything she could to help, Tess knew that. And she was depending on Sarah. Women willing to perform abortions were two a penny in the back streets of Bethnal Green, but she couldn't risk being seen down there. No, it would have to be somewhere round here. Sarah could make some discreet inquiries. It was either that or a button hook. Tess shuddered and shifted uncomfortably in her chair. No, she could never do that to herself, she was far too squeamish . . . But it wouldn't come to that . . . Sarah would help her . . .

And when it was all over she'd get a job, either as a companion or secretary. Or there were department stores . . . except, of course, that they'd want a reference. Until that moment she hadn't given a thought to Virginia. Now she had a sudden picture of her going to Tess's room, getting no reply to her knock and easing open the door. What would her feelings be when she found empty drawers and cupboards and all the untidy evidence of her hasty departure, but no note, no explanation, nothing? Her immediate reaction, Tess felt, would be to contact the police or, even worse, her mother.

At the thought of her mother, Tess broke out in a cold sweat. Virginia would have to be stopped.

Rising from the chair she went to the writing desk by the window. Florence had the unhappy knack of putting two and two together and getting the right answer. In another week or so, please God, she would be her normal self, able to think rationally, and have a plausible explanation for leaving Lennox Street.

Wondering how to word the letter, Tess slowly dipped

the pen into the ink and wrote, 'Dear Miss Virginia'. Then at a loss she sat chewing on the wooden pen holder. What on earth could she say that wasn't a downright lie? Five minutes later she still hadn't written another word but there was a large blot in the middle of the page. Screwing it up, she aimed it at the fire and started again.

Dear Miss Virginia, You are probably wondering why I left so suddenly today without any explanation or even saying goodbye. After all your kindness you must find it inexcusable, which of course it is. However, I had no other choice and my reasons are entirely personal. All I ask is that you don't contact my mother, it would cause her a great deal of unnecessary worry. I'm quite safe and when I've sorted myself out I shall get in touch with her myself in about a week's time.

I'm very sorry for all the distress I must have caused you. I'll always remember my time working with you as one of great benefit and happiness.

By the time Tess wrote her signature the writing was a little unsteady. As she sealed the envelope, large tears rolled down her cheeks.

'Why couldn't she have come here?' They were in the morning room having breakfast and in front of Tess stood a boiled egg, as yet untouched.

'I'm sorry, Tess, but I just couldn't take the risk,' Sarah explained patiently, tapping her egg with a spoon.

Tess gazed at Sarah suspiciously. 'What do you mean, risk? You told me she was a good woman, this Mrs Meads, and clean.'

Avoiding her gaze, Sarah picked the shell off her egg. 'Oh, she's all of those things, don't worry. But I couldn't let her do it here . . . just in case.'

'Just in case of what?' Beneath the tablecloth, Tess felt the palms of her hands begin to sweat.

'Well, something could . . . you know . . . might go wrong. I'm not saying it will,' Sarah added hastily when she saw her friend's frightened expression. 'But you must remember Sally Noakes.'

Tess remembered Sally Noakes all right. She had bled to death after a botched abortion and the woman responsible was now in prison.

'But don't worry, she was an old drunk who used dirty instruments. Mrs Meads is much more particular, I've seen her house and she comes well recommended.'

Although she had hoped all along that Tess wouldn't go through with the abortion, Sarah tried to keep her tone encouraging. Personally she thought Tess was being foolish and pig-headed. She had far more to gain financially by keeping the child, and one had to be practical in this world. Even if Rupert denied that he was the father, Virginia and David knew that Tess was no liar and eventually he would have to face up to his responsibilities with a nice little settlement, enough to keep Tess and the child in comfortable circumstances. As it was, her future was uncertain. But Tess, stubborn and proud as ever, had refused to listen to any of these arguments.

Looking at her now, though, there was little of that proud spirit to be seen. 'Aren't you going to eat your egg?' Sarah asked, for it still sat uneaten in its cup.

'I'm . . . not very hungry, I'll leave it if you don't mind.' Tess pushed the plate away from her.

Sarah stood up. 'Well, when you're ready, then . . . might as well get it over with.'

Tess shuddered. Over with. They got their coats and with dragging feet she followed Sarah out of the house.

It was a hazy autumn day, people went about their business, windows were cleaned, coal and groceries delivered, while Tess felt like a condemned prisoner or her way to the gallows. All her early certainties had been replaced by fear and the ghost of Sally Noakes. Cold, sharp instruments and unstaunchable blood, that was all she could see.

Sarah, who could only guess at her friend's terror, took her arm to give it a comforting squeeze, caught the tremor of fear and began to feel exasperated. Stopping, she stood facing Tess, hands on hips. 'You are in no state to be going through with this. Why don't we just go home?'

But although Tess's face was a chalky white it still wore a set, stubborn look. 'No, I'm not turning back, not after I've got this far. It'll soon be over with now.' She pulled her shoulders back and began to walk on. Sarah watched her, infuriated by such obduracy, then with a hopeless shrug, followed after her.

Mrs Meads's manner as she opened the door to them was brisk and businesslike, which did, briefly, bolster Tess's flagging spirit. Wasting no time, the woman led her into a room at the back of the house, where she handed her a long white robe. Then she pointed to a screen. 'You can get undressed behind there.'

Tess took the robe from her but didn't move. In the middle of the room, which had darkened windows and a tomb-like chill to it, stood a high, narrow table spread with a white sheet. Beside it, laid out with sharp metal instruments, was a trolley and underneath a bucket. Tess, who knew she was going to vomit, felt bile, bitter as aloes, rise in her throat. Already she could feel those torturous-looking instruments with their cold, sharp fingers, pushing and probing at her insides. It would take only one false move ... She gave a small moan and clutched instinctively at her stomach while the room began to tilt and spin. She saw Mrs Meads's lips moving but heard only a great rushing sound like the sea in her ears. Then the world began to recede and darken and in a frantic attempt to save herself, Tess grabbed at Mrs Meads. But the woman pushed her angrily away and she sank to the floor in a swoon.

Mrs Meads stood gazing down at her yellow-livered patient with compressed lips, then going to the door she called to Sarah in a harsh voice, 'Come and get your friend out of here, and look quick about it. And it'll be five pounds anyway, for my trouble.'

17

Tess stood gazing out at the winter-dead garden too preoccupied even to notice that a small clump of snowdrops, early harbingers of spring, had managed to push their way through a tangle of dead flowers and rotting leaves. She had just been stunned by a letter from her mother with the news that the police had finally found her father, floating face down in the Thames and quite dead. The shock she felt wasn't caused by his death, only a hypocrite would pretend any grief. What had shaken her was her mother's extraordinary decision to give him a full Roman Catholic burial. And she expected Tess to be there to pay her last respects.

Tess read the letter again with a growing sense of incredulity. She doubted whether her father had entered a church willingly more than three times in his life and guessed this last homage to her husband was an act of atonement for a soured and ruined life. Perhaps, too, there was a slight shadow of guilt.

Unfortunately, Florence's pious decision had thrown Tess into a state of turmoil; there was absolutely no way she could attend the funeral and hide her condition from her mother. Crumpling the letter in her hand she cursed her father for his sense of timing. And she thought she had everything worked out so well, too.

After the fiasco at Mrs Meads's she had no choice but to resort to lies and subterfuge when writing to her mother. Fortunately her explanation that she'd left Virginia for a more highly paid situation seemed to satisfy her mother, particularly when she enclosed more money each week. Over the months she'd become quite adept at fabricating stories about her new employer, Mrs Wallis, and she and Sarah congratulated themselves on their cleverness. This news had taken the wind out of her sails completely.

They'd worked out, she and Sarah, that Florence need never know about the baby. After it was born Tess would look for a job and accommodation locally so that Sarah could mind the baby during the day. If the worst did happen and Florence discovered the existence of the child, they would pass it off as Sarah's. It had all been so neatly worked out, and now this. Tess felt she wanted to scream, except that it might bring Annie running from the scullery convinced she had gone into early labour.

Not that this wasn't an eagerly awaited event for both Annie and Sarah. The little maid spent all her spare time stitching together tiny flannelette nightdresses of indeterminate colour while Sarah was forever rushing up to Whiteley's to buy baby clothes. There was now a drawerful of tiny garments upstairs and although Tess had tried to stop her, she'd gone out again that afternoon to look for baby carriages.

Tess herself awaited the birth with mixed feelings. The baby was a little life to her now because it moved and kicked, yet she hated waddling around like an ungainly elephant. But there was only about two more months to go and she would be glad to get it over with. Whether she could actually love the little thing that had devastated her life, she didn't know. And it just had to be a girl so that she could bring her up to be strong and independent and give her the best education she could afford . . . perhaps even send her to university.

Tess turned from the window and sat down heavily. She was daydreaming when she should be thinking up an excuse for not going to her father's funeral. Something plausible enough to convince a sceptical mother.

The idea, when it came, was brilliant yet simple. She would tell her mother she was about to leave on an extended visit to France with Mrs Wallis, that the tickets had already been bought and there was no way she could get out of it.

Feeling grateful to Mrs Wallis, a lady Tess had built up quite a picture of over the months, she sat down to answer her mother's letter. When she heard the front doorbell ring she waited for Annie to answer it and then come scuttling back to announce who it was. It rang again and since there was no movement from the kitchen, Tess went out and peered down the hall, deciding if it was one of Sarah's customers, she would ignore it. Through the glass-panelled door she could see the outline of a woman. It must be Sarah, she thought as she lumbered down the hall, she'll have forgotten her keys again.

But the woman standing on the step wasn't Sarah and when Tess saw who it was, her hand flew to her mouth in stunned surprise. 'You,' she managed to say eventually.

'Hello, Tess,' said Virginia, and smiled. 'I've come to see you.'

'What for?' said Tess guardedly.

Virginia looked up at the cold sky. 'I'd prefer not to talk on the doorstep.'

'Sorry, you'd better come in.' Tess held the door open, glad that for once Sarah wasn't entertaining a client, but her mind churning as to why Virginia should be here or had even found her, and dreading that her mother was in some way implicated. That would be the end, that would, she thought as she invited Virginia to sit down and watched as with a thoughtful expression, she slowly pulled off her gloves.

'When is the baby due?' Virginia asked at last.

Heck, she doesn't beat about the bush, thought Tess. She knew there was no disguising her condition but she felt Virginia could have approached the subject rather more delicately. 'April, some time, I think,' she answered dully, then feeling ashamed, turned away.

Sounding rather emotional, Virginia sat forward in her chair and took Tess's hand. 'Oh my dear, why didn't you tell me? When I received your letter I rather thought you might be pregnant, that's why I didn't make any attempt to contact your mother. But I had no idea Rupert was the father.'

Shaking her hand off, Tess swung round and stared at her suspiciously. 'Who told you that?'

'Sarah came to see me.'

'Sarah . . .?'

'Yes, she felt, quite rightly, that Rupert should be made to face up to his responsibilities and that this wasn't a burden you should be carrying alone.'

'She had no right to do that,' Tess declared hotly with an angry stamp of her foot. 'Knowing how I feel . . . and behind my back.'

'She did it out of the best possible motives, Teresa. She thinks you're entitled to some sort of financial help, and I agree with her.'

'I certainly have no intention of taking scraps from a rich man's table,' Tess answered coldly, still smarting from Sarah's betrayal. 'What's done is done and I'll take care of myself and the child in my own way. We might go hungry occasionally but I'm used to that.' She turned away from Virginia again, hoping she would go.

But Virginia stayed put. 'Tess, we must talk, can't you sit down?'

'I've nothing more to say.'

'But I have. You are carrying Rupert's child, perhaps his heir.'

'It's going to be a girl,' Tess said unnecessarily. 'Besides, Sarah's told you it's Rupert's child, I haven't.'

'Rupert's already admitted it.'

Such honesty seemed so uncharacteristic of Rupert that Tess was quite lost for words.

'I didn't think Sarah was lying but had to wait until he came back from Scotland, then I tackled him about it. He accepts full responsibility. He was very put out last September when I told him of your flight, wanted to get in touch with the police and everything. I never made the connection, though, which was stupid of me I suppose, knowing Rupert's reputation. But you should have told me and not run off like that. You gave me a few sleepless nights, I can tell you.'

'I'm sorry, I just panicked. I didn't think you'd believe me anyway. All I could think about was getting rid of it.'

'I'm very glad you didn't. I know he's treated you badly, Tess, but Rupert's not quite the heartless cad you think he is.

It's just that he's always been spoilt, always had everything he wanted, including women. But this is his day of reckoning. From now on he will have to face up to life. And it will do him good, be the making of him probably. He'll have other people to think about now rather than just himself.' She tugged Tess's hand. 'Look at me, Teresa, please, I've got something rather important to say. I want you and Rupert to be married.'

Tess's head shot round in surprise. 'Married?' she squeaked. 'Rupert would never marry me. Besides, we don't love each other.'

'You must have felt something for each other, for, for . . . this to happen.' She indicated Tess's bulge.

Bewildered, emotional and near to tears, Tess answered in a reproachful voice. 'It would never have happened if you hadn't left me on my own.'

Virginia went pale. 'I had no choice, David needed me. What are you trying to tell me? Rupert . . . he didn't . . . force you . . . against your will?'

Remembering those nights when she'd waited so impatiently for him to come to her room and the power of her own need, Tess felt her body grow warm. 'No, it wasn't like that.'

Virginia sighed with relief. 'Thank heavens. I didn't think even Rupert would be that unscrupulous.'

Tess turned on Virginia angrily. 'No, but he didn't care what happened to me afterwards, did he?' Those days after he'd left were still painfully vivid in her mind and still had the power to hurt.

'He's not as indifferent as you think. In fact he's quite happy for the marriage to go ahead if you are . . . but on certain conditions.'

'But it's impossible. We belong to different worlds.' Tess spread her hands in a helpless gesture.

'Tess, my maternal grandfather left school at twelve and had made a fortune out of coal by the time he was forty. The St Clairs, when my mother came along, had very little, apart from a title and a crumbling house. Their great gift is for

261

spending money, not making it, a trait, unfortunately, which Rupert has inherited.'

'I would never fit into Rupert's life . . . all that gambling and drinking . . . and those friends of his, I could never like them.'

Virginia, who was beginning to feel sorely tried by Tess's obstinacy, decided to speak bluntly. 'You won't be marrying his friends. And do you want your child to be called a bastard and carry that stigma all his life?'

Tess studied her fingernails. 'No, not particularly.'

'There will be no need to mix with Rupert's friends. As I've said, there are conditions to this marriage. One is that you maintain separate establishments. Rupert has always had a certain predilection for other men's wives and his present mistress is the wife of a Member of Parliament. There's no question of divorce since this lady's husband has hopes of high office. You would, of course, be expected to turn a blind eye to this liaison.'

'But that's not a good enough reason for him to want to marry me.'

'Well, I must admit there are certain financial inducements. Grandfather was a wily old character who tied up his money very carefully. There's money in trust which Rupert gets only on marriage, plus some more if and when he produces a male heir.'

'I might not have a boy.'

'But you'll have other children.'

'What, living in separate establishments?' Even Rupert Tess felt, wasn't that virile.

Virginia coughed delicately. 'Ah . . . well, if you had a gir something would have to be arranged, of course.'

'I'm beginning to feel like a prize breeding sow,' Tess said indignantly.

'I wouldn't put it quite as crudely as that, but you are both young and healthy, the pair of you, and you'll produce strong, healthy stock. I know you don't love him but you would still have quite a good life unfettered by domesti routine. Besides, what are the alternatives? You must know

262

it wouldn't be easy trying to find work and look after a demanding baby. Think of him, too. Don't let your pride stand in the way of that poor innocent's future.'

Tess's shoulders slumped. From the start, Sarah had cast Rupert in the role of bounder, blaming him entirely for her friend's condition. Tess herself had never been able to analyse her feelings for Rupert. Her own personal lodestar, in matters of the heart, was the novels she read, where passion, for women at least, only followed after love. And thankfully, over the months he'd grown more dim in her mind as her world shrank to the small life growing and kicking inside her. And now here was Virginia with this extraordinary proposition that she should marry Rupert, upsetting her plans and all the brave talk about bringing a baby up on her own. But the world was hostile to an illegitimate child, and she did worry about the future. And did she have the right to deny her baby the name and privileges it was entitled to? Perhaps not, yet there was a dogged streak in Tess that wanted to hold out. But people like the St Clairs knew everybody had their price, hers being the welfare of her child.

'You say Rupert and I would lead separate lives, so I could come back and live with you at Lennox Street?'

'Yes, my dear.'

'Right, I'll marry Rupert, but on that condition only.'

'Good.' It was all Virginia said but as she eased on her gloves and stood up to go, Tess was taken aback by her look of quiet satisfaction.

After Virginia had left, Tess took a turn round the garden to clear her muddled thoughts. Preoccupied and nervously biting her lip, she moved restlessly up and down the short path, her gown trailing in the dank, rotting leaves. Dear God, what had she committed herself to? And she could hardly believe Rupert was in favour of the union. No, only Virginia wanted it, and that was what baffled her. After all, in the fullness of time Rupert would probably marry and even if he didn't there was always David. A sharp rap on the window pane made her look up. It was Sarah, with an eager look on her face, gesticulating for her to come in. And she'll get a tongue sandwich from me, too, thought Tess, going behind my back like that.

As Tess turned to go back into the house, she noticed the snowdrops, and stooped to study the modest white flowers, balancing one of the small bells on her fingers and wondering how they had managed to push their way through, and thrive, in the sour London soil. Admiring their tenacity, she cleared away some of the vegetation, giving them a chance to breathe. Perhaps they were a sign of better days to come, she thought as she stood up again. Then wistfully: But why did it have to be the wrong brother?

The church, a Gothic soot-laden structure, was gloomy and cold, a smell of incense hung on the chill air and a drumming rain echoed on the high, vaulted roof. As the vicar conducting the marriage ceremony tried to lead the faltering and meagre congregation in the hymn 'Lead us, Heavenly Father, Lead us', Tess glanced down at the heavy gold ring on her left hand then up at her husband's profile as he robustly joined in the singing. Once she'd agreed to the marriage, everything had seemed to proceed with indecent haste.

'It's imperative we have you married before your accouchement,' Virginia had said and the banns were called the following Sunday.

It had been difficult, that first meeting with Rupert. His abandonment still hurt but she'd steeled herself, deliberately keeping her distance and making sure they were never alone together. She had no idea how he felt about their union so here she stood, next to a man who was now her husband and with whom she'd spent some very intimate hours and yet who was almost a stranger to her; his deeper thoughts and feelings a mystery still to be unravelled.

Mr Appleby, who had just given her away, stood behind them and in the front pew sat her mother, hostile and unforgiving.

That had been one of the most terrible days of her life, facing Florence, and it had taken almost a week to brace herself for the ordeal.

'You've got to tell her so you might as well get it over with,' Sarah had said when she continued to delay her visit.

'But what about all those lies I've told her ... about my job ... Mrs Wallis? You know how Mum hates liars.'

Sarah regarded her friend with some amusement. 'I imagine that'll be the least of your problems when she sees the size of you,' she retorted bluntly, an observation which in no way helped Tess's flagging spirits.

'It might help sweeten the pill when you tell her who you're going to marry.'

'I doubt it.' In fact Tess knew her condition would override any other consideration. She would have besmirched Florence's good name, that was the only thing that would matter.

Eventually finding the courage from somewhere, Tess waited until it was evening and growing dark, then took a hansom to her old home. It was over a year and a half since she'd been there and the whole area seemed even grimmer than she remembered. Whatever else happens in my life, at least I've got away from this, Tess thought thankfully. Nothing could be as bad, not even a loveless marriage, as being condemned to spend your days in a place like this. She'd see she got her mother out of it soon, too. The family wouldn't want her staying here, in these squalid back streets.

They were having supper, Florence and Mr Appleby, and Tess watched them for a moment through the window, saw their cosy intimacy and wondered, not for the first time, what the relationship was between them. Without much hope that whatever it was it would ease her way, Tess swallowed hard and pushed open the door.

They both jumped up from the table in delight when they saw her, but Florence's greeting died on her lips and her expression darkened as she saw her daughter's ungainly form. 'What's this, then?' she asked unnecessarily, standing back and eyeing her daughter up and down.

Tess's mouth was dry with fear but she managed to stutter, 'I'm ... I'm in the family ... way ...' Her voice trailed away as her nerve failed her.

Florence advanced towards her threateningly. 'I can see that, you stupid bitch!' she shrieked. 'And I suppose you've been messing about with the servants? I always knew you would come to no good, it's that tinker blood. The badness was born in you like it was your father, I've known it since the day you were born.' That this prediction had come true seemed to afford her some comfort, and she was silent for a moment.

In the brief respite from an anger that had been honed to a fine edge over the years, Tess found her voice. Lifting her chin proudly, she declared, 'The father of my child is Sir Rupert St Clair.'

But the name neither impressed nor mollified Florence. 'Well then, you're nothing but a common little harlot, giving yourself to a man like that.'

At these deeply wounding words, Tess's chin went a little higher. 'And we're to be married. I shall be a Lady then.'

This was just too much for Florence. 'You. A Lady. Huh. You'll never be a Lady. The shame of it. I ought to disown you.'

Mr Appleby, who had remained silent so far, came over and put a placating hand on Florence, trying to calm her down. 'Now my dear, I think you've said enough.' He spoke with an unusual firmness. 'What's done is done, and you heard what the lass said. She's to be wed and into a good family, things could be a lot worse.'

'Oh Arthur,' said Florence, wringing her hands distractedly, 'I don't think I'll ever get over this. I've always been respectable, tried to bring my children up that way, in spite of their old man, and now this ...' Her voice trembled, then she did something Tess had rarely seen and was more frightening than all her anger; she broke down and cried.

But there'd been no forgiveness in those tears and she'd come to the wedding today, Tess knew, because Mr Appleby insisted. The hymn ended, the priest gave his blessing to the marriage and then led them into the vestry to sign the register. Here Mr Appleby embraced her and shook Rupert's hand, wishing them both luck. But when Tess turned, seeking

266

benediction from her mother, the grim features stopped her in her tracks and brought tears to her eyes.

Seeing his young wife's distress, Rupert took her hand and pulled it through his arm. 'Come along, my dear, we're going home,' he said gently and led her out of the vestry, down the aisle and into a waiting carriage.

When they arrived back at Lennox Street the servants were waiting for them in the hall and a chorus of 'Good luck, madam, good luck, sir' followed them up the stairs. But Tess, knowing all eyes were on her, felt hot and embarrassed, and wondered how much of the good will was genuine. She'd caught the sly looks of the maids, heard the occasional snigger, and she could imagine the gossip and crude jokes that went on behind those green baize doors. No doubt Rupert, with his taste for fast living, had often set their tongues wagging in the past, but this . . . well, it would add spice to their daily lives for years. After all, it was acceptable for a gentleman to dally with a girl from the lower classes, but to marry her, that was quite a different kettle of fish.

But Rupert was smiling and enjoying it all and when they reached the first landing he slipped his arm around Tess's waist and, turning, called expansively to the staff, 'There will be champagne for everyone later on and I hope you will drink the health of my new wife and myself.' Then to a cheer of encouragement from his friends, he bent and kissed Tess rather lingeringly on the mouth.

Once in the drawing room Rupert's friends wasted no time in opening the champagne, and as a toast was drunk to the bride and groom Tess watched with a growing exasperation as her mother took a sip of the sparkling wine then give an exaggerated shudder and hand the glass to Pip. Glasses were refilled, social distinctions began to blur but Florence stood there, implacably unyielding in a sea of grape-induced good will. Considering her an accessory to her daughter's deception, she wouldn't give Sarah the time of day. Pip had wandered off to get something to eat, while Tom was surrounded by an admiring group, eager for racing tips.

267

Tess studied her brother with some concern. She hadn't seen him since the previous summer and she was struck by how gaunt he looked. She really must talk to him, find out if he was eating properly, she thought, and then was distracted again by her mother.

Florence looked so small and lonely Tess's heart went out to her. It was time, she decided, for them to settle their differences. She had just put down her glass when she saw Virginia go over to her mother, take her arm and lead her to a chair. When Florence saw the pot of tea, her expression lightened for the first time that day. How clever of Virginia to think of the one thing that would cheer Florence up: a cup of tea. That was the nice thing about her new sister-in-law, she was kind, perceptive, and would never condescend. Her mother was in safe hands.

Tess shifted uncomfortably from one leg to another. There were a dull ache in her limbs, the tensions of the day and the wine were beginning to take their toll and she had difficulty stifling a yawn. She looked round the room. I wonder if anyone would miss me if I went? Certainly Rupert wouldn't because, with noisy support from his friends, he was endeavouring to fill his best man's glass with champagne, a task made more difficult by the fact that the glass was balanced on top of his head. Cyril, as he was called, was the young man who had fallen in the fountain the previous summer, and Tess found him as unappealing sober as she had done drunk. She knew the two brothers didn't get on but she'd still expected David to be best man. When she heard he wasn't even coming over from France for the wedding she blamed herself, since it seemed obvious he couldn't bring himself to watch his brother, scion of a great family, marry a common factory girl. Because that was how David ultimately viewed her, she knew that now, in spite of his great kindnesses to her.

There was a burst of applause as Rupert successfully concluded his trick and Tess could see that it might develop into one of those parties, the sort that went on all night. She edged her way to the door. I'll just slip quietly away. Nobody called her back and she soon reached the sanctuary of her bedroom. Collapsing on the bed she gave a loud uninhibited yawn.

Tomorrow, or the day after, she and Rupert would go down to Elms Court to await the birth of the baby. Then she'd come back here, take up her life with Virginia, and she and Rupert need never impinge on each other again ... unless, of course, she thought sleepily, the baby was a girl ... but before the implications of that had hit her she was fast asleep.

18

Her personal maid was lighting the gas when she awoke. Tess stretched lazily and rubbed her eyes. 'What time is it, Ethel?'

'Nine o'clock, madam.' The young woman adjusted the gas flame then busied herself lining up brushes, tweaking drawn curtains into order and piling coal on an already roaring fire.

'Gosh, I've been asleep for three hours.'

Ethel came and stood by the bed. 'Well, it has been a rather tiring day for you, madam, hasn't it?'

'I suppose it has,' answered Tess and stretched again.

'Shall I help you to undress, madam?'

'No, thank you, Ethel.' Then when the young woman looked hurt, 'But you can run me a bath if you like.'

'And bring you up a hot milky drink and brush your hair?' the girl asked hopefully. 'You know how you like me to brush your hair,' she added persuasively.

'Just run my bath,' Tess spoke firmly. 'Then you can go.' Ethel's face fell but, doing as she was told, went into the adjoining bathroom and as steam began to seep under the door, Tess wondered how long it would take to get used to, or even accept, being waited on hand and foot.

Ethel had been with her just three weeks. She had come from a reputable domestic agency, had impeccable testimonials and had been engaged by Tess herself. This last task had been at Virginia's insistence.

'It will be good experience for you, Tess. You'll be engaging staff a lot in the future. Let me give you one word of advice, though, pick the plainest girl you can find. Pretty ones have a habit of running off and getting married just as you have them trained in your ways.'

Well, with her small, currant-black eyes embedded in

a face puffy as well-risen dough, Ethel was certainly plain, poor girl. But she was also the soul of moral rectitude and so discreet she hadn't once alluded to Tess's pregnancy. She didn't even seem to find it strange that on the first night of their marriage, she and Rupert were sleeping in separate bedrooms. However, her outstanding attribute as far as Tess was concerned was her ability to deal with Mrs Bradshaw.

Poor Mrs Bradshaw. There she was, thinking she'd seen the last of Tess, then a few months later she's back, heavily pregnant and, unforgivably, about to marry her beloved Rupert! No longer able to address cutting remarks to Tess, she tried sharpening her tongue on Ethel instead. But here she had met her match.

Tess had heard their verbal tussle in the hall one day with Mrs Bradshaw barking out an order and Ethel answering in a voice equally as acid as the housekeeper's. 'Madam tells me what to do, nobody else.'

There'd been a shocked silence, an audible indrawing of breath, then, 'How dare you speak to me like that ... you ... you chit of a girl.' Tess had been delighted to hear Ethel answer, 'I'll speak to you in exactly the same way as you speak to me. If you want me to keep a civil tongue in my head you'd best do the same.' And after this exchange, Tess, who found her maid's constant solicitude rather wearing, began to warm to the girl.

Swinging her legs clumsily off the bed, Tess stood up and began unbuttoning her beige silk wedding dress, hand made and cunningly draped to hide her burgeoning figure. But she'd hardly undone the first button when Ethel came bustling back into the room. 'Now madam, I'll do that for you.'

'I'm really quite capable of doing it myself, thank you. You can go now, Ethel, good night.'

'You're sure you don't want a drink?'

'No, nothing.'

But the maid continued to hover. 'Oh ... well, good night then, madam.' As the door closed behind her Tess gave an enormous sigh of relief, let the dress fall in a defiant,

271

untidy heap and then kicked it away with her toe, trying not to think that the cost of it would have fed a family in Bethnal Green for a year. Stepping into the bath, she lay regarding her swollen belly with distaste. How much longer had she to carry this lump around with her? Not more than a few weeks, surely. If she got any larger, she'd have trouble walking. She had a leisurely soak then, getting out, wrapped her bulk in a large towel. Using the corner of it, she rubbed away the steam from the mirror and was reassured by her reflection. At least her face was all right even if the rest of her wasn't up to much at the moment. In fact her skin, dewy and pink from the steam, had never looked better, while her hair hung in damp ringlets around her shoulders. She was rubbing cologne on to her skin when she heard the bedroom door open and close. Tess gave an exasperated sigh. Not Ethel back again. Hadn't that girl got a life of her own? Prolonging her toilet, she cleaned her teeth, brushed her hair vigorously and then pulled a pretty oyster satin and lace nightdress over her head, delighting in the feel of it against her skin. 'A Lady, who'd have thought it,' she said to her image in the mirror, and then giggled at the whole preposterous idea of it.

Hearing no sound and deciding Ethel must have gone, Tess opened the door cautiously and the last person she expected to see that evening rose to greet her.

'Oh . . . oh, it's you, Rupert,' she said guardedly, wondering what he was doing in a long, frogged, silk dressing gown so early in the evening.

'Were you expecting someone else then, my dear?'

'Only my maid,' Tess retorted sharply, nettled by the implication that she behaved like him and his friends. 'Was there something you wanted?' Her manner was cool, distant.

'Only a few kind words from my wife,' Rupert answered. He sat down on the chaise longue and held out his hand to her. 'Come and keep me company.'

Ignoring his invitation, Tess put her hand to her mouth in an exaggerated yawn. 'I'm sorry, Rupert, but I am very tired, it's been a long day and as you can see I'm ready for bed.' Since she'd managed to avoid being alone with Rupert in the few weeks prior to their marriage, Tess saw no reason why it shouldn't continue that way. Besides, surely he hadn't forgotten the terms of their marriage already. 'Why aren't you at your club?' she continued. Or with your mistress, she thought to herself, and then wondered what she was like. Was she that beautiful, imperious creature she'd seen him riding with in Hyde Park? Most probably, she decided and felt a stab of jealousy. With her air of breeding, she was certainly Rupert's type of woman.

Rupert considered her remark for a moment before answering. 'I thought, since it was the first night of our marriage it might be more appropriate if I spent it with you.'

'Oh, you don't have to worry about me,' Tess hastily assured him, alarmed at the implication of this statement.

Tess had never been able to understand why Rupert should even consider marrying her. He'd desired her once, briefly, and then left her. It had never occurred to her in all that time that perhaps his feelings ran deeper than mere desire; that the reason for his abrupt flight had been fear of emotional involvement. Managing to maintain a patient expression, Rupert stood up, took his wife's hand and led her to the chaise longue.

As she sat down, Tess primly adjusted her voluminous nightdress, then asked, 'Has everyone gone?'

'Yes, I threw them out hours ago. I've been in to see you several times but you were dead to the world.'

'How did my mother seem when she left?'

'Remarkably cheerful. Do you know, I think she's taken quite a shine to me, although of course, it could be the deeds to that house in Hackney that made her regard me in a more favourable light.'

Tess had quite forgotten about the house in the turmoil of the day. It was one she and Virginia had driven out to look at quite recently, newly built and complete with bathroom, parlour and very modern kitchen.

'Do you think your mother will like it?' Virginia had asked as they were shown round by the builder. Since the villa was the epitome of luxury and therefore beyond her mother's most optimistic dreams, it was a question that hardly needed to be asked. Whether she would accept such a gift was entirely a different matter, of course. Now it seemed that she had.

'She hasn't forgiven me yet,' said Tess bitterly, remembering her mother's coldness at the wedding. 'I have to be made to pay for my fall from grace.'

'I shouldn't worry, babies have a remarkable ability to heal rifts. And she said before she left that she wanted to know immediately her first grandchild was born. Which shouldn't be long, looking at you.' Rupert placed a hand on her rounded belly, massaging it gently. 'He's a hefty little beggar, isn't he?'

It was a sharp reminder of just how gross she must look to him. 'Yes, I hate looking like this, being ugly,' Tess burst out petulantly.

Rupert lifted her chin so that she was gazing straight into his eyes. 'Don't say that. You're as beautiful now as I've ever seen you.' He pulled her closer, running his finger lightly around the full line of her mouth, and immediately that old familiar charge went through her so that when he murmured huskily, 'Come and sit on my lap,' she went willingly, already in the thrall of his dark compelling eyes that made no secret of his desire for her.

Slipping the low-cut nightgown down over her shoulders he moved his lips and tongue lightly but skilfully over her soft skin, over her shoulders and neck and her heavy breasts. With a shiver of delight, Tess closed her eyes and when he drew her head down and covered his mouth with hers, she was no longer capable of protest. Pulling impatiently at her nightdress, his hand slid between her thighs, caressing her into a frantic response. Underneath his dressing gown Rupert was naked and as it fell open, Tess could feel him hard and erect against her. Easing her round and away from him, he entered her and there was silence except for her erratic breathing and the slight creaking of the chaise longue as with his hands pressed down on her thighs, he moved insistently inside her.

Unexpectedly and sharply she felt a pincer-like pain in her lower abdomen, then a second spasm and another accompanied this time by a tearing sensation at the base of her spine. With a frightened cry, Tess pulled herself away from Rupert and, bent almost double, stumbled to the bed.

Rupert started up from the chaise in alarm, and through the great waves of pain she was dimly aware of his voice, vibrating with terror. 'What is it, Tess? What's the matter?'

'The baby . . . I think it's coming,' she gasped.

'Oh my God, what can I do?'

'Fetch someone, quickly,' she managed to order as the contractions momentarily lessened their grip. 'The doctor, Mrs Bradshaw, anyone . . .'

Bells summoned, there was a sound of running feet and frightened voices. Between her legs there was the sensation of something large, and Tess felt an uncontrollable urge to push. The contractions were fierce now and through the sweating waves of pain she was aware of Mrs Bradshaw standing over her, still in her nightcap. But the safe delivery of her baby had become the most important thing in the universe. Gathering up all her strength she bore down, there was one more great searing contraction, and on what felt like a great gush of water the baby emerged and Mrs Bradshaw only just managed to catch the slippery mass before it slid to the floor.

Through a pain-induced haze she then heard Rupert's voice and saw his frightened, excited face. 'Dear God, there's another little bugger coming,' and as Mrs Bradshaw pressed down on her, a second infant was ejected protesting into an uncertain world.

Recognizing the doctor's voice as, too late, he swept into the room and began issuing orders, Tess struggled to hold on. She lifted her head weakly from the pillow. 'What are they?' she asked, as the doctor severed the cord and the afterbirth was taken away.

'A wee boy and a wee girl,' Dr Henderson answered.

Tess sank back on the pillows. 'Twins?' Then fearfully: 'They're not dead, are they?'

'Good heavens, no, alive and kicking,' replied the doctor, snapping his black bag shut. 'A wee bit on the small side like all premature babies, but they'll soon catch up.' He leaned over her. 'Now don't worry, Mrs Bradshaw is looking after them and they're in capable hands. You just get some sleep.'

'How do you feel, my dear?' Rupert reached for her hand as she opened her eyes, a look of anxious solicitude on his gaunt, unshaven face.

'A lot thinner,' Tess answered with a smile. Then as she gazed round the room, 'But where are my babies?' She'd expected to have them sleeping in their cots beside her and she was impatient to see them, anxious to check that they really were all right.

'They're with Mrs Bradshaw. She'll bring them down shortly but there's something I want to say to you first about last night. I feel such a selfish brute subjecting you to my advances like that. You might have died.'

Rupert contrite and humble was such a new experience Tess felt compelled to reassure him. She lifted her hand and rubbed it across the black stubble with a feeling almost of affection. 'Don't worry, Rupert. I might not have come with much to commend me but at least I'm bred from hardy stock. We hurried their entry into the world, that was all. There can't be many couples who produce twins on their honeymoon, it must be some sort of record. And now that you have a son and heir and your settlement, you must be a happy man.'

'I'm equally happy to have a daughter, and the settlement is unimportant.' He stroked the black curls away from her face, then leaning forward, kissed her tenderly on both cheeks. When she pushed him away he looked faintly surprised.

'Rupert,' she said thoughtfully, 'I have now fulfilled my obligation to you – and the arrangement was, we went our separate ways.'

'I've no plans to dash off, if that's what you mean. Why we haven't even decided on names for the babies yet. The there's the baptism, and a nanny to be found. It will all have to be arranged.'

Tess shrugged. 'Well, there is all that to be settled, of course, but after that . . .'

'Yes?' Rupert's tone was wary.

'. . . Virginia and I have talked this over and I want to help the women who work in the East End sweatshops, try and organize them into some sort of union.'

Rupert stood up abruptly. 'Why is Ginny always putting these damn silly ideas in your head?' he demanded loudly and began striding up and down the room.

'They are not damn silly ideas,' Tess answered through clenched teeth, fighting to keep her temper under control. 'And it's something I'm determined to do.'

'You are a wife and mother now. You have other duties, duties to me and your babies.'

Tess was speechless. Of all the nerve, she thought, and then found her voice. 'I don't intend to live with you as your wife. You lead your life, I lead mine, that was the agreement and you're trying to interfere already, it's unreasonable.' She began to sound tearful.

He turned away from her and she waited for the great explosion of anger. But when he finally did speak, his voice was quiet and controlled. 'You're quite right, I am being unreasonable. It's just that I had hoped we might work something out between us. I see now you don't even want to try.'

'Family life would bore you in two days, Rupert,' Tess said gently but realistically to his unresponsive back.

He turned to face her again, his usually expressive features cold and remote. 'Very well, I shall do as you wish and remove myself from your life as soon as possible.'

Well I never, thought Tess as the door slammed behind him. It wasn't enough to have an heir, a mistress and a settlement, he wanted to dabble in domesticity as well – until the novelty palled. She, in the meantime, would have grown used to having a husband around, and as her affection for him grew the sexual desire Rupert felt for her now would grow stale, because nothing held his interest for long. Soon he'd be out filly-hunting and seeking other diversions while she was left with the pain of jealousy and rejection. She shook her head to cast away any lingering doubts. No, she couldn't stand that, no matter how strongly she felt drawn to him physically. But she was never very resolute where Rupert was concerned, and when the bedroom door opened again, her lips parted in an indulgent smile.

But it was Ethel, and by the look of her anxious to take control. 'How are you this morning, madam?' she asked, tucking in the bedclothes firmly and anchoring Tess to the bed.

'Well enough to get up,' replied Tess, loosening the sheets around her again.

Ethel looked aghast. 'Oh, you can't do that, madam. You must rest for a few days, you've been through quite an ordeal.'

Tess thought of all the women she knew, women like her mother, who only a few hours after a difficult labour and birth, weak, tired and undernourished, would still be back working at a factory bench or scrubbing floors. But Ethel must know women like this too and Tess wondered if she ever thought about the divisions between rich and poor or questioned the morality of it. Possibly not, for Ethel was a regular churchgoer and, as Tess remembered from an incident when she was at school, the clergy were concerned to see that the working classes didn't get above themselves.

It had been during a scripture lesson when, for the benefit of a visiting curate, the class had been singing 'All Things Bright and Beautiful'. When they'd finished the young cleric had asked them if they had any questions to ask about Jesus, and Tess had been the only one to put up her hand.

The curate smiled at her benevolently. 'Yes, little girl.'

'Please, sir,' she'd piped innocently, 'it says in that hymn that God made some men 'igh and some lowly. Now why should 'e do that?' These words had genuinely puzzled Tess for some time, and she waited bright-eyed for his answer.

278

The smile went from the cleric's face and he regarded her sternly. 'My dear child, it is quite obvious that some of us are infinitely more superior than others. God ordained it that way, quite rightly I think, and it is not for us to question his ways. And be warned,' he continued, waving an admonishing finger at her, 'to think otherwise would be extremely dangerous.'

She'd been given detention that day and kept in after school for her cheek, but in spite of the curate's dire warning, Tess *had* continued to think otherwise. But she doubted whether Ethel asked herself such questions. Certainly, looking at her as she stood primly awaiting orders by the bed, she didn't appear to be a girl smouldering with revolutionary ideas. 'Is there anything I can get you, madam?'

'Yes, my babies. It doesn't seem to have occurred to anyone that I would like to see them – and feed them.'

Ethel's pale eyebrows nearly vanished into her hairline. '*Feed* them, madam?' Disbelief rang in every syllable. 'But they have a wet nurse.'

'And who said they were to have a wet nurse?' Tess demanded icily.

'Why . . . no one . . . we . . . Mrs Bradshaw and me . . . just assumed . . .' Ethel spluttered lamely.

'Well, you both assumed wrong. My babies were born early, they need a mother's milk. And knowing the habits of these wet nurses, they're more likely to be supping gin from her than milk.'

'Oh no, this woman's very respectable,' Ethel assured her.

'Get rid of her just the same and tell Mrs Bradshaw to bring them down to me. Immediately,' Tess instructed, feeling a certain pleasure in being able to put Mrs Bradshaw in her place.

But when the housekeeper did enter the bedroom carrying two flannel-wrapped bundles, there was actually a smile on her flinty features.

Tess reached out her arms eagerly, hungrily. 'Let me see them.'

279

'They're still asleep,' Mrs Bradshaw whispered, handing over one of the bundles. 'Isn't he the image of the Master?' she simpered. Tess gazed down at the crumpled red features of her son with his black fuzz of hair, and searched in vain for any resemblance to Rupert. 'He's so tiny,' she exclaimed in awe.

'They both weigh five pounds, which isn't a bad weight.'

When Tess had her son tucked safely into her arm, Mrs Bradshaw handed over her daughter who resembled no one but her twin brother. But she did briefly open her eyes, which were blue and unfocused. Then she yawned, her small, pink mouth opening like a flower, and Tess was overcome with such a feeling of tenderness she thought she might cry.

She wanted Mrs Bradshaw to go now, to leave her alone with her babies, but she didn't quite have the courage to dismiss her. So the housekeeper continued to hover, obviously feeling Tess was a totally inadequate mother. Fortunately Rupert made a timely reappearance, which left Mrs Bradshaw with no choice but to leave.

Tess was half expecting him to continue with their earlier argument but instead he sat down in a chair, his chin resting on his hands, his expression thoughtful. Finally he spoke. 'I've been thinking about what you said and of course, you're right, I'm not cut out for the tedium of married life. However, I shall still want to see my children and be involved in their lives, which means you and me spending some time together. Otherwise I won't impose on you in any other way. Do you feel you will be able to accommodate me to this extent, my dear wife?' He smiled but his voice had a cutting edge.

'You have every right to see the children, they're as much yours as mine.' Tess kept her tone brisk but in the deep recesses of her heart she grieved that she hadn't the courage to commit herself to Rupert totally.

'Good.' Rupert slapped his knee with satisfaction and stood up. 'That's what I like, amicable compromise. No point in fighting.' Moving to the bed he bent down and lifted one of the babies from Tess's tired arms. 'Blowed if I know which one is which,' he said, holding it gingerly.

'That's the little boy you're holding,' said Tess, who had no difficulty in telling them apart.

'I think it's about time the little tinkers had names, don't you? Have you any preference?'

'I like the name Caroline.'

'Sounds fine to me. What about the boy?'

'You choose his name.'

'How about William?'

'Caroline and William,' Tess mused. 'Yes, the names seem to go well together.'

'At least something's been settled to our mutual satisfaction.' Rupert handed William back to Tess. 'If it's all right with you, I'll go ahead and make arrangements for them to be baptized down at Elms Court.'

But his wife's dark head was bent to her babies and she wasn't listening to what he said. Standing by the door, he saw her rapt expression and, knowing he was excluded from that love, Rupert was gripped by an intense feeling of jealousy. Childishly he rattled the door handle to try and gain her attention. Tess looked up, caught his expression and was surprised. Rupert jealous, surely not, at least not of her.

As it was the twins weren't baptized until late June because, although Caroline forged healthily ahead, gaining weight by the day, William lagged some way behind and Tess worried over him constantly. In the end, Dr Henderson suggested some country air might do him good and Tess removed them swiftly to Elms Court. Shortly afterwards they were baptized in the small village church of St Peter's where the souls of their ancestors lay at rest.

It was a strictly family affair with none of Rupert's carousing friends. Florence, Pip and Tom came down and to Tess's surprise and delight, David turned up unexpectedly.

Tess had to acknowledge that Rupert had been entirely accurate in his prediction about babies healing rifts. As soon as Florence set eyes on her grandchildren and Tess saw her face relax into a rare expression of tenderness, she knew she was about to be forgiven for her unfortunate moral lapse.

There was a small luncheon party after the christening and Tess noticed that although Tom turned food over on his plate, nothing actually went in his mouth. She would have to speak to Florence about it, surely she must see how ill her son was looking. She was still watching Tom out of the corner of her eye when Pip stood up and tapped his glass for silence, then, embarrassed by his own presumption, he took a quick sip of water.

'I have an announcement to make,' he said at last and smiled down at Florence who was staring fixedly at her plate. 'Today I consider myself a most fortunate man, for Florence has agreed to become my wife.' Beaming, he sat down again and amid everyone's congratulations and good wishes he leaned over and kissed his bride-to-be soundly on the cheek.

'Arthur, really!' Florence exclaimed, but without much conviction.

It wasn't news that was totally unexpected but it still gladdened Tess's heart. Getting up she rushed round the table and gave her mother an enormous hug. 'Oh Mum, I am pleased.'

'It's for practical reasons only. It wouldn't be respectable, me and Arthur living in that posh house together and not wed, it would start tongues wagging. After all, Hackney's not like Bethnal Green, it matters how you behave there.'

'Whatever the reasons, I'm glad anyway,' Tess said, and moved on to speak to Pip. She had already decided to say nothing to Florence about Tom that day, so she had to get him alone and tackle him herself.

'I can't afford to put on weight, Tess.' Tom's voice was irritable and he was dismissive of her concern. 'Every ounce counts in this game.'

'You're just skin and bones. Can't you see what you're doing to yourself?'

'Tess, don't fuss. I don't tell you how to run your life and I'm not your little brother any longer. I'm a grown man, I make my own decisions.'

He was right, of course, he was too old for a clip round the ear, but she watched him walk away with a mixture of exasperation and love. When her family left she had to blow her nose hard several times, then remembered David was staying, and cheered up a bit. In fact he seemed in no hurry to leave Elms Court at all, developed a great interest in his nephew and niece and would entertain them for hours.

Watching him one day as they sat on the lawn together with the twins, Tess thought a trifle wistfully what a marvellous father he would have made. Not that Rupert was a bad one, but since he was not a person to deny himself any pleasure, he was often an absent one. But that was the arrangement, she told herself firmly, and she couldn't quarrel with it.

David was leaning over Caroline trying to amuse her with a silver rattle and as she clutched at the air, trying to grab it, Tess was struck by the likeness between the two of them. 'Do you know, I think Carrie's going to end up looking like you. She's lost all that black hair she was born with and . . .'

'Nonsense.' It was Rupert's voice and she looked up, squinting into the sun, then continued as if she hadn't been interrupted. '. . . And I think it's coming through fair.'

'I don't think Rupert could bear it if one of his children were to look like me,' said David with a chilly smile.

Smelling strongly of horses and sweat, Rupert flopped down beside them and picked up his daughter, who lay in his arms gurgling happily. He pretended to study her features intently. 'No, happily I can see no resemblance. If there was, I might be asking a few questions.' The idea seemed to cause him a great deal of mirth and David sprang to his feet, the muscles in his jaw working furiously.

'If you're going to be offensive, I'll spare you the bother of my company.'

Tess glared at her husband and then turned quickly to David, clasping his hand and shaking it persuasively. 'Don't leave yet, David, you've only just come. You haven't told me about your trip to France or anything.' If he went now she knew it would be several months before she saw him again.

'You needn't go on my behalf, old man,' Rupert said carelessly. 'I'm off to London anyway this afternoon. My wife prefers anyone's company to mine.'

283

'Please . . . stay,' Tess pleaded, ignoring Rupert's remark.

'Well . . . I'll see,' said David uncertainly, his eyes moving from husband to wife. Then he turned and walked away and Tess watched him with an ache in her heart, sharing his pain. She waited until he was out of sight before she turned on her husband.

'How could you be so coarse and suggestive, say things like that in front of David . . . in front of me? I'm not one of your floozies, you know.'

'No, you're my wife, but I've seen you mooning over David. I suppose you wish you were married to him. Huh, a fat lot of good that would do you,' he jeered.

'Shut up,' she yelled back at him, 'I don't want to hear any more of your smut.' Tess felt a great churning anger and she longed to lash out at Rupert and harm him physically. She was restrained only by the fact that they were in full view of the house and she had no wish to provide a free spectacle for the servants.

Just then William, who a moment before had been lying kicking his feet in the air, began to wail. Tess snatched him up, hugging him protectively against her. 'Now look what you've done.' She glared accusingly at Rupert and stood up. 'Bring Caroline, please,' she said in a peremptory manner. 'It's time for their feed.'

Without a word of protest Rupert followed Tess across the lawn, into the house and up the stairs to her bedroom. Once there she took Caroline from him and laid her down on the bed beside William. 'You'll have to go now, I want to feed them.'

'I think I'll stay.' He sat down in a chair, immovable as a rock. 'It's not often I have the chance to enjoy these little domestic scenes.'

Tess shrugged with pretended indifference and swept past him into her dressing room to change into the peignoir she always wore when breast feeding. Although she was now weaning the twins she was glad she had fed them herself. She found it intensely satisfying and she was sure the twins had benefited immeasurably from it. With the top of her peignoir

284

loose, she went back into the bedroom and, propping a baby in either arm, sat down on a low chair with her back to her husband, while the infants hungrily sought her breasts.

Rupert immediately moved his chair so that he was sitting directly in front of her. With legs sprawled out in front of him he regarded her lazily through half-closed eyes.

Although she refused to look directly at him there was growing physical evidence that the small domestic scene was having a profoundly disturbing effect on Rupert. By the time the babies had finished their feed, they were almost asleep and Tess rang for the young nanny they had recently hired.

As soon as she had taken them away to the nursery, Rupert went and turned the key in the lock. Going over to where Tess sat, he held out both hands to her and led her to the bed. He undressed hurriedly, flinging his clothes untidily round the room, then lying down beside her, tore off the flimsy gown and with a groan, gathered her hungrily in his arms.

He was lying on top of her when the luncheon gong went but neither of them heard it. Afterwards, as she lay against his shoulder, warm, damp and naked, Tess knew it would be hopeless to fight against her love for Rupert any longer. Because no matter how much unhappiness he might cause her in the future, she was inextricably linked to him for ever.

'Are you there, madam?' The sound of Ethel's anxious voice through the locked door and her insistent tapping made Tess start guiltily.

Easing herself up on one elbow she called back, 'I'm just resting, Ethel,' and Rupert gave her such a knowing wink, she had to stuff her hand in her mouth to gag her laughter.

'But you haven't been down to luncheon . . .' the maid whined.

Tess glanced at the ormolu clock on the chimneypiece. 'Good heavens, it's three o'clock,' she hissed at Rupert. And then to Ethel: 'I wasn't hungry.'

'Only for her husband,' Rupert growled, and then grabbing her, started nibbling the lobe of her ear.

Tess giggled audibly and half-heartedly pushed him away. There was a short silence and Tess was sure Ethel had her ear pressed against the door.

'I could bring you something up on a tray.'

'Perhaps later, Ethel,' replied Tess patiently, thinking to herself that if there were any medals going for persistence then surely Ethel would win one.

'Well, if you're quite sure . . .' The maid's voice sounded doubtful but eventually they heard her walk away.

'You didn't have to tell her lies, you know,' Rupert said after she'd gone. 'We're not doing anything illegal and we are husband and wife.'

'In the middle of the day though, she'd probably consider that highly improper.' Tess started searching around amongst the crumpled sheets for her peignoir. 'Anyway I'd better get up.'

'Not just yet, you're not,' Rupert said, pulling her back down beside him. Tess tried to wriggle free but he pinned her to the bed so that it was another hour before she finally got up and ran a bath.

When she went back into the bedroom Rupert was still lying stretched out on the bed and smoking a strongly smelling Turkish cigarette. He blew three smoke rings into the air, admired their brief perfection and then without turning said, 'I think I'll take Hector out again. Are you coming?'

It was a casual request, and after several hours of Rupert's ardour she hardly felt like getting on to a horse. But she had been made vulnerable by her need for him and she knew just how easily he fell prey to boredom. If she couldn't provide the diversions Rupert needed, then he would find them elsewhere, probably with unsuitable friends in London. At present she had youth and passion, potent weapons with which to hold on to him, but always now there would be that uncertainty, the constant fear of losing him; and when they were apart, she would never be quite sure who he was with. Tess began to understand the painful cost of loving. Resenting this dependence, she watched as he finished his

286

cigarette and flicked it into the empty fireplace. Did he love her? He never said so and her own pride wouldn't allow her to ask. Anyway, perhaps hopeful ignorance was preferable to brutal truth.

He rolled off the bed and, picking up strewn clothing, started to dress. 'Well,' he said, his voice muffled as he pulled his shirt over his head, 'shall I get Johnson to saddle Poppy for you?'

'That sounds a very good idea, Rupert.' She forced herself to sound enthusiastic.

'Good,' he said, looking pleased with her. 'I'll see you in the stableyard in about a quarter of an hour.' Giving her a quick kiss, he unlocked the door and then swore profusely as he collided with Ethel carrying a large tray.

Rupert's profanities produced a slight trembling of Ethel's lower lip as she placed the tray on the table. To pacify her, Tess swallowed some cake and tea and even allowed Ethel to help her into her riding habit. When she was dressed, Tess stood studying herself critically in the mirror, lifting her chin, pulling in her bottom and splaying her fingers across her flat belly. Not bad, she thought, her figure was almost back to normal. And that was how she intended to stay. Then she remembered the last few hours and prayed there was some truth in the story that a nursing mother couldn't conceive.

But she shouldn't be standing here admiring herself, Rupert was probably already down in the stables, and he soon grew impatient. Adjusting her hat, she ran swiftly down the stairs and out through the side door that led to the yard. She'd expected to see the horses already saddled and Rupert and Johnson waiting for her. But Hector and Poppy were still in their boxes and the yard was empty. Where was everyone? She spun round on her heels feeling slightly perplexed.

Hearing a slight noise from the tack room, Tess moved lightly across to the door, thinking to herself that it was probably Billy and Johnson brewing up again. As she stood poised on the threshold waiting for her pupils to adjust to the light, she heard irregular, heavy breathing. Stepping down inside she saw, pressed against the wall amid the clutter of harnesses and saddles, the figures of two men, who turned to stare at her in slack-mouthed sweating surprise. At the sight of flapping shirt tails and bare flesh, Tess froze. Then knowing there was something appallingly wrong she started to back out of the door while the two men hastily bent to grab their trousers which were concertinaed incongruously around their ankles. Whimpering like an animal in pain, Tess turned and, stumbling over the step, fled across the yard, hounded by something unspeakable but only dimly understood.

She reached the corner of the house and cannoned so violently against Rupert he had to put out his hands to steady her. 'What's the matter?' he asked when he saw her white, stricken face. But great rasping sobs tore at her throat and she could only roll her head from side to side.

He gave her a slight shake. 'Tell me what's happened?'

Still sobbing and with a terrible feeling of betrayal, she pointed to the tack room. 'It's ... David ... over there ... with a footman.'

'What?' With a roar, Rupert pushed her aside, negotiating the yard in a couple of strides. The screams were terrible but even worse was the sound of riding crop on bare flesh.

'Oh no, oh no,' she moaned and, unable to endure the pitiful pleas for mercy any longer, she pinned her hands against her ears and fled across the park. When she reached the sanctuary of the lake, she fell on her hands and knees and was violently sick. Then sobbing and retching she crawled to a tree and, unable to cope with the implications of what she had just seen, lapsed into a semi-conscious state. And that was where Rupert found her almost an hour later. Picking his wife up in his arms, he carried her back to her room. Here he sat her in a chair, washed her hands and face and then poured a brandy which she was ordered to drink.

Neither of them spoke and in the lengthening, brooding silence, Tess glared at her husband with a hostile expression. She had blanked out most of what had happened that afternoon, except for the beating and David's screams. Everything now had become Rupert's fault. Unable to contain herself any longer she blurted out, 'You shouldn't have done that, you know.' Her voice held a high accusing note and Rupert turned from filling his glass with a puzzled expression.

'Done what?' he asked.

'Thrashed David so brutally. I think you enjoyed it. In fact I think it's something you've been wanting to do for a long time. I know you've never liked him.'

Rupert looked flabbergasted. 'Have you any idea at all what he was up to with that servant?'

She didn't answer and her expression was so sullen and unresponsive, Rupert wanted to shake her. He put down his glass and, yanking her to her feet, glared at her fiercely. 'Well, I shall tell you anyway. I know you've always had a soft spot for David but you're wasting your time.' His face was hardly an inch from Tess's now and he enunciated each word carefully. 'You see, he doesn't like women, in fact they disgust him – even you, my dear Tess. What he does like is to bugger boys, the rougher the better.' He shook her. 'Do you understand what I am talking about?'

The tears welled up in Tess's eyes and she thought she might be sick again but still she refused to answer.

'Well, we'll use the biblical term, shall we? David, my brother, is a sodomite.'

Tess began to beat her fists against Rupert's chest. 'Stop it! Stop it!' she screamed hysterically.

'No, I will not stop it, you'll hear me to the end. I've been prepared to put up with David's sordid little practices as long as he conducts them in private. What I will not tolerate is him seducing the servants, and in public. A whipping was too good for him, he should be in prison. Virginia and I are forever bailing him out of trouble, paying off blackmailers, but that's the last time.'

Tess wiped her eyes and blew her nose. 'But what will become of him?' Why two men should want to have sex together or even how they had it was a mystery to her. She had a vision of David destitute, burdened with a terrible guilt and without family or friends.

289

'Don't worry yourself, he'll go running to Virginia. She's always protected him since he was a little boy. Probably arrange for him to take another trip abroad until things cool down.' He gave a contemptuous snort. 'But he'd better not show his face here again.'

As Rupert spoke, fragments of the past came back to Tess. The lowly young men who turned up regularly at the Settlement, David's rather hasty departure for France the previous year and Virginia's insistence that she and Rupert should be married. She understood the reason for that now. She had been made pregnant by Rupert and in spite of her background her fertility was assured. A barren wife, even an aristocratic one, might have been a blow from which the family would never recover.

In their own way, all three of them had used and exploited her. But she was part of that clan now, her children even more so, and she understood their motives. After all a dynasty had to be maintained, even if the cracks were beginning to show in its structure.

19

Tess sat on the terrace at Elms Court trying to enjoy the late October sun but, instead, counting the weeks on her fingers and doing some quick mental arithmetic. Five-month-old Thomas lay in the nursery with the twins and if her calculations were right, a brother or sister would be joining them in seven months' time. That would make four children in only four years of marriage. Rupert, of course, would be delighted, he considered it quite natural that his wife should be filling the nursery with healthy, lusty St Clairs.

But she had other ideas. Tess loved her children and her husband, deeply, but she loathed pregnancy; the sickness and general malaise seemed to sap her creative energy and reduce her to a bovine passivity. So she'd made a decision; after this there would be no more. Tess was entirely ignorant as to how she might achieve this blissful state, but she had implicit faith in Sarah's knowledge of such matters and had already made up her mind to have a quiet word with her friend about it, without bothering to let Rupert know.

In marriage and parenthood, Rupert had discovered a role that suited him perfectly and he pursued the life of country squire and paterfamilias with the same dedication he'd given to being a man about town. He delighted in the company of his family, spent hours playing with the children and had sat the twins on ponies almost as soon as they could walk. He saw no reason either why Tess shouldn't be content in her role of wife and mother. And by and large she was, although there were restrictions she couldn't have dreamed of. She had nothing in common with the local stuffy gentry, who bored her with their talk of shoots and hunting, and in the early days of her marriage, entertaining had been an ordeal.

To remember one such encounter could still make her smart. Mrs Compton-Brown and her daughter, Phoebe, had called one afternoon. Tess quickly gathered by her manner that Mrs Compton-Brown had seen Rupert as a possible husband for her daughter. Phoebe had a large inheritance coming her way, although she had little else to commend her, being both ugly and fat. But Mrs Compton-Brown was piqued that a mere secretary had carried away the prize and she condescended just as much as she dare.

Tea had arrived while they were there so Tess was obliged to offer them some. She'd been called away briefly by a worried nursemaid, and when she returned she could hear them discussing her through the half-open door. They made no effort to lower their voices and she stood listening, clenching and unclenching her hands and wanting to throttle them both.

'She tries to hide it, but there's definitely a cockney accent there.'

'Breeding counts for nothing these days, Mama,' mumbled Phoebe, through a mouthful of cake.

'I know she was pregnant, but why on earth did Rupert marry *her*? He could have easily paid her off.'

'I'll tell you why he married me,' muttered Tess, 'for sex. He likes doing it to me. Frequently. He likes my naked body and watching me undress makes him randy as a goat, which is something you, poor Phoebe, with your bad complexion and pendulous breasts, could never do.'

Tess longed to march in and proclaim these facts in crude, gutter language and she was tempted, just for the pleasure of seeing their scandalized faces. But she knew she couldn't, she was Lady St Clair now and must choose her words carefully. So instead, she coughed slightly and when she pushed open the door, her smile was bright even if a trifle fixed. However, even though a lady, Tess was still no hypocrite, and she made sure she never returned the Compton-Browns' call or invited them again to the house.

As well as weathering those early days of social unease, she'd also had to cope with her often stormy relationship with Rupert. He'd made it quite clear, soon after they were married, that he didn't want to hear any more 'damn silly nonsense about the enfranchisement of women', and he was quite likely to fly into a rage against Virginia, her hairbrained schemes and the unsettling influence she had on his wife. Tess was quite as strong-willed as Rupert, but she tried to avoid incurring his wrath, which could be alarming. Any object could go flying, punctuated by obscenities even Tess was unfamiliar with. He calmed down as quickly as he flared up, then, slightly ashamed, he would take her in his arms and apologize. But Tess never enjoyed these eruptions, even when they were resolved in bed. So she occasionally escaped to London and Virginia. Here, well away from Rupert's ears, the two sisters would gossip all afternoon about the movement and Virginia's book, which was now finished and about to be published. And when Tess came back from London, she would bring with her articles and pamphlets, carefully stuffing them away behind bookcases and cabinets like a secret drinker.

Also during the past year there had been the tragic but inevitable consequences of Tom's dieting to cope with. Her mother's frantic letter had come as no surprise. Tom had purged himself with castor oil so frequently and denied himself proper food for so long, he'd eventually collapsed. Pip had gone to Suffolk to fetch him, and found Tom so frail he'd had to carry him into his mother's house.

But even Tess was unprepared for the wraith-like figure lying in the bed, his complexion the same colour as the linen sheets. The whole situation reminded her so vividly of Milly, she knew her brother must be dying.

But his family weren't going to let that happen. Florence called in an apothecary who, being an honest man, insisted Tom needed nothing more than nourishing food. Starting him on a very light diet, they fed him calf's-foot jelly and beef tea, and as Tom grew a little stronger, steamed fish and breast of chicken. Because of his lack of flesh, he got bed sores which had to be dressed and since he hadn't the strength to move, he had to be turned constantly.

With all the worry of it Florence lost weight, so as soon as Tom had some flesh back on his bones and was able to walk, Tess took him back down to Elms Court with her to convalesce. Here he'd spent all his time in the stables with Johnson. But all the hard work in restoring him to full health seemed a waste of time when he told Tess he was going back to racing.

Angry at his stupidity, Tess remonstrated with him. But Tom was adamant. 'It's all I can do, Tess, and I've got used to the money.'

'You'll kill yourself next time, Tom,' she warned. 'Please, none of that stupid dieting, for Mum's sake.'

He held up his hands in surrender. 'All right, I promise and I'll be very sensible.' And off he'd gone back to Suffolk, leaving Tess to wonder and worry about what he was getting up to.

The weak sun had now gone behind a cloud and Tess shivered and stood up. Why couldn't everything always be perfect, she thought. Why did the sun have to go in, why did Tom have to be stupid and why did she have to be pregnant again? Rupert would be pleased, of course. He'd spent the morning in the office going over accounts, a job he detested. He found sitting at a desk, worrying about money, irksome. The news that he was to be a father again would cheer him up. She'd break it to him over luncheon. Imagining his delighted reaction, Tess smiled as she climbed the stairs to the bedroom.

Unexpectedly, Rupert was there and when he turned, Tess was taken aback by the thunderous expression on his face. Then she saw that he was holding a bundle of papers, and thought, Oh Lor', he's found some leaflets. But as he waved the bundle at her, Tess saw the blue ribbon and realized they were Liam's letters, the ones he had written to her before she was married and which lay forgotten at the back of her writing desk along with the Brighton photograph.

'What are these?' Rupert demanded, thrusting the opened letters under her nose.

'You've obviously just read them, so you must know,' Tess answered coldly, and tried to snatch the package back from him. Swiftly he held the letters above his head, well out of her reach.

'This man, whoever he is, says he loves you.'

'That's right, and he wanted to marry me,' Tess answered provocatively, fuming at Rupert's invasion of her privacy.

Rupert's face went beetroot red and in one furious movement he turned and tossed the letters and photograph into the fire.

'No, don't,' screamed Tess and darted forward to retrieve the letters, which had suddenly assumed a tremendous significance. As the flames curled round the paper she picked up a poker and raked desperately at the coals, dashing her feet against the letters as they lay smouldering in the hearth.

'You stupid girl, what are you doing? You'll set yourself alight,' Rupert yelled, grabbing her arm and trying to yank her away.

'Leave me alone,' she screamed. Shaking herself free, Tess continued to stamp on the letters until they were just a few charred fragments. Then with an acute sense of loss she sorted amongst the ash with her toe, found a remnant of photograph and picked it up. Cupping it protectively against her heaving breast, she turned on her husband. 'How dare you go through my desk, pry into my personal belongings?'

Biting back an angry retort, Rupert suddenly, and with a flash of insight, saw his behaviour for what it was, childish and petty. He knew by the set of her jaw that he'd gone too far with Tess, and he struggled to contain his anger and the jealousy he felt towards the unknown young man who'd dared to make a declaration of love to *his* wife and to whom, unwittingly, he'd lost his own heart. It still surprised Rupert that since that first night when he'd so carelessly taken her to bed, his need for Tess had in no way diminished. He never deliberately engineered a row, but reconciliation always gave an exquisite edge to their lovemaking. Her earthy sexuality was a constant source of delight, her response always total, and as she stood there, angry and imperious, grey eyes flashing, Rupert felt a pleasurable stirring in his groin. He must have her. Now.

With a penitent expression he stepped forward and opened his arms. 'Come here, Tess, I'm sorry.'

Her rebuff took him totally unawares. Her back stiff with resentment, Tess walked to the door. 'Being sorry's not enough,' she answered coldly, and a shaken Rupert heard her rejection reiterated in the enraged bang of the door.

Feeling weepy and unforgiving at Rupert's jealous destructiveness and knowing she would have choked on any food, Tess went to her own small sitting room and stayed there all afternoon. The rescued scrap of photograph was a head and shoulders of Liam and herself, earnest young faces now streaked with soot. Finding some scissors, she trimmed away the curled, burnt border with care then hid it between the pages of a heavy book.

Rupert returned at six but she sat with her head in a book, studiously ignoring him. With a vexed expression he came and stood in front of her, placing a large hand over the page she was reading and forcing her to look up.

'Aren't you going to get changed for dinner?' he asked.

'You'll be dining alone tonight. I shall have something sent up on a tray,' Tess answered briefly.

The muscles began to work in Rupert's jaw. 'Tess, I've said I'm sorry but I'm damned if I'll go down on my hands and knees and beg.'

By way of rejoinder, Tess snapped the book shut on his hand.

He was furious now. 'By God, I could shake you sometimes, you're so stubborn.' He stormed out, slamming the door so violently the whole room trembled and a small Meissen shepherd parted company from his shepherdess and shattered into a thousand pieces on the floor.

'Oh no,' cried Tess, and leapt from the chair. She was particularly attached to the two small ornaments which had been a gift from Rupert on the birth of Thomas. 'You and me,' he'd said tenderly when she'd unwrapped them. She found herself sobbing quietly as she stooped to pick up the figure, smashed beyond repair.

That night, Tess had Ethel make up a spare bed in her dressing room, then very pointedly turned the key in the lock. He came and rattled the handle, calling through the door, 'Tess, this is ridiculous.'

'Go away,' she shouted back, then knew she was only punishing herself when she spent a restless night tossing and turning.

Next morning she waited until she heard him go out before emerging from her room. He was off to inspect some property that needed repairing and she knew he wouldn't be back until midday. Crossing to the window, Tess watched as he rode away across the park with his steward, observed the powerful thrust of his shoulders, the strong straight back and the way his thighs clasped and controlled the large horse.

How I do love him, she thought, and was filled with such an urgent need to express these feelings openly and make her peace with him, she hurriedly pushed open the window. With a dangerous disregard for her safety, Tess leaned out, calling after him, 'Rupert, I'm sorry, please . . . please come back,' at the same time waving frantically. But it was too late, the two men were already obscured by a hedge and her entreaties were carried away by a brisk wind.

Feeling wretched, Tess lowered the window. It had been stupid to quarrel about Liam's letters. Time and distance had blurred her affection and she felt nothing for him now.

Rupert was the only man she ever had loved – ever would love, although she always held back from telling him so. He was generous, affectionate and, as far as she knew, faithful, but she had to remind herself frequently that theirs was, after all, a marriage of convenience, for both of them, and love certainly hadn't been part of the contract.

But today she would make a gift of her love, tell him about the baby, and everything would be all right between them again. Humming to herself and impatient for Rupert's return, Tess rang for Ethel.

Anticipating their reconciliation, she sat down in front of the mirror. 'Make me look pretty, Ethel.'

So it's like that, is it, thought the prim maid, remembering the locked door. Aloud and obsequiously, she said, 'You always look pretty, madam.' And no luncheon for either of them today. Disapprovingly she teased and tweaked the dark hair before finally securing it with tortoiseshell combs . . . It didn't seem nice somehow, that sort of thing, particularly in the middle of the day . . . Still, it always put the master in a cheerful frame of mind, and often he would slip her a sovereign, which was better any day than his awesome rages.

'What dress today, madam?' the maid asked when she'd finished arranging Tess's hair.

Tess, who was rubbing eau de Cologne on to her skin, paused for a moment. 'The sage green with the leg-of-mutton sleeves, please, Ethel.' It was a dress Rupert particularly liked and he always commented on it whenever she wore it.

As she did up the back fastenings on the close-fitting bodice, Ethel's sharp eyes noticed the thickening waistline. Mmm, in the family way again, is she? She won't like that . . Could have been the cause of those tantrums last night. It's all right now, but if she goes on like this, she won't have any figure left and I wouldn't give much for her chances of holding on to him then, the girl thought spitefully as she struggled with the last hook.

Ethel hovered for so long after Tess was dressed that she felt like pushing her bodily out of the door. 'I'm going up to see the children now,' Tess said and eventually the maid went. She was just on her way upstairs to the nursery when she saw that Ethel had brought some mail in with her. I'll look at it later, Tess thought, then saw the foreign stamp and her maiden name, and almost snatched it up. She turned the envelope over and over in her hand. It was uncanny hearing from Liam like this and after so long . . what was it, four years? Fearful that the letter would cast a shadow over her reunion with Rupert, she was tempted to toss it into the flames along with the others. But curiosity got the better of her. She would read it first, then destroy

298

t. Perching herself on the window seat, Tess slit open the
nvelope.

It was soon obvious why there'd been such a prolonged
ilence. Liam had been beset with nothing but misfortune
n Africa. He'd been robbed, beaten up and when he and
is uncle had gone into the interior, they'd both succumbed
o a malarial fever from which the older man had died.
he letter ran to several pages and Tess was only halfway
hrough when she happened to glance up and saw Rupert
nd the steward riding back across the park. Her heart leapt
ith pleasure. He's come back early to see me, she thought.
orgetting Liam and his problems, she stuffed the letter into
pocket and ran downstairs and out on the terrace to wait for
er husband, waving as they approached.

But there was no answering salute from Rupert, and
s the horses drew nearer Tess noticed that he was sitting
wkwardly on Hector. He's had a fall, she thought with
ismay and was already running down the steps when the
eward called in a worried voice, 'Your Ladyship, I think
ir Rupert is ill.'

She reached them just as Rupert slid from his horse,
most falling to the ground as his legs buckled under
m.

'Whatever is the matter, darling?' Tess cried in alarm, for
stead of his normal robust colouring, Rupert's had a ghastly
eenish pallor and his face was damp with sweat.

'It's nothing . . .' Caught in mid sentence by the pain, he
utched his stomach. '. . . Just something I've eaten, no need
make a fuss.'

Barely managing to keep her voice calm, Tess turned to
e steward. 'Mr Campbell, go to the village immediately
d get the doctor. Tell him it's extremely urgent and he's
return with you.'

The man hesitated. 'Shall I help you with Sir Rupert
st?'

'Go now,' Tess commanded. 'I can manage.' Then to
pert: 'Put your arm round me, darling, I think we'd better
t you to bed.'

The steward touched his cap. 'Yes, ma'am,' and as he rode off with the two horses, Tess struggled with Rupert, who was now leaning heavily against her, up the terrace steps.

By the time she reached the house she was almost collapsing under his solid weight. She'd expected a servant to come running out to help her, but the house seemed deserted. Sitting Rupert down carefully in a chair, she flew upstairs to find his valet. Between them they got him to the bedroom, although they almost dragged him the last part of the way. Laying him down on the bed they loosened his collar and removed his boots but when Tess tried to cover him with a blanket he swore obscenely and threw the blanket away from him. His agony was terrible and as he thrashed and flailed and his features contorted in pain, Tess and the valet stared at each other helplessly across the bed, reading abject fear in each other's eyes.

But the need to do something, to relieve her husband's terrible suffering, gave Tess some sort of strength. Wringing out a towel in cold water, she sponged his sweating body. 'The doctor will be here shortly, darling, just hold on,' she whispered in his ear, willing him to stay alive for he had suddenly gone quiet and she was sure he was slipping away from her.

But where was the doctor, why was he taking so long? First she went to the window, then the door and then downstairs into the hall. Helpless and unable to bear it any longer, Tess closed her eyes and prayed. 'Please God, let the doctor come quickly ... don't let Rupert die ...' When she went back into the bedroom he was vomiting and his hands were like ice. He opened his eyes briefly and gazed at her through a confusion of pain. Tess almost lost a grip on herself then and only an enormous effort of will prevented her from collapsing in a flood of tears.

After what seemed an eternity the doctor did arrive, by which time Rupert was delirious and rambling and muttering unintelligibly. But at least the doctor's diagnosis was swift. He took Rupert's temperature, gently pressed his abdomen and asked Tess a few questions.

'The appendix is badly inflamed. We could get a surgeon out here to operate but I think it would be quicker to get him to hospital. But he must lie flat. Can you arrange for a mattress and blankets to be put on a waggon?'

Glad to be able to do something for Rupert, Tess nodded. 'I'll go now. But please, will you give him something to lessen the pain ... I ... can't bear to see him suffering like that.' She looked across at her sick husband then at the doctor, and as she placed a trembling hand on his sleeve, her eyes pleaded with him. 'He will be all right, won't he?'

Clasping her hand, the doctor spoke gently, too cautious to promise miracles but trying to sound optimistic. 'I'll ride on and alert the hospital. They have a very good surgeon there, he will do all he can for Sir Rupert. Morphine will ease his pain but we haven't a moment to lose and it's at least five miles to Chichester.'

Tess had a superstitious dread of leaving Rupert, fearing he would slip away while she was out of the room, so she was shouting her instructions to Johnson even as she crossed the yard. 'Quickly, get one of the farm waggons and bring it round to the front of the house.'

'Whatever for?' asked an astonished Johnson who had been having a quiet smoke.

'It's Sir Rupert, he's ill and we must get him to hospital. Oh hurry ... please, Mr Johnson,' she begged, weeping openly now.

'Give me five minutes,' he answered, jumping up and stamping on his cigarette, and by the time the valet had directed two servants to get a mattress and blankets downstairs, he was outside with two large Clydesdales hitched to a farm waggon.

A makeshift stretcher had been prepared and at the doctor's instruction Rupert was carried downstairs and placed carefully in the cart. The doctor rode off to alert the hospital, Tess got into the cart beside her husband and the sad little procession made its way down the drive, watched by a silent household.

The waggon, with its large wooden wheels, swayed and jolted over every stone and rut in the road, but mercifully Rupert was now heavily drugged and he lay stretched out gaunt and still under the blankets, his head resting on Tess's lap. Lifting his hand, she pressed it to her cheek staring down with blank-eyed misery at her husband's features already shrivelled and made old by pain. If only there had been some hint, some warning, she might have coped better. Where were the vitality, vigour and lustiness now? All sapped away by this terrible malady, and he seemed to be fading away in front of her eyes.

Tess looked around at the rolling countryside and clenched her fists in helpless frustration. They seemed to be miles yet from the hospital and she was suddenly aware of the slow, measured tread of the horses.

'Couldn't you persuade the horses to get a move on, Mr Johnson?' she asked impatiently, feeling she would like to take a whip to them herself.

Johnson turned and gave her a brief sympathetic glance. 'It would do more harm than good to the Master if I did. Besides, they're covering the ground more quickly than you think. See, there's the spire of the cathedral coming into view. Try not to fret, he'll be in good hands soon.'

Ten minutes later they were trundling down the hill and as the waggon turned into the forecourt of the hospital several white-robed figures came running down the steps and Rupert was lifted from the cart and carried by stretcher into the hospital. Tess ran along beside him holding his hand until they reached the doors of the operating theatre where a nursing sister barred her way.

'I'm sorry, Lady St Clair, but you can't go in there. Dr Williams is ready to operate on Sir Rupert immediately.'

'He's very ill, my husband, isn't he?' Tess's voice was so tense with emotion it barely rose above a whisper.

The nursing sister was a practical woman who had to face death and grief almost every day of her life, and she saw little point in raising false hopes. But she saw such undisguised fear in the young woman's eyes that she felt compelled reassure her. 'Dr Williams is an excellent surgeon, the best there is, he will do all he can. In the meantime the best thing you can do is to come and sit down and try and rest.' She led Tess along a green-tiled corridor and into a small office where she offered her a chair and some journals. 'I'll have to leave you now but directly there's any news, I'll let you know.'

As soon as she had gone, Tess flung the journals aside and went and stood by the window, one hand pressed to her aching throat and her body tensing each time a footfall sounded in the stone corridor.

The passage of time for her that day was marked only by tradespeople coming and going, by their commonplace, cheerful remarks drifting up from below; by the delivery of milk, bread and mail. Then a silence fell over the town, shops shut, a horse in the street had a nose bag stuffed with oats hitched to its harness and the unpalatable smell of cabbage water seeped through the hospital.

Her ears had strained all day for footsteps to slow down outside her door and yet when they did she was still taken off guard and she swung round with a startled expression when a man's voice called her name. He was tall, distinguished and silver-haired, and Tess knew immediately by the carefully composed set of his features, the mixture of gravity and sympathy, that something was wrong.

The great man stood hesitating by the door. He often felt he'd been cast in the role of God and wasn't quite up to it, and the desperate look of hope on Tess's face was almost too much for him. He took several deep breaths and with carefully measured strides, crossed the floor to her.

As he advanced, Tess shrank fearfully against the window. 'What is it?' she managed to say at last.

'I'm sorry, Lady St Clair, there is nothing we can do.' He found himself unable to look at her.

'What . . . what . . . are you saying?'

'The appendix had already ruptured and the poison was spreading through his body by the time he reached hospital.'

Tess leapt at him. 'No, no,' she screamed. 'You must do something.' She had grabbed his arm and her nails bit into his flesh. Gently he tried to release her. 'You don't know how sorry I am, but I can't. All I can do now is relieve his suffering.'

Tess closed her eyes, swaying slightly. When she opened them again she had found a sort of courage from somewhere and spoke calmly enough. 'Can I see my husband, please?'

'You realize he might not recognize you?'

'I still want to see him,' Tess repeated, and then followed the doctor down a labyrinth of corridors, past the sick and dying, but aware only of her own intolerable suffering.

A watery, almost subterranean light filtered through the dark green blinds in the room where Rupert lay, and as she stood leaning against the closed door, Tess almost gagged on the sickly smell of ether and carbolic. Her body shook with an involuntary tremor she couldn't control and she had to force herself to walk to the bed. He lay very still. His skin had the patina of wax in the dim light and only a slight movement in his chest told Tess he was still alive. Helplessly trying to curb her tears, she pressed her hands against her mouth and rocked backwards and forwards on her heels. Then finally succumbing to her grief, she sank to the floor, her head resting on the bed, and wept silent, bitter tears.

She had always sensed their time together would be brief, that tiring of her he would turn to someone else. That she could have accepted, but to be cheated of him like this, with such brutal finality . . .

A slight movement of his fingers against her temple made Tess look up. Rupert's eyes were open and they were clear and free of pain. With a reckless hope she scrambled joyously to her feet. His lips moved slightly, and desperate to hear just one word from him, she leaned over the bed.

'I . . . lo . . .' But the effort was too much for him and he closed his eyes again.

'I love you, Rupert, with all my heart. Please say you love me,' Tess pleaded, her tears falling like a benediction on his dry, cracked lips.

With a tremendous effort of will, he managed to form the words. 'I . . . love . . . you,' he breathed, and then closed his eyes with a deep sigh. It was the first time Rupert had ever told her he loved her ... It was also the last, and when Dr Williams returned a short time later, he had slipped away from her for ever.

It was the last day of October, All Hallow's Eve. Smoke rose from chimneys straight as an exclamation mark and berries, strung out along hedgerows, were brighter than a robin's breast. As a mark of respect, curtains had been drawn across windows of tenants' cottages and men stood thigh deep in autumn gardens of chrysanthemum and michaelmas daisy, heads bowed and with caps clutched self-consciously in large, calloused fists.

Even the children had ceased their games and as yet, unaware of their own mortality, hung over gates gazing in awe at the two ghastly mutes leading the cortège, at the glass-sided hearse piled high with flowers and at the black-plumed horses drawing a seemingly endless line of carriages and mourners through the narrow Sussex lanes.

But heavily veiled and immured in a world where nothing registered but her own grief, Tess saw none of this, neither the almost intolerable beauty of the day, nor the genuine sense of loss of the estate workers.

In the church she couldn't even bring herself to look up at the coffin raised on its bier, nor the stone effigies of St Clair forebears, their eyes closed for ever, like Rupert's, their hands clasped piously in prayer.

She heard nothing of the service, either in the church or afterwards when Virginia and her mother helped her to the family vault where Rupert would be interred. But throughout it all, even driving back to Elms Court, Tess maintained a steadfast dry-eyed dignity.

Even when accepting the final condolences of the mourners as they departed, Tess kept her self-control, although her complexion was the colour of alabaster against the heavy black widow's weeds.

But when the last person had finally taken his leave, she went to her room and, dismissing Ethel, locked the door and refused to see anyone – not Virginia, not her mother, not even the three children.

Although his clothes had been discreetly removed there was evidence everywhere in the room of Rupert. His brushes lay on the dressing table by hers, the Turkish cigarettes he smoked were still in their silver box and the scent of his sandalwood soap hung on the air.

Her throat tight with an unspeakable misery, Tess went and stood by the window from where, on that last day, she'd watched Rupert ride off across the park and had waited so eagerly for his return. She hadn't known then that she'd dissipated their last day together by prolonging a stupid quarrel. And now it was too late to heal the rift between them. All she had was a lifetime in which to regret all the loving words that had been left unsaid. It was too late to tell him about the baby and watch his dark eyes light up with pleasure and pride, and gratitude too for what she gave him.

But there'd be no lavish gift from Rupert when this baby was born, for she was a widow now. Such a barren word that, conjuring up a desolate landscape of empty days and cold lonely nights devoid of tenderness and the companionship of a shared bed.

Tess stood by the window for so long that birds, coming in to roost, began to darken the sky like tea leaves as they wheeled and turned in unison before settling noisily for the night. Not until the last grey splinter of light had been extinguished did she draw the curtains. Then, without bothering to undress, Tess lay down on the bed. Reaching out to the empty space beside her, she gave way to a wild anguished sobbing.

A dull, dragging pain low in her back and abdomen woke Tess from an uneasy half sleep. Instinctively she drew her legs up and pressed her hands into her sides as she did when she had painful courses. It gripped her again, but so sharply this time she let out an involuntary exclamation of painful protest. It was pitch dark and she had no idea what time was. As she got off the bed to light a candle and find a clock she felt a warm sticky sensation between her legs and knew

306

she had started to bleed. Frightened, she tugged urgently on the bell for Ethel, realized the door was locked and dragged herself across to turn the key.

When the maid finally reached her, Tess was bleeding heavily and very distraught. 'You must get the doctor, Ethel, I think I'm losing the baby.'

'Oh, no,' cried Ethel, unable to hide her terror, and ran to wake Virginia and Florence.

Florence arrived first, still in her flannel nightgown and with her greying hair in a single braid down her back. Immediately she took control and while they waited for the doctor the quiet, mourning household was jolted into action. Issuing curt orders, Florence demanded hot water and clean towels. Then between them she and Virginia removed the blood-soaked undergarments and the barely formed small life, Tess's last link with Rupert.

Semi-conscious and in pain, Tess saw various faces swimming vaguely in front of her ... Florence's, Virginia's, Ethel's and finally the doctor's. She was still haemorrhaging badly when he arrived, but the terrified man, certain he was about to lose another patient, could do nothing to staunch the flow.

Virginia, watching the doctor intently as he attended to Tess, saw how his fingers trembled, the film of sweat on his brow as he fumbled in his black bag, and felt a true terror. Inwardly cursing his incompetence, she tried to hide her own sense of panic. Unless something was done, and quickly, Tess would be following Rupert to the grave. So she decided to take matters into her own hands. Ordering a pony and trap to be made ready, Virginia dressed hurriedly then whipped the horse through the dark night to the village. Here she roused a disgruntled postmaster from his bed and dictated a telegram to Dr Spencer Harcourt, an eminent Harley Street surgeon.

Dr Harcourt, who arrived late the following afternoon, was a bearded gentleman with a cold, patrician air. He discreetly attended to the unwanted pregnancies of society ladies and counted among his patients the Prince of Wales' current mistress, so he could name his price, which was exorbitant.

He administered a liquid solution of quinine to Tess to stop the bleeding, and laudanum to sedate her. For Tess, however, one grief had been swallowed up by another and, lacking the will to recover, she clung precariously to life for a few days while the whole household held its breath, as unprepared for this tragedy as it had been the first. But as well as his medicines, Dr Harcourt brought with him his expertise, and the promise of a further generous payment if his patient recovered encouraged him to deploy all his learning and skill.

Fortunately, too, Tess had youth on her side and a strong constitution. After a week she was out of danger and the house gave a collective sigh of relief. The doctor left with the stern command that his patient was not to move from her bed for at least a month, although Tess, weakened by the enormous loss of blood, had no wish to anyway.

She was fussed over by her mother, Ethel and Virginia for a couple of weeks, although Virginia, who was depending on Tess's natural resilience, imagined it was only a question of time before she was back on her feet. At the end of the prescribed month, however, Tess made no effort to leave her room but spent her days lying on the chaise longue, pretending to read a book although Virginia never once saw her turn a page.

As her body healed, Tess was becoming assailed by an overwhelming sense of guilt which she couldn't bring herself to speak about. She could think of nothing but her last angry words with Rupert. Going over in microscopic detail every move and turn in their argument, she knew she could only blame herself that it had remained unresolved. And the loss of the baby, that was God's judgement on her for scheming to defy the natural order of things . . . pregnancy . . . mother hood. So like a noxious plant the depression grew, her personality became fragmented and she had unpredictable swings of mood; morose and introspective at one moment, tearful and angry the next.

Every night, too, she had the same vivid dream. In it Rupert was just out of reach or in another room and she was calling frantically for him to wait for her as he walked away. Always she woke sobbing her heart out.

Florence watched her daughter's downward spiral with great disquiet. She'd convinced herself that it was madness that had driven Patrick Kelly to commit his unspeakable acts of violence and she was terrified Tess would succumb to the same malady. Florence had never had much time to indulge in inward looking self-reproach, but she knew the love she had for her children was unequally divided and that she'd often wounded Tess with her hasty tongue. So she tried to make amends by spending hours with Tess, talking to her, willing her to get better, although the response was almost nil.

Tess's affliction scared Virginia, too. Against impossible odds, Rupert and Tess had achieved a successful marriage, had perhaps even loved each other, so grief was normal. Tess's anguish, though, seemed to take her beyond those normal bounds which were part of the mourning process. So she searched for ways to shake her out of her apathy and knowing demanding children couldn't be ignored, Virginia made sure that each day they were brought down to play in the room where Tess sat. Thomas was placed in her arms, the twins put to play at her feet.

But William wanted the huge, strong father who, to his terror and delight, flung him high in the air and tried to sit him on the back of a pony, not his silent weeping mother. 'Where's my dada?' he demanded.

'Yes, where's Dada?' parroted Caroline.

'Oh William, my love,' Tess said helplessly and her eyes filled with tears as she gazed at Virginia over the top of Tom's head.

'Caroline, William, come here.' Obediently the twins trotted over to their aunt and she drew their tubby little bodies into the security of her arms. 'Dada's gone away,' she said gently.

'Gone 'way?' repeated Caroline.

'Yes, darling, to heaven.' Virginia herself could hardly speak now for the ache in her throat.

Satisfied, the twins toddled back to their bricks. At three and a half they were too young to comprehend the meaning of death. Dada often went away so they didn't mind him going to heaven, just as long as when he came back he brought them a present. Perhaps then, too, Mama would stop crying.

At the end of November, although she was unhappy about leaving Tess, Florence knew she couldn't neglect her husband any longer and reluctantly returned to London. Left on her own with Tess, Virginia became a little impatient of her quixotic moods. She shared her desolation of spirit, but life had to go on. And Tess was responsible for three young lives who needed her love and guidance, even more so now that Rupert was gone.

Virginia put these points to her rather briskly one day, but Tess was deaf to her blandishments and she might as well have been talking to a post. So as the year moved slowly to its close, Virginia decided to move Tess and the children back to London. She had an almost religious faith in new ideas and had heard that a Herr Schmidt, one of Sigmund Freud's disciples, had achieved some success in healing minds by psychoanalysis. If she could persuade Tess to undergo a course of treatment with this gentleman, he might find the key to her melancholia. It was her last hope.

20

Virginia had imagined she might have trouble persuading Tess to see Herr Schmidt. Surprisingly, though, she was quite amenable to the idea. It was unfortunate, then, that she took an instant dislike to the gentleman, hating his guttural accent, unctuous manner and bad breath. Above all, she resented the way he delved and pried into her childhood and marriage, asking her intimate questions. So after only two sessions, Tess told him, rather emphatically, to 'mind his own business', whereupon Herr Schmidt rushed from the room in high dudgeon, declaring rather unprofessionally to Virginia that he thought Lady St Clair should be committed to a lunatic asylum.

At first, Virginia saw in the outburst a faint glimmer of Tess's old spirit, and inwardly rejoiced. But it was a false hope. The crushing sorrow returned, so that Virginia began to wonder if it actually was possible to die of a broken heart.

Coinciding as it did with Tess's wedding anniversary, Virginia knew the twins' fourth birthday would be a particularly bad day to get through. She rarely admitted defeat but when Florence arrived with the children's presents and mouthed 'How is she?' Virginia gave a deep, sad sigh.

'To tell you the truth, Mrs Appleby, I'm at my wits' end.'

Although she forbore to say so, it was Florence's considered opinion that her daughter should be pulling herself together a bit now. This depression business was all very well, but it was only something the rich could afford. Realizing she was perhaps being a trifle cold-hearted, Florence put a check on her uncharitable thoughts and said instead, 'I was wondering ... do you think seeing a friend might cheer Tess up?'

'Possibly.'

311

'It's Sarah. She wrote because she hadn't heard from Tess for such a long time. How would you feel about her coming here?'

Florence ventured these suggestions with some diffidence because she wasn't sure how much Virginia knew about Sarah, and didn't want to insult her by proposing she invite a common prostitute to the house. Of course Arthur was always telling her she should be more tolerant of folk's weaknesses. 'Let him who is without sin cast the first stone, Florence,' he would quote, and Sarah's life had been tough. But she couldn't really understand why Tess had bothered to maintain the friendship, not when she could mix with gentry, and Sarah was no lady. Still she was on her way to being respectable now that she'd got herself a dress shop, even if it had been bought from her ill-got gains.

Anyway, she was preferable to that Liam O'Sullivan, back from Africa, looking fairly well heeled and making inquiries about Tess. She'd never liked his family and she didn't want her daughter to be associated with them in any way, so she'd given him short shrift. Besides, after all these years, Tess wouldn't want to see him, she was sure of that ... Her thoughts, meandering like a stream, were halted just then by Virginia's response to her suggestion, which she seemed to be eagerly taking up.

'I should be very pleased to see Sarah. Doubly pleased if she can bring a smile to Tess's lips. I'll send her a note, shall I?'

Virginia's carefully worded letter had referred in an oblique way to Tess's state of mind. But it was the stark contrast of widow's weeds against the milk-white skin that really brought Sarah up short. Coo blimey, she thought in dismay, her old friend, who'd once been so buxom and bonny, come to this and all for a man.

When her awkward letter of condolence had gone unanswered and further inquiries were ignored, Sarah finally accepted that they'd come to the parting of the ways. But it was a bitter rather than a philosophical acceptance, and she

312

felt her friend's perfidy deeply. And all the time Tess had been ill and no one had bothered to tell her – at least, not until it suited them.

In a rush of compassion Sarah crossed the room to hug her friend, but when she spoke her tone was jovial and she deliberately accentuated her cockney vowels. 'Hello, luv. How yer doin' then?' she said and was gratified to see a ghost of a smile.

'Fine, just fine.'

Well, that's a lie for a start, thought Sarah. Fancy loving a man that much to be in this state six months after he'd died. Still, she remembered her own sense of desolation when Milly passed on. The feeling she would never get over it and even now, something familiar from the past, the sight of bluebells, a child in a pram, would catch her unawares and all the hurt and misery would surface again. No, it never left you, that pain, not if you loved someone, she understood that perfectly.

But she wasn't here to wallow in a pool of mutual self-pity with Tess. Her brief was to 'Try and take Tess out of herself', and that's what she had every intention of doing, so she heard *her* question with a sense of surprise.

'How's the shop going, Sarah?'

'It's going great guns. I've got a gold-lettered sign outside saying: Madame Sarah, Gowns and Mantles.' She giggled. 'I've a good selection of dresses, too: morning dresses, tea gowns, ball gowns. You name it, we've got it. You must come over one day and try some on.'

'I couldn't just yet . . . but perhaps later.'

Realizing Tess was referring to her period of mourning, Sarah felt rather embarrassed. 'Oh, yes . . . of course. Well, just come and look anyway, and Annie would like to see you, too.'

'How is Annie?' Tess asked, remembering the timid little maid.

'You'd hardly recognize her. She's in the shop with me now and quite the young lady. Some of my clients have got more money than taste and she's very tactful with them, guides them to the right styles. Trouble is, I might lose her soon, she's walking out with a young bobby. I've tried to warn her against getting wed too young but she's in love at the moment and all starry eyed.'

'Will you ever marry, Sarah?'

Sarah, momentarily startled by this question, laughed. 'Who's going to marry me, with my past? You know what men are like with their double standards. It's all right for them to have a little bit on the side, but women must keep themselves pure. And the capers some of them got up to . . . if only their wives knew . . .' She shook her head in disbelief. 'No, I'm fine as I am and answerable to nobody. I'd have liked kids, of course, but Annie's policeman will probably give her a quiverful and I'll be auntie to them.'

After months of morbid introspection, Tess found Sarah's blunt, down to earth opinions so refreshing, she actually laughed. And with the laughter came a lifting of the spirit, so that Virginia, coming in to join them for tea, felt that a small miracle had taken place.

Anxious to take advantage of Sarah's mysterious restorative powers, Virginia walked with her to the door. 'You will come again, won't you, Sarah?'

'Course I will. Tell you what, though, there's someone else Tess might like to see even more than me.'

'Oh, who's this?'

'A friend of hers from way back, Liam O'Sullivan.'

'Wasn't he the young man who went to South Africa? I remember Tess being quite down in the dumps after he left.'

'That's right. But he's been home for some time now. I'm really surprised Tess's mum hasn't mentioned it. Anyway, I know where he lives so I can easily get in touch with him. But just in case . . . I shouldn't say anything to Tess about it,' Sarah finished conspiratorially.

'Look who's come to see you, Tess,' said Virginia brightly, coming through the door, then turning to beckon to someone behind her.

Liam entered the room with a certain hesitancy. 'Hello, Tess.'

In the worst days in Africa, ill and homesick and often hallucinating, a dream of being reunited with Tess was the only thing that had sustained him. And he thought he'd prepared himself but now, here he was and his heart was beating uncomfortably and he felt as anxious as a schoolboy.

And he could see by her startled expression, the way a book went flying as she sprang from the chair, that his visit was totally unexpected. 'Liam! Good heavens! What on earth are you doing here?' she exclaimed.

'I've come to see you,' he answered, misinterpreting her question.

'I mean in England.'

'Ah . . . well, that's a longish story. Although I did write and tell you I was coming back.'

'Oh . . . did you . . .?' She sat down again, twisting her gold wedding ring round and round on her finger.

Liam pulled up a chair and sat as close to Tess as he dare, and each was studying the other so intently that neither heard Virginia leave the room and quietly close the door.

In that memory he had of her, Tess had remained plump cheeked and pretty, now she seemed insubstantial as a shadow. He'd been warned by Sarah about her ill health but it didn't seem like her to get in this state and he wanted to say, 'Come on, Tess, where's that fighting spirit?' for she'd always seemed so certain of where she was going.

Tess's utter astonishment at Liam walking so unexpectedly back into her life had now given way to a certain natural curiosity. Interested in the change the years had brought, she noticed the well-cut suit, the gold watch chain hanging from his waistcoat pocket, the hand-made shoes. But most of all she noticed the air of natural self-assurance. The face was maturer too and it suited him. The lines round his eyes and mouth gave character to his good looks and he still had a thick thatch of hair. Altogether the years had treated him well, she decided.

'It's good to see you again, Tess. How long has it been?'

She spread her hands helplessly. 'Four . . . five years. I hardly remember, so much has happened.'

You're telling me, Liam thought feelingly. He'd been devastated when he received the news that she was married. He'd seriously thought of postponing his return to England then. Except that he didn't like Africa, hated the eternal sunshine that made him ill and longed only for rain-washed skies. So he'd returned home to learn with an equal sense of shock that she was already a widow. He wasn't callous enough to rejoice in this news and knew anyway that the dead often exerted a tremendous power over the living. For they have the advantage of remaining eternally young and with the passing of time their virtues multiply while their faults are conveniently forgotten.

A small tortoiseshell cat jumped on Tess's lap and began kneading away with her paws before curling up to sleep. 'Anyway, now that you are back, what are you doing?' As she talked, Tess stroked the cat's silky coat. Liam longed, at that moment, to reach out and take her hand, hold it to him and let her feel the power of his love. But the black dress put a curb on these emotions and he remembered how he'd often mucked things up in the past with his incautious behaviour. Exercising tremendous self-control, Liam swallowed hard and answered her question.

'I'm going to try and get into Parliament. I'm not short of the odd bob or two now,' he couldn't resist adding.

'A man of independent means, eh?'

'You could say that. Uncle Josh, God rest his soul, was a bachelor and he left everything to me, and if Keir Hardie can get himself elected so can I.'

'Good for you, Liam. Wait till I tell Virginia. You'll be supporting the feminist cause, of course.'

'Hey, hold on, I'm not in yet,' he answered with a laugh, but relishing her interest.

'Don't worry, you will be before long,' Tess answered confidently. For she could sense that Liam was on his way to achieving those ambitions he'd predicted for himself – and she'd so scornfully dismissed – all those years ago

316

when they'd walked home in the fog together. But the brash boy had been replaced by a man who exuded an unforced certainty and confidence, which she had to admit was attractive. It would be interesting watching his career take shape.

Feeling relaxed in her company now, Liam was about to let the conversation drift in a more personal direction when the door burst open and two small children galloped in, hurling themselves upon Tess and covering her with damp, rapturous kisses. Wisely the cat took cover but Liam saw the closed-in expression on Tess's face lighten as she gathered them up in her arms and returned their kisses.

The little boy, he could see, had Tess's dark curly hair, but although the girl was fair, it was she, Liam guessed, who had Tess's assertive character. For suddenly aware there was someone else in the room, she got down from her mother's lap and marched over to him, studying him silently with direct grey eyes.

'Who are you?' she asked finally.

'Caroline!' said her mother sharply. 'Where are your manners?'

Liam laughed. 'It's all right, Tess, she's entitled to ask.' He bent towards the small girl, who with her resourceful chin was a miniature version of her mother. 'I'm Mr Liam O'Sullivan, a very old friend of your mama's.'

'Will you be coming to see her again?' the inquisitive child asked.

'You'll have to ask your mama that,' Liam replied, with a hopeful glance at Tess.

What her answer was he never found out because once again there was a distracting flurry at the door. There must be better times to call, Liam mused ruefully, as this time a nursemaid entered carrying a smaller, younger child.

'Hello my cherub,' breathed Tess and with an ecstatic expression of love, held out her arms. The nurse put the infant down and he stumbled towards his adoring mother on fat little legs. But his progress was unsteady and suddenly he wobbled and landed with a bump on a well-padded bottom.

317

He might have got himself up again but with exclamations of alarm, both Tess and the nurse ran to him. Now the enjoyable centre of attention, he opened his mouth and proceeded to howl.

Feeling excluded from this loving family group and knowing he wouldn't even be missed in the general mayhem of nannies and children, Liam took his leave. As he descended the stairs, he was overwhelmed by the hopelessness of his situation. Others could engage her affections, David ... Rupert ... her children, but never himself in spite of years of unwavering love. Occasionally he had met girls he thought might cast out Tess's image, but it was only a brief amnesia and she would return again to haunt his mind. And anything he'd ever done had only been to impress her, right from their first meeting, but he could see now it was all a waste of time.

A servant was opening the door for him when he heard her call over the stair well. 'Liam, could you hold on a moment?' and he waited, wondering what it was he had left behind, as she came running down the stairs.

Tess had been so busy pacifying Tom, she hadn't noticed Liam's departure and as she reached him and put her question, there was the slightest stain of pink on her cheeks. 'Will you be calling again, Liam?'

'Do you want me to?' A smile formed on his lips but his eyes were serious. He needed some sort of commitment from her.

With a tentative, almost shy gesture, Tess put out her hand and touched his sleeve. 'Of course I do.'

'When?'

'Tomorrow afternoon if you're free.'

'I'm free,' Liam answered, his soaring spirits ignoring the fact that several appointments would have to be cancelled.

The features of the servant hovering at the door were impassive but Liam knew by his attentive stance that every word of their conversation was being noted and very soon would be relayed below stairs. Having no wish to make Tess a subject for servants' title tattle, Liam decided to go.

Tess followed him outside, calling to him as he ran down the steps, 'You won't forget, Liam, will you?'

He turned and in one long stride was beside her again. 'Do you really think I could?' he asked quietly, disregarding the servant this time.

Confused by the look of love in his eyes, Tess shook her head. 'No, not really.'

Liam lightly touched her fingers in a gesture of farewell. 'Tomorrow then.' Clinging to the rail, he made a backward descent of the steps, reluctant to leave her.

Tess watched him as he swung off down the street. Half-way down he stopped and dropped a coin into a beggar's tin, turned to check that she was still there, then to Tess's amusement and the tramp's toothless, open-mouthed surprise, Liam executed a joyous Irish jig along the pavement.

Tess heard her own unforced laughter with a sense of release and as she lifted her hand to wave to Liam there came unbidden, but sharply etched, that golden day on the Downs; skylarks, the fragrance of wild thyme and Liam's mouth on hers. With a sharp intake of breath, cool hands flew to her warm cheeks, thankful that after one last wave, Liam had turned the corner and gone.

Pull yourself together, Tess reprimanded herself sternly. All that happened years ago and like the silly pretence with the photographer that they were engaged, just some childish fun, nothing deep or serious . . . .

The street was deserted now. The tramp had emptied his tin, counted his earnings and gone to look for the nearest hostelry. But Tess continued to linger on the steps, enjoying a soft southerly breeze on her face. It had been a cold spring, with leaden, weeping skies, but now the sun was out. In the yearly cycle this was a time of regeneration, with a quickening in the rhythm of the days.

Already Tess knew, ducks would be marshalling their fluffy offspring on the Serpentine, while trees greening the park would be interspersed with beds of tulips, bright as daubs on an artist's palette.

As she stood there, Tess could feel some of the inertia, the self-absorbing black depression begin to lift. A small flame, fluttering like a candle in the wind, was warming and nourishing her soul and stirring within her was the desire to once again explore the potential of life and everything it had to offer. Of course, it could fall prey to the first cold draught but she would take that chance and maybe in a day or two, if the weather remained fine, she would take a walk in the park with the children, perhaps visit Sarah . . . even help Virginia. Small accomplishments but, taking one day at a time, she *could* forge a future out of past sorrow. And a sudden intuitive notion that some of her future might be closely interwoven with Liam's, caused a surge of optimism in her heart and brought a smile of happiness to Tess's lips.